wheels

The most complete and the most fascinating novel ever written about what really goes on in America's richest, most complex, and fiercely competitive industry—automobiles!

"He's done it again . . . He has somehow sensed the pounding pulse of America's biggest factory town . . . It's great reading!"
—Newsday

"The author of **Airport** and **Hotel** has the natural storyteller's gift of keeping a reader avidly turning the pages . . . In my judgment, the chances of **Wheels** escaping blockbusterdom are nil."
—The New York Times Book Review

"Unfolds with action and drama—the kind of behind-the-scenes lore that only Arthur Hailey could discover. It is a novel in depth in the best Hailey tradition!"
—The Literary Guild Magazine

"Excitement, action, suspense . . . with eight cylinders."
—Detroit News

Soon to be a major motion picture from United Artists Corporation!

ARTHUR HAILEY
WHEELS

BANTAM BOOKS
TORONTO · NEW YORK · LONDON

A NATIONAL GENERAL COMPANY

WHEELS

A Bantam Book/published by arrangement with
Doubleday & Company, Inc.

PRINTING HISTORY

Doubleday edition published September 1971

2nd printing	..	September 1971
3rd printing	..	September 1971
4th printing	..	September 1971
5th printing	....	October 1971
6th printing	..	November 1971
7th printing	..	November 1971
8th printing	..	December 1971
9th printing	...	February 1972
10th printing	......	April 1972

Literary Guild selection for October 1971

Doubleday Book Club selection for July 1972

Bantam edition published January 1973

Bantam Books are published by Bantam Books, Inc., a
National General company. Its trade-mark, consisting
of the words "Bantam Books" and the portrayal of a
bantam, is registered in the United States Patent Office
and in other countries. Marca Registrada. Bantam
Books, Inc., 666 Fifth Avenue, New York, N.Y. 10019.

PRINTED IN THE UNITED STATES OF AMERICA

Henceforward, no wheeled vehicles whatsoever will be allowed within the precincts of the City, from sunrise until the hour before dusk . . . Those which shall have entered during the night, and are still within the City at dawn, must halt and stand empty until the appointed hour . . .

—*Senatus consultum of Julius Caesar, 44 B.C.*

It is absolutely impossible to sleep anywhere in the City. The perpetual traffic of wagons in the narrow winding streets . . . is sufficient to wake the dead . . .

—*The Satires of Juvenal, A.D. 117*

wheels

chapter one

The president of General Motors was in a foul humor. He had slept badly during the night because his electric blanket had worked only intermittently, causing him to awaken several times, feeling cold. Now, after padding around his home in pajamas and robe, he had tools spread on his half of the king-size bed where his wife still slept, and was taking the control mechanism apart. Almost at once he observed a badly joined connection, cause of the night's on-again off-again performance. Muttering sourly about poor quality control of blanket manufacturers, the GM president took the unit to his basement workshop to repair.

His wife, Coralie, stirred. In a few minutes more her alarm clock would sound and she would get up sleepily to make breakfast for them both.

Outside, in suburban Bloomfield Hills, a dozen miles north of Detroit, it was still dark.

The GM president—a spare, fast-moving, normally even-tempered man—had another cause for ill humor besides the electric blanket. It was Emerson Vale. A few minutes ago, through the radio turned on softly beside his bed, the GM chief had heard a news broadcast which included the hated, astringent, familiar voice of the auto industry's arch critic.

Yesterday, at a Washington press conference, Emerson Vale had blasted anew his favorite targets—General Motors, Ford, and Chrysler. The press wire services, probably due to a lack of hard news from other sources, had obviously given Vale's attack the full treatment.

The big three of the auto industry, Emerson Vale charged, were guilty of "greed, criminal conspiracy, and self-serving abuse of public trust." The conspiracy was their continuing failure to develop alternatives to gasoline-powered autobiles—namely electric and steam vehicles—which, Vale asserted, "are available now."

The accusation was not new. However, Vale —a skilled hand at public relations and with the press—had injected enough recent material to make his statement newsworthy.

The president of the world's largest corporation, who had a Ph.D. in engineering, fixed the blanket control, in the same way that he enjoyed doing other jobs around the house when time permitted. Then he showered, shaved, dressed for the office, and joined Coralie at breakfast.

A copy of the *Detroit Free Press* was on the dining-room table. As he saw Emerson Vale's name and face prominently on the front page, he swept the newspaper angrily to the floor.

"Well," Coralie said. "I hope that made you feel better." She put a cholesterol-watcher's breakfast in front of him—the white of an egg on dry toast, with sliced tomatoes and cottage cheese. The GM president's wife always made breakfast herself and had it with him, no matter how early his departure. Seating herself opposite, she retrieved the *Free Press* and opened it.

Presently she announced, "Emerson Vale says if we have the technical competence to land men on the moon and Mars, the auto industry should be able to produce a totally safe, defect-free car that doesn't pollute its environment."

Her husband laid down his knife and fork. "Must you spoil my breakfast, little as it is?"

Coralie smiled. "I had the impression something else had done that already." She continued, unperturbed, "Mr. Vale quotes the Bible about air pollution."

"For Christ's sake! Where does the Bible say anything about *that*?"

"Not Christ's sake, dear. It's in the Old Testament."

His curiosity aroused, he growled, "Go ahead, read it. You intended to, anyway."

"From Jeremiah," Coralie said, " '*And I brought you into a plentiful country, to eat the fruit thereof and the goodness thereof; but when ye entered, ye defiled my land, and made mine heritage an abomination.*' " She poured more coffee for them both. "I do think that rather clever of him."

"No one's ever suggested the bastard isn't clever."

Coralie went back to reading aloud. " 'The auto and oil industries, Vale said, have together delayed technical progress which could have led, long before now, to an effective electric or steam car. Their reasoning is simple. Such a car would nullify their enormous capital investment in the pollutant-spreading internal combustion engine.' " She put the paper down. "Is any of that true?"

"Obviously Vale thinks it's all true."

"But you don't?"

"Naturally."

"None of it whatever?"

He said irritably, "There's sometimes a germ of truth in any outrageous statement. That's how people like Emerson Vale manage to sound plausible."

"Then you'll deny what he says?"

"Probably not."

"Why not?"

"Because if General Motors takes on Vale, we'll be accused of being a great monolith trampling down an individual. If we don't reply we'll be damned too, but at least that way we won't be misquoted."

"Shouldn't someone answer?"

"If some bright reporter gets to Henry Ford, he's apt to." The GM president smiled. "Except

Henry will be damned forceful and the papers won't print all his language."

"If I had your job," Coralie said, "I think I'd say something. That is, if I really was convinced of being right."

"Thank you for your advice."

The GM president finished his breakfast, declining to rise any further to his wife's bait. But the exchange, along with the needling which Coralie seemed to feel was good for him occasionally, had helped get the bad temper out of his system.

Through the door to the kitchen the GM president could hear the day maid arriving, which meant that his car and chauffeur—which picked up the girl on their way—were now waiting outside. He got up from the table and kissed his wife goodbye.

A few minutes later, shortly after 6 A.M., his Cadillac Brougham swung onto Telegraph Road and headed for the Lodge Freeway and the midtown New Center area. It was a brisk October morning, with a hint of winter in a gusty northwest wind.

Detroit, Michigan—the Motor City, auto capital of the world—was coming awake.

Also in Bloomfield Hills, ten minutes from the GM president's house, as a Lincoln Continental glides, an executive vice-president of Ford was preparing to leave for Detroit Metropolitan Airport. He had already breakfasted, alone. A housekeeper had brought a tray to his desk in the softly lighted study where, since 5 A.M., he had been alternately reading memoranda (mostly on special blue stationery which Ford vice-presidents used in implementing policy) and dictating crisp instructions into a recording machine. He had scarcely looked up, either as the meal arrived, or while eating, as he accomplished in an hour what would have taken most other executives a day, or more.

The majority of decisions just made concerned new plant construction or expansion and involved expenditures of several billion dollars. One of the executive vice-president's responsibilities was to approve or veto projects, and allocate priorities. He had once been asked if such rulings, on the disposition of immense wealth, worried him. He replied, "No, because mentally I always knock off the last three figures. That way it's no more sweat than buying a house."

The pragmatic, quick response was typical of the man who had risen, rocket-like, from a lowly car salesman to be among the industry's dozen top decision makers. The same process, incidentally, had made him a multimillionaire, though some might ponder whether the penalties for success and wealth were out of reason for a human being to pay.

The executive vice-president worked twelve and sometimes fourteen hours a day, invariably at a frenetic pace, and as often as not his job claimed him seven days a week. Today, at a time when large segments of the population were still abed, he would be en route to New York in a company Jetstar, using the journey time for a marketing review with subordinates. On landing, he would preside at a meeting on the same subject with Ford district managers. Immediately after, he would face a tough-talking session with twenty New Jersey dealers who had beefs about warranty and service problems. Later, in Manhattan, he would attend a bankers' convention luncheon and make a speech. Following the speech he would be quizzed by reporters at a freewheeling press conference.

By early afternoon the same company plane would wing him back to Detroit where he would be in his office for appointments and regular business until dinnertime. At some point in the afternoon, while he continued to work, a barber would come in to cut his hair. Dinner—in the penthouse, one floor above the executive suite—would include a critical discussion about new models with division managers.

Later still, he would stop in at the William R. Hamilton Funeral Chapel to pay respects to a company colleague who had dropped dead yesterday from a coronary occlusion brought on by overwork. (The Hamilton funeral firm was *de rigueur* for top echelon auto men who, rank conscious to the end, passed through, en route to exclusive Woodlawn Cemetery, sometimes known as "Executive Valhalla.")

Eventually the executive vice-president would go home—with a filled briefcase to be dealt with by tomorrow morning.

Now, pushing his breakfast tray away and shuffling papers, he stood up. Around him, in this personal study, were book-lined walls. Occasionally—though not this morning—he glanced at them with a trace of longing; there was a time, years ago, when he had read a good deal, and widely, and could have been a scholar if chance had directed his life differently. But nowadays he had no time for books. Even the daily newspaper would have to wait until he could snatch a moment to skim through it. He picked up the paper, still folded as the housekeeper had brought it, and stuffed it into his bag. Only later would he learn of Emerson Vale's latest attack and privately curse him, as many others in the auto industry would do before the day was out.

At the airport, those of the executive vice-president's staff who would accompany him were already in the waiting lounge of the Ford Air Transportation hangar. Without wasting time, he said, "Let's go."

The Jetstar engines started as the party of eight climbed aboard and they were taxiing before the last people in had fastened seatbelts. Only those who traveled by private airfleets knew how much time they saved compared with scheduled airlines.

Yet, despite the speed, briefcases were out and opened on laps before the aircraft reached the takeoff runway.

The executive vice-president began the discussion. "Northeast Region results this month are unsatisfactory. You know the figures as well as I do. I want to know why. Then I want to be told what's being done."

As he finished speaking, they were airborne.

The sun was halfway over the horizon; a dull red, brightening, amid scudding gray clouds.

Beneath the climbing Jetstar, in the early light, the vast sprawling city and environs were becoming visible: downtown Detroit, a square mile oasis like a miniature Manhattan; immediately beyond, leagues of drab streets, buildings, factories, housing, freeways—mostly dirt encrusted: an Augean work town without petty cash for cleanliness. To the west, cleaner, greener Dearborn, abutting the giant factory complex of the Rouge; in contrast, in the eastern extremity, the Grosse Pointes, tree-studded, manicured, havens of the rich; industrial, smoky Wyandotte to the south; Belle Isle, hulking in the Detroit River like a laden gray-green barge. On the Canadian side, across the river, grimy Windsor, matching in ugliness the worst of its U.S. senior partner.

Around and through them all, revealed by daylight, traffic swirled. In tens of thousands, like armies of ants (or lemmings, depending on a watcher's point of view) shift workers, clerks, executives, and others headed for a new day's production in countless factories, large and small.

The nation's output of automobiles for the day—controlled and masterminded in Detroit—had already begun, the tempo of production revealed in a monster Goodyear signboard at the car-jammed confluence of Edsel Ford and Walter Chrysler Freeways. In figures five feet high, and reading like a giant odometer, the current year's car production was recorded minute by minute, with remarkable accuracy, through a nationwide reporting system. The total grew as completed cars came off assembly lines across the country.

Twenty-nine plants in the Eastern time zone were operating now, their data feeding in. Soon, the figures would whirl faster as thirteen assembly plants in the Midwest swung into operation, followed by six more in California. Local motorists checked the Goodyear sign the way a physician read blood pressure or a stockbroker the Dow Jones. Riders in car pools made bets each day on the morning or the evening tallies.

The car production sources closest to the sign were those of Chrysler—the Dodge and Plymouth plants in Hamtramck, a mile or so away, where more than a hundred cars an hour began flowing off assembly lines at 6 A.M.

There was a time when the incumbent chairman of the board of Chrysler might have dropped in to watch a production start-up and personally check out a finished product. Nowadays, though, he did that rarely, and this morning was still at home, browsing through *The Wall Street Journal* and sipping coffee which his wife had brought before leaving, herself, for an early Art Guild meeting downtown.

In those earlier days the Chrysler chief executive (he was president then, newly appointed) had been an eager-beaver around the plants, partly because the declining, dispirited corporation needed one, and partly because he was determined to shed the "bookkeeper" tag which clung to any man who rose by the financial route instead of through sales or engineering. Chrysler, under his direction, had gone both up and down. One long six-year cycle had generated investor confidence; the next rang financial alarm bells; then, once more, with sweat, drastic economies and effort, the alarm had lessened, so there were those who said that the company functioned best under leanness or adversity. Either way, no one seriously believed any more that Chrysler's slim-pointed Pentastar would fail to stay in orbit—a reasonable achievement on its own, prompting the chairman of the board to hurry less nowadays, think more, and read what he wanted to.

At this moment he was reading Emerson Vale's latest outpouring, which *The Wall Street Journal* carried, though less flamboyantly than the *Detroit Free Press*. But Vale bored him. The Chrysler chairman found the auto critic's remarks repetitive and unoriginal, and after a moment turned to the real estate news which was decidedly more cogent. Not everyone knew it yet, but within the past few years Chrysler had been building a real estate empire which, as well as diversifying the company, might a few decades hence (or so the dream went), make the present "number three" as big or bigger than General Motors.

Meanwhile, as the chairman was comfortably aware, automobiles continued to flow from the Chrysler plants at Hamtramck and elsewhere.

Thus, the Big Three—as on any other morning—were striving to remain that way, while smaller American Motors, through its factory to the north in Wisconsin, was adding a lesser tributary of Ambassadors, Hornets, Javelins, Gremlins, and their kin.

chapter two

At a car assembly plant north of the Fisher Freeway, Matt Zaleski, assistant plant manager and a graying veteran of the auto industry, was glad that today was Wednesday.

Not that the day would be free from urgent problems and exercises in survival—no day ever was. Tonight, like any night, he would go homeward wearily, feeling older than his fifty-three years and convinced he had spent another day of his life inside a pressure cooker. Matt Zaleski sometimes wished he could summon back the energy he had had as a young man, either when he was new to auto production or as an Air Force bombardier in World War II. He also thought sometimes, looking back, that the years of war—even though he was in Europe in the thick of things, with an impressive combat record—were less crisis-filled than his civil occupation now.

Already, in the few minutes he had been in his glass-paneled office on a mezzanine above the assembly plant floor, even while removing his coat, he had skimmed through a red-tabbed memo on the desk—a union grievance which he realized immediately could cause a plant-wide walkout if it wasn't dealt with properly and promptly. There was undoubtedly still more to worry about in an adjoining pile of papers—other headaches, including critical material shortages (there were always some, each day), or quality control demands, or machinery failures, or some new conundrum which no one had thought of before, any or all of which could halt the assembly line and stop production.

Zaleski threw his stocky figure into the chair at his gray metal desk, moving in short, jerky movements, as he always had. He heard the chair protest—a reminder of his growing overweight and the big belly he carried around nowadays. He thought ashamedly: he could never squeeze it now into the cramped nose dome of a B-17. He wished that worry would take off pounds; instead, it seemed to put them on, especially since Freda died and loneliness at night drove him to the refrigerator, nibbling, for lack of something else to do.

But at least today was Wednesday.

First things first. He hit the intercom switch for the general office; his secretary wasn't in yet. A timekeeper answered.

"I want Parkland and the union committeeman," the assistant plant manager commanded. "Get them in here fast."

Parkland was a foreman. And outside they would be well aware which union committeeman he meant because they would know about the red-tabbed memo on his desk. In a plant, bad news traveled like burning gasoline.

The pile of papers—still untouched, though he would have to get to them soon—reminded Zaleski he had been thinking gloomily of the many causes which could halt an assembly line.

Halting the line, stopping production for whatever reason, was like a sword in the side to Matt Zaleski. The function of his job, his personal *raison d'être*, was to keep the line moving, with finished cars being driven off the end at the rate of one car a minute, no matter how the trick was done or if, at times, he felt like a juggler with fifteen balls in the air at once. Senior management wasn't interested in the juggling act, or excuses either. Result were what counted: quotas, daily production, manufacturing costs. But if the line stopped he heard about it soon enough. Each single minute of lost time meant that an entire car didn't get produced, and the loss would never be made up. Thus, even a two- or three-minute stoppage cost thousands of dollars because, while an assembly line stood still, wages and other costs went rollicking on.

But at least today was Wednesday.

The intercom clicked. "They're on their way, Mr. Zaleski."

He acknowledged curtly.

The reason Matt Zaleski liked Wednesday was simple. Wednesday was two days removed from Monday, and Friday was two more days away.

Mondays and Fridays in auto plants were management's most harrowing days because of absenteeism. Each Monday, more hourly paid employees failed to report for work than on any other normal weekday; Friday ran a close second. It happened because after paychecks were handed out, usually on Thursday, many workers began a long boozy or drugged weekend, and afterward, Monday was a day for catching up on sleep or nursing hangovers.

Thus, on Mondays and Fridays, other problems were eclipsed by one enormous problem of keeping production going despite a critical shortage of people. Men were moved around like marbles in a game of Chinese checkers. Some were removed from tasks they were accustomed to and given jobs they had never done before. A worker who normally tightened wheel nuts might find himself fitting front fenders, often with the briefest of instruction or sometimes none at all. Others, pulled in hastily from labor pools or less skilled duties—such as loading trucks or sweeping— would be put to work wherever gaps remained. Sometimes they caught on quickly in their temporary roles; at other times they might spend an entire shift installing heater hose clamps, or something similar—upside down.

The result was inevitable. Many of Monday's and Friday's cars were shoddily put together, with built-in legacies of trouble for their owners, and those in the know avoided them like contaminated meat. A few big city dealers, aware of the problem and with influence at factories because of volume sales, insisted that cars for more valued customers be built on Tuesday, Wednesday, or Thursday, and customers who knew the ropes sometimes went to big dealers with this objective. Cars for company executives and their friends were invariably scheduled for one of the midweek days.

The door of the assistant plant manager's office flung open abruptly. The foreman he had sent for, Parkland, strode in, not bothering to knock.

Parkland was a broad-shouldered, big-boned man in his late thirties, about fifteen years younger than Matt Zaleski. He might have been a football fullback if he had gone to college, and, unlike many foremen nowadays, looked as if he could handle authority. He also looked, at the moment, as if he expected trouble and was prepared to meet it. The foreman's face was glowering. There was a darkening bruise, Zaleski noted, beneath his right cheekbone.

Ignoring the mode of entry, Zaleski motioned him to a chair. "Take the weight off your feet, then simmer down."

They faced each other across the desk.

"I'm willing to hear your version of what happened," the assistant plant chief said, "but don't waste time because the way this reads"— he fingered the red-tabbed grievance report— "you've cooked us all a hot potato."

"The hell I cooked it!" Parkland glared at his superior; above the bruise his face flushed red. "I fired a guy because he slugged me. What's more, I'm gonna make it stick, and if you've got any guts or justice you'd better back me up."

Matt Zaleski raised his voice to the bull roar he had learned on a factory floor. "Knock off that goddam nonsense, right now!" He had no intention of letting this get out of hand. More reasonably, he growled, "I said simmer down, and meant it. When the time comes I'll decide who to back and why. And there'll be no more crap from you about guts and justice. Understand?"

Their eyes locked together. Parkland's dropped first.

"All right, Frank," Matt said. "Let's start over, and this time give it to me straight, from the beginning."

He had known Frank Parkland a long time. The foreman's record was good and he was usually fair with men who worked under him. It had taken something exceptional to get him as riled as this.

"There was a job out of position," Parkland said. "It was steering column bolts, and there was this kid doing it; he's new, I guess. He was crowding the next guy. I wanted the job put back."

Zaleski nodded. It happened often enough. A worker with a specific assignment took a few seconds longer than he should on each operation. As successive cars moved by on the assembly line, his position gradually changed, so that soon he was intruding on the area of the next operation. When a foreman saw it happen he made it his business to help the worker back to his correct, original place.

Zaleski said impatiently, "Get on with it."

Before they could continue, the office door opened again and the union committeeman came in. He was a small, pink-faced man, with thick-lensed glasses and a fussy manner. His name was Illas and, until a union election a few months ago, had been an assembly line worker himself.

"Good morning," the union man said to Zaleski. He nodded curtly to Parkland, without speaking.

Matt Zaleski waved the newcomer to a chair. "We're just getting to the meat."

"You could save a lot of time," Illas said, "if you read the grievance report."

"I've read it. But sometimes I like to hear the other side." Zaleski motioned Parkland to go on.

"All I did," the foreman said, "was call another guy over and say, 'Help me get this man's job back in position.'"

"And I say you're a liar!" The union man hunched forward accusingly; now he swung toward Zaleski. "What he really said was 'get this *boy's* job back.' And it so happened that the person he was speaking of, and calling 'boy,' was one of our black brothers to whom that word is a very offensive term."

"Oh, for God's sake!" Parkland's voice combined anger with disgust. "D'you think I don't know that? D'you think I haven't been around here long enough to know better than to use that word that way?"

"But you *did* use it, didn't you?"

"Maybe, just maybe, I did. I'm not saying yes, because I don't remember, and that's the truth. But if it happened, there was nothing meant. It was a slip, that's all."

The union man shrugged. "That's your story now."

"It's no story, you son-of-a-bitch!"

Illas stood up. "Mr. Zaleski, I'm here officially, representing the United Auto Workers. If that's the kind of language . . ."

"There'll be no more of it," the assistant plant manager said. "Sit down, please, and while we're on the subject, I suggest you be less free yourself with the word 'liar.'"

Parkland slammed a beefy fist in frustration

on the desk top. "I said it was no story, and it isn't. What's more, the guy I was talking about didn't even give a thought to what I said, at least before all the fuss was made."

"That's not the way *he* tells it," Illas said.

"Maybe not now." Parkland appealed to Zaleski. "Listen, Matt, the guy who was out of position is just a kid. A black kid, maybe seventeen. I've got nothing against him; he's slow, but he was doing his job. I've got a kid brother his age. I go home, I say, 'Where's the boy?' Nobody thinks twice about it. That's the way it was with this thing until this other guy, Newkirk, cut in."

Illas persisted, "But you're admitting you used the word 'boy.'"

Matt Zaleski said wearily, "Okay, okay, he used it. Let's all concede that."

Zaleski was holding himself in, as he always had to do when racial issues erupted in the plant. His own prejudices were deep-rooted and largely anti-black, and he had learned them in the heavily Polish suburb of Wyandotte where he was born. There, the families of Polish origin looked on Negroes with contempt, as shiftless and troublemakers. In return, the black people hated Poles, and even nowadays, throughout Detroit, the ancient enmities persisted. Zaleski, through necessity, had learned to curb his instincts; you couldn't run a plant with as much black labor as this one and let your prejudices show, at least not often. Just now, after the last remark of Illas, Matt Zaleski had been tempted to inject: *So what if he did call him "boy"? What the hell difference does it make? When a foreman tells him to, let the bastard get back to work.* But Zaleski knew it would be repeated and maybe cause more trouble than before. Instead, he growled, "What matters is what came after."

"Well," Parkland said, "I thought we'd never

get to that. We almost had the job back in place, then this heavyweight, Newkirk, showed up."

"He's another black brother," Illas said.

"Newkirk'd been working down the line. He didn't even hear what happened; somebody else told him. He came up, called me a racist pig, and slugged me." The foreman fingered his bruised face which had swollen even more since he came in.

Zaleski asked sharply, "Did you hit him back?"

"No."

"I'm glad you showed a little sense."

"I had sense, all right," Parkland said. "I fired Newkirk. On the spot. Nobody slugs a foreman around here and gets away with it."

"We'll see about that," Illas said. "A lot depends on circumstances and provocation."

Matt Zaleski thrust a hand through his hair; there were days when he marveled that there was any left. This whole stinking situation was something which McKernon, the plant manager, should handle, but McKernon wasn't here. He was ten miles away at staff headquarters, attending a conference about the new Orion, a super-secret car the plant would be producing soon. Sometimes it seemed to Matt Zaleski as if McKernon had already begun his retirement, officially six months away.

Matt Zaleski was holding the baby now, as he had before, and it was a lousy deal. Zaleski wasn't even going to succeed McKernon, and he knew it. He'd already been called in and shown the official assessment of himself, the assessment which appeared in a loose-leaf, leather-bound book which sat permanently on the desk of the Vice-president, Manufacturing. The book was there so that the vice-president could turn its pages whenever new appointments or promotions were considered. The entry for Matt Zaleski, along with his photo and other details, read: "This individual is well placed at his present level of management."

Everybody in the company who mattered knew that the formal, unctious statement was a "kiss off." What it really meant was: *This man has gone as high as he's going. He will probably serve his time out in his present spot, but will receive no more promotions.*

The rules said that whoever received that deadly summation on his docket had to be told; he was entitled to that much, and it was the reason Matt Zaleski had known for the past several months that he would never rise beyond his present role of assistant manager. Initially the news had been a bitter disappointment, but now that he had grown used to the idea, he also knew why: He was old shoe, the hind end of a disappearing breed which management and boards of directors didn't want any more in the top critical posts. Zaleski had risen by a route which few senior plant people followed nowadays—factory worker, inspector, foreman, superintendent, assistant plant manager. He hadn't had an engineering degree to start, having been a high school dropout before World War II. But after the war he had armed himself with a degree, using night school and GI credits, and after that had started climbing, being ambitious, as most of his generation were who had survived *Festung Europa* and other perils. But, as Zaleski recognized later, he had lost too much time; his real start came too late. The strong comers, the top echelon material of the auto companies—then as now—were the bright youngsters who arrived fresh and eager through the direct college-to-front office route.

But that was no reason why McKernon, who was still plant boss, should sidestep this entire situation, even if unintentionally. The assistant manager hesitated. He would be within his rights to send for McKernon and could do it here and now by picking up a phone.

Two things stopped him. One, he admitted to himself, was pride; Zaleski knew he could handle this as well as McKernon, if not better. The other: His instinct told him there simply wasn't time.

Abruptly, Zaleski asked Illas, "What's the union asking?"

"Well, I've talked with the president of our local . . ."

"Let's save all that," Zaleski said. "We both know we have to start somewhere, so what is it you want?"

"Very well," the committeeman said. "We insist on three things. First, immediate reinstatement of Brother Newkirk, with compensation for time lost. Second, an apology to both men involved. Third, Parkland to be removed from his post as foreman."

Parkland, who had slumped back in his chair, shot upright. "By Christ! You don't want much." He inquired sarcastically, "As a matter of interest, am I supposed to apologize before I'm fired, or after?"

"The apology would be an official one from the company," Illas answered. "Whether you had the decency to add your own would be up to you."

"I'll say it'd be up to me. Just don't anyone hold their breath waiting."

Matt Zaleski snapped, "If you'd held your own breath a little longer, we wouldn't be in this mess."

"Are you trying to tell me you'll go along with all that?" The foreman motioned angrily to Illas.

"I'm not telling anybody anything yet. I'm trying to think, and I need more information than has come from you two." Zaleski reached behind him for a telephone. Interposing his body between the phone and the other two, he dialed a number and waited.

When the man he wanted answered, Zaleski asked simply, "How are things down there?"

The voice at the other end spoke softly. "Matt?"

"Yeah."

In the background behind the other's guarded response, Zaleski could hear a cacophony of noise from the factory floor. He always marveled how men could live with that noise every day of their working lives. Even in the years he had worked on an assembly line himself, before removal to an office shielded him from most of the din, he had never grown used to it.

His informant said, "The situation's real bad, Matt."

"How bad?"

"The hopheads are in the saddle. Don't quote me."

"I never do," the assistant plant manager said. "You know that."

He had swung partially around and was aware of the other two in the office watching his face. They might guess, but couldn't know, that he was speaking to a black foreman, Stan Lathruppe, one of the half dozen men in the plant whom Matt Zaleski respected most. It was a strange, even paradoxical, relationship because, away from the plant, Lathruppe was an active militant who had once been a follower of Malcolm X. But here he took his responsibility seriously, believing that in the auto world he could achieve more for his race through reason than by anarchy. It was this second attitude which Zaleski —originally hostile to Lathruppe—had eventually come to respect.

Unfortunately for the company, in the present state of race relations, it had comparatively few black foremen or managers. There ought to be more, many more, and everybody knew it, but right now many of the black workers didn't want responsibility, or were afraid of it because of young militants in their ranks, or simply weren't ready. Sometimes Matt Zaleski, in his less prejudiced moments, thought that if the industry's top brass had looked ahead a few years, the way senior executives were supposed to do, and had launched a meaningful training program for black workers in the 1940s and '50s, there would be more Stan Lathruppes now. It was everybody's loss that there were not.

Zaleski asked, "What's being planned?"

"I think, a walkout."

"When?"

"Probably at break time. It could be before, but I don't believe so."

The black foreman's voice was so low Zaleski had to strain to hear. He knew the other man's problem, added to by the fact that the telephone he was using was alongside the assembly line where others were working. Lathruppe was already labeled a "white nigger" by some fellow blacks who resented even their own race when in authority, and it made no difference that the charge was untrue. Except for a couple more questions, Zaleski had no intention of making Stan Lathruppe's life more difficult.

He asked, "Is there any reason for the delay?"

"Yes. The hopheads want to take the whole plant out."

"Is word going around?"

"So fast you'd think we still used jungle drums."

"Has anyone pointed out the whole thing's illegal?"

"You got any more jokes like that?" Lathruppe said.

"No." Zaleski sighed. "But thanks." He hung up.

So his first instinct had been right. There wasn't any time to spare, and hadn't been from the beginning, because a racial labor dispute always burned with a short fuse. Now, if a walkout happened, it could take days to settle and get everybody back at work; and even if only black workers became involved, and maybe not all of them, the effect would still be enough to halt production. Matt Zaleski's job was to keep production going.

As if Parkland had read his thoughts, the foreman urged, "Matt, don't let them push you! So a few may walk off the job, and we'll have trouble. But a principle's worth standing up for, sometimes, isn't it?"

"Sometimes," Zaleski said. "The trick is to know which principle, and when."

"Being fair is a good way to start," Parkland said, "and fairness works two ways—up and down." He leaned forward over the desk, speaking earnestly to Matt Zaleski, glancing now and then to the union committeeman, Illas. "Okay, I've been tough with guys on the line because I've had to be. A foreman's in the middle, catching crap from all directions. From up here, Matt, you and your people are on our necks every day for production, production, more production; and if it isn't you it's Quality Control who say, build 'em better, even though you're building faster. Then there are those who are working, doing the jobs—including some like Newkirk, and others—and a foreman has to cope with them, along with the union as well if he puts a foot wrong, and sometimes when he doesn't. So it's a tough business, and I've been tough; it's the way to survive. But I've been fair, too. I've never treated a guy who worked for me differently because he was black, and I'm no plantation overseer with a whip. As for what we're talking about now, all I did—so I'm told—is call a black man 'boy.' I didn't ask him to pick cotton, or ride Jim Crow, or shine shoes, or any other thing that's supposed to go with that word. What I did was help him with his job. And I'll say another thing: if I did call him 'boy'—so help me, by a slip!—I'll say I'm sorry for that, because I am. But not to Newkirk. Brother Newkirk stays fired. Because if he doesn't, if he gets away with slugging a foreman without reason, you can stuff a surrender flag up your ass and wave goodbye to any discipline around this place from this day on. That's what I mean when I say be fair."

"You've got a point or two there," Zaleski said. Ironically, he thought, Frank Parkland *had* been fair with black workers, maybe fairer than a good many others around the plant. He asked Illas, "How do you feel about all that?"

The union man looked blandly through his thick-lensed glasses. "I've already stated the union's position, Mr. Zaleski."

"So if I turn you down, if I decide to back up Frank the way he just said I should, what then?"

Illas said stiffly, "We'd be obliged to go through further grievance procedure."

"Okay." The assistant plant manager nodded. "That's your privilege. Except, if we go through a full grievance drill it can mean thirty days or more. In the meantime, does everybody keep working?"

"Naturally. The collective bargaining agreement specifies . . ."

Zaleski flared, "I don't need you to tell me what the agreement says! It says everybody stays on the job while we negotiate. But right now a good many of your men are getting ready to walk off their jobs in violation of the contract."

For the first time, Illas looked uneasy. "The UAW does not condone illegal strikes."

"Goddamit, then! Stop this one!"

"If what you say is true, I'll talk to some of our people."

"Talking won't do any good. You know it, and I know it." Zaleski eyed the union committeeman whose pink face had paled slightly; obviously Illas didn't relish the thought of arguing with some of the black militants in their present mood.

The union—as Matt Zaleski was shrewdly aware—was in a tight dilemma in situations of this kind. If the union failed to support its black militants at all, the militants would charge union leaders with racial prejudice and being "management lackeys." Yet if the union went too far with its support, it could find itself in an untenable position legally, as party to a wildcat strike. Illegal strikes were anathema to UAW leaders like Woodcock, Fraser, Greathouse, Bannon, and others, who had built reputations for tough negotiating, but also for honoring agreements once made, and settling grievances through due process. Wildcatting debased the union's word and undermined its bargaining strength.

"They're not going to thank you at Solidarity House if we let this thing get away from us," Matt Zaleski persisted. "There's only one thing can stop a walkout, and that's for us to make a decision here, then go down on the floor and announce it."

Illas said, "That depends on the decision." But it was plain that the union man was weighing Zaleski's words.

Matt Zaleski had already decided what the ruling had to be, and he knew that nobody would like it entirely, including himself. He thought sourly: these were lousy times, when a man had to shove his convictions in his pocket along with pride—at least, if he figured to keep an automobile plant running.

He announced brusquely, "Nobody gets fired. Newkirk goes back to his job, but from now on he uses his fists for working, nothing else." The assistant plant manager fixed his eyes on Illas. "I want it clearly understood by you and by Newkirk—one more time, he's out. And before he goes back, I'll talk to him myself."

"He'll be paid for lost time?" The union man had a slight smile of triumph.

"Is he still at the plant?"

"Yes."

Zaleski hesitated, then nodded reluctantly. "Okay, providing he finishes the shift. But there'll be no more talk about anybody replacing Frank." He swung to face Parkland. "And you'll do what you said you would—talk to the young guy. Tell him what was said was a mistake."

"An apology is what it's known as," Illas said.

Frank Parkland glared at them both. "Of all the crummy, sleazy backdowns!"

"Take it easy!" Zaleski warned.

"Like hell I'll take it easy!" The burly foreman was on his feet, towering over the assistant plant manager. He spat words across the desk between them. "You're the one taking it easy—the easy out because you're too much a goddam coward to stand up for what you know is right."

His face flushing deep red, Zaleski roared, "I don't have to take that from you! That'll be enough! You hear?"

"I hear." Contempt filled Parkland's voice and eyes. "But I don't like what I hear, or what I smell."

"In that case, maybe you'd like to be fired!"

"Maybe," the foreman said. "Maybe the air'd be cleaner some place else."

There was a silence between them, then Zaleski growled, "It's no cleaner. Some days it stinks everywhere."

Now that his own outburst was over, Matt

Zaleski had himself in hand. He had no intention of firing Parkland, knowing that if he did, it would be a greater injustice piled on another; besides, good foremen were hard to come by. Nor would Parkland quit of his own accord, whatever he might threaten; that was something Zaleski had calculated from the beginning. He happened to know that Frank Parkland had obligations at home which made a continuing paycheck necessary, as well as too much seniority in the company to throw away.

But for a moment back there, Parkland's crack about cowardice had stung. There had been an instant when the assistant plant manager wanted to shout that Frank Parkland had been ten years old, a snot-nosed kid, when he, Matt Zaleski, was sweating bomber missions over Europe, never knowing when a hunk of jagged flak would slice through the fuselage, then horribly through his guts or face or pecker, or wondering if their B-17F would go spinning earthward from 25,000 feet, burning, as many of the Eighth Air Force bombers did while comrades watched . . . *So think again about who you're taunting with cowardice, sonny; and remember I'm the one, not you, who has to keep this plant going, no matter how much bile I swallow doing it!* . . . But Zaleski hadn't said any of that, knowing that some of the things he had thought of happened a long time ago, and were not relevant any more, that ideas and values had changed in screwy, mixed-up ways; also that there were different kinds of cowardice, and maybe Frank Parkland was right, or partly right. Disgusted with himself, the assistant plant manager told the other two, "Let's go down on the floor and settle this."

They went out of the office—Zaleski first, followed by the union committeeman, with Frank Parkland, dour and glowering, in the rear. As they clattered down the metal stairway from the office mezzanine to the factory floor, the noise of the plant hit them solidly, like a barrage of bedlam.

The stairway at factory floor level was close to a section of assembly line where early subassemblies were welded onto frames, becoming the foundations on which finished cars would rest. The din at this point was so intense that men working within a few feet of one another had to shout, heads close together, to communicate. Around them, showers of sparks flew upward and sideways in a pyrotechnic curtain of intense white-blue. Volleys from welding machines and rivet guns were punctuated by the constant hiss of the power tools' lifeblood—compressed air. And central to everything, focus of activity like an ambling godhead exacting tribute, the moving assembly line inched inexorably on.

The union committeeman fell in beside Zaleski as the trio moved forward down the line. They were walking considerably faster than the assembly line itself, so that cars they passed were progressively nearer completion. There was a power plant in each chassis now, and immediately ahead, a body shell was about to merge with a chassis sliding under it in what auto assembly men called the "marriage act." Matt Zaleski's eyes swung over the scene, checking key points of operation, as he always did, instinctively.

Heads went up, or turned, as the assistant plant manager, with Illas and Parkland, continued down the line. There were a few greetings, though not many, and Zaleski was aware of sour looks from most workers whom they passed, white as well as black. He sensed a mood of resentment and unrest. It happened occasionally in plants, sometimes without reason, at other times through a minor cause, as if an eruption would have happened anyway and was merely seeking the nearest outlet. Sociologists, he knew, called it a reaction to unnatural monotony.

The union committeeman had his face set in a stern expression, perhaps to indicate that he hobnobbed with management only through duty, but did not enjoy it.

"How's it feel," Matt Zaleski asked him, "now you don't work on the line any more?"

Illas said curtly, "Good."

Zaleski believed him. Outsiders who toured auto plants often assumed that workers there became reconciled, in time, to the noise, smell, heat, unrelenting pressure, and endless repetition of their jobs. Matt Zaleski had heard touring visitors tell their children, as if speaking of inmates of a zoo: *They all get used to it. Most of them are happy at that kind of work. They wouldn't want to do anything else.*

When he heard it, he always wanted to cry out: *Kids, don't believe it! It's a lie!*

Zaleski knew, as did most others who were close to auto plants, that few people who worked on factory production lines for long periods had ever intended to make that work a lifetime's occupation. Usually, when hired, they looked on the job as temporary until something better came along. But to many—especially those with little education—the better job was always out of reach, forever a delusive dream. Eventually a trap was sprung. It was a two-pronged trap, with a worker's own commitments on one side—marriage, children, rent, installment payments—and on the other, the fact that pay in the auto industry was high compared with jobs elsewhere.

But neither pay nor good fringe benefits could change the grim, dispiriting nature of the work. Much of it was physically hard, but the greatest toll was mental—hour after hour, day after day of deadening monotony. And the nature of their jobs robbed individuals of pride. A man on a production line lacked a sense of achievement; he never made a car; he merely made, or put together, pieces—adding a washer to a bolt, fastening a metal strip, inserting screws. And always it was the identical washer or strip or screws, over and over and over and over and over and over and over again, while working conditions—including an overlay of noise—made communication difficult, friendly association between individuals impossible. As years went by, many, while hating, endured. Some had mental breakdowns. Almost no one liked his work.

Thus, a production line worker's ambition, like that of a prisoner, was centered on escape. Absenteeism was a way of partial escape; so was a strike. Both brought excitement, a break in monotony—for the time being the dominating drive.

Even now, the assistant plant manager realized, that drive might be impossible to turn back.

He told Illas, "Remember, we made an agreement. Now, I want this thing cleaned up fast." The union man didn't answer, and Zaleski added, "Today should do you some good. You got what you wanted."

"Not all of it."

"All that mattered."

Behind their words was a fact of life which both men knew: An escape route from the production line which some workers chose was through election to a full-time union post, with a chance of moving upward in UAW ranks. Illas, recently, had gone that way himself. But once elected, a union man became a political creature; to survive he must be re-elected, and between elections he maneuvered like a politician courting favor with constituents. The workers around a union committeeman were his voters, and he strove to please them. Illas had that problem now.

Zaleski asked him, "Where's this character Newkirk?"

They had come to the point on the assembly line where this morning's blow-up had occurred.

Illas nodded toward an open area with several plastic-topped tables and chairs, where line workers took their meal breaks. There was a bank of vending machines for coffee, soft drinks, candy. A painted line on the floor served in lieu of a surrounding wall. At the moment the only occupant of the area was a husky, big-featured black man; smoke drifted from a cigarette in his hand as he watched the trio which had just arrived.

The assistant plant manager said, "All right, tell him he goes back to work, and make sure you fill in all the rest. When you're through talking, send him over to me. "

"Okay," Illas said. He stepped over the painted line and was smiling as he sat down at the table with the big man.

Frank Parkland had already gone directly to a younger black man, still working on the line. Parkland was talking earnestly. At first the other looked uncomfortable, but soon after grinned sheepishly and nodded. The foreman touched the younger man's shoulder and motioned in the direction of Illas and Newkirk, still at the lunch area table, their heads close together. The young assembly worker grinned again. The foreman put out his hand; after hesitating briefly, the young man took it. Matt Zaleski found himself wondering if he could have handled Parkland's part as gracefully or as well.

"Hi, boss man!" The voice came from the far side of the assembly line. Zaleski turned toward it.

It was an interior trim inspector, an old-timer on the line, a runtish man with a face extraordinarily like that of Hitler. Inevitably, fellow workers called him Adolf and, as if enjoying the joke, the employee—whose real name Zaleski could never remember—even combed his short hair forward over one eye.

"Hi, Adolf." The assistant plant manager crossed to the other side of the line, stepping carefully between a yellow convertible and a mist-green sedan. "How's body quality today?"

"I've seen worse days, boss man. Remember the World Series?"

"Don't remind me."

World Series time and the opening days of the Michigan hunting season were periods which auto production men dreaded. Absenteeism was at a peak; even foremen and supervisors were guilty of it. Quality plummeted, and at World Series time the situation was worsened by employees paying more attention to portable radios than to their jobs. Matt Zaleski remembered that at the height of the 1968 Series, which the Detroit Tigers won, he confided grimly to his wife, Freda—it was the year before she died—"I wouldn't wish a car built today on my worst enemy."

"This special's okay, anyway." Adolf (or whatever his name was) had hopped nimbly in and out of the mist-green sedan. Now, he turned his attention to the car behind—a bright orange sports compact with white bucket seats. "Bet this one's for a blonde," Adolf shouted from inside the car. "An' I'd like to be the one to screw her in it."

Matt Zaleski shouted back, "You've got a soft job already."

"I'd be softer after her." The inspector emerged, rubbing his crotch and leering; factory humor was seldom sophisticated.

The assistant plant manager returned the grin, knowing it was one of the few human exchanges the worker would have during his eight-hour shift.

Adolf ducked into another car, checking its interior. It was true what Zaleski had said a moment earlier: an inspector did have a softer job than most others on the line, and usually got it through seniority. But the job, which carried no extra pay and gave a man no real authority, had disadvantages. If an inspector was conscientious and drew attention to all bad work, he aroused the ire of fellow workers who could make life miserable for him in other ways. Foremen, too, took a dim view of what they conceived to be an overzealous inspector, resenting anything which held up their particular area of production. All foremen were under pressure from superiors— including Matt Zaleski—to meet production quotas, and foremen could, and often did, overrule inspectors. Around an auto plant a classic phrase was a foreman's grunted, "Let it go," as a substandard piece of equipment or work moved onward down the line—sometimes to be caught by Quality Control, more often not.

In the meal break area, the union committeeman and Newkirk were getting up from their table.

Matt Zaleski looked forward down the line; something about the mist-green sedan, now several cars ahead, caused his interest to sharpen. He decided to inspect that car more closely before it left the plant.

Also down the line he could see Frank Parkland near his regular foreman's station; presumably Parkland had gone back to his job, assuming his own part in the now-settled dispute to be over. Well, Zaleski supposed it was, though he suspected the foreman would find it harder, from now on, to maintain discipline when he had to. But, hell!—everybody had their problems. Parkland would have to cope with his.

As Matt Zaleski recrossed the assembly line, Newkirk and the union committeeman walked to meet him. The black man moved casually; standing up, he seemed even bigger than he had at the table. His facial features were large and prominent, matching his build, and he was grinning.

Illas announced, "I've told Brother Newkirk about the decision I won for him. He's agreed to go back to work and understands he'll be paid for time lost."

The assistant plant manager nodded; he had no wish to rob the union man of kudos, and if Illas wanted to make a small skirmish sound like the Battle of the Overpass, Zaleski would not object. But he told Newkirk sharply, "You can take the grin off. There's nothing funny." He queried Illas, "You told him it'll be even less funny if it happens again?"

"He told me what he was supposed to," Newkirk said. "It won't happen no more, not if there ain't no cause."

"You're pretty cocky," Zaleski said. "Considering you've just been fired and unfired."

"Not cocky, mister, *angry!*" The black man made a gesture which included Illas. "That's a thing you people, all of you, won't ever understand."

Zaleski snapped, "I can get pretty damned angry about brawls upsetting this plant."

"Not deep soul angry. Not so it burns, a *rage.*"

"Don't push me. I might show you otherwise."

The other shook his head. For one so huge, his voice and movements were surprisingly gentle; only his eyes burned—an intense gray-green. "Man, you ain't black, you don't know what it means; not rage, not anger. It's a million goddam pins bein' stuck in from time you was born, then one day some white motha' calls a man 'boy,' an' it's a million 'n one too many."

"Now then," the union man said, "we settled all that. We don't have to get into it again."

Newkirk dismissed him. "You hush up!" His eyes remained fixed, challengingly, on the assistant plant manager.

Not for the first time, Matt Zaleski wondered: Had the whole free-wheeling world gone crazy? To people like Newkirk and millions of others, including Zaleski's own daughter, Barbara, it seemed a basic credo that everything which used to matter—authority, order, respect, moral decency—no longer counted in any recognizable way. Insolence was a norm—the kind Newkirk used with his voice and now his eyes. The familiar phrases were a part of it: Newkirk's *rage* and *deep soul angry* were interchangeable, it seemed, with a hundred others like *generation gap, strung out, hanging loose, taking your own trip, turned on,* most of which Matt Zaleski didn't comprehend and—the more he heard them—didn't want to. The changes which, nowadays, he could neither keep pace with nor truly understand, left him subdued and wearied.

In a strange way, at this moment, he found himself equating the big black man, Newkirk, with Barbara who was pretty, twenty-nine, college educated, and white. If Barbara Zaleski were here now, automatically, predictably, she would see things Newkirk's way, and not her father's. Christ!—he wished he were half as sure of things himself.

Tiredly, though it was still early morning, and not at all convinced that he had handled this situation the way he should, Matt Zaleski told Newkirk brusquely, "Get back to your job."

When Newkirk had gone, Illas said, "There'll be no walkout. Word's going around."

"Am I supposed to say thanks?" Zaleski asked sourly. "For not being raped?"

The union man shrugged and moved away.

The mist-green sedan which Zaleski had been

curious about had moved still farther forward on the line. Walking quickly, the assistant plant manager caught up with it.

He checked the papers, including a scheduling order and specifications, in a cardboard folder hanging over the front grille. As he had half-expected, as well as being a "special"—a car which received more careful attention than routine—it was also a "foreman's friend."

A "foreman's friend" was a *very* special car. It was also illegal in any plant and, in this case, involved more than a hundred dollars' worth of dishonesty. Matt Zaleski, who had a knack of storing away tidbits of information and later piecing them together, had more than a shrewd idea who was involved with the mist-green sedan, and why.

The car was for a company public relations man. Its official specifications were Spartan and included few, if any, extras, yet the sedan was (as auto men expressed it) "loaded up" with special items. Even without a close inspection, Matt Zaleski could see a de-luxe steering wheel, extra-ply whitewall tires, styled steel wheels and tinted glass, none of which were in the specifications he was holding. It looked, too, as if the car had received a double paint job, which helped durability. It was this last item which had caught Zaleski's eye earlier.

The almost-certain explanation matched several facts which the assistant plant manager already knew. Two weeks earlier the daughter of a senior foreman in the plant had been married. As a favor, the public relations man, whose car this was, had arranged publicity, getting wedding pictures featured prominently in Detroit and suburban papers. The bride's father was delighted. There had been a good deal of talk about it around the plant.

The rest was easy to guess.

The p.r. man could readily find out in advance which day his car was scheduled for production. He would then have telephoned his foreman friend, who had clearly arranged special attention for the mist-green sedan all the way through assembly.

Matt Zaleski knew what he ought to do. He ought to check out his suspicions by sending for the foreman concerned, and afterward make a written report to the plant manager, McKernon, who would have no choice except to act on it. After that there would be seventeen kinds of hell let loose, extending—because of the p.r. man's involvement—all the way up to staff headquarters.

Matt Zaleski also knew he wasn't going to.

There were problems enough already. The Parkland-Newkirk-Illas embroilment had been one; and predictably, by now, back in the glass-paneled office were others requiring decisions, in addition to those already on his desk this morning. These, he reminded himself, he still hadn't looked at.

On his car radio, driving to work an hour or so ago from Royal Oak, he had heard Emerson Vale, the auto critic whom Zaleski thought of as an idiot, firing buckshot at the industry again. Matt Zaleski had wished then, as now, that he could install Vale on a production hot seat for a few days and let the son-of-a-bitch find out what it really took, in terms of effort, grief, compromise, and human exhaustion to get cars built at all.

Matt Zaleski walked away from the mist-green sedan. In running a plant, you had to learn that there were moments when some things had to be ignored, and this was one.

But at least today was Wednesday.

chapter three

At 7:30 A.M., while tens of thousands in greater Detroit had been up for hours and were already working, others—either through choice or the nature of their work—were still abed.

One who remained there by choice was Erica Trenton.

In a wide, French Provincial bed, between satin sheets which were smooth against the firm surface of her young body, she was awake, but drifting back to sleep, and had no intention of getting up for at least two hours more.

Drowsily, only half-conscious of her own thoughts, she dreamed of a man . . . no particular man, simply a vague figure . . . arousing her sensually, thrusting her deeply—*again! again!* . . . as her own husband had not, for at least three weeks and probably a month.

While she drifted, as on a gently flooding tide between wakefulness and a return to sleep, Erica mused that she had not always been a late riser. In the Bahamas, where she was born, and lived until her marriage to Adam five years ago, she had often risen before dawn and helped launch a dinghy from the beach, afterward running the outboard while her father trolled and the sun rose. Her father enjoyed fresh fish at breakfast and, in her later years at home, it was Erica who cooked it when they returned.

During her initiation to marriage, in Detroit, she had followed the same pattern, rising early with Adam and preparing breakfast which they ate together—he zestfully, and loudly appreciative of Erica's natural talent for cooking which she used with imagination, even for simplest meals. By her own wish they had no live-in help, and

Erica kept busy, especially since Adam's twin sons, Greg and Kirk, who were at prep school nearby, came home during most weekends and holidays.

That was the time when she had been worried about her acceptance by the boys—Adam had divorced their mother earlier the same year, only a few months before meeting Erica and the beginning of their brief, jet-speed courtship. But Erica had been accepted at once by Greg and Kirk —even gratefully, it seemed, since they had seen little of either of their parents over several preceding years, Adam being immersed in his work, and the boys' mother, Francine, traveling frequently abroad, as she still did. Besides, Erica was closer to the boys' own age. She had been barely twenty-one then, Adam eighteen years her senior, though the differences in ages hadn't seemed to matter. Of course, the gap of years between Adam and Erica was still the same, except that nowadays—five years later—it *seemed* wider.

A reason, obviously, was that at the beginning they had devoured each other sexually. They first made love—tempestuously—on a moonlit Bahamas beach. Erica remembered still: the warm, jasmine-scented night, white sand, softly lapping water, a breeze stirring palm trees, music drifting from a lighted cruise ship in Nassau harbor. They had known each other for a few days only. Adam had been holidaying—an aftermath to his divorce —with friends at Lyford Cay who introduced him to Erica at a Nassau night spot, Charley Charley's. They spent all next day together, and others afterward.

The night on the beach was not their first time there. But on the earlier occasions she had resisted Adam; now, she learned, she could resist no longer, and only whisper helplessly, "I can get pregnant."

He had whispered back, "You're going to marry me. So it doesn't matter."

She had not become pregnant, though many times since she wished she had.

From then on, and into marriage a month later, they made love frequently and passionately —almost unfailingly each night, then expending themselves further (but, oh, how gloriously) on awakening in the morning. Even back in Detroit the night and morning love-making persisted, despite Adam's early work start which, Erica quickly discovered, was part of an auto executive's life.

But as months went by and, after that, the first few years, Adam's passion lessened. For either of them it could never have sustained itself at the original fevered pace; Erica realized that. But what she had not expected was that the decline would come as early as it had, or be so near-complete. Undoubtedly she became more conscious of the change because other activities were less. Greg and Kirk now came home seldom, having left Michigan for college—Greg to Columbia, en route to medical school; Kirk to the University of Oklahoma to major in journalism.

She was still drifting . . . Still not quite asleep. The house, near Quarton Lake in the northern suburb of Birmingham, was quiet. Adam had gone. Like most in the auto industry's top echelon, he was at his desk by half-past seven, had done an hour's work before the secretaries came. Also, as usual, Adam had risen in time to do exercises, take a ten-minute run outside, then, after showering, get his own breakfast, as he always did these days. Erica had slipped out of the habit of preparing it after Adam told her candidly that the meal was taking too long; unlike their early years together, he chafed impatiently, wanting to be on his way, no longer enjoying their relaxed quarter hour together at the table. One morning he had simply said, "Honey, you stay in bed. I'll get breakfast for myself." And he had, doing the same thing next day, and on other mornings after that, so they had drifted into the present pattern, though it depressed Erica to know she was no longer useful to Adam at the beginning of his day, that her imaginative breakfast menus, the cheerfully set table and her own presence there, were more irritating to him than pleasing.

Erica found Adam's diminishing concern about what went on at home, along with total dedication to his job, more and more an aggravating combination nowadays. He was also tediously considerate. When his alarm clock sounded, Adam snapped it off promptly before it could penetrate Erica's sleep too deeply, and got out of bed at once, though it seemed not long ago that they had reached for each other instinctively on waking, and sometimes coupled quickly, finding that each could bring the other, feverishly, to a swifter climax than at night. Then, while Erica still lay, lingering for a moment breathlessly, her heart beating hard, Adam would whisper as he slipped from her and from the bed, "What better way to start a day?"

But not any more. Never in the morning, and only rarely, now, at night. And in the mornings, for all the contact they had, they might as well be strangers. Adam awakened quickly, performed his swift routines, and then was gone.

This morning, when Erica heard Adam moving around in the bathroom and downstairs, she considered changing the routine and joining him. Then she reminded herself that all he wanted was to move fast—like the go-go cars his Product Planning team conceived; the latest, the soon-to-be-unveiled Orion—and be on his way. Also, with

his damned efficiency, Adam could make breakfast just as speedily as Erica—for a half-dozen
people if necessary, as he sometimes had. Despite
this, she debated getting up, and was still debating
when she heard Adam's car start, and leave. Then
it was too late.

Where have all the flowers gone? Where the
love, the life, the vanished idyll of Adam and Erica
Trenton, young lovers not so long ago? *O where,
O where!*

Erica slept.

When she awakened it was midmorning, and
a watery autumn sun was slanting in through
slats of the venetian blinds.

Downstairs, a vacuum cleaner whined and
thumped, and Erica was relieved that Mrs. Gooch,
who cleaned twice a week, had let herself in and
was already at work. It meant that today Erica
need not bother with the house, though lately, in
any case, she had paid much less attention to it
than she used to do.

A morning paper was beside the bed. Adam
must have left it there, as he sometimes did.
Propping herself up with pillows, her long ash-
blond hair tumbling over them, Erica unfolded it.

A sizable portion of page one was given over
to an attack on the auto industry by Emerson
Vale. Erica skipped most of the news story, which
didn't interest her, even though there were times
when she felt like attacking the auto world herself. She had never cared for it, not since first
coming to Detroit, though she had tried, for
Adam's sake. But the all-consuming interest in
their occupations which so many auto people had,
leaving time for little else, repelled her. Erica's
own father, an airline captain, had been good at
his job, but always put it behind him mentally
when he left an Island Airways cockpit to come

home. His greater interests were being with his family, fishing, pottering at carpentry, reading, strumming a guitar, and sometimes just sitting in the sun. Erica knew that even now her own mother and father spent far more time together than she and Adam did.

It was her father who had said, when she announced her sudden plans to marry Adam: *"You're your own girl and always have been. So I won't oppose this because, even if I did, it would make no difference and I'd sooner you go with my blessing than without. And maybe, in time, I'll get used to having a son-in-law almost my own age. He seems a decent man; I like him. But one thing I'll warn you of: He's ambitious, and you don't know yet what ambition means, especially up there in Detroit. If the two of you have trouble, that'll be the cause of it."* She sometimes thought how observant—and how right—her father had been.

Erica's thoughts returned to the newspaper and Emerson Vale, whose face glared out from a two-column cut. She wondered if the youthful auto critic was any good in bed, then thought: probably not. She had heard there were no women in his life, nor men either, despite abortive efforts to smear him with a homosexual tag. Humanity, it seemed, had a depressing proportion of capons and worn-out males. Listlessly, she turned the page.

There was little that held interest, from international affairs—the world was in as much a mess as on any other day—through to the social section, which contained the usual auto names: the Fords had entertained an Italian princess, the Roches were in New York, the Townsends at the Symphony, and the Chapins duck hunting in North Dakota. On another page Erica stopped at Ann Landers' column, then mentally began composing a letter of her own: *My problem, Ann, is a married woman's cliché. There are jokes about it, but the jokes are made by people it isn't happening to. The plain truth is—if I can speak frankly as one woman to another—I'm simply not getting enough . . . Just lately I've not been getting any . . .*

With an impatient, angry gesture Erica crumpled the newspaper and pulled the bed-clothes aside. She slid from the bed and went to the window where she tugged vigorously at the blind cord so that full daylight streamed in. Her eyes searched the room for a brown alligator handbag she had used yesterday; it was on a dressing table. Opening the bag, she riffled through until she found a small, leather-covered notebook which she took—turning pages as she went—to a telephone by Adam's side of the bed.

She dialed quickly—before she could change her mind—the number she had found in the book. As she finished, Erica found her hand trembling and put it on the bed to steady herself. A woman's voice answered, "Detroit Bearing and Gear."

Erica asked for the name she had written in the notebook, in handwriting so indecipherable that only she could read it.

"What department is he in?"

"I think—sales."

"One moment, please."

Erica could still hear the vacuum cleaner somewhere outside. At least, while that continued, she could be sure Mrs. Gooch was not listening.

There was a click and another voice answered, though not the one she sought. She repeated the name she had asked for.

"Sure, he's here." She heard the voice call "Ollie!" An answering voice said, "I got it," then, more clearly, "Hullo."

"This is Erica." She added uncertainly, "You know; we met . . ."

"Sure, sure; I know. Where are you?"

"At home."

"What number?"

She gave it to him.

"Hang up. Call you right back."

Erica waited nervously, wondering if she would answer at all, but when the ring back came, she did so immediately.

"Hi, baby!"

"Hullo," Erica said.

"Some phones are better'n other phones for special kindsa calls."

"I understand."

"Long time no see."

"Yes. It is."

A pause.

"Why'd you call, baby?"

"Well, I thought . . . we might meet."

"Why?"

"Perhaps for a drink."

"We had drinks last time. Remember? Sat all afternoon in that goddam Queensway Inn bar."

"I know, but . . ."

"An' the same thing the time before that."

"That was the very first time; the time we met there."

"Okay, so you don't put out the first time. A dame cuts it the way she sees; fair enough. But the second time a guy expects to hit the coconut, not spend an afternoon of his time in a big gab-fest. So I still say—what's on your mind?"

"I thought . . . if we could talk, just a little, I could explain . . ."

"No dice."

She let her hand holding the phone drop down. *In God's name, what was she doing, even*

*talking with this . . . There must be other men.
But where?*

The phone diaphragm rasped, "You still there,
baby?"

She lifted her hand again. "Yes."

"Listen, I'll ask you something. You wanna
get laid?"

Erica was choking back tears; tears of humiliation, self-disgust.

"Yes," she said. "Yes, that's what I want."

"You're sure, this time. No more big gabfest?"

Dear God! Did he want an affidavit? She
wondered: Were there really women so desperate,
they would respond to an approach so crude?
Obviously, yes.

"I'm sure," Erica said.

"That's great, kiddo! How's if we hit the sack
next Wednesday?"

"I thought . . . perhaps sooner." Next
Wednesday was a week away.

"Sorry, baby; no dice. Gotta sales trip. Leave
for Cleveland in an hour. Be there five days." A
chuckle. "Gotta keep them Ohio dolls happy."

Erica forced a laugh. "You certainly get
around."

"You'd be surprised."

She thought: *No, I wouldn't. Not at anything, any more.*

"Call you soon's I get back. While I'm gone,
you keep it warm for me." A second's pause, then:
"You be all right Wednesday? You know what I
mean?"

Erica's control snapped. "Of course I know.
Do you think I'm so stupid not to have thought of
that?"

"You'd be surprised how many don't."

In a detached part of her mind, as if she
were a spectator, not a participant, she marveled:

Has he ever tried making a woman feel good, instead of awful?

"Gotta go, baby. Back to the salt mines! Another day, another dollar!"

"Goodbye," Erica said.

"S' long."

She hung up. Covering her face with her hands, she sobbed silently until her long, slim fingers were wet with tears.

Later, in the bathroom, washing her face and using make-up to conceal the signs of crying as best she could, Erica reasoned: There *was* a way out.

It didn't have to happen a week from now. Adam could prevent it, though he would never know.

If only, within the next seven nights he would take her, as a husband could and should, she would weather this time, and afterward, somehow, tame her body's urgency to reasonableness. All she sought—all she had ever sought—was to be loved and needed, and in return to give love. She still loved Adam. Erica closed her eyes, remembering the way it was when he first loved and needed her.

And she would help Adam, she decided. Tonight, and other nights if necessary, she would make herself irresistibly attractive, she'd wash her hair so it was sweet-smelling, use a musky perfume that would tantalize, put on her sheerest negligee . . . Wait! She would buy a new negligee—today, this morning, *now* . . . in Birmingham.

Hurriedly, she began to dress.

chapter four

The handsome, gray stone staff building, which could have done duty as a state capitol, was quiet in the early morning as Adam Trenton wheeled his cream sport coupe down the ramp from outside. Adam made a fast "S" turn, tires squealing, into his stall in the underground, executive parking area, then eased his lanky figure out of the driver's seat, leaving the keys inside. A rain shower last night had slightly spotted the car's bright finish; routinely it would be washed today, topped off with gas, and serviced if necessary.

A personal car of an executive's own choice, replaced every six months, and each time with all the extras he wanted, plus fuel and constant attention, was a fringe benefit which went with the auto industry's higher posts. Depending on which company they worked for, most senior people made their selections from the luxury ranges—Chrysler Imperials, Lincolns, Cadillacs. A few, like Adam, preferred something lighter and sportier, with a high performance engine.

Adam's footsteps echoed as he walked across the black, waxed garage floor, gleaming and immaculate.

A spectator would have seen a gray-suited, lithe, athletic man, a year or two past forty, tall, with broad shoulders and a squarish head thrust forward, as if urging the rest of the body on. Nowadays, Adam Trenton dressed more conservatively than he used to, but still looked fashionable, with a touch of flashiness. His facial features were clean-cut and alert, with intense blue eyes and a straight, firm mouth, the last tempered by a hint of humor and a strong impression, over-all, of open honesty. He backed up this impression, when he talked, with a blunt directness which sometimes threw others off balance—a tactic he had learned to use deliberately. His manner of walking was confident, a no-nonsense stride suggesting a man who knew where he was going.

Adam Trenton carried the auto executive's symbol of office—a filled attaché case. It contained papers he had taken home the night before and had worked on, after dinner, until bedtime.

Among the few executive cars already parked, Adam noticed two limousines in vice-presidents' row—a series of parking slots near an exclusive elevator which rose nonstop to the fifteenth floor, preserve of the company's senior officers. A parking spot closest to the elevator was reserved for the chairman of the board, the next for the president; after that came vice-presidents in descending order of seniority. Where a man parked was a significant prestige factor in the auto industry. The higher his rank, the less distance he was expected to walk from his car to his desk.

Of the two limousines already in, one belonged to Adam's own chief, the Product Development vice-president. The other was the car of the Vice-President Public Relations.

Adam bounded up a short flight of stairs, two at a time, entered a doorway to the building's main lobby, then continued briskly to a regular staff elevator where he jabbed a button for the tenth floor. Alone in the elevator, he waited impatiently while the computer-controlled mechanism took its time about starting, then on the way up experienced the eagerness he always felt to become immersed in a new day's work. As always, through most of the past two years, the Orion was at the forefront of his thoughts. Physically, Adam felt good. Only a sense of tension troubled him—a mental tautness he had become aware of lately, a nuisance, illogical, yet increasingly difficult to shake off. He took a small, green-and-black capsule from an inside pocket, slipped it into his mouth and gulped it down.

From the elevator, along a silent, deserted corridor which would see little activity for another hour, Adam strode to his own office suite—a corner location, also a token of rank, rating only a little lower than a vice-president's parking slot.

As he went in, he saw a pile of newly delivered mail on his secretary's desk. There was a time, earlier in his career, when Adam would have stopped to riffle through it, to see what was interesting and new, but he had long since shed the habit, nowadays valuing his time too much for that kind of indulgence. One of the duties of a top-notch secretary was—as Adam once heard the company president declare—to "filter out the crap" from the mountain of paper which came her boss's way. She should be allowed to go through everything first, using her judgment about what to refer elsewhere, so that an executive mind could concern itself with policy and ideas, unencumbered by detail which others, in lowlier posts, could be trusted to handle.

That was why few of the thousands of letters yearly which individual car owners addressed to heads of auto companies ever reached the person whom the sender named. All such letters were screened by secretaries, then sent to special departments which dealt with them according to set routines. Eventually the sum of all complaints and comments in a year was tabulated and studied, but no senior executive could cope with them individually and do his job as well. An occasional exception was where a correspondent was shrewd enough to write to an executive's home address—not hard to find, since most were listed in Who's Who, available in public libraries.

Then an executive, or his wife, might well read the letter, become interested in a particular case, and follow through personally.

The first thing Adam Trenton noticed in his office was a glowing orange light on an intercom box behind his desk. It showed that the Product Development vice-president had called, almost certainly this morning. Adam touched a switch above the light and waited.

A voice, metallic through the intercom, demanded, "What's the excuse today? Accident on the freeway, or did you oversleep?"

Adam laughed, his eyes flicking to a wall clock which showed 7:23. He depressed the key connecting him with the vice-president's office five floors above. "You know my problem, Elroy. Just can't seem to get out of bed."

It was rarely that the head of Product Development beat Adam in; when he did, he liked to make the most of it.

"Adam, how are you fixed for the next hour?"

"I've a few things. Nothing I can't change around."

From the windows of his office, as they talked, Adam could see the early morning freeway traffic. At this time the volume was moderately heavy, though not so great as an hour ago when production workers were heading in to factories to begin day shifts. But the traffic pattern would change again soon as thousands of office employees, now breakfasting at home, added their cars to the hurrying stream. The pressures and easings of traffic density, like variations in the wind, always fascinated Adam—not surprisingly, since automobiles, the traffic's chief constituent, were the *idée fixe* of his own existence. He had devised a scale of his own—like the Beaufort wind scale, ranging from one to ten degrees of volume—which he applied to traffic as he viewed it. Right now, he decided, the flow was at Volume Five.

"I'd like you up here for a while," Elroy Braithwaite, the vice-president, said. "I guess you know our buddy, Emerson Vale, is off in orbit again."

"Yes." Adam had read the *Free Press* report of Vale's latest charges before leaving the newspaper beside the bed where Erica was sleeping.

"Some of the press have asked for comments. This time Jake thinks we should make a few."

Jake Earlham was the Vice-President Public Relations, whose car had also been parked below as Adam came in.

"I agree with him," Adam said.

"Well, I seem to have been elected, but I'd like you in on the session. It'll be informal. Somebody from AP, the *Newsweek* gal, *The Wall Street Journal,* and Bob Irvin from the *Detroit News*. We're going to see them all together."

"Any ground rules, briefing?" Usually, in advance of auto company press conferences, elaborate preparations were made, with public relations departments preparing lists of anticipated questions, which executives then studied. Sometimes rehearsals were staged at which p.r. men played reporters. A major press conference took weeks in planning, so that auto company spokesmen were as well prepared as a U.S. President facing the press, sometimes better.

"No briefing," Elroy Braithwaite said. "Jake and I have decided to hang loose on this one. We'll call things the way we see them. That goes for you too."

"Okay," Adam said. "Are you ready now?"

"About ten minutes. I'll call you."

Waiting, Adam emptied his attaché case of last night's work, then used a dictating machine to leave a series of instructions for his secretary,

Ursula Cox, who would deal with them with predictable efficiency when she came in. Most of Adam's homework, as well as the instructions, concerned the Orion. In his role as Advanced Vehicles Planning Manager he was deeply involved with the new, still-secret car, and today a critical series of tests involving a noise-vibration problem with the Orion would be reviewed at the company's proving ground thirty miles outside Detroit. Adam, who would have to make a decision afterward, had agreed to drive to the test review with a colleague from Design-Styling. Now, because of the press conference just called, one of Ursula's instructions was to reschedule the proving ground arrangements for later in the day.

He had better, Adam decided, reread the Emerson Vale news story before the press session started. Along with the pile of mail outside were some morning newspapers. He collected a *Free Press* and a *New York Times*, then returned to his office and spread them out, this time memorizing, point by point, what Vale had said in Washington the day before.

Adam had met Emerson Vale once when the auto critic was in Detroit to make a speech. Like several others from the industry, Adam Trenton had attended out of curiosity and, on being introduced to Vale ahead of the meeting, was surprised to find him an engagingly pleasant young man, not in the least the brash, abrasive figure Adam had expected. Later, when Vale faced his audience from the platform, he was equally personable, speaking fluently and easily while marshaling arguments with skill. The entire presentation, Adam was forced to admit, was impressive and, from the applause afterward, a large part of the audience—which had paid for admission—felt the same way.

There was one shortcoming. To anyone with

specialized knowledge, many of Emerson Vale's arguments were as porous as a leaky boat.

While attacking a highly technical industry, Vale betrayed his own lack of technical know-how and was frequently in error in describing mechanical functions. His engineering pronouncements were capable of several interpretations; Vale gave one, which suited his own viewpoint. At other moments he dealt in generalities. Even though trained in law, Emerson Vale ignored elementary rules of evidence. He offered assertion, hearsay, unsupported evidence as fact; occasionally the young auto critic—it seemed to Adam—distorted facts deliberately. He resurrected the past, listing faults in cars which manufacturers had long since admitted and rectified. He presented charges based on no more than his own mail from disgruntled car users. While excoriating the auto industry for bad design, poor workmanship, and lack of safety features, Vale acknowledged none of the industry's problems nor recent genuine attempts to improve its ways. He failed to see anything good in auto manufacturers and their people, only indifference, neglect, and villainy.

Emerson Vale had published a book, its title: *The American Car: Unsure in Any Need*. The book was skillfully written, with the attention-commanding quality which the author himself possessed, and it proved a bestseller which kept Vale in the spotlight of public attention for many months.

But subsequently, because there seemed little more for him to say, Emerson Vale began dropping out of sight. His name appeared in newspapers less frequently, then, for a while, not at all. This lack of attention goaded Vale to new activity. Craving publicity like a drug, he seemed willing to make any statement on any subject, in return for keeping his name before the public. Describing

himself as "a consumers' spokesman," he launched
a fresh series of attacks on the auto industry,
alleging design defects in specific cars, which the
press reported, though some were later proved untrue. He coaxed a U.S. senator into quoting pil-
fered information on auto company costs which
soon after was shown to be absurdly incomplete.
The senator looked foolish. A habit of Vale's
was to telephone reporters on big city dailies—
collect, and sometimes in the night—with suggestions for news stories which just incidentally
would include Emerson Vale's name, but which
failed to stand up when checked out. As a result,
the press, which had relied on Vale for colorful
copy, became more wary and eventually some reporters ceased trusting him at all.

Even when proved wrong, Emerson Vale—
like his predecessor in the auto critic field, Ralph
Nader—was never known to admit an error or to
apologize, as General Motors had once apologized
to Nader after the corporation's unwarranted intrusion into Nader's private life. Instead, Vale
persisted with accusations and charges against
all automobile manufacturers and, at times, could
still draw nationwide attention, as he had succeeded in doing yesterday in Washington.

Adam folded the newspapers. A glance outside showed him that the freeway traffic had increased to Volume Six.

A moment later the intercom buzzed. "The
fourth estate just got here," the Product Development vice-president said "You want to make a
fifth?"

On his way upstairs, Adam reminded himself
that he must telephone his wife sometime today.
He knew that Erica had been unhappy lately, at
moments more difficult to live with than during
the first year or two of their marriage which

began so promisingly. Adam sensed that part of the trouble was his own tiredness at the end of each day, which took its toll physically of them both. But he wished Erica would get out more and learn to be enterprising on her own. He had tried to encourage her in that, just as he had made sure she had all the money she needed. Fortunately there were no money problems for either of them, thanks to his own steady series of promotions, and there was a good chance of even bigger things to come, which any wife ought to be pleased about.

Adam was aware that Erica still resented the amount of time and energy which his job demanded, but she had been an automotive wife for five years now, and ought to have come to terms with that, just as other wives learned to.

Occasionally, he wondered if it had been a mistake to marry someone so much younger than himself, though intellectually they had never had the slightest problem. Erica had brains and intelligence far beyond her years, and—as Adam had seen—was seldom *en rapport* with younger men.

The more he thought about it, the more he realized they would have to find some resolution to their problems soon.

But at the fifteenth floor, as he entered high command territory, Adam thrust personal thoughts away.

In the office suite of the Product Development vice-president, Jake Earlham, Vice-President Public Relations, was performing introductions. Earlham, bald and stubby, had been a newspaperman many years ago and now looked like a donnish Mr. Pickwick. He was always either smoking a pipe or gesturing with it. He waved the pipe now to acknowledge Adam Trenton's entry.

"I believe you know Monica from *Newsweek*."

"We've met." Adam acknowledged a petite brunette, already seated on a sofa. With shapely ankles crossed, smoke rising lazily from a cigarette, she smiled back coolly, making it plain that a representative of New York would not be taken in by Detroit charm, no matter how artfully applied.

Beside *Newsweek*, on the sofa, was *The Wall Street Journal*, a florid, middle-aged reporter named Harris. Adam shook his hand, then that of AP, a taut young man with a sheaf of copy paper, who acknowledged Adam curtly, plainly wanting the session to get on. Bob Irvin, bald and easygoing, of the *Detroit News*, was last.

"Hi, Bob," Adam said. Irvin, whom Adam knew best, wrote a daily column about automotive affairs. He was well-informed and respected in the industry, though no sycophant, being quick to jab a needle when he felt occasion warranted. In the past, Irvin had given a good deal of sympathetic coverage to both Ralph Nader and Emerson Vale.

Elroy Braithwaite, the Product Development vice-president, dropped into a vacant armchair in the comfortable lounge area where they had assembled. He asked amiably, "Who'll begin?"

Braithwaite, known among intimates as "The Silver Fox" because of his mane of meticulously groomed gray hair, wore a tightly cut Edwardian mode suit and sported another personal trademark—enormous cuff links. He exuded a style matching his surroundings. Like all offices for vice-presidents and above, this one had been exclusively designed and furnished; it had African avodire wood paneling, brocaded drapes, and deep broadloom underfoot. Any man who attained this eminence in an auto company worked long and fiercely to get here. But once arrived, the working conditions held pleasant perquisites including an office like this, with adjoining dressing room and sleeping quarters, plus—on the floor above—a personal dining room, as well as a steam bath and masseur, available at any time.

"Perhaps the lady should lead off." It was Jake Earlham, perched on a window seat behind them.

"All right," the *Newsweek* brunette said. "What's the latest weak alibi for not launching a meaningful program to develop a nonpollutant steam engine for cars?"

"We're fresh out of alibis," the Silver Fox said. Braithwaite's expression had not changed; only his voice was a shade sharper. "Besides, the job's already been done—by a guy named George Stephenson—and we don't think there's been a lot of significant progress since."

The AP man had put on thin-rimmed glasses; he looked through them impatiently. "Okay, so we've got the comedy over. Can we have some some straight questions and answers now?"

"I think we should," Jake Earlham said. The p.r. head added apologetically, "I should have remembered. The wire services have an early deadline for the East Coast afternoon papers."

"Thank you," AP said. He addressed Elroy Braithwaite. "Mr. Vale made a statement last night that the auto companies are guilty of conspiracy and some other things because they haven't made serious efforts to develop an alternative to the internal combustion engine. He also says that steam and electric engines are available now. Would you care to comment on that?"

The Silver Fox nodded. "What Mr. Vale said about the engines being available now is true. There are various kinds; most of them work, and we have several ourselves in our test center. What

Vale didn't say—either because it would spoil his argument or he doesn't know—is that there still isn't a hope in hell of making a steam or electric engine for cars, at low cost, low weight, and good convenience, in the foreseeable future."

"How long's that?"

"Through the 1970s. By the 1980s there'll be other new developments, though the internal combustion engine—an almost totally nonpolluting one—still *may* dominate."

The Wall Street Journal interjected, "But there've been a lot of news stories about all kinds of engines here and now . . ."

"You're damn right," Elroy Braithwaite said, "and most of 'em should be in the comics section. If you'll excuse my saying so, newspaper writers are about the most gullible people afloat. Maybe they want to be; I guess, that way, the stories they write are more interesting. But let some inventor—never mind if he's a genius or a kook—come up with a one-only job, and turn the press loose on him. What happens? Next day all the news stories say this 'may' be the big breakthrough, this 'may' be the way the future's going. Repeat that a few times so the public reads it often, and everybody thinks it must be true, just the way newspaper people, I suppose, believe their own copy if they write enough of it. It's that kind of hoopla that's made a good many in this country convinced theyll have a steam or electric car, or maybe a hybrid, soon in their own garages."

The Silver Fox smiled at his public relations colleague, who had shifted uneasily and was fidgeting with his pipe. "Relax, Jake. I'm not taking off at the press. Just trying to fix a perspective."

Jake Earlham said dryly, "I'm glad you told me. For a minute I was wondering."

"Aren't you losing sight of some facts, Mr. Braithwaite?" AP persisted. "There are reputable people who still believe in steam power. Some big outfits other than auto companies are working on it. The California government is putting money on the line to get a fleet of steam cars on the road. And there are legislative proposals out there to ban internal combustion engines five years from now."

The Product Development vice-president shook his head decisively, his silver mane bobbing. "In my book, the only reputable guy who believed in a steam car was Bill Lear. Then he gave up publicly, calling the idea 'utterly ridiculous.' "

"But he's since changed his mind," AP said.

"Sure, sure. And carries around a hatbox, saying his new steam engine is inside. Well, *we* know what's inside; it's the engine's innermost core, which is like taking a spark plug and saying 'there's an engine from our present cars.' What's seldom mentioned, by Mr. Lear and others, is that to be added are combusters, boiler, condenser, recuperation fans . . . a long list of heavy, expensive, bulky hardware, with dubious efficiency."

Jake Earlham prompted, "The California government's steam cars . . ."

The Silver Fox nodded. "Okay, California. Sure the state's spending lots of money; what government doesn't? If you and half a million others were willing to pay a thousand dollars more for *your* cars, maybe—just maybe—we could build a steam engine, with all its problems and disadvantages. But most of our customers—and our competitors' customers, which we have to think about too—don't have that kind of moss to sling around."

"You're still ducking electric cars," *The Wall Street Journal* pointed out

Braithwaite nodded to Adam "You take that one."

"There are electric cars right now," Adam

told the reporters. "You've seen golf carts, and it's conceivable that a two-passenger vehicle can be developed soon for shopping or similar use within a small local area. At the moment, though, it would be expensive and not much more than a curiosity. We've also built, ourselves, experimental trucks and cars which are electric powered. The trouble is, as soon as we give them any useful range we have to fill most of the inside space with heavy batteries, which doesn't make a lot of sense."

"The small, lightweight battery—zinc-air or fuel cells," AP questioned. "When is it coming?"

"You forgot sodium sulphur," Adam said. "That's another that's been talked up. Unfortunately, there's little more than talk so far."

Elroy Braithwaite put in, "Eventually we believe there *will* be a breakthrough in batteries, with a lot of energy stored in small packages. What's more, there's a big potential use for electric vehicles in downtown traffic. But based on everything we know, we can't see it happening until the 1980s."

"And if you're thinking about air pollution in conjunction with electric cars," Adam added, "there's one factor which a lot of people overlook. Whatever kind of batteries you had, they'd need recharging. So with hundreds of thousands of cars plugged into power sources, there'd be a requirement for many more generating stations, each spewing out its own air pollution. Since electric power plants are usually built in the suburbs, what could happen is that you'd end up taking the smog from the cities and transferring it out there."

"Isn't all that still a pretty weak alibi?" The cool *Newsweek* brunette uncrossed her legs, then twitched her skirt downward, to no effect, as she undoubtedly knew; it continued to ride high on shapely thighs. One by one, the men dropped their eyes to where the thighs and skirt joined.

She elaborated, "I mean an alibi for not having a crash program to make a good, cheap engine —steam or electric, or both. That's how we got to the moon, isn't it?" She added pertly, "If you'll remember, that was my first question."

"I remember," Elroy Braithwaite said. Unlike the other men, he did not remove his gaze from the junction of skirt and thighs, but held it there deliberately. There were several seconds of silence in which most women would have fidgeted or been intimidated. The brunette, self-assured, entirely in control, made clear that she was not. Still not looking up, the Silver Fox said slowly, "What was the question again, Monica?"

"I think you know." Only then did Braithwaite, outmaneuvered, lift his head.

He sighed. "Oh, yes—the moon. You know, there are days I wish we'd never got there. It's produced a new cliché. Nowadays, the moment there's any kind of engineering hangup, anywhere, you can count on somebody saying: We got to the moon, didn't we? Why can't we solve this?"

"If she hadn't asked," *The Wall Street Journal* said, "I would. So why can't we?"

"I'll tell you," the vice-president snapped. "Quite apart from the space gang having unlimited public money—which we haven't—they had an objective: Get to the moon. You people are asking us, on the vague basis of things you've read or heard, to give development of a steam or electric engine for cars that kind of all-or-nothing, billions-in-the-kitty priority. Well, it so happens that some of the best engineering brains in this business think it isn't a practical objective, or even a worthwhile one. We have better ideas and other objectives."

Braithwaite passed a hand over his silver

mane, then nodded to Adam. He gave the impression of having had enough.

"What we believe," Adam said, "is that clean air—at least air not polluted by motor vehicles—can be achieved best, fastest, and most cheaply through refinements of the present gasoline internal combustion engine, along with more improvements in emission control and fuels. That includes the Wankel engine which is also an internal combustion type." He had deliberately kept his voice low key. Now he added, "Maybe that's not as spectacular as the idea of steam or electric power but there's a lot of sound science behind it."

Bob Irvin of the *Detroit News* spoke for the first time. "Quite apart from electric and steam engines, you'd admit, wouldn't you, that before Nader, Emerson Vale, and their kind, the industry wasn't nearly as concerned as it is now about controlling air pollution?"

The question was asked with apparent casualness, Irvin looking blandly through his glasses, but Adam knew it was loaded with explosive. He hesitated only momentarily, then answered, "Yes, I would."

The three other reporters looked at him, surprised.

"As I understand it," Irvin said, still with the same casual manner, "we're here because of Emerson Vale, or in other words, because of an auto critic. Right?"

Jake Earlham intervened from his window seat. "We're here because your editors—and in your case, Bob, you personally—asked if we would respond to some questions today, and we agreed to. It was our understanding that some of the questions would relate to statements which Mr. Vale had made, but *we* did not schedule a press conference specifically because of Vale."

Bob Irvin grinned. "A bit hair-splitty, aren't you, Jake?"

The Vice-President Public Relations shrugged. "I guess."

From Jake Earlham's doubtful expression now and earlier, Adam suspected he was wondering if the informal press meeting had been such a good idea.

"In that case," Irvin said, "I guess this question wouldn't be out of order, Adam." The columnist seemed to ruminate, shambling verbally as he spoke, but those who knew him were aware how deceptive this appearance was. "In your opinion have the auto critics—let's take Nader and safety—fulfilled a useful function?"

The question was simple, but framed so it could not be ducked. Adam felt like protesting to Irvin: *Why pick me?* Then he remembered Elroy Braithwaite's instructions earlier: *"We'll call things the way we see them."*

Adam said quietly, "Yes, they have fulfilled a function. In terms of safety, Nader booted this industry, screaming, into the second half of the twentieth century."

All four reporters wrote that down.

While they did, Adam's thoughts ranged swiftly over what he had said and what came next. Within the auto industry, he was well aware, plenty of others would agree with him. A strong contingent of younger executives and a surprising sprinkling at topmost echelons conceded that basically—despite excesses and inaccuracies—the arguments of Vale and Nader over the past few years made sense. The industry *had* relegated safety to a minor role in car design, it *had* focused attention on sales to the exclusion of most else, it *had* resisted change until forced to change through government regulation or the threat of it. It seemed, looking back, as if auto makers had become drunken on their own immensity and power, and had behaved like Goliaths, until in the end they were humbled by a David—Ralph Nader and, later, Emerson Vale.

The David-Goliath equation, Adam thought, was apt. Nader particularly—alone, unaided, and with remarkable moral courage—took on the entire U.S. auto industry with its unlimited resources and strong Washington lobby, and, where others had failed, succeeded in having safety standards raised and new consumer-oriented legislation passed into law. The fact that Nader was a polemicist who, like all polemicists, took rigid poses, was often excessive, ruthless, and sometimes inaccurate, did not lessen his achievement. Only a bigot would deny that he had performed a valuable public service. Equally to the point: to achieve such a service, against such odds, a Nader-type was necessary.

The Wall Street Journal observed, "So far as I know, Mr. Trenton, no auto executive has made that admission publicly before."

"If no one has," Adam said, "maybe it's time someone did."

Was it imagination, or had Jake Earlham—apparently busy with his pipe—gone pale? Adam detected a frown on the face of the Silver Fox, but what the hell; if necessary, he would argue with Elroy later. Adam had never been a "yes man." Few who rose high in the auto industry were, and those who held back their honest opinions, fearing disapproval from seniors, or because of insecurity about their jobs, seldom made it higher than middle management, at best. Adam had not held back, believing that directness and honesty were useful contributions he could make to his employers. The important thing, he had learned, was to stay an individual. A misguided notion which outsiders had of auto executives was that they conformed to a standard pattern, as if stamped out by cookie cutters. No concept could be more wrong. True, such men had certain traits in common—ambition, drive, a sense of organization, a capacity for work. But, apart from that, they were highly individual, with a better-than-average sprinkling of eccentrics, geniuses, and mavericks.

Anyway, it had been said; nothing would undo it now. But there were postscripts.

"If you're going to quote that"—Adam surveyed the quartet of reporters—"some other things should be said as well."

"Which are?" It was the *Newsweek* girl's query. She seemed less hostile than before, had stubbed out her cigarette and was making notes. Adam stole a glance: her skirt was as high as ever, her thighs and legs increasingly attractive in filmy gray nylon. He felt his interest sharpen, then tore his thoughts away.

"First," Adam said, "the critics have done their job. The industry is working harder on safety than it ever did; what's more, the pressure's staying on. Also, we're consumer oriented. For a while, we weren't. Looking back, it seems as if we got careless and indifferent to consumers without realizing it. Right now, though, we're neither, which is why the Emerson Vales have become shrill and sometimes silly. If you accept their view, nothing an automobile maker does is ever right. Maybe that's why Vale and his kind haven't recognized yet—which is my second point—that the auto industry is in a whole new era."

AP queried, "If that's true, wouldn't you say the auto critics forced you there?"

Adam controlled his irritation. Sometimes auto criticism became a fetish, an unreasoning cult, and not just with professionals like Vale. "They helped," he admitted, "by establishing directions and goals, particularly about safety and pollution. But they had nothing to do with the technological revolution which was coming anyway. It's that that's going to make the next ten years more exciting for everybody in this business than the entire half century just gone."

"Just how?" AP said, glancing at his watch.

"Someone mentioned breakthroughs," Adam answered. "The most important ones, which we can see coming, are in materials which will let us design a whole new breed of vehicles by the mid- or late '70s. Take metals. Instead of solid steel which we're using now, honeycomb steel is coming; it'll be strong, rigid, yet incredibly lighter—meaning fuel economy; also it'll absorb an impact better than conventional steel—a safety plus. Then there are new metal alloys for engines and components. We anticipate one which will allow temperature changes from a hundred degrees to more than two thousand degree Fahrenheit, in seconds, with minor expansion only. Using that, we can incinerate the remainder of unburned fuel causing air pollution. Another metal being worked on is one with a retention technique to 'remember' its original shape. If you crumple a fender or a door, you'll apply heat or pressure and the metal will spring back the way it was before. Another alloy we expect will allow cheap production of reliable, high-quality wheels for gas turbine engines."

Elroy Braithwaite added, "That last is one to watch. If the internal combustion engine goes eventually, the gas turbine's most likely to move in. There are plenty of problems with a turbine for cars—it's efficient only at high power output, and you need a costly heat exchanger if you aim not to burn pedestrians. But they're *solvable* problems, and being worked on."

"Okay," *The Wall Street Journal* said. "So that's metals. What else is new?"

"Something significant, and coming soon for

every car, is an on-board computer." Adam glanced at AP. "It will be small, about the size of a glove compartment."

"A computer to do what?"

"Just about anything; you name it. It will monitor engine components—plugs, fuel injection, all the others. It will control emissions and warn if the engine is polluting. And in other ways it will be revolutionary."

"Name some," *Newsweek* said.

"Part of the time the computer will think for drivers and correct mistakes, often before they realize they're made. One thing it will mastermind is sensory braking—brakes applied individually on every wheel so a driver can never lose control by skidding. A radar auxiliary will warn if a car ahead is slowing or you're following too close. In an emergency the computer could decelerate and apply brakes automatically, and because a computer's reactions are faster than human there should be a lot less rear-end collisions. There'll be the means to lock on to automatic radar control lanes on freeways, which are on the way, with space satellite control of traffic flow not far behind."

Adam caught an approving glance from Jake Earlham and knew why. He had succeeded in turning the talk from defensive to positive, a tactic which the public relations department was constantly urging on company spokesmen.

"One effect of all the changes," Adam went on, "is that interiors of cars, especially from a driver's viewpoint, will look startlingly different within the next few years. The in-car computer will modify most of our present instruments. For example, the gas gauge as we know it is on the way out; in its place will be an indicator showing how many miles of driving your fuel is good for at present speed. On a TV-type screen in front of the

driver, route information and highway warning
signs will appear, triggered by magnetic sensors
in the road. Having to look out for highway signs
is already old-fashioned and dangerous; often a
driver misses them; when they're inside the car,
he won't. Then if you travel a route which is new,
you'll slip in a cassette, the way you do a tape
cartridge for entertainment now. According to
where you are, and keyed in a similar way to the
road signs, you'll receive spoken directions and
visual signals on the screen. And almost at once
the ordinary car radio will have a transmitter,
as well as a receiver, operating on citizens' band.
It's to be a nationwide system, so that a driver can
call for aid—of any kind—whenever he needs it."

AP was on his feet, turning to the p.r. vice-
president. "If I can use a phone . . ."

Jake Earlham slipped from his window seat
and went around to the door. He motioned with
his pipe for AP to follow him. "I'll find you somewhere private."

The others were getting up.

Bob Irvin of the *News* waited until the wire
service reporter had left, then asked, "About that
on-board computer. Are you putting it in the
Orion?"

God damn that Irvin! Adam knew that he
was boxed. The answer was "yes," but it was
secret. On the other hand, if he replied "no,"
eventually the journalists would discover he had
lied.

Adam protested, "You know I can't talk about
the Orion, Bob."

The columnist grinned. The absence of an
outright denial had told him all he needed.

"Well," the *Newsweek* brunette said; now that
she was standing, she appeared taller and more
lissome than when seated. "You trickily steered

the whole thing away from what we came here to talk about."

"Not me." Adam met her eyes directly; they were ice blue, he noted, and derisively appraising. He found himself wishing they had met in a different way and less as adversaries. He smiled. "I'm just a simple auto worker who tries to see both sides."

"Really!" The eyes remained fixed, still mirroring derision. "Then how about an honest answer to this: Is the outlook inside the auto industry really changing?" *Newsweek* glanced at her notebook. "Are the big auto makers truly responding to the times—accepting new ideas about community responsibility, developing a social conscience, being realistic about changing values, including values about cars? Do you genuinely believe that consumerism is here to stay? Is there really a new era, the way you claim? Or is it all a front-office dress-up, staged by public relations flacks, while what you really hope is that the attention you're getting now will go away, and everything will slip back the way it was before, when you did pretty much what you liked? Are you people really tuned in to what's happening about environment, safety, and all those other things, or are you kidding yourselves and us? *Quo Vadis?*—do you remember your Latin, Mr. Trenton?"

"Yes," Adam said, "I remember." *Quo Vadis? Whither goest thou?* . . . The age-old question of mankind, echoing down through history, asked of civilizations, nations, individuals, groups and, now, an industry.

Elroy Braithwaite inquired, "Say, Monica, is that a question or a speech?"

"It's a mélange question." The *Newsweek* girl gave the Silver Fox an unwarmed smile. "If it's too complicated for you, I could break it into simple segments, using shorter words."

The public relations chief had just returned after escorting AP. "Jake," the Product Development vice-president told his colleague, "somehow these press meetings aren't what they used to be."

"If you mean we're more aggressive, not deferential any more," *The Wall Street Journal* said, "it's because reporters are being trained that way, and our editors tell us to bore in hard. Like everything else, I guess there's a new look in journalism." He added thoughtfully, "Sometimes it makes me uncomfortable, too."

"Well, it doesn't me," *Newsweek* said, "and I still have a question hanging." She turned to Adam. "I asked it of you."

Adam hesitated. *Quo Vadis?* In other forms, he sometimes put the same interrogation to himself. But in answering now, how far should open honesty extend?

Elroy Braithwaite relieved him of decision.

"If Adam doesn't mind," the Silver Fox interposed, "I believe I'll answer that. Without accepting all your premises, Monica, this company—as it represents our industry—has always accepted community responsibility; what's more, it does have a social conscience and has demonstrated this for many years. As to consumerism, we've always believed in it, long before the word itself was coined by those who . . ."

The rounded phrases rolled eloquently on. Listening, Adam was relieved he hadn't answered. Despite his own dedication to his work, he would have been compelled, in honesty, to admit some doubts.

He was relieved, though, that the session was almost done. He itched to get back to his own bailiwick where the Orion—like a loving but demanding mistress—summoned him.

chapter five

In the corporate Design-Styling Center—a mile or so from the staff building where the press session was now concluding—the odor of modeling clay was, as usual, all-pervading. Regulars who worked in Design-Styling claimed that after a while they ceased to notice the smell—a mild but insistent mix of sulphur and glycerin, its source the dozens of security-guarded studios ringing the Design-Styling Center's circular inner core. Within the studios, sculptured models of potential new automobiles were taking shape.

Visitors, though, wrinkled their noses in distaste when the smell first hit them. Not that many visitors got close to the source. The majority penetrated only as far as the outer reception lobby, or to one of the half-dozen offices behind it, and even here they were checked in and out by security guards, never left alone, and issued color-coded badges, defining—and usually limiting severely—the areas where they could be escorted.

On occasions, national security and nuclear secrets had been guarded less carefully than design details of future model cars.

Even staff designers were not allowed unhampered movement. Those least senior were restricted to one or two studios, their freedom increasing only after years of service. The precaution made sense. Designers were sometimes wooed by other auto companies and, since each studio held secrets of its own, the fewer an individual entered, the less knowledge he could take with him if he left. Generally, what a designer was told about activity on new model cars was based on the military principle of "need to know." However, as designers grew older in the company's service, and also more "locked in" financially through stock options and pension plans, security was relaxed and a distinctive badge —worn like a combat medal—allowed an individual past a majority of doors and guards. Even then, the system didn't always work because occasionally a top-flight, senior designer would move to a competitive company with a financial arrangement so magnanimous as to outweigh everything else. Then, when he went, years of advance knowledge went with him. Some designers in the auto industry had worked, in their time, for all major auto companies, though Ford and General Motors had an unwritten agreement that neither approached each other's designers— at least, directly—with job offers. Chrysler was less inhibited.

Only a few individuals—design directors and heads of studios—were allowed everywhere within the Design-Styling Center. One of these was Brett DeLosanto. This morning he was strolling unhurriedly through a pleasant, glass-enclosed courtyard which led to Studio X. This was a studio which, at the moment, bore somewhat the same relationship to others in the building as the Sistine Chapel to St. Peter's nave.

A security guard put down his newspaper as Brett approached.

"Good morning, Mr. DeLosanto." The man looked the young designer up and down, then whistled softly. "I shoulda brought dark glasses."

Brett DeLosanto laughed. A flamboyant figure at any time with his long—though carefully styled —hair, deep descending sideburns and precisely trimmed Vandyke beard, he had added to the effect today by wearing a pink shirt and mauve tie, with slacks and shoes matching the tie, the ensemble topped by a white cashmere jacket.

"You like the outfit, eh?"

The guard considered. He was a grizzled ex-Army noncom, more than twice Brett's age. "Well, sir, you could say it was different."

"The only difference between you and me, Al, is that I design my uniforms." Brett nodded toward the studio door. "Much going on today?"

"There's the usual people in, Mr. DeLosanto. As to what goes on, they told me when I came here: Keep my back to the door, eyes to the front."

"But you know the Orion's in there. You must have seen it."

"Yes, sir, I've seen it. When the brass came in for the big approval day, they moved it to the showroom."

"What do you think?"

The guard smiled. "I'll tell you what I think, Mr. DeLosanto. I think you and the Orion are a lot alike."

As Brett entered the studio, and the outer door clicked solidly behind him, he reflected: If true, it would scarcely be surprising.

A sizable segment of his life and creative talent had gone into the Orion. There were times, in moments of self-appraisal, when he wondered if it had been too much. On more hundreds of occasions than he cared to think about, he had passed through this same studio door, during frenetic days and long, exhausting nights—times of agony and ecstasy—while the Orion progressed from embryo idea to finished car.

He had been involved from the beginning.

Even before studio work began, he and others from Design had been apprised of studies—market research, population growth, economics, social changes, age groups, needs, fashion trends. A cost target was set. Then came the early concept of a completely new car. During months that followed, design criteria were hammered out at meeting after meeting of product planners, designers, engineers. After that, and working together, engineers devised a power package while designers —of whom Brett was one—doodled, then became specific, so that lines and contours of the car took shape. And while it happened, hopes advanced, receded; plans went right, went wrong, then right again; doubts arose, were quelled, arose once more. Within the company, hundreds were involved, led by a top half-dozen.

Endless design changes occurred, some prompted by logic, others through intuition only. Later still, testing began. Eventually—too soon, it always seemed to Brett—management approval for production came and, after that, Manufacturing moved in. Now, with production planning well advanced, in less than a year, the Orion would undergo the most critical test of all: public acceptance or rejection. And through all the time so far, while no individual could ever be responsible for an entire car, Brett DeLosanto, more than anyone else on the design team, had implanted in the Orion his own ideas, artistic flair, and effort.

Brett, with Adam Trenton.

It was because of Adam Trenton that Brett was here this morning—far earlier than his usual time of starting work. The two had planned to go together to the company proving ground, but a message from Adam, which had just come in, announced that he would be delayed. Brett, less disciplined than Adam in his working habits, and preferring to sleep late, was annoyed at having got up needlessly, then decided on a short solitude with the Orion, anyway. Now, opening an inner door, he entered the main studio.

In several brightly lighted work areas, design development was in progress on clay models of Orion derivatives—a sports version to appear three years from now, a station wagon, and on other variations of the original Orion design which might, or might not, be used in future years.

The original Orion—the car which would have its public introduction only a year from now —was at the far end of the studio on soft gray carpeting under spotlights. The model was finished in *bleu céleste*. Brett walked toward it, a sense of excitement gripping him, which was why he had come here, knowing that it would.

The car.was small, compact, lean, slim-lined. It had what sales planners were already calling a "tucked under, tubular look," clearly influenced by missile design, giving a functional appearance, yet with élan and style. Several body features were revolutionary. For the first time in any car, above the belt line there was all-around vision. Auto makers had talked bubble tops for decades, and experimented with them timidly, but now the Orion had achieved the same effect, yet without loss of structural strength. Within the clear glass top, vertical members of thin, high tensile steel— A and C pillars to designers—had been molded almost invisibly, crossing to join unobtrusively overhead. The result was a "greenhouse" (another design idiom for the upper body of any automobile) far stronger than conventional cars, a reality which a tough series of crashes and rollovers had already confirmed. The tumblehome—angle at which the body top sloped inward from the vertical—was gentle, allowing spacious headroom inside. The same spaciousness, surprising in so small a car, extended below the belt line where design was rakish and advanced, yet not bizarre, so that the Orion, from every angle, melded into an eye-pleasing whole.

Beneath the exterior, Brett knew, engineering innovations would match the outward look. A notable one was electronic fuel injection, replacing a conventional carburetor—the latter an anachronistic hangover from primitive engines and overdue for its demise. Controlling the fuel injection system was one of the many functions of the Orion's on-board, shoe-box-size computer.

The model in Studio X, however, contained nothing mechanical. It was a Fiberglas shell only, made from the cast of an original clay sculpture, though even with close scrutiny it was hard to realize that the car under the spotlights was not real. The model had been left here for comparison with other models to come later, as well as for senior company officers to visit, review, worry over, and renew their faith. Such faith was important. A gigantic amount of stockholders' money, plus the careers and reputations of all involved, from the chairman of the board downward, was riding on the Orion's wheels. Already the board of directors had sanctioned expenditures of a hundred million dollars for development and production, with more millions likely to be budgeted before introduction time.

Brett was reminded that he had once heard Detroit described as "more of a gambling center than Las Vegas, with higher stakes." The earthy thought drew his mind to practicalities, of which one was the fact that he had not yet had breakfast.

In the design directors' dining room, several others were already breakfasting when Brett DeLosanto came in. Characteristically, instead of ordering from a waitress, Brett dropped into the kitchen where he joshed with the cooks, who knew him well, then coerced them into preparing Eggs Benedict, which was never on the standard menu. Emerging, he joined his colleagues at the dining room's large, round table.

Two visitors were at the table—students from Los Angeles Art Center College of Design, from where, not quite five years ago, Brett DeLosanto himself had graduated. One of the students was a pensive youth, now tracing curves on the tablecloth with a fingernail, the other a bright-eyed, nineteen-year-old girl.

Glancing around to make sure he would be listened to, Brett resumed a conversation with the students which had begun yesterday.

"If you come to work here," he advised them, "you should install brain filters to keep out the antediluvian ideas the old-timers will throw at you."

"Brett's idea of an old-timer," a designer in his early thirties said from across the table, "is anyone old enough to vote when Nixon was elected."

"The elderly party who just spoke," Brett informed the students, "is our Mr. Robertson. He designs fine family sedans which would be even better with shafts and a horse in front. By the way, he endorses his paycheck with a quill, and is hanging on for pension."

"A thing we love about young DeLosanto," a graying designer put in, "is his respect for experience and age." The designer, Dave Heberstein, who was studio head for Color and Interiors, surveyed Brett's carefully groomed but dazzling appearance. "By the way, where *is* the masquerade ball tonight?"

"If you studied my exteriors more carefully," Brett retorted, "then used them for your interiors, you'd start customer stampedes."

Someone else asked, "To our competitors?"

"Only if I went to work for them."

Brett grinned. He had maintained a brash repartee with the majority of others in the design studios since coming to work there as a novice, and most seemed to enjoy it still. Nor had it affected Brett's rise as an automobile designer, which had been phenomenal. Now, at age twenty-six, he ranked equal with all but a few senior studio heads.

A few years ago it would have been inconceivable that anyone looking like Brett DeLosanto could have got past the main gate security guards, let alone be permitted to work in the stratified atmosphere of a corporate design studio. But concepts had changed. Nowadays, management realized that avant-garde cars were more likely to be created by "with it" designers who were imaginative and experimental about fashion, including their own appearance. Similarly, while stylist-designers were expected to work hard and produce, seniors like Brett were allowed, within reason, to decide their own working hours. Often Brett DeLosanto came late, idled or sometimes disappeared entirely during the day, then worked through lonely hours of the night. Because his record was exceptionally good, and he attended staff meetings when told to specifically, nothing was ever said.

He addressed the students again. "One of the things the ancient ones will tell you, including some around this table eating sunny side ups . . . Ah, many thanks!" Brett paused while a waitress placed his Eggs Benedict in front of him, then resumed. "A thing they'll argue is that major changes in car design don't happen any more. From now on, they say, we'll have only transitions and ordered development. Well, that's what the gas works thought just before Edison invented electric light. I tell you there are disneyesque design changes coming. One reason: We'll be getting fantastic new materials to work with soon, and that's an area where a lot of people aren't looking because there aren't any flashing lights."

"But you're looking, Brett, aren't you?" someone said. "You're looking out for the rest of us."

"That's right." Brett DeLosanto cut himself a substantial portion of Eggs Benedict and speared it with his fork. "You fellows can relax. I'll help you keep your jobs." He ate with zest.

The bright-eyed girl student said, "Isn't it true that most new designs from here on will be largely functional?"

Speaking through a full mouth, Brett answered, "They can be functional *and* fantastic."

"You'll be functional like a balloon tire if you eat a lot of that." Heberstein, the Color and Interiors chief, eyed Brett's rich dish with distaste, then told the students, "Almost all good design is functional. It always has been. The exceptions are pure art forms which have no purpose other than to be beautiful. It's when design isn't functional that it becomes either bad design or bordering on it. The Victorians made their designs ponderously unfunctional, which is why so many were appalling. Mind you, we still do the same thing sometimes in this business when we put on enormous tail fins or excess chrome or protruding grillwork. Fortunately we're learning to do it less."

The pensive male student stopped making patterns on the tablecloth. "The Volkswagen is functional—wholly so. But you wouldn't call it beautiful."

Brett DeLosanto waved his fork and swallowed hastily, before anyone else could speak. "That, my friend, is where you and the rest of the world's public are gullibly misled. The Volkswagen is a fraud, a gigantic hoax."

"It's a good car," the girl student said. "I have one."

"Of course it's a good car." Brett ate some more of his breakfast while the two young, would-be designers watched him curiously. "When the landmark autos of this century are added up, the Volkswagen will be there along with the Pierce-Arrow, the Model T Ford, 1929 Chevrolet 6, Packard before the 1940s, Rolls-Royce until the '60s, Lincoln, Chrysler Airflow, Cadillacs of the '30s, the Mustang, Pontiac GTO, 2-passenger

Thunderbirds, and some others. But the Volkswagen is still a fraud because a sales campaign has convinced people it's an ugly car, which it isn't, or it wouldn't have lasted half as long as it has. What the Volkswagen really has is form, balance, symmetrical sense and a touch of genius; if it were a sculpture in bronze instead of a car it could be on a pedestal alongside a Henry Moore. But because the public's been beaten on the head with statements that it's ugly, they've swallowed the hook and so have you. But then, all car owners like to deceive themselves."

Somebody said, "Here's where I came in."

Chairs were eased back. Most of the others began drifting out to their separate studios. The Color and Interiors chief stopped beside the chairs of the two students. "If you filter Junior's output— the way he advised to begin with—you might just find a pearl or two."

"By the time I'm through"—Brett checked a spray of egg and coffee with a napkin—"they'll have enough to make pearl jam."

"Too bad I can't stay!" Heberstein nodded amiably from the doorway. "Drop in later, Brett, will you? We've a fabric report I think you'll want to know about."

"Is it always like that?" The youth, who had resumed drawing finger parabolas on the tablecloth, looked curiously at Brett.

"In here it is, usually. But don't let the kidding fool you. Under it, a lot of good ideas get going."

It was true. Auto company managements encouraged designers, as well as others in creative jobs, to take meals together in private dining rooms; the higher an individual's rank, the more pleasant and exclusive such privileges became. But, at whatever level, the talk at table inevitably turned to work. Then, keen minds sparked one another and brilliant ideas occasionally had genesis over entree or dessert. Senior staff dining rooms operated at a loss, but managements made up deficits cheerfully, regarding them as investments with a good yield.

"Why did you say car owners deceive themselves?" the girl asked.

"We know they do. It's a slice of human nature you learn to live with." Brett eased from the table and tilted back his chair. "Most Joe Citizens out there in communityland love snappy-looking cars. But they also like to think of themselves as rational, so what happens? They kid themselves. A lot of those same Joe C.'s won't admit, even in their minds, their real motivations when they buy their next torpedo."

"How can you be sure?"

"Simple. If Joe wants just reliable transportation—as a good many of his kind say they do— all he needs is the cheapest, simplest, stripped economy job in the Chev, Ford, or Plymouth line. Most, though, want more than that—a better car because, like a sexy-looking babe on the arm, or a fancy home, it gives a good warm feeling in the gut. Nothing wrong with that! But Joe and his friends seem to think there is, which is *why they fool themselves.*"

"So consumer research . . ."

"Is for the birds! Okay, we send out some dame with a clipboard who asks a guy coming down the street what he wants in his next car. Right away he thinks he'll impress her, so he lists all the square stuff like reliability, gas mileage, safety, trade-in value. If it's a written quiz, unsigned, he does it so he impresses himself. Down at the bottom, both times, he may put appearance, if he mentions it at all. Yet, when it comes to buy-time and the same guy's in a showroom, whether he admits it or not, appearance will be right there on top."

Brett stood, and stretched. "You'll find some who'll tell you that the public's love affair with cars is over. Nuts! We'll all be around for a while, kids, because old Joe C., with his hangups, is still a designer's friend."

He glanced at his watch; there was another half hour until he would meet Adam Trenton en route to the proving ground, which left time to stop at Color and Interiors.

On their way out of the dining room, Brett asked the students, "What do you make of it all?"

The curiosity was genuine. What the two students were doing now, Brett had done himself not many years ago. Auto companies regularly invited design school students in, treating them like VIPs, while the students saw for themselves the kind of aura they might work in later. The auto makers, too, courted students at their schools. Teams from the Big Three visited design colleges several times a year, openly competing for the most promising soon-to-be graduates, and the same was true of other industry areas—engineering, science, finance, merchandising, law—so that auto companies with their lavish pay scales and benefits, including planned promotion, skimmed off a high proportion of the finer talents. Some—including thoughtful people in the industry itself—argued that the process was unjust, that auto makers corralled too much of the world's best brainpower, to the detriment of civilization generally, which needed more thinkers to solve urgent, complex human problems. Just the same, no other agency or industry succeeded in recruiting a comparable, constant flow of top-flight achievers. Brett DeLosanto had been one.

"It's exciting," the bright-eyed girl said, answering Brett's question. "Like being in on creation, the real thing. A bit scary, of course. All those other people to compete with, and you know how good they must be. But if you make it here, you've really made it big."

She had the attitude it took, Brett thought. All she needed was the talent, plus some extra push to overcome the industry's prejudice against women who wanted to be more than secretaries.

He asked the youth, "How about you?"

The pensive young man shook his head uncertainly. He was frowning. "I'm not sure. Okay, everything's big time, there's plenty of bread thrown around, a lot of effort, and I guess it's exciting all right"—he nodded toward the girl— "just the way she said. I keep wondering, though: Is it all worth it? Maybe I'm crazy, and I know it's late; I mean, having done the design course and all, or most of it. But you can't help asking: For an artist, does it matter? Is it what you want to give blood to, a lifetime?"

"You have to love cars to work here," Brett said. "You have to care about them so much that they're the most important thing there is. You breathe, eat, sleep cars, sometimes remember them when you're making love. You wake up in the night, it's cars you think about—those you're designing, others you'd like to. It's like a religion." He added curtly, "If you don't feel that way, you don't belong here."

"I do love cars," the youth said. "I always have, as long as I remember, in just the way you said. It's only lately . . ." He left the sentence hanging, as if unwilling to voice heresy a second time.

Brett made no other comment. Opinions, appraisals of that kind were individual, and decisions because of them, personal. No one else could help because in the end it all depended on your own ideas, values, and sometimes conscience. Besides, there was another factor which Brett had no intention of discussing with these two: Lately he had experienced some of the same questioning and doubts himself.

The chief of Color and Interiors had a skeleton immediately inside his office, used for anatomy studies in relation to auto seating. The skeleton hung slightly off the ground, suspended by a chain attached to a plate in the skull. Brett DeLosanto shook hands with it as he came in. "Good morning, Ralph."

Dave Heberstein came from behind his desk and nodded toward the main studio. "Let's go through." He patted the skeleton affectionately in passing. "A loyal and useful staff member who never criticizes, never asks for a raise."

The Color Center, which they entered, was a vast, domed chamber, circular and constructed principally of glass, allowing daylight to flood in. The overhead dome gave a cathedral effect, so that several enclosed booths—for light-controlled viewing of color samples and fabrics—appeared like chapels. Deep carpeting underfoot deadened sound. Throughout the room were display boards, soft and hard trim samples, and a color library comprising every color in the spectrum as well as thousands of subcolors.

Heberstein stopped at a display table. He told Brett DeLosanto, "Here's what I wanted you to see."

Under glass, a half-dozen upholstery samples had been arranged, each identified by mill and purchase number. Other similar samples were loose on the table top. Though variously colored, they bore the generic name "Metallic Willow." Dave Heberstein picked one up. "Remember these?"

"Sure." Brett nodded. "I liked them; still do."

"I did, too. In fact, I recommended them for use." Heberstein fingered the sample which was pleasantly soft to the touch. It had—as had all the others—an attractive patterned silver fleck. "It's crimped yarn with a metallic thread."

Both men were aware that the fabric had been introduced as an extra cost option with the company's top line models this year. It had proven popular and soon, in differing colors, would be available for the Orion. Brett asked, "So what's the fuss?"

"Letters," Heberstein said. "Customers' letters which started coming in a couple of weeks ago." He took a key ring from his pocket and opened a drawer in the display table. Inside was a file containing about two dozen photocopied letters. "Read a few of those."

The correspondence, which was mainly from women or their husbands, though a few lawyers had written on behalf of clients, had a common theme. The women had sat in their cars wearing mink coats. In each case when they left the car, part of the mink had adhered to the seat, depleting and damaging the coat. Brett whistled softly.

"Sales ran a check through the computer," Heberstein confided. "In every case the car concerned had Metallic Willow seats. I understand there are still more letters coming in."

"Obviously you've made tests." Brett handed back the folder of letters. "So what do they show?"

"They show the whole thing's very simple; trouble is, nobody thought of it before it happened. You sit on the seat, the cloth depresses and opens up. That's normal, of course, but what also open up in this case are the metallic threads, which is still okay, providing you don't happen to be wearing mink. But if you are, some of the fine hairs go down between the metallic threads. Get up, and the threads close, holding the mink hairs so they pull out from the coat. You can ruin a three-thousand-dollar coat in one trip around the block."

Brett grinned. "If word gets around, every woman in the country with an old mink will rush out for a ride, then put in a claim for a new coat."

"Nobody's laughing. Over at staff they've pushed the panic button."

"The fabric's out of production?"

Heberstein nodded. "As of this morning. And from now on we have another test around here with new fabrics. Rather obviously, it's known as the mink test."

"What's happening about all the seats already out?"

"God knows! And I'm glad that part's not my headache. The last I heard, it had gone as high as the chairman of the board. I do know the legal department is settling all claims quietly, as soon as they come in. They've figured there'll be a few phony ones, but better to pay if there's a chance of keeping the whole thing under wraps."

"Mink wraps?"

The studio head said dourly, "Spare me the lousy jokes. You'll get all this through channels, but I thought you and a few others should know right away because of the Orion."

"Thanks." Brett nodded thoughtfully. It was true—changes would have to be made in Orion plans, though the particular area was not his responsibility. He was grateful, however, for another reason.

Within the next few days, he now decided, he must change either his car or the seats in his present one. Brett's car had Metallic Willow fabric and, coincidentally, he planned a birthday gift of mink next month which he had no wish to see spoiled. The mink, which undoubtedly would be worn in his car, was for Barbara.

Barbara Zaleski.

chapter six

"Dad," Barbara said, "I'll be staying over in New York for a day or two. I thought I'd let you know."

In the background, through the telephone, she could hear an overlay of factory noise. Barbara had had to wait several minutes while the operator located Matt Zaleski in the plant; now, presumably, he had taken the call somewhere close to the assembly line.

Her father asked, "Why?"

"Why what?"

"Why do you have to stay?"

She said lightly, "Oh, the usual kind of thing. Client problems at the agency. Some meetings about next year's advertising; they need me here for them." Barbara was being patient. She really shouldn't have to explain, as if she were still a child requiring permission to be out late. If she decided to stay a week, a month, or forever in New York, that was it.

"Couldn't you come home nights, then go back in the morning?"

"No, Dad, I couldn't."

Barbara hoped this wasn't going to develop into another argument in which it would be necessary to point out that she was twenty-nine, a legal adult who had voted in two presidential elections, and had a responsible job which she was good at. The job, incidentally, made her financially free so that she could set up a separate establishment any time she wanted, except that she lived with her father, knowing he was lonely after her mother's death, and not wanting to make things worse for him.

"When will you be home then?"

"By the weekend for sure. You can live without me till then. And take care of your ulcer. By the way, how is it?"

"I'd forgotten it. Too many other things to think about. We had some trouble in the plant this morning."

He sounded strained, she thought. The auto industry had that effect on everybody close to it, including herself. Whether you worked in a plant, in an advertising agency, or on design, like Brett, the anxieties and pressures got to you in the end. The same kind of compulsion told Barbara Zaleski at this moment that she had to get off the telephone and back into the client meeting. She had slipped out a few minutes ago, the men assuming, no doubt, that she had left to do whatever women did in washrooms, and instinctively Barbara put a hand to her hair—chestnut brown and luxuriant, like her Polish mother's; it also grew annoyingly fast so she had to spend more time than she liked in beauty salons. She patted her hair into place; it would have to do. Her fingers encountered the dark glasses which she had pushed upward above her forehead hours ago, reminding her that she had heard someone recently deride dark glasses in hair as the hallmark of the girl executive. Well, why not? She left the glasses where they were.

"Dad," Barbara said, "I haven't much time. Would you do something for me?"

"What's that?"

"Call Brett. Tell him I'm sorry I can't make our date tonight, and if he wants to call me later, I'll be at the Drake Hotel."

"I'm not sure I can . . ."

"Of course you can! Brett's at the Design Center, as you know perfectly well, so all you have to do is pick up an inside phone and dial. I'm not asking you to like him; I know you don't, and you've made that clear plenty of times to both of us. All I'm asking is that you pass a message. You may not even have to speak to him."

She had been unable to keep the impatience out of her voice, so now they were having an argument after all, one more added to many others.

"All right," Matt grumbled. "I'll do it. But keep your shirt on."

"You keep yours on, too. Goodbye, Dad. Take care, and I'll see you at the weekend."

Barbara thanked the secretary whose phone she had been using and slid her full, long-limbed body from the desk where she had perched. Barbara's figure, which she was aware that men admired, was another legacy from her mother who had managed to convey a strong sexuality— characteristically Slavic, so some said—until the last few months before she died.

Barbara was on the twenty-first floor of the Third Avenue building which was New York head- quarters of the Osborne J. Lewis Company—or more familiarly, OJL—one of the world's half- dozen largest advertising agencies, with a staff of two thousand, more or less, on three skyscraper floors. If she had wanted to, instead of phoning Detroit from where she had, Barbara could have used an office in the jam-packed, creative rabbit warren one floor down, where a few windowless, cupboard-size offices were kept available for out- of-town staffers like herself while working tem- porarily in New York. But it had seemed simpler to stay up here, where this morning's meeting was being held. This floor was client country. It was also where account executives and senior agency officers had their lavishly decorated and broad- loomed office suites, with original Cézannes, Wyeths, or Picassos on the walls as well as built-in bars—the latter remaining hidden or activated according to a client's known and carefully re-

membered preferences. Even secretaries here enjoyed better working conditions than some of the
best creative talent down below. In a way, Barbara
sometimes thought, the agency resembled a
Roman galley ship, though at least those below
had their martini lunches, went home at nights,
and—if senior enough—were sometimes allowed
topside.

She walked quickly down a corridor. In the
austere Detroit offices of OJL, where Barbara
worked mostly, her heels would have "tip-tapped,"
but here, deep carpeting deadened their sound.
Passing a door partially open, she could hear a
piano and a girl singer's voice:

> *"One more happy user*
> *Has joined the millions who*
> *Say Brisk!—please bring it briskly;*
> *It satisfies me too."*

Almost certainly a client was in there listening,
and would make a decision about the jingle—aye
or nay, involving vast expenditures—based on
hunch, prejudice, or even whether he felt good or
breakfast had given him dyspepsia. Of course, the
lyric was awful, probably because the client preferred it to be banal, being afraid—as most were
—of anything more imaginative. But the music
had an ear-catching lilt; recorded with full orchestra and chorus, a large part of the nation might be
humming the little tune a month or two from
now. Barbara wondered what Brisk was. A drink?
A new detergent? It could be either, or something
more outlandish. The OJL agency had hundreds
of clients in diverse businesses, though the auto
company account which Barbara worked on was
among its most important and lucrative. As auto
company men were fond of reminding agency

people, the car advertising budget alone exceeded a hundred million dollars annually.

Outside Conference Room 1 a red MEETING IN PROGRESS sign was still flashing. Clients loved the flashing signs for the aura of importance they created.

Barbara went in quietly and slipped into her chair halfway down the long table. There were seven others in the dignified, rosewood-paneled room with Georgian furnishings. At the table's head was Keith Yates-Brown, graying and urbanely genial, the agency management supervisor whose mission was to keep relations between the auto company and the Osborne J. Lewis agency friction free. To the right of Yates-Brown was the auto company advertising manager from Detroit, J. P. Underwood ("Call me J.P., please"), youngish, recently promoted and not entirely at ease yet with the top-rank agency crowd. Facing Underwood was bald and brilliant Teddy Osch, OJL creative director and a man who spewed ideas the way a fountain disgorges water. Osch, unflappable, schoolmasterish, had outlasted many of his colleagues and was a veteran of past, successful car campaigns.

The others comprised J. P. Underwood's assistant, also from Detroit, two other agency men —one creative, one executive—and Barbara, who was the only woman present, except for a secretary who at the moment was refilling coffee cups.

Their subject of discussion was the Orion. Since yesterday afternoon they had been reviewing advertising ideas which the agency had developed so far. The OJL group at the meeting had taken turns in presentations to the client—represented by Underwood and his assistant.

"We've saved one sequence until last, J.P." Yates-Brown was speaking directly though informally to the auto company advertising manager.

"We thought you'd find them original, even interesting perhaps." As always, Yates-Brown managed an appropriate mix of authority and deference, even though everyone present knew that an advertising manager had little real decision power and was off the mainstream of auto company high command.

J. P. Underwood said, more brusquely than necessary, "Let's see it."

One of the other agency men placed a series of cards on an easel. On each card a tissue sheet was fixed, the tissue having a sketched layout, in preliminary stage. Each layout, as Barbara knew, represented hours, and sometimes long nights of thought and labor.

Today's and yesterday's procedure was normal in the early stages of any new car campaign and the tissue sheets were called a "rustle pile."

"Barbara," Yates-Brown said, "will you skipper this trip?"

She nodded.

"What we have in mind, J.P.," Barbara told Underwood with a glance to his assistant, "is to show the Orion as it will be in everyday use. The first layout, as you see, is an Orion leaving a car wash."

All eyes were on the sketch. It was imaginative and well executed. It showed the forward portion of the car emerging from a wash tunnel like a butterfly from a chrysalis. A young woman was waiting to drive the car away. Photographed in color, whether still or on film, the scene would be arresting.

J. P. Underwood gave no reaction, not an eyelid flicker. Barbara nodded for the next tissue.

"Some of us have felt for a long time that women's use of cars has been underemphasized in advertising. Most advertising, as we know, has been directed at men."

She could have added, but didn't, that her own assignment for the past two years had been to push hard for women's point of view. There were days, however, after reading the masculine-oriented advertising (the trade called it "muscle copy") which continued to appear, when Barbara was convinced that she had failed totally.

Now she commented, "We believe that women are going to use the Orion a great deal."

The sketch on the easel was a supermarket parking lot. The artist's composition was excellent—the storefront in background, an Orion prominently forward with other cars around it. A woman shopper was loading groceries into the Orion's back seat.

"Those other cars," the auto company ad manager said. "Would they be ours or competitors'?"

Yates-Brown answered quickly, "I'd say ours, J.P."

"There should be *some* competitive cars, J.P.," Barbara said. "Otherwise the whole thing would be unreal."

"Can't say I like the groceries." The remark was from Underwood's assistant. "Clutters everything up. Takes the eye away from the car. And if we did use that background it should be Vaselined."

Barbara felt like sighing dispiritedly. Vaseline smeared around a camera lens when photographing cars was a photographer's trick which had become a cliché; it made background misty, leaving the car itself sharply defined. Though auto companies persisted in using it, many advertising people thought the device as dated as the Twist. Barbara said mildly, "We're attempting to show actual use."

"All the same," Keith Yates-Brown injected, "that was a good point. Let's make a note of it."

"The next layout," Barbara said, "is an Orion in the rain—a real downpour would be good, we think. Again, a woman driver, looking as if she's going home from the office. We'd photograph after dark to get best reflections from a wet street."

"Be hard not to get the car dirty," J. P. Underwood observed.

"The whole idea *is* to get it a little dirty," Barbara told him. "Again—reality. Color film could make it great."

The assistant ad manager from Detroit said softly, "I can't see the brass going for it."

J. P. Underwood was silent.

There were a dozen more. Barbara went through each, briefly but conscientiously, knowing how much effort and devotion the younger agency staff members had put into every one. That was the way it always went. The creative oldsters like Teddy Osch held back and—as they put it—"let the kids exhaust themselves," knowing from experience that the early work, however good it was, would always be rejected.

It was rejected now. Underwood's manner made that clear, and everyone in the room shared the knowledge, as they had shared it yesterday, before this session started. In her early days at the agency Barbara had been naïve enough to inquire why it always happened that way. Why were so much effort and quality—frequently excellent quality—utterly wasted?

Afterward, some facts of life about auto advertising had been quietly explained. It was put to her: If the ad program burgeoned quickly, instead of painfully slowly—far slower than advertising for most other products—then how would all the auto people in Detroit involved with it justify their jobs, the endless meetings over months, fat expense accounts, the out-of-town junkets? Furthermore, if an auto company chose to burden itself with that kind of inflated cost, it was not the agency's business to suggest otherwise, far less to go crusading. The agency did handsomely out of the arrangement; besides, there was always approval in the end. The advertising process for each model year started in October or November. By May-June, decisions had to be firm so that the agency could do its job; therefore, auto company people began making up their minds because they could read a calendar too. This was also the time that the Detroit high brass came into the picture, and they made final decisions about advertising, whether talented in that particular direction or not.

What bothered Barbara most—and others too, she discovered later—was the appalling waste of time, talent, people, money, the exercise in nothingness. And, from talking with people in other agencies, she knew that the same process was true of all Big Three companies. It was as if the auto industry, normally so time-and-motion conscious and critical of bureaucracy outside, had created its own fat-waxing bureaucracy within.

She had once asked: Did any of the original ideas, the really good ones, ever get reinstated? The answer was: No, because you can't accept in June what you rejected last November. It would be embarrassing to auto company people. That kind of thing could easily cost a man—perhaps a good friend to the agency—his job.

"Thank you, Barbara." Keith Yates-Brown had smoothly taken charge. "Well, J.P., we realize we still have a long way to go." The management supervisor's smile was warm and genial, his tone just the right degree apologetic.

"You sure do," J. P. Underwood said. He pushed his chair back from the table.

Barbara asked him, "Was there nothing you liked? Absolutely nothing at all?"

Yates-Brown swung his head toward her sharply and she knew she was out of line. Clients were not supposed to be harassed that way, but Underwood's brusque superiority had needled her. She thought, even now, of some of the talented youngsters in the agency whose imaginative work, as well as her own, had just gone down the drain. Maybe what had been produced so far wasn't the ultimate answer to Orion needs, but neither did it rate a graceless dismissal.

"Now, Barbara," Yates-Brown said, "no one mentioned not liking anything." The agency supervisor was still suave and charming, but she sensed steel beneath his words. If he wanted to, Yates-Brown, essentially a salesman who hardly ever had an original idea himself, could squash creative people in the agency beneath his elegant alligator shoes. He went on, "However, we'd be less than professional if we failed to agree that we have not yet caught the true Orion spirit. It's a wonderful spirit, J.P. You've given us one of the great cars of history to work with." He made it sound as if the ad manager had designed the Orion singlehanded.

Barbara felt slightly sick. She caught Teddy Osch's eye. Barely perceptibly, the creative director shook his head.

"I'll say this," J. P. Underwood volunteered. His tone was friendlier. For several years previously he had been merely a junior at this table; perhaps the newness of his job, his own insecurity, had made him curt a moment earlier. "I think we've just seen one of the finest rustle piles we ever had."

There was a pained silence through the room. Even Keith Yates-Brown betrayed a flicker of shocked surprise. Clumsily, illogically, the company ad man had stomped on their agreed pretense, revealing the elaborate charade for what it was. On the one hand—automatic dismissal of everything submitted; an instant later, fulsome praise. But nothing would be changed. Barbara was an old enough hand to know that.

So was Keith Yates-Brown. He recovered quickly.

"That's generous of you, J.P. Damn generous! I speak for us all on the agency side when I tell you we're grateful for your encouragement and assure you that next time around we'll be even more effective." The management supervisor was standing now; the others followed his example. He turned to Osch. "Isn't that so, Teddy?"

The creative chief nodded with a wry smile. "We do our best."

As the meeting broke up, Yates-Brown and Underwood preceded the others to the door.

Underwood asked, "Did somebody get on the ball about theater tickets?"

Barbara, close behind, had heard the ad manager ask earlier for a block of six seats to a Neil Simon comedy for which tickets, even through scalpers, were almost impossible to get.

The agency supervisor guffawed genially. "Did you ever doubt me?" He draped an arm companionably around the other's shoulders. "Sure we have them, J.P. You picked the toughest ticket in town, but for you we pulled every string. They're being sent to our lunch table at the Waldorf. Is that okay?"

"That's okay."

Yates-Brown lowered his voice. "And let me know where your party would like dinner. We'll take care of the reservation."

And the bill, *and* all tips, Barbara thought. As for the theater tickets, she imagined Yates-Brown must have paid fifty dollars a seat, but the agency would recoup that, along with other expenses, a thousandfold through Orion advertising.

On some occasions when clients were taken to lunch by agency executives, people from creative side were invited along. Today, for reasons of his own, Yates-Brown had decided against this. Barbara was relieved.

While the agency executive-J. P. Underwood group was no doubt heading for the Waldorf, she walked, with Teddy Osch and Nigel Knox, the other creative staffer who had been at the client meeting, a few blocks uptown on Third Avenue. Their destination was Joe & Rose, an obscure but first-rate bistro, populated at lunchtime by advertising people from big agencies in the neighborhood. Nigel Knox, who was an effeminate young man, normally grated on Barbara, but since his work and ideas had been rejected too, she regarded him more sympathetically than usual.

Teddy Osch led the way, under a faded red awning, into the restaurant's unpretentious interior. En route, no one had said more than a word or two. Now, on being shown to a table in a small rear room reserved for habitués, Osch silently raised three fingers. Moments later three martinis in chilled glasses were placed before them.

"I'm not going to do anything stupid like cry," Barbara said, "and I won't get drunk because you always feel so awful after. But if you both don't mind, I intend to get moderately loaded." She downed the martini. "I'd like another, please."

Osch beckoned a waiter. "Make it three."

"Teddy," Barbara said, "how the hell do you stand it?"

Osch passed a hand pensively across his baldness. "The first twenty years are hardest. After that, when you've seen a dozen J. P. Underwoods come and go . . ."

Nigel Knox exploded as if he had been bottling up a protest. "He's a beastly person. I tried to like him, but I couldn't possibly."

"Oh shut up, Nigel," Barbara said.

Osch continued, "The trick is to remind yourself that the pay is good, and most times—except today—I like the work. There isn't a business more exciting. I'll tell you something else: No matter how well they've built the Orion, if it's a success, and sells, it'll be because of us and advertising. They know it; we know it. So what else matters?"

"Keith Yates-Brown matters," Barbara said. "And he makes me sick."

Nigel Knox mimicked in a high-pitched voice, *"That's generous of you, J.P. Damn generous! Now I'm going to lie down, J.P., and I hope you'll pee all over me."*

Knox giggled. For the first time since this morning's meeting, Barbara laughed.

Teddy Osch glared at them both. "Keith Yates-Brown is my meal ticket and yours, and let's none of us forget it. Sure, I couldn't do what he does—keep snugged up to Underwood's and other people's anuses and look like I enjoyed it, but it's a part of this business which somebody has to take care of, so why fault him for a thorough job? Right now, and plenty of other times while we're doing the creative bit, which we like, Yates-Brown is in bed with the client, stroking whatever's necessary to keep him warm and happy, and telling him about *us*, how great we are. And if you'd ever been in an agency which lost an automotive account, you'd know why I'm glad he is."

A waiter bustled up. "Veal Parmigiana's good today." At Joe & Rose no one bothered with frills like menus.

Barbara and Nigel Knox nodded. "Okay, with noodles," Osch told the waiter. "And martinis all around."

Already, Barbara realized, the liquor had relaxed them. Now, the session was following a familiar pattern—at first gloomy, then self-consoling; soon, after one more martini probably, it would become philosophic. In her own few years at the OJL agency she had attended several post-mortems of this kind, in New York at advertising "in" places like Joe & Rose, in Detroit at the Caucus Club or Jim's Garage, downtown. It was at the Caucus she had once seen an elderly advertising man break down and sob because months of his work had been brusquely thrown out an hour earlier.

"I worked at an agency once," Osch said, "where we lost a car account. It happened just before the weekend; nobody expected it, except the other agency which took the account away from us. We called it 'Black Friday.'"

He fingered the stem of his glass, looking back across the years. "A hundred agency people were fired that Friday afternoon. Others didn't wait to be fired; they knew there was nothing left for them, so they scurried up and down Madison and Third, trying for jobs at other places before they closed. Guys were scared. A good many had fancy homes, big mortgages, kids in college. Trouble is, other agencies don't like the smell of losers; besides, some of the older guys were just plain burned out. I remember, two hit the bottle and stayed on it; one committed suicide."

"You survived," Barbara said.

"I was young. If it happened now, I'd go the way the others did." He raised his glass. "To Keith Yates-Brown."

Nigel Knox placed his partially drunk martini on the table. "Oh no, really. I couldn't possibly."

Barbara shook her head. "Sorry, Teddy."

"Then I'll drink the toast alone," Osch said. And did.

"The trouble with our kind of advertising,"

Barbara said, "is that we offer a nonexistent car to an unreal person." The three of them had almost finished their latest martinis; she was aware of her own speech slurring. "We all know you couldn't possibly buy the car that's in the ads, even if you wanted to, because the photographs are lies. When we take pictures of the real cars we use a wide-angle lens to balloon the front, a stretch lens to make the side view longer. We even make the color look better than it is with spray and powder puffs and camera filters."

Osch waved a hand airily. "Tricks of the trade."

A waiter saw the hand wave. "Another round, Mr. Osch? Your food will be here soon."

The creative chief nodded.

Barbara insisted, "It's still a nonexistent car."

"That's jolly good!" Nigel Knox clapped vigorously, knocking over his empty glass and causing occupants of other tables to glance their way amusedly. "Now tell us who's the unreal person we advertise it to."

Barbara spoke slowly, her thoughts fitting together less readily than usual. "Detroit executives who have the final word on advertising don't understand people. They work too hard; there isn't time. Therefore most car advertising consists of a Detroit executive advertising to another Detroit executive."

"I have it!" Nigel Knox bobbed up and down exuberantly. "Everybody knows a Detroit panjandrum is an unreal person. Clever! Clever!"

"So are you," Barbara said. "I don't think, at this point, I could even think panjan . . . wotsit, let alone say it." She put a hand to her face, wishing she had drunk more slowly.

"Don't touch the plates," their waiter warned, "they're hot." The Veal Parmigiana, with savoury steaming noodles was put before them, plus another three martinis. "Complimentsa the next table," the waiter said.

Osch acknowledged the drinks, then sprinkled red peppers liberally on his noodles.

"My goodness," Nigel Knox warned, "those are terribly hot."

The creative chief told him, "I need a new fire in me."

There was a silence while they began eating, then Teddy Osch looked across at Barbara. "Considering the way you feel, I guess it's all to the good you're coming off the Orion program."

"What?" Startled, she put down her knife and fork.

"I was supposed to tell you. I hadn't got around to it."

"You mean I'm fired?"

He shook his head. "New assignment. You'll hear tomorrow."

"Teddy," she pleaded, "you have to tell me now."

He said firmly, "No. You'll get it from Keith Yates-Brown. He's the one who recommended you. Remember?—the guy you wouldn't drink a toast to."

Barbara had an empty feeling.

"All I can tell you," Osch said, "is I wish it were me instead of you." He sipped his fresh martini; of the three of them, he was the only one still drinking. "If I was younger I think it might have been me. But I guess I'll go on doing what I always have: advertising that nonexistent car to the unreal person."

"Teddy," Barbara said, "I'm sorry."

"No need to be. The sad thing is, I think you're right." The creative chief blinked. "Christ! Those peppers are hotter than I thought." He produced a handkerchief and wiped his eyes.

chapter seven

Some thirty miles outside Detroit, occupying a half thousand acres of superb Michigan countryside, the auto company's proving ground lay like a Balkan state bristling with defended borders. Only one entrance to the proving ground existed —through a security-policed double barrier, remarkably similar to East-West Berlin's Checkpoint Charlie. Here, visitors were halted to have credentials examined; no one, without prearranged authority, got in.

Apart from this entry point, the entire area was enclosed by a high, chain-link fence, patrolled by guards. Inside the fence, trees and other protective planting formed a visual shield against watchers from outside.

What the company was guarding were some of its more critical secrets. Among them: experiments with new cars, trucks, and their components, as well as drive-to-destruction performance tests on current models.

The testing was carried out on some hundred and fifty miles of roads—routes to nowhere— ranging from specimens of the very best to the absolute worst or most precipitous in the world. Among the latter was a duplicate of San Francisco's horrendously steep Filbert Street, appropriately named (so San Franciscans say) since only nuts drive down it. A Belgian block road jolted every screw, weld, and rivet in a car, and set drivers' teeth chattering. Even rougher, and used for truck trials, was a replica of an African game trail, with tree roots, rocks, and mud holes.

One road section, built on level ground, was known as Serpentine Alley. This was a series of sharp S-bends, closely spaced and absolutely flat, so that absence of any banking in the turns strained a car to its limits when cornering at high speed.

At the moment, Adam Trenton was hurling an Orion around Serpentine Alley at 60 mph.

Tires screamed savagely, and smoked, as the car flung hard left, then right, then left again. Each time, centrifugal force strained urgently, protestingly, against the direction of the turn. To the three occupants it seemed as if the car might roll over at any moment, even though knowledge told them that it shouldn't.

Adam glanced behind him. Brett DeLosanto, sitting centrally in the rear seat, was belted in, as well as bracing himself by his arms on either side.

The designer called over the seatback, "My liver and spleen just switched sides. I'm counting on the next bend to get them back."

Beside Adam, Ian Jameson, a slight, sandy-haired Scot from Engineering, sat imperturbably. Jameson was undoubtedly thinking what Adam realized—that there was no necessity for them to be going around the turns at all; professional drivers had already put the Orion through grueling tests there which it survived handily. The trio's real purpose at the proving ground today was to review an NVH problem (the initials were engineerese for Noise, Vibration, and Harshness) which prototype Orions had developed at very high speed. But on their way to the fast track they had passed the entry to Serpentine Alley, and Adam swung on to it first, hoping that throwing the car around would release some of his own tension, which he had continued to be aware of since his departure from the press session an hour or two earlier.

The tension, which started early this morning, had occurred more frequently of late. So a few weeks ago Adam made an appointment with a physician who probed, pressed, performed assorted tests, and finally told him there was nothing wrong organically except, possibly, too much acid in his system. The doctor then talked vaguely of "ulcer personality," the need to stop worrying, and added a kindergarten bromide, "A hill is only as steep as it looks to the man climbing it."

While Adam listened impatiently, wishing that medics would assume more knowledge and intelligence on the part of patients, the doctor pointed out that the human body had its own built-in warning devices and suggested easing up for a while, which Adam already knew was impossible this year. The doctor finally got down to what Adam had come for and prescribed Librium capsules with a recommended dosage. Adam promptly exceeded the dosage, and continued to. He also failed to tell the doctor that he was taking Valium, obtained elsewhere. Today, Adam had swallowed several pills, including one just before leaving downtown, but without discernible effect. Now, since the S-turns had done nothing to release his tension either, he surreptitiously transferred another pill from a pocket to his mouth.

The action reminded him that he still hadn't told Erica, either about the visit to the doctor, or the pills, which he kept in his briefcase, out of sight.

Near the end of Serpentine Alley, Adam swung the car sharply, letting the speed drop only slightly before heading for the track which was used for high-speed runs. Outside, the trees, meadows, and connecting roads sped by. The speedometer returned to 60, then edged to 65.

With one hand, Adam rechecked the tightness of his own lap straps and shoulder harness. Without turning his head, he told the others, "Okay, let's shake this baby out."

They hurtled on the fast track, sweeping past another car, their speed still climbing. It was 70 mph, and Adam caught a glimpse of a face as the driver of the other car glanced sideways.

Ian Jameson craned left to watch the speed-ometer needle, now touching 75. The sandy-haired engineer had been a key figure in studying the Orion's present NVH problem.

"We'll hear it any moment," Jameson said.

Speed was 78. The wind, largely of their own creating, roared as they flew around the track. Adam had the accelerator floored. Now he touched the automatic speed control, letting the computer take over, and removed his foot. Speed crept up. It passed 80.

"Here she comes," Jameson said. As he spoke, the car shuddered violently—an intense pulsation, shaking everything, including occupants. Adam found his vision blurring slightly from the rapid movement. Simultaneously a metallic hum rose and fell.

The engineer said, "Right on schedule." He sounded complacent, Adam thought, as if he would have been disappointed had the trouble not appeared.

"At fair grounds . . ." Brett DeLosanto raised his voice to a shout to make himself heard; his words came through unevenly because of the shaking. "At fair grounds, people pay money for a ride like this"

"And if we left it in," Adam said, "most drivers would never know about it. Not many take their cars up to eighty"

Ian Jameson said, "But some do."

Adam conceded gloomily: it was true. A handful of madcap drivers would hit eighty, and among them one or two might be startled by the sudden vibration, then lose control, killing or maiming themselves and others. Even without accident, the NVH effect could become known, and people like Emerson Vale would make the most of it. It was a few freak accidents at high speed, Adam recalled, with drivers who over- or understeered in emergencies, which had killed the Corvair only a few years ago. And although by the time Ralph Nader published his now-famous indictment of the Corvair, early faults had been corrected, the car had still gone to a precipitate end under the weight of publicity which Nader generated.

Adam, and others in the company who knew about the high-speed shake, had no intention of allowing a similar episode to mar the Orion's record. It was a reason why the company high command was being close-mouthed so that rumors of the trouble did not leak outside. A vital question at this moment was: How could the shake be eliminated and what would it cost? Adam was here to find out and, because of the urgency, had authority to make decisions.

He took back control from the car's computer and allowed the speed to fall off to 20 mph. Then, twice more, at differing rates of acceleration he took it up to 80. Each time, both the vibration and the point at which it occurred were identical.

"There's a difference in sheet metal on this car." Adam remembered that the Orion he was driving was an early prototype, handmade—as were all prototypes so far—because assembly line manufacture had not yet started.

"Makes no difference to the effect," Ian Jameson declared flatly. "We've had an exact Orion out here, another on the dynamometer. They all do it. Same speed, same NVH."

"It feels like a woman having an orgasm," Brett said. "Sounds like it, too." He asked the engineer, "Does it do any harm?"

"As far as we can tell, no."

"Then it seems a shame to take it out."

Adam snapped, "For Christ's sake, cut the stupidity! Of course we have to take it out! If it were an appearance problem, you wouldn't be so goddam smug."

"Well, well," Brett said. "Something else appears to be vibrating."

They had left the fast track. Abruptly, Adam braked the car, skidding so that all three were thrown forward against their straps. He turned onto a grass shoulder. As the car stopped, he unbuckled, then got out and lit a cigarette. The others followed.

Outside the car, Adam shivered slightly. The air was briskly cool, fall leaves were blowing in a gusty wind, and the sun, which had been out earlier, had disappeared behind an overcast of gray nimbostratus. Through trees, he could see a lake, its surface ruffled bleakly.

Adam pondered the decision he had to make. He was aware it was a tough one for which he would be blamed—justly or unjustly—if it went wrong.

Ian Jameson broke the uncomfortable silence. "We're satisfied that the effect is induced by tire and road surfaces when one or the other becomes in phase with body harmonics, so the vibration is natural body frequency."

In other words, Adam realized, there was no structural defect in the car. He asked, "Can the vibration be overcome?"

"Yes," Jameson said. "We're sure of that, also that you can go one of two ways. Either redesign the cowl side structure and underbody torque boxes"—he filled in engineering details—"or add braces and reinforcement."

"Hey!" Brett was instantly alert. "That first one means exterior body changes. Right?"

"Right," the engineer acknowledged. "They'd

be needed at the lower body side near the front door cut and rocker panel areas."

Brett looked gloomy, as well he might, Adam thought. It would require a crash redesign and testing program at a time when everyone believed the Orion design was fixed and final. He queried, "And the add-ons?"

"We've experimented, and there'd be two pieces—a front floor reinforcement and a brace under the instrument panel." The engineer described the brace which would be out of sight, extending from the cowl side structure on one side, to the steering column, thence to the cowl on the opposite side.

Adam asked the critical question. "Cost?"

"You won't like it." The engineer hesitated, knowing the reaction his next words would produce. "About five dollars."

Adam groaned. "God Almighty!"

He was faced with a frustrating choice. Whichever route they went would be negative and costly. The engineer's first alternative—redesign —would be less expensive, costing probably half a million to a million dollars in retooling. But it would create delays, and the Orion's introduction would be put off three to six months which, in itself, could be disastrous for many reasons.

On the other hand, on a million cars, cost of the two add-ons—the floor reinforcement and brace—would be five million dollars, and it was expected that many more Orions than a million would be built and sold. Millions of dollars to be added to production expense, to say nothing of lost profit, and all for an item wholly negative! In auto construction, five dollars was a major sum, and auto manufacturers thought normally in pennies, shaving two cents here, a nickel there, necessary because of the immense total numbers involved. Adam said in deep disgust, "Goddam!"

He glanced at Brett. The designer said, "I guess it isn't funny."

Adam's outburst in the car was not the first clash they had had since the Orion project started. Sometimes it had been Brett who flared up. But through everything so far they had managed to remain friends. It was as well, because there was a new project ahead of them, at the moment codenamed Farstar.

Ian Jameson announced, "If you want to drive over to the lab, we've a car with the add-ons for you to see."

Adam nodded sourly. "Let's get on with it."

Brett DeLosanto looked upward incredulously. "You mean that hunk of scrap, and the other, 'll cost five bucks!"

He was staring at a steel strip running across the underside of an Orion, and secured by bolts.

Adam Trenton, Brett, and Ian Jameson were inspecting the proposed floor reinforcement from an inspection area beneath a dynamometer, so that the whole of the car's underside was open to their view. The dynamometer, an affair of metal plates, rollers, and instrumentation, with a vague resemblance to a monstrous service station hoist, allowed a car to be operated as if on the road, while viewed from any angle.

They had already inspected, while above, the other cowl-to-steering column-to-cowl brace.

Jameson conceded, "Possibly you could save a few cents from cost, but no more, after allowing for material, machining, then bolt fittings and installation labor."

The engineer's manner, a kind of pedantic detachment as if cost and economics were really none of his concern, continued to irritate Adam, who asked, "How much is Engineering protecting itself? Do we really need all that?"

It was a perennial question from a product planner to an engineer. The product men regularly accused engineers of building in, everywhere, greater strength margins than necessary, thus adding to an automobile's cost and weight while diminishing performance. Product Planning was apt to argue: *If you let the Iron Rings have their way, every car would have the strength of Brooklyn Bridge, ride like an armored truck, and last as long as Stonehenge.* Taking an adversary view, engineers declaimed: *Sure, we allow margins because if something fails we're the ones who take the rap. If product planners did their own engineering, they'd achieve light weight—most likely with a balsawood chassis and tinfoil for the engine block.*

"There's no engineering protection there." It was Jameson's turn to be huffy. "We've reduced the NVH to what we believe is an acceptable level. If we went a more complicated route—which would cost more—we could probably take it out entirely. So far we haven't."

Adam said noncommittally, "We'll see what this does."

Jameson led the way as the trio climbed a metal stairway from the inspection level to the main floor of the Noise and Vibration Laboratory above.

The lab—a building at the proving ground which was shaped like an airplane hangar and divided into specialist work areas, large and small —was busy as usual with NVH conundrums tossed there by various divisions of the company. One problem now being worked on urgently was a high-pitched, girlish-sounding scream emitted by a new-type brake on diesel locomotives. Industrial Marketing had enjoined sternly: The stopping power must be retained, but locomotives should sound as if being braked, not raped.

Another poser—this from Household Products Division—was an audible click in a kitchen oven control clock; a competitor's clock, though less efficient, was silent. Knowing that the public distrusted new or different sounds and that sales might suffer if the click remained, Household Products had appealed to the NVH lab to nix the click but not the clock.

Automobiles, however, produced the bulk of the laboratory's problems. A recent one stemmed from revised styling of an established model car. The new body produced a drum sound while in motion; tests showed that the sound resulted from a windshield which had been reshaped. After weeks of hit-and-miss experimentation, NVH engineers eliminated the drum noise by introducing a crinkle in the car's metal floor. No one, including the engineers, knew exactly why the crinkle stopped the windshield drumming; the important thing was—it did.

The present stage of Orion testing in the lab had been set up on the dynamometer. Hence the car could be operated at any speed, either manually or by remote control, for hours, days, or weeks continuously, yet never move from its original position on the machine's rollers.

The Orion which they had looked at from beneath was ready to go. Stepping over the steel floor plates of the dynamometer, Adam Trenton and Ian Jameson climbed inside, Adam at the wheel.

Brett DeLosanto was no longer with them. Having satisfied himself that the proposed add-ons would not affect the car's outward appearance, Brett had returned outside to review a minor change made recently in the Orion grille. Designers liked to see results of their work out of doors—"on the grass," as they put it. Sometimes, in open surroundings and natural light, a design had unexpected visual effects, compared with its appearance in a studio. When the Orion, for example, was first viewed in direct sunlight the front grille had unexpectedly appeared black instead of bright silver, as it should. A change of angle in the grille had been necessary to correct it.

A girl technician in a white coat came out from a glass-lined control booth alongside the car. She inquired, "Is there any special kind of road you'd like, Mr. Trenton?"

"Give him a bumpy ride," the engineer said. "Let's take one from California."

"Yes, sir." The girl returned to the booth, then leaned out through the doorway, holding a magnetic tape reel in her hand. "This is State Route 17, between Oakland and San Jose." Going back into the booth, she pressed the reel onto a console and passed the tape end through a take-up spool.

Adam turned the ignition key. The Orion's engine sprang to life.

The tape now turning inside the glass booth would, Adam knew, transfer the real road surface, electronically, to the dynamometer rollers beneath the car. The tape was one of many in the lab's library, and all had been made by sensitive recording vehicles driven over routes in North America and Europe. Thus, actual road conditions, good and bad, could be reproduced instantly for test and study.

He put the Orion in drive and accelerated.

Speed rose quickly to 50 mph. The Orion's wheels and the dynamometer rollers were racing, the car itself standing still. At the same time, Adam felt an insistent pounding from below.

"Too many people think California freeways are great," Ian Jameson observed. "It surprises them when we demonstrate how bad they can be."

The speedometer showed 65.

Adam nodded. Auto engineers, he knew, were critical of California road building because the state roads—due to the absence of frost—were not made deep. The lack of depth allowed concrete slabs to become depressed at the center and curled and broken at the edges—a result of pounding by heavy trucks. Thus, when a car came to the end of a slab, in effect it fell off and bounced onto the next. The process caused continuous bumps and vibrations which cars had to be engineered to absorb.

The Orion's speed nudged 80. Jameson said, "Here's where it happens."

As he spoke, a hum and vibration—additional to the roughness of the California freeway—extended through the car. But the effect was slight, the hum low-pitched, vibration minor. The NVH would no longer be startling to a car's occupants, as it had been on the test track earlier.

Adam queried, "And that's all of it?"

"That's all that's left," Ian Jameson assured him. "The braces take the rest out. As I said, we consider what remains to be at an acceptable level." Adam allowed speed to drop off, and the engineer added, "Let's try it on a smooth road."

With another tape on the control console—a portion of Interstate 80 in Illinois—the road unevenness disappeared while the hum and vibration seemed correspondingly lower.

"We'll try one more road," Jameson said, "a really tough one." He signaled to the lab assistant in the booth, who smiled.

As Adam accelerated, even at 60 mph the Orion jolted alarmingly. Jameson announced, "This is Mississippi—U.S. 90, near Biloxi. The road wasn't good to start with, then Hurricane Camille loused it up completely. The portion we're on now still hasn't been fixed. Naturally, no one would do this speed there unless they had suicide in mind."

At 80 mph the road, transmitted through the dynamometer, was so bad that the car's own vibration was undetectable. Ian Jameson looked pleased.

As speed came off, he commented, "People don't realize how good our engineering has to be to cope with all kinds of roads, including plenty of others like that."

Jameson was off again, Adam thought, in his abstract engineer's world. Of more practical importance was the fact that the Orion's NVH problem could be solved. Adam had already decided that the add-on route, despite its appalling cost, was the one they would have to travel, rather than delay the Orion's debut. Of course, the company's executive vice-president, Hub Hewitson, who regarded the Orion as his own special baby, would go through the ceiling when he heard about the five dollars added cost. But he would learn to live with it, as Adam had—almost—already.

He got out of the car, Ian Jameson following. On the engineer's instructions, Adam left the motor running. Now, the girl in the booth took over, operating the Orion by remote control. At 80 on the dynamometer, the vibration was no more serious outside than it had been within.

Adam asked Jameson, "You're sure the bracing will stand up to long use?"

"No question about it. We've put it through every test. We're satisfied."

So was Jameson, Adam thought; too damn satisfied. The engineer's detachment—it seemed like complacency—still irritated him. "Doesn't it ever bother you," Adam asked, "that everything you people do here is negative? You don't produce anything. You only take things out, eliminate."

"Oh, we produce something." Jameson pointed to the dynamometer rollers, still turning swiftly, impelled by the Orion's wheels. "See those? They're connected to a generator; so are the other dynamometers in the lab. Every time we operate a car, the rollers generate electricity. We're coupled in to Detroit Edison, and we sell the power to them." He looked challengingly at Adam. "Sometimes I think it's as useful as a few things which have come out of Product Planning."

Adam smiled, conceding. "But not the Orion."

"No," Jameson said. "I guess we all have hopes for that."

chapter eight

The nightgown which Erica Trenton finally
bought was in Laidlaw-Beldon's on Somerset Mall
in Troy. Earlier, she had browsed through stores
in Birmingham without seeing anything that appealed to her as sufficiently special for the purpose
she had in mind, so she continued to cruise the
district in her sports convertible, not really mind-
ing because it was pleasant, for a change, to have
something special to do.

Somerset Mall was a large, modern plaza,
east on Big Beaver Road, with quality stores,
drawing much of their patronage from well-to-do
auto industry families living in Birmingham and
Bloomfield Hills. Erica had shopped there often
and knew her way around most of the stores,
including Laidlaw-Beldon's.

She realized, the instant she saw it, that the
nightgown was exactly right. It was a sheer
nylon with matching peignoir, in pale beige, almost the color of her hair. The total effect, she
knew, would be to project an image of honey
blondeness. A frosted orange lipstick, she decided,
would round out the sensual impression she intended to create, tonight, for Adam.

Erica had no charge account at the store,
and paid by check. Afterward she went to Cosmetics to buy a lipstick since she was uncertain
if she had one at home, quite the right shade.

Cosmetics was busy. While waiting, glancing
over a display of lipstick colors, Erica became
aware of another shopper at the perfume counter
close by. It was a woman in her sixties who was
informing a salesclerk, "I want it for my daughter-
in-law. I'm really not sure . . . Let me try the
Norell."

Using a sample vial, the clerk—a bored brunette—obliged.

"Yes," the woman said. "Yes, that's nice. I'll take that. An ounce size."

From a mirror-faced store shelf behind her, out of reach of customers, the clerk selected a white, black-lettered box and placed it on the counter. "That's fifty dollars, plus sales tax. Will it be cash or charge?"

The older woman hesitated. "Oh, I hadn't realized it would be that much."

"We have smaller sizes, madam."

"No . . . Well, you see, it's a gift. I suppose I ought . . . But I'll wait and think it over."

As the woman left the counter, so did the perfume salesclerk. She moved through an archway, momentarily out of sight. On the counter, the boxed perfume remained where the clerk had left it.

Irrationally, incredibly, in Erica's mind a message formed: *Norell's my perfume. Why not take it?*

She hesitated, shocked at her own impulse. While she did, a second message urged: *Go on! You're wasting time! Act now!*

Afterward, she remembered that she waited long enough to wonder: Was it really her own mind at work? Then deliberately, unhurriedly, but as if a magnetic force were in control, Erica moved from Cosmetics to Perfume. Without haste or waste motion, she lifted the package, opened her handbag and dropped it in. The handbag had a spring fastener which snapped as it closed. The sound seemed to Erica like the firing of a gun. *It would draw attention!*

What had she done?

She stood trembling, waiting, afraid to move, expecting an accusing voice, a hand on her shoulder, a shouted *"Thief!"*

Nothing happened. But it would; she knew it would, at any moment.

How could she explain? *She couldn't. Not with the evidence in her handbag.* She reasoned urgently: Should she take the package out, return it to where it was before the foolish, *unbelievable impulse* swept over her and made her act as she had? She had never done this before, *never*, nor anything remotely like it.

Still trembling, conscious of her own heart-beat, Erica asked herself: *Why*? What reason was there, if any, for what she had just done? The most absurd thing was, she didn't need to steal— the perfume or anything else. There was money in her purse, a checkbook.

Even now she could call the salesclerk to the counter, could spill out money to pay for the package, and that would be that. *Providing that she acted quickly. Now!*

No.

Obviously, because still nothing had happened, no one had seen her. If they had, Erica thought, by now she would have been accosted, questioned, perhaps taken away. She turned. Casually, feigning indifference, she surveyed the store in all directions. Business was going on as usual. No one seemed in the least interested in her, or was even looking her way. The perfume salesclerk had not reappeared. Unhurriedly, as before, Erica moved back to Cosmetics.

She reminded herself: she had wanted some perfume anyway. The way she had got it had been foolish and dangerous and she would never, ever, do the same thing again. But she had it now, and what was done was done. Trying to undo it would create difficulties, require explanations, perhaps followed by accusation, all of which were best avoided.

A salesclerk at Cosmetics was free. With her

most engaging smile and manner Erica asked to try some orange lipstick shades.

One danger, she knew, still remained: the clerk at the perfume counter. Would the girl miss the package she had put down? If so, would she remember that Erica had been close by? Erica's instinct was to leave, to hurry from the store, but reason warned her: she would be less conspicuous where she was. She deliberately dawdled over the lipstick choice.

Another customer had stopped at Perfumes. The salesclerk returned, acknowledged the newcomer, then, as if remembering, looked at the counter where the Norell package had been left. The salesgirl seemed surprised. She turned quickly, inspecting the stock shelf from where she had taken the package to begin with. Several others were on the shelf; some, the ounce-size Norell. Erica sensed the girl's uncertainty: Had she put the package back or not?

Erica, being careful not to watch directly, heard the customer who had just arrived ask a question. The perfume clerk responded, but seemed worried and was looking around her. Erica felt herself inspected. As she did, she smiled at the cosmetics clerk and told her, "I'll take this one." Erica sensed the inspection by the other salesclerk finish.

Nothing had happened. The salesgirl was probably more worried about her own carelessness, and what might happen to her as a result of it, than anything else. As Erica paid for the lipstick, opening her handbag only a little to extract a billfold, she relaxed.

Before leaving, with a sense of mischief, she even stopped at the perfume counter to try a sample of Norell.

Only when Erica was nearing the store's outer door did her nervousness return. It became terror as she realized: She might have been seen after all, then watched and allowed to get this far so that the store would have a stronger case against her. She seemed to remember reading somewhere that that kind of thing happened. The parking mall, visible outside, seemed a waiting, friendly haven—near, yet still far away.

"Good afternoon, madam." From nowhere, it seemed to Erica, a man had appeared beside her. He was middle-aged, graying, and had a fixed smile revealing prominent front teeth.

Erica froze. Her heart seemed to stop. So after all . . .

"Was everything satisfactory, madam?"

Her mouth was dry. "Yes . . . yes, thank you."

Deferentially, the man held a door open. "Good day."

Then, relief flooding through her, she was in the open air. Outside.

Driving away, at first, she had a let-down feeling. Now that she knew how unnecessary all the worrying had been, that there was nothing whatever she need have become concerned about, her fears while in the store seemed foolishly excessive. She still wondered, though: What had made her do it?

Suddenly, her mood became buoyant; she felt better than she had in weeks.

Erica's buoyancy persisted through the afternoon and carried over while she prepared dinner for Adam and herself. No carelessness in the kitchen tonight!

She had chosen Fondue Bourguignonne as the main course, partly because it was one of Adam's favorites, but mostly because the idea of them eating together out of the same fondue pot suggested an intimacy which she hoped would continue through the evening. In the dining room, Erica planned her table setting carefully. She chose yellow taper candles in spiral silver holders, the candles flanking an arrangement of chrysanthemums. She had bought the flowers on the way home, and now put those left over in the living room so that Adam would see them when he came in. The house gleamed, as it always did after a day's sprucing by Mrs. Gooch. About an hour before Adam was due, Erica lit a log fire.

Unfortunately, Adam was late, which was not unusual; what *was* unusual was his failure to telephone to let Erica know. When 7:30 came and went, then 7:45 and eight o'clock, she became increasingly restless, going frequently to a front window which overlooked the driveway, then rechecking the dining room, after that the kitchen where she opened the refrigerator to satisfy herself that the salad greens, prepared over an hour ago, had retained their crispness. The beef tenderloin for the fondue, which Erica had cut into bite-size pieces earlier, as well as condiments and sauces already in serving dishes were in there too. When Adam did arrive, it would take only minutes to have dinner ready.

She had already replenished the living-room fire a couple of times, so that now the living and dining rooms, which opened into each other, were excessively hot. Erica opened a window, allowing cold air to blow in, which in turn made the fire smoke, so she closed the window, then wondered about the wine—a '61 Château Latour, one of a few special bottles they had squirreled away— which she had opened at six o'clock, expecting to serve it at half-past seven. Now Erica took the wine back to the kitchen and recorked it.

Returning, with everything completed, she switched on a stereo tape player. A cassette was already inserted; the last bars of a recording finished, another began.

It was *Bahama Islands,* a song she loved, which her father used to strum on his guitar while Erica sang. But tonight the soft calypso melody made her sad and homesick.

Gentle breezes swirl the shifting strand,
Clear blue waters lap this fragrant land;
    Fair Bahamas!
    Sweet Bahamas!
Sun and sand.

Arc of islands, set in shining seas,
White sand beaches rim these sun-kissed cays;
    Island living,
    Island loving,
Sand and trees

Bright hibiscus line the path to shore,
Coral grottos grace the ocean floor—
    Nature's treasure,
    Life's sweet pleasure,
Evermore.

She snapped the machine off, leaving the song unfinished, and dabbed quickly at sudden tears before they spoiled what little make-up she was wearing.

At five past eight the telephone rang and Erica hurried to it expectantly. It was not Adam, as she hoped, but long distance for "Mr. Trenton," and during the exchange with the operator, Erica realized that the caller was Adam's sister, Teresa, in Pasadena, California. When the West Coast operator asked, "Will you speak with anyone else?", Teresa, who must have been aware that her sister-in-law was on the line, hesitated, then said, "No, I need Mr. Trenton. Please leave a message for him to call."

Erica was irritated by Teresa's parsimony in not letting the call go through; tonight she would have welcomed a conversation. Erica was aware that since Teresa became a widow a year ago, with four children to take care of, she needed to watch finances, but certainly not to the point of worrying about the cost of a long-distance phone call.

She made a note for Adam, with the Pasadena operator's number, so he could return the call later.

Then, at twenty past eight, Adam called on Citizens Band radio from his car to say he was on the Southfield Freeway, en route home. It meant he was fifteen minutes away. By mutual arrangement Erica always had a Citizens receiver in the kitchen switched to standby during early evening, and if Adam called it was usually to include a code phrase "activate olive." He used it now, which meant he would be ready for a martini as soon as he came in. Relieved, and glad she had not chosen the kind of dinner which the long delay would have spoiled, Erica put two martini glasses into the kitchen freezer and began mixing the drinks.

There was still time to hurry to the bedroom, check her hair, freshen lipstick, and renew her perfume—*the* perfume. A full-length mirror told her that the Paisley lounging pajamas which she had chosen as carefully as everything else, looked as good as earlier. When she heard Adam's key in the lock, Erica ran downstairs, irrationally nervous as a young bride.

He came in apologetically. "Sorry about the time."

As usual, Adam appeared fresh, unrumpled, and clear-eyed, as if ready to begin a day's work instead of having just completed one. Lately, though, Erica had detected a tension at times beneath the outward view; she wasn't sure about it now.

"It doesn't matter." She dismissed the lateness as she kissed him, knowing that the worst thing she could do was to be *Hausfrau*-ish about the delayed dinner. Adam returned the kiss absently, then insisted on explaining what had delayed him while she poured their martinis in the living room.

"Elroy and I were with Hub. Hub was firing broadsides. It wasn't the best time to break off and phone."

"Broadsides at you?" Like every other company wife, Erica knew that Hub was Hubbard J. Hewitson, executive vice-president in charge of North American automotive operations, and an industry crown prince with tremendous power. The power included ability to raise up or break any company executive other than the chairman of the board and president, the only two who outranked him. Hub's exacting standards were well known. He could be, and was, merciless to those who failed them.

"Partly at me," Adam said. "But mostly Hub was sounding off. He'll be over it tomorrow." He told Erica about the Orion add-ons, and the cost, which Adam had known would trigger the blast it had. On returning from the proving ground to staff headquarters, Adam had reported to Elroy Braithwaite. The Product Development vice-president decided they should go to Hub immediately and get the fireworks over with, which was the way it happened.

But however rough Hub Hewitson might be, he was a fair man who had probably accepted by now the inevitability of the extra items and their cost. Adam knew he had made the right decision at the proving ground, though he was still aware of tension within himself, which the martini had eased a little, but not much.

He held out his glass for refilling, then dropped into a chair. "It's damn hot in here tonight. Why did you light a fire?"

He had seated himself alongside the table which held some of the flowers which Erica had bought this afternoon. Adam pushed the flower vase aside to make a space for his glass.

"I thought a fire might be cheerful."

He looked at her directly. "Meaning it isn't usually?"

"I didn't say that."

"Maybe you should have." Adam stood up, then moved around the room, touching things in it, familiar things. It was an old habit, something he did when he was restless. Erica wanted to tell him: *Try touching me! You'll get a lot more response!*

Instead she said, "Oh, there's a letter from Kirk. He wrote it to us both. He's been made features editor of the university paper."

"Um." Adam's grunt was unenthusiastic.

"It's important to him." She could not resist adding, "As important as when a promotion happens to you."

Adam swung around, his back to the fire. He said harshly, "I've told you before, I'm used to the idea of Greg being a doctor. In fact, I like it. It's tough to qualify, and when he does he'll be contributing—doing something useful. But don't expect me, now or later, to be pleased about Kirk becoming a newspaperman, or anything that happens to him on the way."

It was a perennial topic, and now Erica wished she hadn't raised it because they were off to a bad start. Adam's boys had had definite ideas about their own careers, long before she came into their lives. Just the same, in discussions afterward Erica had supported their choices, making clear that she was glad they were not following Adam into the auto industry.

Later, she knew she had been unwise. The boys would have gone their own ways in any case, so all she succeeded in doing was to make Adam bitter because his own career, by implication, had been denigrated to his sons.

She said as mildly as she could, "Surely being a newspaper writer is doing something useful."

He shook his head irritably. The memory of this morning's press conference, which he liked less and less the more he thought about it, was still with Adam. "If you saw as much of press people as I do, you might not think so. Most of what they do is superficial, out of balance, prejudiced when they claim impartiality, and riddled with inaccuracies. They blame the inaccuracies on an obsession with speed, which is used the way a cripple uses a crutch. It never seems to occur to newspaper managements and writers that being slower, checking facts before they storm into print, might be a better public service. What's more, they're critics and self-appointed judges of everybody's failings except their own."

"Some of that's true," Erica said. "But not of all newspapers or everybody working for them."

Adam looked ready for an argument which she sensed could turn into a quarrel. Determined to snuff it out, Erica crossed the room and took his arm. She smiled. "Let's hope Kirk will do better than those others and surprise you."

The physical contact, of which they had had so little lately, gave her a sense of pleasure which, if she had her way, would be even greater before the evening was over. She insisted, "Leave all that for another time. I have your favorite dinner waiting."

"Let's make it as quick as we can," Adam said. "I've some papers I want to go over afterward, and I'd like to get to them."

Erica let go his arm and went to the kitchen, wondering if he realized how many times he had used almost the same words in identical circumstances until they seemed a litany.

Adam followed her in. "Anything I can do?"

"You can put the dressing on the salad and toss it."

He did it quickly, competently as always, then saw the note about Teresa's call from Pasadena. Adam told Erica, "You go ahead and start. I'll see what Teresa wants."

Once Adam's sister was on the phone she seldom talked briefly, long distance or not. "I've waited this long," Erica objected, "I don't want to have dinner alone now. Can't you call later? It's only six o'clock out there."

"Well, if we're really ready."

Erica had rushed. The oil-butter mix, which she had heated in the fondue pot over the kitchen range, was ready. She carried it to the dining room, set the pot on its stand and lit the canned heat beneath. Everything else was on the dining table, which looked elegant.

As she brought a taper near the candles, Adam asked, "Is it worth lighting them?"

"Yes." She lit them all.

The candlelight revealed the wine which Erica had brought in again. Adam frowned. "I thought we were keeping that for a special occasion."

"Special like what?"

He reminded her, "The Hewitsons and Braithwaites are coming next month."

"Hub Hewitson doesn't know the difference between a Château Latour and Cold Duck, and couldn't care. Why can't *we* be special, just the two of us?"

Adam speared a piece of beef tenderloin and left it in the fondue pot while he began his salad. At length he said, "Why is it you never lose a chance to take a dig at the people I work with, or the work I do?"

"Do I?"

"You know you do. You have, ever since our marriage."

"Perhaps it's because I feel as if I fight for every private moment that we have."

But she conceded to herself: Sometimes she did throw needless slings and arrows, just as she had a moment ago about Hub Hewitson.

She filled Adam's wineglass and said gently, "I'm sorry. What I said about Hub was snobbish and unnecessary. If you'd like him to have Château Latour, I'll go shopping for some more." The thought occurred to her: *Maybe I can get an extra bottle or two the way I got the perfume.*

"Forget it," Adam said. "It doesn't matter."

During coffee, he excused himself and went to his upstairs study to telephone Teresa.

"Hi there, bigshot? Where were you? Counting your stock options?" Teresa's voice came clearly across the two thousand miles between them, the big-sister contralto Adam remembered from their childhood long ago. Teresa had been seven when Adam was born. Yet, for all their gap in ages, they had always been close and, strangely, from the time Adam was in his early teens, Teresa had sought her younger brother's advice and often heeded it.

"You know how it is, sis. I'm indispensable, which makes it hard to get home. Sometimes I wonder how they ever started this industry without me."

"We're all proud of you," Teresa said. "The kids often talk about Uncle Adam. They say he'll be company president someday." Another thing about Teresa was her unconcealed pleasure at her brother's success. She had always reacted to his progress and promotions that way, with far more enthusiasm—he admitted reluctantly—than Erica had ever shown.

He asked, "How have you been, sis?"

"Lonely." A pause. "You were expecting some other answer?"

"Not really. I wondered if, by now . . ."

"Somebody else had shown up?"

"Something like that."

"A few have. I'm still not a bad-looking broad for a widow lady."

"I know that." It was true. Though she would be fifty in a year or so, Teresa was statuesque, classically beautiful, and sexy.

"The trouble is, when you've had a man—a real one—for twenty-two years, you start comparing others with him. They don't come out of it well."

Teresa's husband, Clyde, had been an accountant with wide-ranging interests. He had died tragically in an airplane accident a year ago, leaving his widow with four young children, adopted late in their marriage. Since then, Teresa had had to make major adjustments both psychologically and in financial management, the latter an area she had never bothered with before.

Adam asked, "Is the money end all right?"

"I think so. But it's that I called you about. Sometimes I wish you were closer."

Though Adam's late brother-in-law had left adequate provision for his family, his financial affairs had been untidy at the time of his death. As best he could from a distance, Adam had helped Teresa unravel them.

"If you really need me," Adam said, "I can fly out for a day or two."

"No. You're already where I need you—in Detroit. I get concerned about that investment Clyde made in Stephensen Motors. It earns money, but it represents a lot of capital—most of what we have—and I keep asking myself: Should I leave it where it is, or sell out and put the money into something safer?"

Adam already knew the background. Teresa's husband had been an auto-racing buff who haunted tracks in Southern California, so that he came to know many racing drivers well. One had been Smokey Stephensen, a consistent winner over the years who, unusually for his kind, had shrewdly held on to his prize money and eventually quit with most of his winnings intact. Later, using his name and prestige, Smokey Stephensen obtained an auto dealership franchise in Detroit, marketing the products of Adam's company. Teresa's husband had gone into silent partnership with the ex-race driver and contributed almost one-half of needed capital. The shares in the business were now owned by Teresa who received them under Clyde's will.

"Sis, you say you're getting money from Detroit—from Stephensen?"

"Yes. I haven't the figures, though I can send them to you, and the accountants who took over Clyde's office say it's a fair return. What worries me is all I read about car dealerships being risky investments, and some of them failing. If it happened to Stephensen's, the kids and I could be in trouble."

"It can happen," Adam acknowledged. "But if you're lucky enough to have shares in a good dealership, you might make a big mistake by pulling out."

"I realize that. It's why I need someone to

advise me, someone I can trust. Adam, I hate to ask this because I know you're working hard already. But do you think you could spend some time with Smokey Stephensen, find out what's going on, form your own opinion about how things look, then tell me what I ought to do? If you remember, we talked about this once before."

"I remember. And I think I explained then, it could be a problem. Auto companies don't allow their staff to be involved with auto dealerships. Before I could do anything, it would have to go before the Conflict of Interest Committee."

"Is that a big thing? Would it embarrass you?"

Adam hesitated. The answer was: It *would* embarrass him. To do what Teresa asked would involve a close study of the Stephensen dealership, which meant looking into its books and reviewing operating methods. Teresa, of course, would provide Adam with authority from her point of view, but the point of view of Adam's company—his employers—was something else again. Before Adam could cozy up with a car dealer, for whatever purpose, he would have to declare what he was doing, and why. Elroy Braithwaite would need to know; so would Hub Hewitson, probably, and it was a safe bet that neither would like the idea. Their reasoning would be simple. A senior executive of Adam's status was in a position to do financial favors for a dealer, hence the strict rules which all auto companies had about outside business interests in this and other areas. A standing Conflict of Interest Committee reviewed such matters, including personal investments of company employees and their families, reported yearly on a form resembling an income tax return. A few people who resented this put investments in their wives' or children's names, and kept them secret. But mostly the rules made sense, and executives observed them.

Well, he would have to go to the committee, Adam supposed, and state his arguments. After all, he had nothing to gain personally; he would merely be protecting the interest of a widow and young children, which gave the request a compassionate overtone. In fact, the more he thought about it, the less trouble he anticipated.

"I'll see what I can work out, sis," Adam said into the telephone. "Tomorrow I'll start things moving in the company, then it may be a week or two before I get approval to go ahead. You do understand I can't do anything without that?"

"Yes, I do. And the delay doesn't matter. As long as I know you're going to be looking out for us, that's the important thing." Teresa sounded relieved. He could picture her now, the small concentrated frown she had when dealing with something difficult had probably gone, replaced by a warm smile, the kind which made a man feel good. Adam's sister was a woman who liked to rely on a male and have him handle decisions, though during the past year she had been forced to make an unaccustomed number on her own.

Adam asked, "How much of the Stephensen Motors stock did Clyde have?"

"It was forty-nine percent, and I still have all of it. Clyde put up about two hundred and forty thousand dollars. That's why I've been so concerned."

"Was Clyde's name on the franchise?"

"No. Just Smokey Stephensen's."

He instructed, "You'd better send me all the papers, including a record of payments you've had as dividends. Write to Stephensen, too. Tell him he'll probably be hearing from me, and that I have your authority to go in and look things over. Okay?"

"I'll do all that. And thank you, Adam dear; thank you very much. Please give my love to Erica. How is she?"

"Oh, she's fine."

Erica had cleared away their meal and was on the sofa in the living room, feet curled beneath her, when Adam returned.

She motioned to an end table. "I made more coffee."

"Thanks." He poured a cup for himself, then went to the hallway for his briefcase. Returning, he sank into an armchair by the fire, which had now burned low, opened his briefcase and began to take out papers.

Erica asked, "What did Teresa want?"

In a few words Adam explained his sister's request and what he had agreed to do.

He found Erica looking at him incredulously. "When will you do it?"

"Oh, I don't know. I'll find time."

"But when? I want to know when."

With a trace of irritation, Adam said, "If you decide to do something, you can always make the time."

"You don't make time." Erica's voice had an intensity which had been lacking earlier. "You take the time from something or somebody else. Won't it mean a lot of visits to that dealer? Questioning people. Finding out about the business. I know how you do everything—always the same way, thoroughly. So it will involve a lot of time. Well, won't it?"

He conceded, "I suppose so."

"Will it be in office time? In the daytime, during the week?"

"Probably not."

"So that leaves evenings and weekends. Car dealers are open then, aren't they?"

Adam said curtly, "They don't open Sundays."

"Well, hooray for that!" Erica hadn't intended to be this way tonight. She had wanted to be patient, understanding, loving, but suddenly bitterness swept over her. She flared on, knowing she would do better to stop, but unable to, "Perhaps this dealer *would* open on Sunday if you asked him nicely, if you explained that you still have a little time left to spend at home with your wife, and you'd like to do something about it, like filling it with work."

"Listen," Adam said, "this won't be work, and I wouldn't do it if I had the choice. It's simply for Teresa."

"How about something simply for Erica? Or would that be too much? Wait!—why not use your vacation time as well, then you could . . ."

"You're being silly," Adam said. He had taken the papers from his briefcase and spread them around him in a semicircle. Like a witch's circle on the grass, Erica thought, to be penetrated only by the anointed, the bewitched. Even voices entering the magic circle became distorted, misunderstood, with words and meanings twisted . . .

Adam was right. She *was* being silly. And now whimsical.

She went behind him, still conscious of the semicircle, skirting its perimeter the way children playing games avoided lines in paving stones.

Erica put her hands lightly on Adam's shoulders, her face against his. He reached up, touching one of her hands.

"I couldn't turn sis down." Adam's voice was conciliatory. "How could I? If things had been the other way around, Clyde would have done as much, or more, for you."

Abruptly, unexpectedly, she realized, their moods had switched. She thought: There *is* a way into a witch's circle. Perhaps the trick was not to expect to find it, then suddenly you did.

"I know," Erica said. "And I'm grateful it *isn't* the other way around." She had a sense of reprieve from her own stupidity only seconds earlier, an awareness of having stumbled without warning into a moment of intimacy and tenderness. She went on softly, "It's just that sometimes I want things between you and me to be the way they were in the beginning. I really do see so little of you." She scratched lightly, with her fingernails, around his ears, something she used to do but hadn't for a long time. "I still love you." And was tempted to add, but didn't: *Please, oh please, make love to me tonight!*

"I haven't changed either," Adam said. "No reason to. And I know what you mean about the time we have. Maybe after the Orion's launched there'll be more of it." But the last remark lacked conviction. As both of them already knew, after Orion would be Farstar, which would probably prove more demanding still. Involuntarily, Adam's eyes strayed back to the papers spread out before him.

Erica told herself: *Don't rush! Don't push too hard!* She said, "While you're doing that, I think I'll go for a walk. I feel like it."

"Do you want me to come with you?"

She shook her head. "You'd better finish." If he left the work now, she knew he would either return to it late tonight or get up ridiculously early in the morning.

Adam looked relieved.

Outside the house, Erica pulled tightly around her the suede jacket she had slipped on, and stepped out briskly. She had a scarf wound around her hair. The air was chilly, though the wind which had buffeted the Motor City through the day had dropped. Erica liked to walk at night. She used to in the Bahamas, and still did here, though friends and neighbors sometimes cautioned that she shouldn't because crime in Detroit had risen alarmingly in recent years, and now even suburban Birmingham and Bloomfield Hills— once considered almost crime-free—had muggings and armed robberies.

But Erica preferred to take her chances and her walks.

Though the night was dark, with stars and moon obscured by clouds, enough light came from the houses of Quarton Lake for Erica to see her way clearly. As she passed the houses, sometimes observing figures inside, she wondered about those other families in their own environments, their hangups, misunderstandings, conflicts, problems. Obviously, all had some, and the difference between most was only in degree. More to the point, she wondered: How fared the marriages inside those other walls, compared with Adam's and her own?

A majority of the neighbors were automotive people among whom the shedding of spouses nowadays seemed routine. American tax laws eased the way, and many a highly paid executive had discovered he could have his freedom by paying large alimony which cost him almost nothing. The alimony came off the top of his salary, so that he merely paid it to his ex-wife instead of to the government as income tax. A few people in the industry had even done it twice.

But it was always the foundered marriages which made the news. Plenty of the other kind existed—lasting love stories which had weathered well. Erica thought of names she had learned since coming to Detroit: Riccardos, Gerstenbergs, Knudsens, Iacoccas, Roches, Brambletts, others. There had been outstanding second marriages, too: the Henry Fords, Ed Coles, Roy Chapins, Bill Mitchells, Pete and Connie Estes, the John DeLoreans. As always, it depended on the individuals.

Erica walked for half an hour. On her way back, a soft rain began to fall. She held her face toward the rain until it was wet and streaming, yet somehow comforting.

She went in without disturbing Adam who was still in the living room, immersed in papers. Upstairs, Erica dried her face, combed out her hair, then undressed and put on the nightgown she had bought earlier today. Surveying herself critically, she was aware that the sheer beige nylon did even more for her than she had expected in the store. She used the orange lipstick, then applied Norell generously.

From the living-room doorway she asked Adam, "Will you be long?"

He glanced up, then down again at a blue-bound folder in his hand. "Maybe half an hour."

Adam had not appeared to notice the see-through nightgown which could not compete, apparently, with the folder, lettered, *Statistical Projection of Automobile and Truck Registration by States*. Hoping that the perfume might prove more effective, Erica came behind his chair as she had earlier, but all that happened was a perfunctory kiss with a muttered, "Good night; don't wait for me." She might as well, she thought, have been drenched in camphorated oil.

She went to bed, and lay with top sheet and blanket turned back, her sexual desire growing as she waited. If she closed her eyes, she could imagine Adam poised above her . . .

Erica opened her eyes. A bedside clock showed that not half an hour, but almost two hours, had passed. It was 1 A.M.

Soon after, she heard Adam climb the stairs.

He came in, yawning, with a, "God, I'm tired," then undressed sleepily, climbed into bed, and was almost instantly asleep.

Erica lay silently beside him, sleep for herself far away. After a while she imagined that she was once more walking, out of doors, the softness of the rain upon her face.

chapter nine

The day after Adam and Erica Trenton failed to bridge the growing gap between them, after Brett DeLosanto renewed his faith in the Orion yet pondered his artistic destiny, after Barbara Zaleski viewed frustrations through the benthos of martinis, and after Matt Zaleski, her plant-boss father, survived another pressure-cooker work day, a minor event occurred in the inner city of Detroit, unconnected with any of those five, yet whose effect, over months ahead, would involve and motivate them all.

Time: 8:30 P.M. *Place:* Downtown, Third Avenue near Brainard. An empty police cruiser parked beside the curb.

"Get your black ass against the wall," the white cop commanded. Holding a flashlight in one hand, a gun in the other, he ran the flashlight's beam down and up Rollie Knight, who blinked as the light reached his eyes and stayed there.

"Now turn around. Hands above your head. Move!—you goddam jailbird."

As Rollie Knight turned, the white cop told his Negro partner, "Frisk the bastard."

The young, shabbily dressed black man whom the policeman had stopped, had been ambling aimlessly on Third when the cruiser pulled alongside and its occupants jumped out, guns drawn. Now he protested, "Wadd' I do?", then giggled as the second policeman's hands moved up his legs, then around his body. "Hey man, oh man, that tickles!"

"Shaddup!" the white cop said. He was an old-timer on the force, with hard eyes and a big belly, the last from years of riding in patrol cars.

He had survived this beat a long time and never relaxed while on it.

The black policeman, who was several years younger and newer, dropped his hands. "He's okay." Moving back, he inquired softly, "What difference does the color of his ass make?"

The white cop looked startled. In their haste since moving from the cruiser he had forgotten that tonight his usual partner, also white, was off sick, with a black officer substituting.

"Hell!" he said hastily. "Don't get ideas. Even if you are his color, you don't rate down with that crumb."

The black cop said drily, "Thanks." He considered saying more, but didn't. Instead, he told the man against the wall, "You can put your hands down. Turn around."

As the instruction was obeyed, the white cop rasped, "Where you been the last half hour, Knight?" He knew Rollie Knight by name, not only from seeing him around here frequently, but from a police record which included two jail convictions, for one of which the officer had made the arrest himself.

"Where I bin?" The young black man had recovered from his initial shock. Though his cheeks were hollowed, and he appeared underfed and frail, there was nothing weak about his eyes, which mirrored hatred. "I bin layin' a white piece o' ass. Doan know her name, except she says her old man's a fat white pig who can't get it up. Comes here when she needs it from a man."

The white cop took a step forward, the blood vessels in his face swelling red. His intention was to smash the muzzle of his gun across the contemptuous, taunting face. Afterward, he could claim that Knight struck him first and his own action was in self-defense. His partner would back up the story, in the same way that they always corroborated each other, except—he remembered abruptly—tonight his partner was one of *them,* who might just be ornery enough to make trouble later. So the policeman checked himself, knowing there would be another time and place, as this smart-aleck nigger would find out.

The black cop growled at Rollie Knight, "Don't push your luck. Tell us where you were."

The young Negro spat on the sidewalk. A cop was an enemy, whatever his color, and a black one was worse because he was a lackey of the Man. But he answered, "In there," motioning to a basement bar across the street.

"How long?"

"An hour. Maybe two. Maybe three." Rollie Knight shrugged. "Who keeps score?"

The black cop asked his partner, "Should I check it out?"

"No, be a wasta time. They'd say he'd been there. They're all damn liars."

The black officer pointed out, "To get here in this time from West Grand and Second he'd have needed wings, anyway."

The call had come in minutes earlier on the prowl car radio. An armed robbery near the Fisher Building, eighteen blocks away. It had just happened. Two suspects had fled in a late model sedan.

Seconds later, the patrolling duo had seen Rollie Knight walking alone on Third Avenue. Though the likelihood of a single pedestrian, here, being involved with the uptown robbery was remote, when the white cop had recognized Knight, he shouted to halt the car, then jumped out, leaving his partner no choice but to follow. The black officer knew why they had acted. The robbery call provided an excuse to "stop and frisk," and the other officer enjoyed stopping people and bullying them when he knew he could get away with it, though it was coincidental, of course, that those he picked on were invariably black.

There was a relationship, the black officer believed, between his companion's viciousness and brutality—which were well-known around the force—and fear, which rode him while on duty in the ghetto. Fear had its own stink, and the black policeman had smelled it strongly from the white officer beside him the moment the robbery call came in, and when they had jumped from the car, and even now. Fear could, and did, make a mean man meaner still. When he possessed authority as well, he could become a savage.

Not that fear was out of place in these surroundings. In fact, for a Detroit policeman not to know fear would betray a lack of knowledge, an absence of imagination. In the inner city, with a crime rate probably the nation's highest, police were targets—always of hate, often of bricks and knives and bullets. Where survival depended on alertness, a degree of fear was rational; so were suspicion, caution, swiftness when danger showed, or seemed to. It was like being in a war where police were on the firing line. And as in any war, the niceties of human behavior—politeness, psychology, tolerance, kindness—got brushed aside as nonessential, so that the war intensified while antagonisms—often with cause on both sides—perpetuated themselves and multiplied.

Yet a few policemen, as the black cop knew, learned to live with fear while remaining decent human beings, too. These were ones who understood the nature of the times, the mood of black people, their frustrations, the long history of injustice behind them. This kind of policeman— whether white or black—helped relieve the war a little, though it was hard to know how much because they were not in a majority.

To make moderates a majority, and to raise

standards of the Detroit force generally, were declared aims of a recently appointed police chief. But between the chief and his objectives was the physical presence of a contingent of officers, numerically strong, who through fear or rooted prejudice were frankly racist like the white cop here and now.

"Where you working, crumb?" he demanded of Rollie Knight

"I'm like you. I ain't workin', just passin' time."

The policeman's face bulged again with anger. If he had not been there, the black cop knew, his partner would have smashed his fist into the frail young black face leering at him.

The black cop told Rollie Knight, "Beat it! You flap your mouth too much."

Back in the prowl car the other policeman fumed, "So help me, I'll nail that bastard."

The black officer thought: *And so you will, probably tomorrow or the next day when you've got your regular sidekick back, and he'll look the other way if there's a beating or an arrest on some trumped-up charge.* There had been plenty of other vendettas of the same kind.

On impulse, the black cop, who was behind the wheel, said, "Hold it! I'll be back."

As he got out of the car, Rollie Knight was fifty yards away.

"Hey, you!" When the young black man turned, the officer beckoned, then walked to meet him.

The black cop leaned toward Rollie Knight, his stance threatening. But he said quietly, "My partner's out to get you, and he will. You're a stupid jerk for letting your mouth run off, and I don't owe you favors. All the same, I'm warning you: Stay out of sight, or better—get out of town 'til the man cools."

"A Judas nigger cop! Why'd I take the word from you?"

"No reason." The policeman shrugged. "So let what's coming come. No skin off me."

"How'd I leave? Where'd I get wheels, the bread?" Though spoken with a sneer, the query was a shade less hostile.

"Then don't leave. Keep out of sight, the way I said."

"Ain't easy here, man."

No, it was not easy, as the black cop knew. Not easy to remain unnoticed through each long day and night when someone wanted you and others knew where you were. Information came cheap if you knew the pipelines of the inner city; all it took was the price of a fix, the promise of a favor, even the right kind of threat. Loyalty was not a plant which flourished here. But being somewhere else, absence for part of the time, at least, would help. The policeman asked, "Why aren't you working?"

Rollie Knight grinned. "You hear me tell your pig friend . . ."

"Save the smart talk. You want work?"

"Maybe." But behind the admission was the knowledge that few jobs were open to those with criminal records like Rollie Knight's.

"The car plants are hiring," the black cop said.

"That's honky land."

"Plenty of the blood work there."

Rollie Knight said grudgingly, "I tried one time. Some whitey fink said no."

"Try again. Here." From a tunic pocket the black cop pulled a card. It had been given him, the day before, by a company employment office man he knew. It had the address of a hiring hall, a name, some hours of opening.

Rollie Knight crumpled the card and thrust it

in a pocket. "When I feel like it, baby, I'll piss on it."

"Suit yourself," the black cop said. He walked back to the car.

His white partner looked at him suspiciously. "What was all that?"

He answered shortly, "I cooled him down," but did not elaborate.

The black policeman had no intention of being bullied, but neither did he want an argument—at least, not now. Though Detroit's population was forty percent black, only in most recent years had its police force ceased to be nearly a hundred percent white, and within the police department old influences still predominated. Since the 1967 Detroit riots, under public pressure the number of black policemen had increased, but blacks were not yet strong enough in numbers, rank, or influence to offset the powerful, white-oriented Detroit Police Officers Association, or even to be sure of a fair deal, departmentally, in any black-white confrontation.

Thus, the patrol continued in an atmosphere of hostile uncertainty, a mood reflecting the racial tensions of Detroit itself.

Bravado in individuals, black or white, is often only skin shallow, and Rollie Knight, inside his soul, was frightened.

He was frightened of the white cop whom he had unwisely baited, and he realized now that his reckless, burning hatred had briefly got the better of ordinary caution. Even more, he feared a return to prison where one more conviction was likely to send him up for a long time. Rollie had three convictions behind him, and two prison terms; whatever happened now, all hope of leniency was gone.

Only a black man in America knows the true

depths of animal despair and degradation to which the prison system can reduce a human being. It is true that white prisoners are often treated badly, and suffer also, but never as consistently or universally as black. It is also true that some prisons are better or worse than others, but this is like saying that certain parts of hell are ten degrees hotter or cooler than others. The black man, whichever prison he is in, knows that humiliation and abuse are standard, and that physical brutality—sometimes involving major injury—is as normal as defecating. And when the prisoner is frail—as Rollie Knight was frail, partly from a poor physique which he was born with, and partly from accumulated malnutrition over years—the penalties and anguish can be greater still.

Coupled, at this moment, with these fears was the young Negro's knowledge that a police search of his room would reveal a small supply of marijuana. He smoked a little grass himself, but peddled most, and while rewards were slight, at least it was a means to eat because, since coming out of prison several months ago, he had found no other way. But the marijuana was all the police would need for a conviction, with jail to follow.

For this reason, later the same night while nervously wondering if he was already watched, Rollie Knight dumped the marijuana in a vacant lot. Now, instead of a tenuous hold on the means to live from day to day, he was aware that he had none.

It was this awareness which, next day, caused him to uncrumple the card which the black cop had given him and go to the auto company hiring center in the inner city. He went without hope because . . . (and this is the great, invisible gap which separates the "have-nots-and-never-hads" of this world, like Rollie Knight, from the "haves," including some who try to understand their less-blessed brothers yet, oh so sadly, fail) . . . he had lived so long without any reason to believe in anything, that hope itself was beyond his mental grasp.

He also went because he had nothing else to do.

The building near 12th Street, like a majority of others in the inner city's grim "black bottom," was decrepit and unkempt, with shattered windows, of which only a few had been boarded over for inside protection from the weather. Until recently the building had been disused and was disintegrating rapidly. Even now, despite patching and rough painting, its decay continued, and those who went to work there daily sometimes wondered if the walls would be standing when they left at night.

But the ancient building, and two others like it, had an urgent function. It was an outpost for the auto companies' "hard core" hiring programs.

So-called hard core hiring had begun after the Detroit riots and was an attempt to provide work for an indigent nucleus of inner city people —mostly black—who, tragically and callously, had for years been abandoned as unemployable. The lead was taken by the auto companies. Others followed. Naturally, the auto companies claimed altruism as their motive and, from the moment the hiring programs started, public relations staffs proclaimed their employers' public spirit. More cynical observers claimed that the auto world was running scared, fearing the effect of a permanently strife-ridden community on their businesses. Others predicted that when smoke from the riot-torn, burning city touched the General Motors Building in '67 (as it did), and flames came close, some form of public service was assured. The prediction came true, except that Ford moved first.

But whatever the motivations, three things generally were agreed: the hard core hiring program was good. It ought to have happened twenty years before it did. Without the '67 riots, it might never have happened at all.

On the whole, allowing for errors and defeats, the program worked. Auto companies lowered their hiring standards, letting former deadbeats in. Predictably, some fell by the way, but a surprising number proved that all a deadbeat needed was a chance. By the time Rollie Knight arrived, much had been learned by employers and employed.

He sat in a waiting room with about forty others, men and women, ranged on rows of chairs. The chairs, like the applicants for jobs, were of assorted shapes and sizes, except that the applicants had a uniformity: all were black. There was little conversation. For Rollie Knight the waiting took an hour. During part of it he dozed off, a habit he had acquired and which helped him, normally, to get through empty days.

When, eventually, he was ushered into an interview cubicle—one of a half dozen lining the waiting area—he was still sleepy and yawned at the interviewer, facing him across a desk.

The interviewer, a middle-aged, chubby black man, wearing horn-rimmed glasses, a sports jacket and dark shirt, but no tie, said amiably, "Gets tiring waiting. My daddy used to say, 'A man grows wearier sitting on his backside than chopping wood.' He had me chop a lot of wood that way."

Rollie Knight looked at the other's hands. "You ain't chopped much lately."

"Well, now," the interviewer said, "you're right. And we've established something else: You're a man who looks at things and thinks. But are *you* interested in chopping wood, or doing work that's just as hard?"

"I dunno." Rollie was wondering why he had come here at all. Soon they would get to his prison record, and that would be the end of it.

"But you're here because you want a job?" The interviewer glanced at a yellow card which a secretary outside had filled in. "That's correct, isn't it, Mr. Knight?"

Rollie nodded. The "Mr." surprised him. He could not remember when he had last been addressed that way.

"Let's begin by finding out about you." The interviewer drew a printed pad toward him. Part of the new hiring technique was that applicants no longer had to complete a pre-employment questionnaire themselves. In the past, many who could barely read or write were turned away because of inability to do what modern society thought of as a standard function: fill in a form.

They went quickly through the basic questions.

Name: Knight, Rolland Joseph Louis. *Age:* 29. *Address:* he gave it, *not mentioning that the mean, walk-up room belonged to someone else who had let him share it for a day or two, and that the address might not be good next week if the occupant decided to kick Rollie out. But then a large part of his life had alternated between that kind of accommodation, or a flophouse, or the streets when he had nowhere else.*

Parents: He recited the names. The surnames differed since his parents had not married or ever lived together. The interviewer made no comment; it was normal enough. Nor did Rollie add: *He knew his father because his mother had told him who he was, and Rollie had a vague impression of a meeting once: a burly man, heavy-jowled and scowling, with a facial scar, who had been neither friendly nor interested in his son. Years ago, Rollie had heard his father was in jail as a lifer. Whether he was still there, or dead, he had no idea. As for his mother, with whom he lived, more or less, until he left home for the streets at age fifteen, he believed she was now in Cleveland or Chicago. He had not seen or heard from her for several years.*

Schooling: Until grade eight. *He had had a quick, bright mind at school, and still had when something new came up, but realized how much a black man needed to learn if he was to beat the stinking honky system, and now he never would.*

Previous employment: He strained to remember names and places. *There had been unskilled jobs after leaving school—a bus boy, shoveling snow, washing cars. Then in 1957, when Detroit was hit by a national recession, there were no jobs of any kind and he drifted into idleness, punctuated by shooting craps, hustling, and his first conviction: auto theft.*

The interviewer asked, "Do you have a police record, Mr. Knight?"

"Yeah."

"I'm afraid I'll need the details. And I think I should tell you that we check up afterward, so it looks better if we get it correctly from you first."

Rollie shrugged. Sure the sons-of-bitches checked. He knew that, without being given all this grease.

He gave the employment guy the dope on the auto theft rap first. He was nineteen then. He'd been put on a year's probation.

Never mind now about the way it happened. Who cared that the others in the car had picked him up, that he'd gone along, as a backseat passenger, for laughs, and later the cops had stopped them, charging all six occupants with theft? Before going into court next day, Rollie was offered a deal: Plead guilty and he'd get probation. Bewildered, frightened, he agreed. The deal was kept. He was in and out of court in seconds. Only later had he learned that with a lawyer to advise him—the way a white kid would have had—a not guilty plea would probably have got him off, with no more than a warning from the judge. Nor had he been told that pleading guilty would ensure a criminal record, to sit like an evil genie on his shoulder the remainder of his life.

It also made the sentence for the next conviction tougher.

The interviewer asked, "What happened after that?"

"I was in the pen." It was a year later. Auto theft again. *This time for real, and there had been two other times he wasn't caught.* The sentence: two years.

"Anything else?"

This was the clincher. Always, after this, they closed the books—no dice, no work. Well, they could stick their stinking job; Rollie still wondered why he had come. "Armed robbery. I drew five to fifteen, did four years in Jackson Pen."

A jewelry store. Two of them had broken in at night. All they got was a handful of cheap watches and were caught as they came out. Rollie had been stupid enough to carry a .22. Though he hadn't pulled it from his pocket, the fact that it was found on him ensured the graver charge.

"You were released for good behavior?"

"No. The warden got jealous. He wanted my cell."

The middle-aged Negro interviewer looked up. "I dig jokes. They make a dull day brighter. But it *was* good behavior?"

"If you say so."

"All right, I'll say so." The interviewer wrote it down.

"Is your behavior good now, Mr. Knight? What I mean is, are you in any more trouble with the police?"

Rollie shook his head negatively. He wasn't going to tell this Uncle Tom about last night, that he *was* in trouble if he couldn't keep clear of the white pig he had spooked, and who would bust him some way, given half a chance, using scum bag honky law. The thought was a reminder of his earlier fears, which now returned: the dread of prison, the real reason for coming here. The interviewer was asking more questions, busier than a dog with fleas writing down the answers. Rollie was surprised they hadn't stopped, baffled that he wasn't already outside on the street, the way it usually went after he mouthed the words "armed robbery."

What he didn't know—because no one had thought to tell him, and he was not a reader of newspapers or magazines—was that hard core hiring had a new, less rigid attitude to prison records, too.

He was sent to another room where he stripped and had a physical.

The doctor, young, white, impersonal, working fast, took time out to look critically at Rollie's bony body, his emaciated cheeks. "Whatever job you get, use some of what they pay you to eat better, and put some weight on, otherwise you won't last at it. You wouldn't last, anyway, in the foundry where most people go from here. Maybe they can put you in Assembly. I'll recommend it."

Rollie listened contemptuously, already hating the system, the people in it. Who in hell did this smug whitey kid think he was? Some kind of God? If Rollie didn't need bread badly, some work for a while, he'd walk out now, and screw 'em. One thing was sure: whatever job these people gave him, he wouldn't stay on it one day longer than he had to.

Back through the waiting room, in the cubicle again. The original interviewer announced, "The doctor says you're breathing, and when you opened your mouth he couldn't see daylight, so we're offering you a job. It's in final assembly. The work is hard, but pay is good—the union sees to that. Do you want it?"

"I'm here, ain't I?" What did the son-of-a-bitch expect? A bootlick job?

"Yes, you're here, so I'll take that to mean yes. There will be some weeks of training; you get paid for that, too. Outside, they'll give you details —when to start, where to go. Just one other thing."

Here came the preaching. Sure as glory, Rollie Knight could smell it. Maybe this white nigger was a Holy Roller on the side.

The interviewer took off his horn-rimmed glasses, leaned over the desk and put his fingertips together. "You're smart. You know the score. You know you're getting a break, and it's because of the times, the way things are. People, companies like this one, have a conscience they didn't always have. Never mind that it's late; it's here, and a lot of other things are changing. You may not believe it, but they are." The chubby, sports-jacketed interviewer picked up a pencil, rolled it through his fingers, put it down. "Maybe you never had a break before, and this is the first. I think it is. But I wouldn't be doing my job if I didn't tell you that with your record it's the only one you'll get, leastways here. A lot of guys pass through this place. Some make it after they leave; others don't. Those who do are the ones who want to." The interviewer looked hard at Rollie. "Stop being a damn fool, Knight, and grab this

chance. That's the best advice you'll get today."
He put out a hand. "Good luck."

Reluctantly, feeling as if he had been suckered but not knowing exactly how, Rollie took the
proffered hand.

Outside, just the way the man said, they told
him how to go to work.

The training course, sponsored jointly by the
company and through federal grants, was eight
weeks long. Rollie Knight lasted a week and a
half.

He received the first week's paycheck, which
was more money than he had possessed in a long
time. Over the following weekend he tied one on.
However, on Monday he managed to awaken early
and catch a bus which took him to the factory
training center on the other side of town.

But on Tuesday, tiredness won. He failed to
wake until, through the curtainless dirty window
of his room, the sun shone directly on his face.
Rollie got up sleepily, blinking, and went to the
window to look down. A clock in the street below
showed that it was almost noon.

He knew he had blown it, that the job was
gone. His reaction was indifference. He did not
experience disappointment because, from the beginning, he had not expected any other outcome.
How and when the ending came were merely
details.

Experience had never taught Rollie Knight—
or tens of thousands like him—to take a long-
term view of anything. When you were born with
nothing, had gained nothing since, had learned
to live with nothing, there *was* no long-term view
—only today, this moment, here and now. Many
in the white world—nescient, shallow thinkers—
called the attitude "shiftless," and condemned it.
Sociologists, with more understanding and some

sympathy, named the syndrome "present time orientation" or "distrust of the future." Rollie had heard neither phrase, but his instincts embraced both. Instinct also told him, at this moment, he was still tired. He went back to sleep.

He made no attempt, later, to return to the training center or the hiring hall. He went back to his haunts and street corner living, making a dollar when he could, and when he couldn't, managing without. The cop he had antagonized—miraculously—left him alone.

There was only one postscript—or so it seemed at the time—to Rollie's employment.

During an afternoon some four weeks later, he was visited at the rooming house, where he was still sharing space on sufferance, by an instructor from the factory training course. Rollie Knight remembered the man—a beefy, florid-faced ex-plant foreman with thinning hair and a paunch, now puffing from the three flights of stairs he had been forced to climb.

He asked tersely, "Why'd you quit?"

"I won the Irish Sweep, man. Doan need no job."

"You people!" The visitor surveyed the dismal quarters with disgust. "To think we have to support your kind with taxes. If I had my way . . ." He left the sentence unfinished and produced a paper. "You have to sign here. It says you're not coming any more."

Indifferently, not wanting trouble, Rollie signed.

"Oh, yes, and the company made out some checks. Now they have to be paid back in." He riffled through some papers, of which there seemed to be a good many. "They want you to sign those, too."

Rollie endorsed the checks. There were four.

"Another time," the instructor said unpleasantly, "try not to cause other people so much trouble."

"Go screw yourself, fatso," Rollie Knight said, and yawned.

Neither Rollie nor his visitor was aware that while their exchange was taking place, an expensive, late-model car was parked across the street from the rooming house. The car's sole occupant was a tall, distinguished-appearing, gray-haired Negro who had watched with interest while the training course instructor went inside. Now, as the beefy, florid-faced man left the building and drove his own car away, the other car followed, unobserved, at a discreet distance, as it had through most of the afternoon.

chapter ten

"C'mon baby, leave the goddam drink. I gotta bottle in the room."

Ollie, the machinery salesman, peered impatiently at Erica Trenton in the semidarkness, across the small black table separating them.

It was early afternoon. They were in the bar of the Queensway Inn, not far from Bloomfield Hills, Erica dawdling over her second drink which she had asked for as a delaying device, even though recognizing that delay was pointless because either they were or weren't going through with what they had come here for, and if they were they might as well get on with it.

Erica touched her glass. "Let me finish this. I need it."

She thought: He wasn't a bad-looking man, in a raffish kind of way. He was trimly built and his body was obviously better than his speech and manners, probably because he worked on it—she remembered him telling her with pride that he went to a gym somewhere for regular workouts. She supposed she could do worse, though wished she had done better.

The occasion when he had told her about workouts in the gym had been at their first meeting, here in this same bar. Erica had come for a drink one afternoon, the way other lonely wives did sometimes, in the hope that something interesting might happen, and Ollie had struck up a conversation—Ollie, cynical, experienced, who knew this bar and why some women came to it. After that, their next meeting had been by arrangement, when he had taken a room in the residential section of the inn, and assumed she would go to it with him. But Erica, torn between a simple physical

need and nagging conscience, had insisted on staying at the bar all afternoon, and in the end left for
home, to Ollie's anger and disgust. He had written
her off, it seemed, until she telephoned him several
weeks ago.

Even since then, they had had to delay their
arrangement because Ollie had not come back
from Cleveland as expected, and instead went on
to two other cities—Erica had forgotten where.
But they *were* here now, and Ollie was becoming
impatient.

He asked, "How about it, baby?"

Suddenly she remembered, with a mixture
of wryness and sadness, a maxim on Adam's office
wall: Do It Today!

"All right," Erica said. She pushed back her
chair and stood up.

Walking beside Ollie, down the inn's attractive, picture-hung corridors—where many others
had walked before her on the same kind of assignation—she felt her heart beat faster, and
tried not to hurry.

Several hours later, thinking about it calmly,
Erica decided the experience was neither as good
as she had hoped for, nor as bad as she had feared.
In a basic, here-and-now way, she had found
sensual satisfaction; in another way, which was
harder to define, she hadn't. She was sure, though,
of two things. First, such satisfaction as she had
known was not lasting, as it had been in the old
days when Adam was an aggressive lover and the
effect of their love-making stayed with her, sometimes for days. Second, she would not repeat the
experience—at least, with Ollie.

In such a mood, from the Queensway Inn in
late afternoon, Erica went shopping in Birmingham. She bought a few things she needed, and
some others she didn't, but most of her pleasure

came from what proved to be an exciting, challenging game—removing items from stores without payment. She did so three times, with increasing confidence, acquiring an ornamental clothes hanger, a tube of shampoo, and—especial triumph!—an expensive fountain pen.

Erica's earlier experience, when she had purloined the ounce of Norell, had showed that successful shoplifting was not difficult. The requirements, she decided now, were intelligence, quickness, and cool nerve. She felt proud of herself for demonstrating that she possessed all three.

chapter eleven

On a dismal, grimy, wet November day, six weeks
after the meeting with Adam Trenton at the proving ground, Brett DeLosanto was in downtown
Detroit—in a gray, bleak mood which matched
the weather.

His mood was uncharacteristic. Normally,
whatever pressures, worries and—more recently
—doubts assailed the young car designer, he remained cheerful and good-natured. But on a day
like today, he thought, to a native Californian like
himself, Detroit in winter was just too much, too
awful.

He had reached his car, moments earlier,
on a parking lot near Congress and Shelby, having
battled his way to it on foot, through wind and
rain and traffic, the last seeming to flow intermina-
bly the instant he sought to cross any intersection,
so that he was left standing impatiently on curbs,
already miserably sodden, and getting wetter still.

As for the inner city around him . . . ugh!
Always dirty, preponderantly ugly and depressing
at any time, today's leaden skies and rain—as
Brett's imagination saw it—were like spreading
soot on a charnel house. Only one worse time of
year existed: in March and April, when winter's
heavy snows, frozen and turned black, began to
melt. Even then, he supposed, there were people
who became used to the city's hideousness eventually. So far, he hadn't.

Inside his car, Brett started the motor and got
the heater and windshield wipers going. He was
glad to be sheltered at last; outside, the rain was
still beating down heavily. The parking lot was
crowded, and he was boxed in, and would have to
wait while two cars ahead of him were moved

to let him out. But he had signaled an attendant as he came into the lot, and could see the man now, several rows of cars away.

Waiting, Brett remembered it was on such a day as this that he had first come to Detroit himself, to live and work.

The ranks of auto company designers were heavy with expatriate Californians whose route to Detroit, like his own, had been through the Art Center College of Design, Los Angeles, which operated on a trimester system. For those who graduated in winter and came to Detroit to work, the shock of seeing the city at its seasonal worst was so depressing that a few promptly returned West and sought some other design field as a livelihood. But most, though jolted badly, stayed on as Brett had done, and later the city revealed compensations. Detroit was an outstanding cultural center, notably in art, music, and drama, while beyond the city, the State of Michigan was a superb sports-vacation arena, winter and summer, boasting some of the lovelier unspoiled lakes and country in the world.

Where in hell, Brett wondered, *was the parking-lot guy to move those other cars?*

It was this kind of frustration—nothing major—which had induced his present bad temper. He had had a luncheon date at the Pontchartrain Hotel with a man named Hank Kreisel, an auto parts manufacturer and friend, and Brett had driven to the hotel, only to find the parking garage full. As a result he had to park blocks away, and got wet walking back. At the Pontchartrain there had been a message from Kreisel, apologizing, but to say he couldn't make it, so Brett lunched alone, having driven fifteen miles to do so. He had several other errands downtown, and these occupied the rest of the afternoon; but in walking from one place to the next, a series of rude, horn-happy drivers refused to give him the slightest break on pedestrian crossings, despite the heavy rain.

The near-savage drivers distressed him most. In no other city that he knew—including New York, which was bad enough—were motorists as boorish, inconsiderate, and unyielding as on Detroit streets and freeways. Perhaps it was because the city lived by automobiles, which became symbols of power, but for whatever reason a Detroiter behind the wheel seemed changed into a Frankenstein. Most newcomers, at first shaken by the "no quarter asked or given" driving, soon learned to behave similarly, in self-defense. Brett never had. Used to inherent courtesy in California, Detroit driving remained a nightmare to him, and a source of anger.

The parking-lot attendant had obviously forgotten about moving the cars ahead. Brett knew he would have to get out and locate the man, rain or not. Seething, he did. When he saw the attendant, however, he made no complaint. The man looked bedraggled, weary, and was soaked. Brett tipped him instead and pointed to the blocking cars.

At least, Brett thought, returning to his car, he had a warm and comfortable apartment to go home to, which probably the attendant hadn't. Brett's apartment was in Birmingham, a part of swanky Country Club Manor, and he remembered that Barbara was coming in tonight to cook dinner for the two of them. The style of Brett's living, plus an absence of money worries which his fifty thousand dollars a year salary and bonus made possible, were compensations which Detroit had given him, and he made no secret of enjoying them.

At last the cars obstructing him were being moved. As the one immediately ahead swung clear, Brett eased his own car forward.

The exit from the parking lot was fifty yards ahead. One other car was in front, also on the way out. Brett DeLosanto accelerated slightly to close the gap and reached for money to pay the exit cashier.

Suddenly, appearing as if from nowhere, a third car—a dark green sedan—shot directly across the front of Brett's, swung sharply right and slammed into second place in the exit line. Brett trod on his brakes hard, skidded, regained control, stopped and swore. "You goddam maniac!"

All the frustrations of the day, added to his fixation about Detroit drivers, were synthesized in Brett's actions through the next five seconds. He leaped from his car, stormed to the dark green sedan and wrathfully wrenched open the driver's door.

"You son-of-a . ." It was as far as he got before he stopped.

"Yes?" the other driver said. He was a tall, graying, well-dressed black man in his fifties. "You were saying something?"

"Never mind," Brett growled. He moved to close the door.

"Please wait! I do mind! I may even complain to the Human Rights Commission. I shall tell them: A young white man opened my car door with every intention of punching me in the nose. When he discovered I was of a different race, he stopped. That's discrimination, you know. The human rights people won't like it."

"It sure would be a new angle." Brett laughed. "Would you prefer me to finish?"

"I suppose, if you must," the graying Negro said. "But I'd much rather buy you a drink, then I can apologize for cutting in front like that, and explain it was a foolish, irrational impulse at the end of a frustrating day."

"You had one of those days, too?"

"Obviously we both did."

Brett nodded. "Okay, I'll take the drink."

"Shall we say Jim's Garage, right now? It's three blocks from here and the doorman will park your car. By the way, my name is Leonard Wingate."

The green sedan led the way.

The first thing they discovered, after ordering Scotches on the rocks, was that they worked for the same company. Leonard Wingate was an executive in Personnel and, Brett gathered from their conversation, about two rungs down from vice-president level. Later, he would learn that his drinking companion was the highest-ranking Negro in the company.

"I've heard your name," Wingate told Brett. "You've been Michelangelo-ing the Orion, haven't you?"

"Well, we hope it turns out that way. Have you seen the prototype?"

The other shook his head.

"I could arrange it, if you'd like to."

"I would like. Another drink?"

"My turn." Brett beckoned a bartender.

The bar of Jim's Garage, colorfully festooned with historic artifacts of the auto industry, was currently an "in" place in downtown Detroit. Now, in early evening, it was beginning to fill, the level of business and voices rising simultaneously.

"A whole lot riding on that Orion baby," Wingate said.

"Damn right."

"Especially jobs for my people."

"Your people?"

"Hourly paid ones, black *and* white. The way the Orion goes, so a lot of families in this city'll go: the hours they work, what their take-home is —and that means the way they live, eat, whether they can meet mortgage payments, have new clothes, a vacation, what happens to their kids."

Brett mused. "You never think of that when you're sketching a new car or throwing clay to shape a fender."

"Don't see how you could. None of us ever knows the half of what goes on with other people; all kinds of walls get built between us—brick, the other kind. Even when you do get through a wall once in a while, and find out what's behind it, then maybe try to help somebody, you find you haven't helped because of other stinking, rotten, conniving parasites . . ." Leonard Wingate clenched his fist and hammered it twice, silently but intensely, on the bar counter. He looked sideways at Brett, then grinned crookedly. "Sorry!"

"Here comes your other drink, friend. I think you need it." The designer sipped his own before asking, "Does this have something to do with those lousy aerobatics in the parking lot?"

Wingate nodded. "I'm sorry about that, too. I was blowing steam." He smiled, this time less tensely. "Now, I guess, I've let the rest of it out."

"Steam is only a white cloud," Brett said. "Is the source of it classified?"

"Not really. You've heard of hard core hiring?"

"I've heard. I don't know all the details." But he did know that Barbara Zaleski had become interested in the subject lately because of a new project she had been assigned by the OJL advertising agency.

The gray-haired Personnel man summarized the hard core hiring program: its objective in regard to the inner city and former unemployables; the Big Three hiring halls downtown; how, in relation to individuals, the program sometimes worked and sometimes didn't.

"It's been worth doing, though, despite some disappointments. Our retention rate—that is, people who've held on to jobs we've given them—has been better than fifty percent, which is more than we expected. The unions have cooperated; news media give publicity which helps; there's been other aid in other ways. That's why it hurts to get knifed in the back by your own people, in your own company."

Brett asked, "Who knifed you? How?"

"Let me go back a bit." Wingate put the tip of a long, lean finger in his drink and stirred the ice. "A lot of people we've hired under the program have never, in their lives before, kept regular hours. Mostly they've had no reason to. Working regularly, the way most of us do, breeds habits: like getting up in the morning, being on time to catch a bus, becoming used to working five days of the week. But if you've never done any of that, if you don't have the habits, it's like learning another language; what's more, it takes time. You could call it changing attitudes, or changing gears. Well, we've learned a lot about all that since we started hard core hiring. We also learned that some people—not all, but some— who don't acquire those habits on their own, can get them if they're given help."

"You'd better help *me*," Brett said. "I have trouble getting up."

His companion smiled. "If we did try to help, I'd send someone from employee relations staff to see you. If you'd dropped out, quit coming to work, he'd ask you why. There's another thing: some of these new people will miss one day, or even be an hour or two late, then simply give up. Maybe they didn't intend to miss; it just happened. But they have the notion we're so inflexible, it means automatically they've lost their jobs."

"And they haven't?"

"Christ, no! We give a guy every possible break because *we* want the thing to work. Something else we do is give people who have trouble getting to work a cheap alarm clock; you'd be surprised how many have never owned one. The company let me buy a gross. In my office I've got alarm clocks the way other men have paper clips."

Brett said, "I'll be damned!" It seemed incongruous to think of a gargantuan auto company, with annual wage bills running into billions, worrying about a few sleepyhead employees waking up.

"The point I'm getting at," Leonard Wingate said, "is that if a hard core worker doesn't show up, either to finish a training course or at the plant, whoever's in charge is supposed to notify one of my special people. Then, unless it's a hopeless case, they follow through."

"But that hasn't been happening? It's why you're frustrated?"

"That's part of it. There's a whole lot more." The Personnel man downed the last of his Scotch. "Those courses we have where the hard core people get oriented—they last eight weeks; there are maybe two hundred on a course."

Brett motioned for a refill to their drinks. When the bartender had gone, he prompted, "Okay, so a course with two hundred people."

"Right. An instructor and a woman secretary are in charge. Between them, those two keep all course records, including attendance. They pass out paychecks, which arrive weekly in a bunch from Headquarters Accounting. Naturally, the checks are made out on the basis of the course records." Wingate said bitterly, "It's the instructor and the secretary—one particular pair. They're the ones."

"The ones what?"

"Who've been lying, cheating, stealing from the people they're employed to help."

"I guess I can figure some of it," Brett said. "But tell me, anyway."

"Well, as the course goes along, there are dropouts—for the reasons I told you, and for others. It always happens; we expect it. As I said, if our department's told, we try to persuade some of the people to come back. But what this instructor and secretary have been doing is *not* reporting the dropouts, and recording them present. So that checks for the dropouts have kept coming in, and then that precious pair has kept those checks themselves."

"But the checks are made out by name. They can't cash them."

Wingate shook his head. "They can and they have. What happens is eventually this pair does report that certain people have stopped coming, so the company checks stop, too. Then the instructor goes around with the checks he's saved and finds the people they're made out to. It isn't difficult; all addresses are on file. The instructor tells a cock-and-bull story about the company wanting the money back, and gets the checks endorsed. After that, he can cash them anywhere. I know it happens that way. I followed the instructor for an afternoon."

"But how about later, when your employee relations people go visiting? You say they hear about the dropouts eventually. Don't they find out about the checks?"

"Not necessarily. Remember, the people we're dealing with aren't communicative. They're dropouts in more ways than one, usually, and never volunteer information. It's hard enough getting answers to questions. Besides that, I happen to think there've been some bribes passed around. I can't prove it, but there's a certain smell."

"The whole thing stinks."

Brett thought: Compared with what Leonard Wingate had told him, his own irritations of today seemed minor. He asked, "Were you the one who uncovered all this?"

"Mostly, though one of my assistants got the idea first. He was suspicious of the course attendance figures; they looked too good. So the two of us started checking, comparing the new figures with our own previous ones, then we got comparable figures from other companies. They showed what was going on, all right. After that, it was a question of watching, catching the people. Well, we did."

"So what happens now?"

Wingate shrugged, his figure hunched over the bar counter. "Security's taken over; it's out of my hands. This afternoon they brought the instructor and the secretary downtown—separately. I was there. The two of them broke down, admitted everything. The guy cried, if you'll believe it."

"I believe it," Brett said. "I feel like crying in a different way. Will the company prosecute?"

"The guy and his girl friend think so, but I know they won't." The tall Negro straightened up; he was almost a head higher than Brett DeLosanto. He said mockingly, "Bad public relations, y'know. Wouldn't want it in the papers, with our company's name. Besides, the way my bosses see it, the main thing is to get the money back; seems there's quite a few thousand."

"What about the other people? The ones who dropped out, who might have come back, gone on working . . ."

"Oh come, my friend, you're being ridiculously sentimental."

Brett said sharply, "Knock it off! I didn't steal the goddam checks."

"No, you didn't. Well, about those people, let me tell you. If I had a staff six times the size I have, and *if* we could go back through all the records and be sure which names to follow up on, and *if* we could locate them after all these weeks . . ."

The bartender appeared. Wingate's glass was empty, but he shook his head. For Brett's benefit he added, "We'll do what we can. It may not be much."

"I'm sorry," Brett said. "Damn sorry." He paused, then asked, "You married?"

"Yes, but not working at it."

"Listen, my girl friend's cooking dinner at my place. Why not join us?"

Wingate demurred politely. Brett insisted.

Five minutes later they left for Country Club Manor.

Barbara Zaleski had a key to Brett's apartment and was there when they arrived, already busy in the kitchen. An aroma of roasting lamb was drifting out.

"Hey, scullion!" Brett called from the hallway. "Come, meet a guest."

"If it's another woman," Barbara's voice sailed back, "you can cook your own dinner. Oh, it isn't. Hi!"

She appeared with a tiny apron over the smart, knit suit she had arrived in, having come directly from the OJL agency's Detroit office. The suit, Brett thought appreciatively, did justice to Barbara's figure; he sensed Leonard Wingate observing the same thing. As usual, Barbara had dark glasses pushed up into her thick, chestnut-brown hair, which she had undoubtedly forgotten. Brett reached out, removed the glasses and kissed her lightly.

He introduced them, informing Wingate, "This is my mistress."

"He'd like me to be," Barbara said, "but I'm not. Telling people I am is his way of getting even."

As Brett had expected, Barbara and Leonard Wingate achieved a rapport quickly. While they talked, Brett opened a bottle of Dom Perignon which the three of them shared. Occasionally Barbara excused herself to check on progress in the kitchen.

During one of her absences, Wingate looked around the spacious apartment living room. "Pretty nice pad."

"Thanks." When Brett leased the apartment a year and a half ago he had been his own interior decorator, and the furnishings reflected his personal taste for modern design and flamboyant coloring. Bright yellows, mauves, vermilions, cobalt greens predominated, yet were used imaginatively, so that they merged as an attractive whole. Lighting complemented the colors, highlighting some areas, diminishing others. The effect was to create—ingeniously—a series of moods within a single room.

At one end of the living room was an open door to another room.

Wingate asked, "Do you do much of your work here?"

"Some." Brett nodded toward the open door. "There's my Thinkolarium. For when I need to get creative and be uninterrupted away from that wired-for-sound Taj Mahal we work in." He motioned vaguely in the direction of the company's Design-Styling Center.

"He does other things there, too," Barbara

said. She had returned as Brett spoke. "Come in, Leonard. I'll show you." Wingate followed her, Brett trailing.

The other room, while colorful and pleasant also, was equipped as a studio, with the paraphernalia of an artist-designer. A pile of tissue flimsies on the floor beside a drafting table showed where Brett had raced through a series of sketches, tearing off each flimsy, using a new one from the pad beneath as the design took shape. The last sketch in the series—a rear fender style—was pinned to a cork board.

Wingate pointed to it. "Will that one be for real?"

Brett shook his head. "You play with ideas, get them out of your system, like belching. Sometimes, that way, you get a notion which will lead to something permanent in the end. This isn't one." He pulled the flimsy down and crumpled it. "If you took all the sketches which precede any new car, you could fill Cobo Hall with paper."

Barbara switched on a light. It was in a corner of the room where an easel stood, covered by a cloth. She removed the cloth carefully.

"And then there's this," Barbara said. "This isn't for discarding."

Beneath the cloth was a painting in oils, almost—but not quite—finished.

"Don't count on it," Brett said. He added, "Barbara's very loyal. At times it warps her judgment."

The tall, gray-haired Negro shook his head. "Not this time, it hasn't." He studied the painting with admiration.

It was of a collection of automotive discards, heaped together. Brett had assembled the materials for his model—laid out on a board ahead of the easel, and lighted by a spotlight—from an auto wrecker's junk pile. There were several burned-brown spark plugs, a broken camshaft, a discarded oil can, the entrails of a carburetor, a battered headlight, a moldy twelve-volt battery, a window handle, a section of radiator, a broken wrench, some assorted rusty nuts and washers. A steering wheel, its horn ring missing, hung lopsidedly above.

No collection could have been more ordinary, less likely to inspire great art. Yet, remarkably, Brett had made the junk assortment come alive, had conveyed to his canvas both rugged beauty and a mood of sadness and nostalgia. These were broken relics, the painting seemed to say: burned-out, unwanted, all usefulness departed; nothing was ahead save total disintegration. Yet once, however briefly, they had had a life, had functioned, representing dreams, ambitions, achievements of mankind. One knew that all other achievements—past, present, future, no matter how acclaimed—were doomed to end similarly, would write their epilogues in garbage dumps. Yet was not the dream, the brief achievement—of itself—enough?

Leonard Wingate had remained, unmoving, before the canvas. He said slowly, "I know a little about art. You're good. You could be great."

"That's what I tell him." After a moment, Barbara replaced the cloth on the easel and turned out the light. They went back into the living room.

"What Barbara means," Brett said, pouring more Dom Perignon, "is that I've sold my soul for a mess of pottage." He glanced around the apartment. "Or maybe a pot of messuage."

"Brett might have managed to do designing *and* fine art," Barbara told Wingate, "if he hadn't been so darned successful at designing. Now, all he has time to do where painting's concerned is to dabble occasionally. With his talent, it's a tragedy."

Brett grinned. "Barbara has never seen the high beam—that designing a car is every bit as creative as painting. Or that cars are my thing." He remembered what he had told the two students only a few weeks ago: *You breathe, eat, sleep cars . . . wake up in the night, it's cars you think about . . . like a religion*. Well, he still felt that way himself, didn't he? Maybe not with the same intensity as when he first came to Detroit. But did *anyone* really keep that up? There were days when he looked at others working with him, wondering. Also, if he were honest, there were other reasons why cars should stay his "thing." Like what you could do with fifty thousand dollars a year, to say nothing of the fact that he was only twenty-six and much bigger loot would come in a few years more. He asked Barbara lightly, "Would you still breeze in to cook dinner if I lived in a garret and smelled of turpentine?"

She looked at him directly. "You know I would."

While they talked of other things, Brett decided: He *would* finish the canvas, which he hadn't touched in weeks. The reason he had stayed away from it was simple. Once he started painting, it absorbed him totally and there was just so much total absorption which any life could stand.

Over dinner, which tasted as good as it had smelled, Brett steered the conversation to what Leonard Wingate had told him in the bar downtown. Barbara, after hearing of the cheating and victimization of hard core workers, was shocked and even angrier than Brett.

She asked the question which Brett DeLosanto hadn't. "What color are they—the instructor and the secretary who took the checks?"

Wingate raised his eyebrows. "Does it make a difference?"

"Listen," Brett said. "You know damn well it does."

Wingate answered tersely, "They're white. What else?"

"They could have been black." It was Barbara, thoughtfully.

"Yes, but the odds are against it." Wingate hesitated. "Look, I'm a guest here . . ."

Brett waved a hand. "Forget it!"

There was a silence between them, then the gray-haired Negro said, "I like to make certain things clear, even among friends. So don't let this uniform fool you: the Oxford suit, a college diploma, the job I have. Oh, sure, I'm the real front office nigger, the one they point to when they say: *You see, a black man can go high.* Well, it's true for me, because I was one of the few with a daddy who could pay for a real education, which is the only way a black man climbs. So I've climbed, and maybe I'll make it to the top and be a company director yet. I'm still young enough, and I'll admit I'd like it; so would the company. I know one thing. If there's a choice between me and a white man, and providing I can cut the mustard, I'll get the job. That's the way the dice are rolling, baby; they're weighted *my* way because the p.r. department and some others would just love to shout: *Look at us! We've got a board room black!*"

Leonard Wingate sipped his coffee, which Barbara had served.

"Well, as I said, don't let the façade fool you. I'm still a member of my race." Abruptly he put the cup down. Across the dining table his eyes glared at Brett and Barbara. "When something happens like it did today, I don't just get angry. I burn and loathe and *hate*—everything that's *white*."

The glare faded. Wingate raised his coffee cup again, though his hand was shaking.

After a moment he said, "James Baldwin wrote this: 'Negroes in this country are treated as none of you would dream of treating a dog or a cat.' And it's true—in Detroit, just as other places. And for all that's happened in the past few years, nothing's really changed in most white people's attitudes, below the surface. Even the little that's being done to ease white consciences—like hard core hiring, which that white pair tried to screw, and did—is only surface scratching. Schools, housing, medicine, hospitals, are so bad here it's unbelievable—unless you're black; then you believe it because you know, the hard way. But one day, if the auto industry intends to survive in this town—because the auto industry *is* Detroit—it will have to come to grips with improving the black life of the community, because no one else is going to do it, or has the resources or the brains to." He added, "Just the same, I don't believe they will."

"Then there's nothing," Barbara said. "Nothing to hope for." There was emotion in her voice.

"No harm in hoping," Leonard Wingate answered. He added mockingly, "Hope don't cost none. But no good fooling yourself either."

Barbara said slowly, "Thank you for being honest, for telling it like it is. Not everyone does that, as I've reason to know."

"Tell him," Brett urged. "Tell him about your new assignment."

"I've been given a job to do," Barbara told Wingate. "By the advertising agency I work for, acting for the company. It's to make a film. An honest film about Detroit—the inner city."

She was aware of the other's instant interest.

"I first heard about it," Barbara explained, "six weeks ago."

She described her briefing in New York by Keith Yates-Brown.

It had been the day after the abortive "rustle pile" session at which the OJL agency's initial ideas for Orion advertising had been routinely presented and, just as routinely, brushed aside.

As the creative director, Teddy Osch, predicted during their martini-weighted luncheon, Keith Yates-Brown, the account supervisor, had sent for Barbara next day.

In his handsome office on the agency's top floor, Yates-Brown had seemed morose in contrast with his genial, showman's manner of the day before. He looked grayer and older, too, and several times in the later stages of their conversation turned toward his office window, looking across the Manhattan skyline toward Long Island Sound, as if a portion of his mind was far away. Perhaps, Barbara thought, the strain of permanent affability with clients required a surly counterbalance now and then.

There had certainly been nothing friendly about Yates-Brown's opening remark after they exchanged "good mornings."

"You were snooty with the client yesterday," he told Barbara. "I didn't like it, and you should know better."

She said nothing. She supposed Yates-Brown was referring to her pointed questioning of the company advertising manager: *Was there nothing you liked? Absolutely nothing at all?* Well, she still believed it justified and wasn't going to grovel now. But neither would she antagonize Yates-Brown needlessly until she heard about her new assignment.

"One of the early things you're supposed to learn here," the account supervisor persisted, "is to show restraint sometimes, and swallow hard."

"Okay, Keith," Barbara said, "I'm swallowing now."

He had had the grace to smile, then returned to coolness.

"What you're being given to do requires restraint; also sound judgment, and, naturally, imagination. I suggested you for the assignment, believing you to possess those qualities. I still do, despite yesterday, which I prefer to think of as a momentary lapse."

Oh, God!, Barbara wanted to exclaim. *Stop making like you're in a pulpit, and get on!* But she had the sense not to say it.

"The project is one which has the personal interest of the client's chairman of the board." Keith Yates-Brown mouthed "chairman of the board" with awe and reverence. Barbara was surprised he hadn't stood, saluting, while he said it.

"As a result," the account chief continued, "you will have the responsibility—a large responsibility affecting all of us at OJL—of reporting, on occasions, to the chairman personally."

Well, Barbara could appreciate his feelings there. Reporting directly to the chairman about anything *was* a large responsibility, though it didn't frighten her. But since the chairman—if he chose to exercise it—had a life and death power over which advertising agency the company used, Barbara could picture Keith Yates-Brown and others hovering nervously in the wings.

"The project," Yates-Brown added, "is to make a film."

He had gone on, filling in details as far as they were known. The film would be about Detroit: the inner city and its people, their problems —racial and otherwise—their way of life, points of view, their needs. It was to be a factual, honest documentary. In no way would it be company or industry propaganda; the company's name would appear only once—on the credits as sponsor. Objective would be to point up urban problems, the need to reactivate the city's role in national life, with Detroit the prime example. The film's first use would be for educational and civic groups and schools across the nation. It would probably be shown on television. If good enough, it might go into movie houses.

The budget would be generous. It would allow a regular film-making organization to be used, but the OJL agency would select the film maker and retain control. A top-flight director could be hired, and a script writer, if needed, though Barbara— in view of her copywriter's experience—might choose to write the script herself.

Barbara would represent the agency and be in over-all charge.

With a sense of rising excitement as Yates-Brown spoke, Barbara remembered Teddy Osch's words of yesterday at lunch. The creative director had said: *All I can tell you is, I wish it were me instead of you.* Now she knew why. Not only was the assignment a substantial compliment to her professionally, it also represented a strong creative challenge which she welcomed. Barbara found herself looking appreciatively—and certainly more tolerantly—on Keith Yates-Brown.

Even the account supervisor's next words diminished her appreciation only slightly.

"You'll work out of the Detroit office as usual," he had said, "but we shall want to be informed here of everything that's going on, and I mean everything. Another thing to bear in mind is what we spoke of earlier—restraint. It's to be an honest film, but don't get carried away. I do not believe we want, or the chairman of the board will want, too much of—shall we say?—a Socialist point of view."

Well, she had let that one go, realizing there

would be plenty of ideas, as well as points of view, she would have to fight for eventually, without wasting time on abstract arguments now.

A week later, after other activities she was involved in had been reassigned, Barbara began work on the project, tentatively titled: *Auto City*.

Across Brett DeLosanto's dining table, Barbara told Leonard Wingate, "Some of the early things have been done, including choosing a production company and a director. Of course, there'll be more planning before filming can begin, but we hope to start in February or March."

The tall, graying Negro considered before answering. At length he said, "I could be cynical and smart, and say that making a film about problems, instead of solving them or trying to, is like Nero fiddling. But being an executive has taught me life isn't always that simple; also, communication is important." He paused, then added, "What you intend might do a lot of good. If there's a way I can help, I will."

"Perhaps there is," Barbara acknowledged. "I've already talked with the director, Wes Gropetti, and something we're agreed on is that whatever is said about the inner city must be through people who live there—individuals. One of them, we believe, should be someone coming through the 'hard core' hiring program."

Wingate cautioned, "Hard core hiring doesn't always work. You might shoot a lot of film about a person who ends up a failure."

"If that's the way it happens," Barbara insisted, "that's the way we'll tell it. We're not doing a remake of *Pollyanna*."

"Then there might be someone," Wingate said thoughtfully. "You remember I told you—one afternoon I trailed the instructor who stole the checks, then lied to get them endorsed."

She nodded. "I remember."

"Next day I went back to see some of the people he'd visited. I'd noted the addresses; my office matched them up with names." Leonard Wingate produced a notebook and turned pages. "One of them was a man I had a feeling about. I'm not sure what kind of feeling, except I've persuaded him to come back to work. Here it is." He stopped at a page. "His name is Rollie Knight."

Earlier, when Barbara arrived at Brett's apartment, she had come by taxi. Late that evening, when Leonard Wingate had gone—after promising that the three of them would meet again soon —Brett drove Barbara home.

The Zaleskis lived in Royal Oak, a middle-class residential suburb southeast of Birmingham. Driving crosstown on Maple, with Barbara on the front seat close beside him, Brett said, "Nuts to this!" He braked, stopped the car, and put his arms around her. Their kiss was passionate and long.

"Listen!" Brett said; he buried his face in the soft silkiness of her hair, and held her tightly. "What the hell are we doing headed this way? Come back and stay with me tonight. We both want it, and there's not a reason in the world why you shouldn't."

He had made the same suggestion earlier, immediately after Wingate left. Also, they had covered this ground many times before.

Barbara sighed. She said softly, "I'm a great disappointment to you, aren't I?"

"How do I *know* if you're a disappointment, when you've never let me find out?"

She laughed lightly. He had the capacity to make her do that, even at unexpected moments. Barbara reached up, tracing her fingers across

Brett's forehead, erasing the frown she sensed was there.

He protested, "It isn't *fair!* Everybody who knows us just *assumes* we're sleeping together, and you and I are the only ones who know we're not. Even your old man thinks we are. Well, doesn't he?"

"Yes," she admitted. "I think Dad does."

"I know damn well he does. What's more, every time we meet, the old buzzard lets me know he doesn't like it. So I lose out two ways, coming and going."

"Darling," Barbara said, "I know, I *know.*"

"Then why aren't we doing something—right now, tonight? Barb, hon, you're twenty-nine; you can't possibly be a virgin, so what's our hangup? Is it me? Do I smell of modeling clay, or offend you in some other way?"

She shook her head emphatically. "You attract me in every way, and I mean that just as much as all the other times I've said it."

"We've said everything so many times." He added morosely, "None of the other times made any more sense than this one."

"Please," Barbara said, "let's go home."

"*My* home?"

She laughed. "No, mine."

When the car was moving, she touched Brett's arm. "I'm not sure either; about making sense, I mean. I guess I'm just not thinking the way everyone else seems to do nowadays; at least, I haven't yet. Maybe it's old-fashioned . . ."

"You mean if I want to get to the honey pot, I have to marry you."

Barbara said sharply, "No, I *don't.* I'm not even sure I want to marry anybody; I'm a career gal, remember? And I *know* you're not marriage-minded."

Brett grinned. "You're right about that. So why don't we live together?"

She said thoughtfully, "We might."

"You're serious?"

"I'm not sure. I think I could be, but I need time." She hesitated. "Brett, darling, if you'd like us not to see each other for a while, if you're going to be frustrated every time we meet . . ."

"We tried that, didn't we? It didn't work because I missed you." He said decisively, "No, we'll go on this way even if I make like a corralled stallion now and then. Besides," he added cheerfully, "you can't hold out forever."

There was a silence as they drove. Brett turned onto Woodward Avenue, heading south, then Barbara said, "Do something for me."

"What?"

"Finish the painting. The one we looked at tonight."

He seemed surprised. "You mean *that* might make a difference to *us*?"

"I'm not sure. I do know it's part of you, a specially important part; something inside that ought to come out."

"Like a tapeworm?"

She shook her head. "A great talent, just as Leonard said. One that the auto industry won't ever give its proper chance to, not if you stay with car designing, and grow old that way."

"Listen!—I'll finish the painting. I intended to, anyway. But you're in the car racket, too. Where's your loyalty?"

"At the office," Barbara said. "I only wear it until five o'clock. Right now I'm me, which is why I want you to be you—the best, real Brett De-Losanto."

"How'd I know him if I met the guy?" Brett mused. "Okay, so painting sends me, sure. But d'you know what the odds are against an artist, any artist, becoming great, getting recognized and, incidentally, well paid?"

They swung into the driveway of the modest bungalow where Barbara and her father lived. A gray hardtop was in the garage ahead of them. "Your old man's home," Brett said. "It suddenly feels chilly."

Matt Zaleski was in his orchid atrium, which adjoined the kitchen, and looked up as Brett and Barbara came in through the bungalow's side door.

Matt had built the atrium soon after buying the house eighteen years ago, on migrating here from Wyandotte. At that time the move northward to Royal Oak had represented Matt's economic advancement from his boyhood milieu and that of his Polish parents. The orchid atrium had been intended to provide a soothing hobby, offsetting the mental stress of helping run an auto plant. It seldom had. Instead, while Matt still loved the exotic sight, texture, and sometimes scent of orchids, a growing weariness during his hours at home had changed the care of them from pleasure to a chore, though one which, mentally, he could never quite discard.

Tonight, he had come in an hour ago, having stayed late at the assembly plant because of some critical materials shortages, and after a sketchy supper, realized there was some potting and rearrangement which could be put off no longer. By the time he heard Brett's car arrive, Matt had relocated several plants, the latest a yellow-purple *Masdevallia triangularis*, now placed where air movement and humidity would be better. He was misting the flower tenderly when the two came in.

Brett appeared at the open atrium doorway. "Hi, Mr. Z."

Matt Zaleski, who disliked being called Mr. Z., though several others at the plant addressed him that way, grunted what could have been a greeting. Barbara joined them, kissed her father briefly, then returned to the kitchen and began making a hot malted drink for them all.

"Gee!" Brett said. Determined to be genial, he inspected the tiers and hanging baskets of orchids. "It's great to have lots of spare time you can spend on a setup like this." He failed to notice a tightening of Matt's mouth. Pointing to a *Catasetum saccatum* growing in fir bark on a ledge, Brett commented admiringly, "That's a beauty! It's like a bird in flight."

For a moment Matt relaxed, sharing the pleasure of the superb purple-brown bloom, its sepals and petals curving upward. He conceded, "I guess it is like a bird. I never noticed that."

Unwittingly, Brett broke the mood. "Was it a fun day in Assembly, Mr. Z.? Did that rolling erector set of yours hold together?"

"If it did," Matt Zaleski said, "it's no thanks to the crazy car designs we have to work with."

"Well, you know how it is. We like to throw you iron pants guys something that's a challenge; otherwise you'd doze off from the monotony." Good-natured banter was a way of life with Brett, as natural as breathing. Unfortunately, he had never realized that with Barbara's father it was not, and was the reason Matt considered his daughter's friend a smart aleck.

As Matt Zaleski scowled, Brett added, "You'll get the Orion soon. Now that's a playpen that'll build itself."

Matt exploded. He said, heavy-handedly, "Nothing builds itself! That's what you cocksure kids don't realize. Because you and your kind come here with college degrees, you think you know it all, believe everything you put on paper will work out. It doesn't! It's those like me—iron pants, you call us; working slobs—who have to fix it so it does . . ." The words roiled on.

Behind Matt's outburst was his tiredness of tonight; also the knowledge that, yes, the Orion would be coming his way soon; that the plant where he was second in command would have to build the new car, would be torn apart to do it, then put together so that nothing worked the way it had; that the ordinary problems of production, which were tough enough, would quickly become monumental and, for months, occur around the clock; that Matt himself would draw the toughest trouble-shooting during model changeover, would have little rest, and some nights would be lucky if he got to bed at all; furthermore, he would be blamed when things went wrong. He had been through it all before, more times than he remembered, and the next time—coming soon—seemed one too many.

Matt stopped, realizing that he had not really been talking to this brash kid DeLosanto—much as he disliked him—but that his own emotions, pent up inside, had suddenly burst through. He was about to say so, awkwardly, and add that he was sorry, when Barbara appeared at the atrium door. Her face was white.

"Dad, you'll apologize for everything you just said."

Obstinacy was his first reaction. "I'll do what?"

Brett interceded; nothing bothered him for long. He told Barbara, "It's okay; he doesn't have to. We had a mild misunderstanding. Right, Mr. Z.?"

"No!" Barbara, usually patient with her father, stood her ground. She insisted, "Apologize! If you don't, I'll leave here now. With Brett. I mean it."

Matt realized she did.

Unhappily, not really understanding anything, including children who grew up and talked disrespectfully to parents, young people generally who behaved the way they did; missing his wife, Freda, now dead a year, who would have never let this happen to begin with, Matt mumbled an apology, then locked the atrium door and went to bed.

Soon after, Brett said goodnight to Barbara, and left.

chapter twelve

Now, winter gripped the Motor City. November had gone, then Christmas, and in early January the snow was deep, with skiing in northern Michigan, and ice heaped high and solidly along the shores of Lakes St. Clair and Erie.

As the new year came in, so preparations intensified for the Orion's debut, scheduled for mid-September. Manufacturing division, already huddled over plans for months, moved closer to plant conversions which would start in June, to produce the first production run Orion—Job One, as it was called—in August. Then, six weeks of production—shrouded in secrecy—would be needed before the car's public unveiling. Meanwhile, Purchasing nervously co-ordinated an armada of materials, ordered, and due on vital days, while Sales and Marketing began hardening their endlessly debated, oft-changed plans for dealer introductions and promotion. Public Relations pressed forward with groundwork for its Lucullan freeload which would accompany the Orion's introduction to the press. Other divisions, in greater or less degree according to their functions, joined in the preparation.

And while the Orion program progressed, many in the company gave thought to Farstar, which would follow Orion, though its timing, shape, and substance were not yet known. Among these were Adam Trenton and Brett DeLosanto.

Something else which Adam was concerned with in January was the review of his sister Teresa's investment, bequeathed by her dead husband, in the auto dealership of Smokey Stephensen.

Approval from the company for Adam to

involve himself with one of its dealers, however tenuously, had taken longer than expected, and had been given grudgingly after discussion by the Conflict of Interest committee. In the end, Hub Hewitson, executive vice-president, made a favorable ruling after Adam approached him personally. However, now that the time had come to fulfill his promise to Teresa, Adam realized how little he really needed, or wanted, an extra responsibility. His work load had grown, and an awareness of physical tension still bothered him. At home, relations with Erica seemed neither better nor worse, though he accepted the justice of his wife's complaint—repeated recently—that nowadays they had scarcely any time together. Soon, he resolved, he would find a way to put that right, but first, having accepted this new commitment, he would see it through.

Thus, on a Saturday morning, after arrangements made by telephone, Adam paid his first call on Smokey Stephensen.

The Stephensen dealership was in the northern suburbs, close to the boundary lines of Troy and Birmingham. Its location was good—on an important crosstown route, with Woodward Avenue, a main northwest artery, only a few blocks away.

Smokey, who had clearly been watching the street outside, strode through the showroom doorway onto the sidewalk, as Adam stepped from his car.

The ex-race driver, heavily bearded and now corpulent in middle-age, boomed, "Welcome! Welcome!" He wore a dark blue silk jacket with carefully creased black slacks and a wide, brightly patterned tie.

"Good morning," Adam said, "I'm . . ."

"No need to tell me! Seen your picture in *Automotive News*. Step in!"

The dealer held the showroom doorway wide.

"We always say there's only two reasons for a man to pass through here—to get out of the rain or buy himself wheels. I guess you're the exception." Inside he declared, "Within half an hour we'll be using first names. I always say, why wait that long?" He held out a bear paw of a hand. "I'm Smokey."

"I'm Adam," Adam said. He managed not to wince as his hand was squeezed.

"Let me have your car keys." Smokey beckoned a young salesman who hurried across the showroom floor. "Park Mr. Trenton's car carefully, and don't sell it. Also, be sure you treat him with respect. His sister owns forty-nine percent of this joint, and if business don't pick up by noon, I may mail her the other fifty-one." He winked broadly at Adam.

"It's an anxious time for all of us," Adam said. He knew, from sales reports, that a post-holiday lull was being felt this year by all auto makers and dealers. Yet, if only car buyers knew, this was the best time in any year to make a favorable financial deal. With dealers heavily stocked with cars forced on them by factories, and sometimes desperate to reduce inventory, a shrewd car buyer might save several hundred dollars on a medium-priced car, compared with buying a month or so later.

"I should be selling color televisions," Smokey growled. "That's what dopes put money in around Christmas and New Year's."

"But you did well at model changeover."

"Sure did." The dealer brightened. "You seen the figures, Adam?"

"My sister sent them to me."

"Never fails. You'd think people'd learn. Fortunately for us, they don't." Smokey glanced at Adam as they walked across the showroom. "You understand, I'm speaking freely?"

Adam nodded. "I think we should both do that."

He knew, of course, what Smokey Stephensen meant. At model introduction time—from September through November—dealers could sell every new car which factories would let them have. Then, instead of protesting the number of cars consigned—as they did at other times of year —dealers pleaded for more. And despite all adverse publicity about automobiles, the public still flocked to buy when models were new, or after major changes. What such buyers didn't know, or didn't care about, was that this was open season on customers, when dealers could be toughest in bargaining; also, the early cars after any production change were invariably less well made than others which would follow a few months later. With any new model, manufacturing snags inevitably arose while engineers, foremen, and hourly workers learned to make the car. Equally predictable were shortages of components or parts, resulting in manufacturing improvisations which ignored quality standards. As a result, an early car was often a poor buy from a quality point of view.

Knowledgeable buyers wanting a new model waited until four to six months after production began. By that time, chances were, they would get a better car because bugs would have been eliminated and production—except for Monday and Friday labor problems which persisted through all seasons—would be smoothly settled down.

Smokey Stephensen declared, "Everything's wide open to you here, Adam—like a whorehouse with the roof off. You can see our books, files, inventories, you name it; just the way your sister would, as she's entitled to. And ask questions, you'll get straight answers."

"You can count on questions," Adam said, "and later I'll need to see those things you mentioned.

What I also want—which may take longer—is to get a feeling about the way you operate."

"Sure, sure; any way you want is fine with me." The auto dealer led the way up a flight of stairs to a mezzanine which ran the length of the showroom below. Most of the mezzanine was occupied by offices. At the top of the stairs the two men paused to look down, viewing the cars of various model lines, polished, immaculate, colorful, which dominated the showroom floor. Along one side of the showroom were several cubicle-type offices, glass-paneled, for use by salesmen. An open doorway gave access to a corridor, leading to Parts and Service, out of sight.

Already, at midmorning, despite the quiet season, several people were viewing the cars, with salesmen hovering nearby.

"Your sister's got a good thing going here— poor old Clyde's dough working for her and all them kids." Smokey glanced at Adam shrewdly. "What's Teresa stewing over? She's been getting checks. We'll have a year-end audited statement soon."

Adam pointed out, "Mostly it's the long term Teresa's thinking of. You know I'm here to advise her: Should she sell her stock or not?"

"Yeah, I know." Smokey ruminated. "I don't mind telling you, Adam, if you advise 'sell,' it'll make things rugged for me."

"Why?"

"Because I couldn't raise the dough to buy Teresa's stock. Not now, with money tight."

"As I understand it," Adam said, "if Teresa decides to sell her share of the business, you have a sixty-day option to buy her out. If you don't, then she's free to sell elsewhere."

Smokey acknowledged, "That's the way of it." But his tone was glum.

What Smokey didn't relish, obviously, was the

possibility of a new partner, perhaps fearing that someone else would want to be active in the business or could prove more troublesome than a widow two thousand miles away. Adam wondered what, precisely, lay behind Smokey's unease. Was it a natural wish to run his own show without interference, or were things happening in the dealership which he preferred others not to know? Whatever the reason, Adam intended to find out if he could.

"Let's go in my office, Adam." They moved from the open mezzanine into a small but comfortable room, furnished with green leather armchairs and a sofa. A desk top and a swivel chair had the same material. Smokey saw Adam look around.

"The guy I got to furnish this wanted it all red. I told him, 'Nuts to that! The only red'll ever get in this business'll be by accident.' "

One side of the office, almost entirely window, fronted the mezzanine. The dealer and Adam stood looking down at the showroom as if from a ship's bridge.

Adam motioned toward the row of sales offices below. "You have a monitoring system?"

For the first time, Smokey hesitated. "Yeah."

"I'd like to listen. The sales booth right there." In one of the glassed enclosures a young salesman, with a boyish face and a shock of blond hair, faced two prospective customers, a man and a woman. Papers were spread over a desk between them."

"I guess you can." Smokey was less than enthusiastic. But he opened a sliding panel near his desk to reveal several switches, one of which he clicked. Immediately, voices became audible through a speaker recessed into the wall.

". . . course, we can order the model you want in Meadow Green." The voice was obviously the young salesman's. "Too bad we don't have one in stock."

Another male voice responded; it had an aggressive nasal quality. "We can wait. That's if we make a deal here. Or we might go someplace else."

"I understand that, sir. Tell me something, merely out of interest. The Galahad model, in Meadow Green; the one you were both looking at. How much more do you think that would cost?"

"I already told you," the nasal voice said. "A Galahad's out of our price range."

"But just out of interest—name any figure. How much more?"

Smokey chuckled. "Attaboy, Pierre!" He seemed to have forgotten his reluctance about Adam listening. "He's selling 'em up."

The nasal voice said grudgingly, "Well, maybe two hundred dollars."

Adam could see the salesman smile. "Actually," he said softly, "it's only seventy-five."

A woman's voice interceded. "Dear, if it's only that much . . ."

Smokey guffawed. "You can hook a woman that way, every time. The dame's already figured she's saved a hundred and twenty-five bucks. Pierre hasn't mentioned a cuppla options extra on that Galahad. But he'll get to it."

The salesman's voice said, "Why don't we take another look at the car? I'd like to show you . . ."

As the trio rose, Smokey snapped off the switch.

"That salesman," Adam said. "I've seen his face . . ."

"Sure. He's Pierre Flodenhale."

Now Adam remembered. Pierre Flodenhale was a race driver whose name, in the past year or two, had become increasingly well-known nationally. Last season he had had several spectacular wins.

"When things are quiet around the tracks," Smokey said, "I let Pierre work here. Suits us both. Some people recognize him; they like to have him sell them a car so they can tell their friends. Either way, he's a good sales joe. He'll cinch that deal."

"Perhaps he'd buy in as a partner. If Teresa drops out."

Smokey shook his head. "Not a chance. The kid's always broke; it's why he moonlights here. All race drivers are the same—blow their dough faster'n they make it, even the big winners. Their brains get flooded like carburetors; they figure the purse money'll keep coming in forever."

"You didn't."

"I was a smart cookie. Still am."

They discussed dealer philosophy. Smokey told Adam, "This never was a sissie business; now it's getting tougher. Customers are smarter. A dealer has to stay smarter still. But it's big, and you can win big."

At talk of consumerism, Smokey bridled. "The 'poor consumer' is taking goddam good care of himself. The public was greedy before; consumerism made it worse. Now, everybody wants the best deal ever, with free service forevermore. How about a little 'dealerism' sometime? A dealer has to fight to survive."

While they talked, Adam continued to watch activity below. Now he pointed to the sales booths again. "That first one. I'd like to hear."

The sliding panel had remained open. Smokey reached out and clicked a switch.

". . . deal. I'm telling you, you won't do better anywhere else." A salesman's voice again; this time an older man than Pierre Flodenhale, graying, and with a sharper manner. The prospective customer, a woman whom Adam judged to be in her thirties, appeared to be alone. Momentarily he had a guilty sense of snooping, then reminded himself that use of concealed microphones by dealers, to monitor exchanges between salesmen and car buyers, was widespread. Also, only by listening as he was doing now, could Adam judge the quality of communication between Smokey Stephensen's dealership and its clients.

"I'm not as sure as you," the woman said. "With the car I'm trading in as good as it is, I think your price is a hundred dollars high." She started to get up. "I'd better try somewhere else."

They heard the salesman sigh. "I'll go over the figures one more time." The woman subsided. A pause, then the salesman again. "You'll be financing the new car, right?"

"Yes."

"And you'd like us to arrange financing?"

"I expect so." The woman hesitated. "Well, yes."

From his own knowledge, Adam could guess how the salesman's mind was working. With almost every financed sale a dealer received a kickback from the bank or finance company, usually a hundred dollars, sometimes more. Banks and others made the payments as a means of getting business, for which competition was keen. In a tight deal, knowledge that the money would be coming could be used to make a last-minute price cut, rather than lose the sale entirely.

As if he had read Adam's mind, Smokey murmured, "Chuck knows the score. We don't like to lose our kickback, but sometimes we have to."

"Perhaps we can do a little better." It was the salesman in the booth again. "What I've done is, on your trade . . ."

Smokey snapped the switch, cutting the details off.

Several newcomers had appeared in the showroom; now a fresh group moved into another sales booth. But Smokey seemed dissatisfied. "To make the joint pay I have to sell two thousand five hundred cars a year, and business is slow, slow."

Knuckles rapped on the office door outside. As Smokey called, "Yeah," it opened to admit the salesman who had been dealing with the woman on her own. He held a sheaf of papers which Smokey took, skimmed over, then said accusingly, "She outbluffed you. You didn't have to use all the hundred. She'd have settled for fifty."

"Not that one." The salesman glanced at Adam, then away. "She's a sharpie. Some things you can't see from up here, boss. Like what's in people's eyes. I tell you, hers are hard."

"How would you know? When you gave my money away, you were probably looking up her skirts, so you let her take you."

The salesman looked pained.

Smokey scribbled a signature and handed the papers back. "Get the car delivered."

They watched the salesman leave the mezzanine and return to the booth where the woman waited.

"Some things to remember about salesmen," Smokey Stephensen said. "Pay 'em well, but keep 'em off balance, and never trust one. A good many'll take fifty dollars under the desk for a sweet deal, or for steering finance business, as soon as blow their nose."

Adam motioned to the switch panel. Once more Smokey touched it and they were listening to the salesman who had left the office moments earlier.

". . . your copy. We keep this one."

"Is it properly signed?"

"Sure is." Now that the deal was made, the

salesman was more relaxed; he leaned across the desk, pointing. "Right there. The boss's fist."

"Good." The woman picked up the sales contract, folded it, then announced, "I've been thinking while you were away, and I've decided not to finance after all. I'll pay cash, with a deposit check now and the balance when I pick up the car on Monday."

There was a silence from the sales booth.

Smokey Stephensen slammed a meaty fist into his palm. "The smartass bitch!"

Adam looked at him inquiringly.

"That lousy broad planned that! She knew all along she wouldn't finance."

From the booth they heard the salesman hesitate. "Well . . . that could make a difference."

"A difference to what? The price of the car?" The woman inquired coolly, "How could it unless there's some concealed charge you haven't told me about? The Truth in Lending Act . . ."

Smokey stormed from the window to his desk, snatched up an inside phone and dialed. Adam saw the salesman reach for a receiver.

Smokey snarled, "Let the cow have the car. We'll stand by the deal." He slammed down the phone, then muttered, "But let her come back for service after warranty's out, she'll be sorry!"

Adam said mildly, "Perhaps she'll think of that, too."

As if she had heard him, the woman looked up toward the mezzanine and smiled.

"There's too many know-it-alls nowadays." Smokey returned to stand beside Adam. "Too much written in the newspapers; too many two-bit writers sticking their noses where they've no goddam business. People read that crap." The dealer leaned forward, surveying the showroom. "So what happens? Some, like that woman, go to a bank, arrange financing before they get here, but don't tell us till the deal is made. They let us think we're to set up the financing. So we figure our take—or some of it—into the sale, then we're hooked, and if a dealer backs out of a signed sales contract, he's in trouble. Same thing with insurance; we like arranging car insurance because our commission's good; life insurance on finance payments is even better." He added moodily, "At least the broad didn't take us on insurance, too."

Each incident so far, Adam thought, had given him a new, inside glimpse of Smokey Stephensen.

"I suppose you could look at it from a customer's point of view," Adam prompted. "They want the cheapest financing, most economical insurance, and people are learning they don't get either from a dealer, and that they're better off arranging their own. When there's a payoff to the dealer—finance or insurance—they know it's the customer who pays because the extra money's incorporated in his rates or charges."

Smokey said dourly, "A dealer's gotta live, too. Besides, what people didn't used to know, they didn't worry after."

In another sales booth below, an elderly couple were seating themselves, a salesman facing them. A moment earlier, the trio had walked from a demonstrator car they had been examining. As Adam nodded, under Smokey's hand a switch clicked once more.

". . . really like to have you folks for clients because Mr. Stephensen runs a quality dealership and we're happiest when we sell to quality people."

"That's a nice thing to hear," the woman said.

"Well, Mr. Stephensen's always telling us salesmen, 'Just don't think of the car you're selling today. Think of how you can give folks good service; also that they'll be coming back two years from now, and perhaps another two or three after that.' "

Adam turned to Smokey. "*Did* you say that?"

The dealer grinned. "If I didn't, I should have."

Over the next several minutes, while they listened, a trade-in was discussed. The elderly couple was hesitant about committing themselves to a final figure—the difference between an allowance for their used car and the price of a new one. They lived on a fixed income, the husband explained—his retirement pension.

At length the salesman announced, "Look, folks, like I said, the deal I've written up is the very best we can give anybody. But because you're nice people, I've decided to try something I shouldn't. I'll write an extra sweet deal for you, then see if I can con the boss into okaying it."

"Well . . ." The woman sounded doubtful. "We wouldn't want . . ."

The salesman assured her, "Let me worry about that. Some days the boss is not as sharp as others; we'll hope this is one. What I'll do is change the figures this way: On the trade . . ."

It amounted to a hundred dollars reduction of the end price. As he switched off, Smokey appeared amused.

Moments later, the salesman knocked on the office door and came in, a filled-in sales contract in his hand.

"Hi, Alex." Smokey took the proffered contract and introduced Adam, adding, "It's okay, Alex; he's one of us."

The salesman shook hands. "Nice to know you, Mr. Trenton." He nodded to the booth below. "Were you tuned in, boss?"

"Sure was. Too bad, ain't it, this is one of my sharp days?" The dealer grinned.

"Yeah." The salesman smiled back. "Too bad."

While they chatted, Smokey made alterations to the figures on the sales papers. Afterward he signed, then glanced at his watch. "Been gone long enough?"

"I guess so," the salesman said. "Nice to have met you, Mr. Trenton."

Together, Smokey and the salesman left the office and stood on the open mezzanine outside.

Adam heard Smokey Stephensen raise his voice to a shout. "What you tryin' on? You wanna make a bankrupt outa me?"

"Now, boss, just let me explain."

"Explain! Who needs it? I read figures; they say this deal means a great fat loss."

In the showroom below, heads turned, faces glanced upward to the mezzanine. Among them were those of the elderly couple in the first booth.

"Boss, these are nice people." The salesman was matching Smokey's voice in volume. "We want their business, don't we?"

"Sure I want business, but this is charity."

"I was just trying . . ."

"How about trying for a job someplace else?"

"Look, boss, maybe I can fix this up. These are reasonable people . . ."

"Reasonable, so they want my skin!"

"I did it, boss; not them. I just thought maybe . . ."

"We give great deals here. We draw the line at losses. Understand?"

"I understand."

The exchange was loud as ever. Two of the other salesmen, Adam observed, were smiling surreptitiously. The elderly couple, waiting, looked perturbed.

Again the dealer shouted. "Hey, gimme back those papers!"

Through the open doorway Adam saw Smokey seize the sales contract and go through motions of writing, though the alterations were already made. Smokey thrust the contract back. "Here's the very best I'll do. I'm being generous because you put me in a box." He winked broadly, though the last was visible only on the mezzanine.

The salesman returned the wink. As he went downstairs, Smokey reentered his office and slammed the door, the sound reverberating below.

Adam said drily, "Quite a performance."

Smokey chuckled. "Oldest ploy in the book, and still works sometimes." The listening switch for the first sales booth was still on; he turned the volume up as the salesman rejoined the elderly couple who had risen to their feet.

"Oh, we're so sorry," the woman said. "We were embarrassed for you. We wouldn't have had that happen . . ."

The salesman's face was suitably downcast. "I guess you folks heard."

"Heard!" the older man objected. "I should think everybody within five blocks heard. He didn't have to talk to you like that."

The woman asked, "What about your job?"

"Don't worry; as long as I make a sale today I'll be okay. The boss is a good guy, really. Like I told you, people who deal here find that out. Let's look at the figures." The salesman spread the contract on the desk, then shook his head. "We're back to the original deal, I'm afraid, though it's still a good one. Well, I tried."

"We'll take it," the man said; he seemed to have forgotten his earlier doubts. "You've gone to enough trouble . . ."

Smokey said cheerfully, "In the bag." He switched off and slumped into one of the green leather chairs, motioning Adam to another. The dealer took a cigar from his pocket and offered one to Adam, who declined and lit a cigarette.

"I said a dealer has to fight," Smokey said, "and so he does. But it's a game, too." He looked at Adam shrewdly. "I guess a different kind of game than yours."

Adam acknowledged, "Yes."

"Not so fancy pants as over at that think factory, huh?"

Adam made no answer. Smokey contemplated the glowing tip of his cigar, then went on. "Remember this: a guy who gets to be a car dealer didn't make the game, he doesn't name the rules. He joins the game and plays the way it's played— for real, like strip poker. You know what happens if you lose at strip poker?"

"I guess so."

"No guessing to it. You end up with a bare ass. It's how I'd end here if I didn't play hard, for real, the way you've seen. And though she'd look nicer 'n me bare-assed"—Smokey chuckled— "so would that sister of yours. I'll ask you to remember that, Adam." He stood up. "Let's play the game some more."

He was, after all, Adam realized, getting an untrammeled inside view of the dealership in operation. Adam accepted Smokey's viewpoint that trading in cars—new and used—was a tough, competitive business in which a dealer who relaxed or was softhearted could disappear from sight quickly, as many had. A car dealership was the firing line of automobile marketing. Like any firing line it was no place for the overly sensitive or anyone obsessed with ethics. On the other hand, an alert, shrewd wheeler-dealer—as Smokey Stephensen appeared to be—could make an exceedingly good living, which was part of the reason for Adam's inquiry now.

Another part was to learn how Smokey might adapt to changes in the future.

Within the next decade, Adam knew, major changes were coming in the present car dealership system, a system which many—inside the industry and out—believed archaic in its present form. So far, existing dealers—a powerful, organized bloc—had resisted change. But if manufacturers and dealers, acting together, failed to initiate reforms in the system soon, it was certain that government would step in, as it had already in other industy areas.

Car dealers had long been the auto industry's least reputable arm, and while direct defrauding had been curbed in recent years, many observers believed the public would be better served if contact between manufacturers and car buyers were more direct, with fewer intermediaries. Likely in the future were central dealership systems, factory-operated, which could deliver cars to customers more efficiently and with less overhead cost than now. For years, a similar system had been used successfully with trucks; more recently, car fleet users and car leasing and rental companies, who bought directly, were demonstrating large economies. Along with such direct sales outlets, factory-operated warranty and service centers were likely to be established, the latter offering more consistent, better-supervised service than many dealers provided now.

What was needed to get such systems started —and what auto companies would secretly welcome—was more external, public pressure.

But while dealerships would change, and some fall by the way, the more efficient, better-operated ones were likely to remain and prosper. One reason was the dealers' most commanding argument for existence—their disposal of used cars.

A question for Adam to decide was: Would Smokey Stephensen's—and Teresa's—dealership progress or decline amid the changes of the next few years? He was already debating the question mentally as he followed Smokey from the mezzanine office down the stairway to the showroom floor.

For the next hour Adam stayed close to Smokey Stephensen, watching him in motion. Clearly, while letting his sales staff do their work, Smokey kept a sensitive finger on the pulse of business. Little escaped him. He had an instinct, too, about when his own intervention might nudge a teetering sale to its conclusion.

A lantern-jawed, cadaverous man who had come in from the street without glancing at the cars displayed, was arguing with a salesman about price. The man knew the car he wanted; equally obviously, he had shopped elsewhere.

He had a small card in his hand which he showed to the salesman, who shook his head. Smokey strolled across the showroom. Adam positioned himself so he could observe and hear.

"Let me see." Smokey reached out, plucking the card deftly from Lantern Jaw's fingers. It was a business card with a dealer insignia on the front; on the back were penciled figures. Nodding amiably, his manner robbing the action of offense, Smokey studied the figures. No one bothered with introductions; Smokey's proprietorial air, plus the beard and blue silk jacket were his identification. As he turned the card his eyebrows went up. "From an Ypsilanti dealer. You live there, friend?"

"No," Lantern Jaw said. "But I like to shop around."

"And where you shop, you ask for a card with the best price difference between your trade-in and the new car. Right?"

The other nodded.

"Be a good sport," Smokey said. "Show me the cards from all the other dealers."

Lantern Jaw hesitated, then shrugged. "Why not?" From a pocket he produced a handful of cards and gave them to Smokey who counted them, chuckling. Including the one he already held, there were eight. Smokey spread the cards on a desk top nearby, then, with the salesman, craned over them.

"The lowest offer is two thousand dollars," the salesman read out, "and the highest twenty-three hundred."

Smokey motioned. "The report on his trade."

The salesman passed over a sheet, which Smokey glanced at, then handed back. He told the lantern-jawed man, "I guess you'd like a card from me, too."

"Sure would."

Smokey took out a business card, turned it over, and scribbled on the back.

Lantern Jaw accepted the card, then looked up sharply. "This says fifteen hundred dollars."

Smokey said blandly, "A nice round figure."

"But you won't sell me a car for that!"

"You're damn right I won't, friend. And I'll tell you something else. Neither will any of those others, not at the prices they put on *their* cards." Smokey swept the business cards into his hand, then returned them one by one. "Go back to this place, they'll tell you their price didn't include sales tax. This one—they've left out the cost of options, maybe sales tax, too. Here, they didn't add dealer prep, license, and some more . . ." He continued through the cards, pointing to his own last. "Me, I didn't include wheels and an engine; I'd have got around to it when you came back to talk for real."

Lantern Jaw looked crestfallen.

"An old dealer trick, friend," Smokey said,

"designed for shoppers like you, and the name of the game is 'Bring 'em back later!'" He added sharply, "Do you believe me?"

"Yeah. I believe you."

Smokey rammed his point home. "So nine dealers after you started—right here and now—is where you got your first honest news, where somebody leveled with you. Right?"

The other said ruefully, "Sure looks that way."

"Great! That's how we run this shop." Smokey draped a hand genially around Lantern Jaw's shoulders. "So, friend, now you got the starting flag. What you do next is drive back to all those other dealers for more prices, the real ones, close as you can get." The man grimaced; Smokey appeared not to notice. "After that, when you're ready for more honest news, like a driveaway price which includes everything, come back to me." The dealer held out a beefy hand. "Good luck!"

"Hold it," Lantern Jaw said. "Why not tell me now?"

"Because you aren't serious yet. Because you'd still be wasting my time and yours."

The man hesitated only briefly. "I'm serious. What's the honest price?"

Smokey warned him, "Higher'n any of those fake ones. But my price has the options you want, sales tax, license, a tank of gas, nothing hidden, the works . . ."

Minutes later they shook hands on twenty-four hundred and fifty dollars. As the salesman began his paper work, Smokey strolled away, continuing to prowl the showroom.

Almost at once Adam saw him stopped by a self-assured, pipe-smoking newcomer, handsomely dressed in a Harris tweed jacket, immaculate slacks and alligator shoes. They talked at length and, after the man left, Smokey returned to Adam, shaking his head. "No sale there! A doctor! They're the worst to do business with. Want giveaway prices; afterwards, priority service, and always with a free loan car, as if I had 'em on the shelf like Band-Aids. Ask any dealer about doctors. You'll touch a nerve."

He was less critical, soon after, of a stockily built, balding man with a gravelly voice, shopping for a car for his wife. Smokey introduced him to Adam as a local police chief, Wilbur Arenson. Adam, who had encountered the chief's name frequently in newspapers, was aware of cold, blue eyes sizing him up, his identity stored away routinely in the policeman's memory. The two retired to Smokey's office where a deal was consummated —Adam suspected a good one for the customer. When the police chief had gone, Smokey said, "Stay friendly with the cops. Could cost me plenty if I got parking tickets for all the cars my service department has to leave on the street some days."

A swarthy, voluble man came in and collected an envelope which was waiting for him in the main floor reception office. On his way out, Smokey intercepted him and shook hands warmly. Afterward he explained, "He's a barber, and one of our bird dogs. Gets people in his chair; while he cuts their hair, he talks about how good a deal he got here, how great the service is. Sometimes his customers say they're coming over, and if we make a sale the guy gets his little cut." He had twenty or so regular bird dogs, Smokey revealed, including service station operators, a druggist, a beauty parlor operator, and an undertaker. As to the last, "A guy dies, his wife wants to sell his car, maybe get something smaller. More often'n not, the undertaker's got her hypnotized, so she'll go where he says, and if it's here, we take care of him."

They returned to the mezzanine office for

coffee, laced with brandy out of a bottle produced by Smokey from a desk drawer.

Over their drinks the dealer introduced a new subject—the Orion.

"It'll be big when it hits, Adam, and that's the time we'll sell as many Orions here as we can get our hands on. You know how it is." Smokey swirled the mixture in his cup. "I was thinking— if you could use your pull to get us an extra allocation, it'd be good for Teresa and them kids."

Adam said sharply, "It would also put money in Smokey Stephensen's pocket."

The dealer shrugged. "So we help each other."

"In this case we don't. And I'll ask you not to bring it up, or anything else like it, ever again."

A moment earlier Adam had tensed, his anger rising at the proposal which was so outrageous that it represented everything the company Conflict of Interest committee was set up to prevent. Then, amusement creeping in, he settled for the moderate reply. Clearly, where sales and business were concerned, Smokey Stephensen was totally amoral and saw nothing wrong in what had been suggested. Perhaps a car dealer had to be that way. Adam wasn't sure; nor was he sure, yet, what he would recommend to Teresa.

But he had gained the first impressions which he came for. They were mixed; he wanted to digest and think about them.

chapter thirteen

Hank Kreisel, lunching in Dearborn with Brett
DeLosanto, represented the out-of-sight portion
of an iceberg.

Kreisel, fifty-five-ish, lean, muscular, and
towering over most other people like a collie in a
pack of terriers, was the owner of his own company which manufactured auto parts.

The world, when it thinks of Detroit, does so
in terms of name-famed auto manufacturers,
dominated by the Big Three. The impression is
correct, except that major car makers represent
the portion of the iceberg in view. Out of sight are
thousands of supplemental firms, some substantial, but most small, and with a surprising segment operating out of holes-in-the-wall on petty
cash financing. In the Detroit area they are anywhere and everywhere—downtown, out in suburbs, on side roads, or as satellites to bigger plants.
Their work quarters range from snazzy compages
to ramshackle warehouses, converted churches or
one-room lofts. Some are unionized, many are not,
although their total payrolls run to billions yearly.
But the thing they have in common is that a Ni-
agara of bits and pieces—some large, but mostly
small, many unrecognizable as to purpose except
by experts—flow outward to create other parts
and, in the end, the finished automobiles. Without
parts manufacturers, the Big Three would be like
honey processors bereft of bees.

In this sense, Hank Kreisel was a bee. In
another sense he was a master sergeant of Marines. He had been a Marine top kick in the Ko-
rean War, and still looked the part, with short
hair only slightly graying, a neatly trimmed mus-
tache, and a ramrod stance when he stood still,

though this was seldom. Mostly he moved in urgent, precise, clipped movements—*go, go, go*—and talked the same way, from the time of rising early in his Grosse Pointe home until ending each active day, invariably well into the next. This and other habits had brought him two heart attacks, with a warning from his physician that one more might be fatal. But Hank Kreisel regarded the warning as he would once have reacted to news of a potential enemy ambush in the jungle ahead. He pressed on, hard as ever, trusting in a personal conviction of indestructibility, and luck which had seldom failed him.

It was luck which had given him a lifetime, so far, filled with the two things Hank Kreisel relished most—work and women. Occasionally the luck had failed. Once had been during a fervid affair in rest camp with a colonel's wife, after which her husband personally busted Master Sergeant Kreisel down to private. And later, in his Detroit manufacturing career, disasters had occurred, though successes well outnumbered them.

Brett DeLosanto had met Kreisel when the latter was in the Design-Styling Center one day, demonstrating a new accessory. They had liked each other and, partly through the young designer's genuine curiosity about how the rest of the auto industry worked and lived, had become friends. It was Hank Kreisel whom Brett had planned to meet on the frustrating day downtown when he had had the parking lot encounter with Leonard Wingate. But Kreisel had failed to make it that day and now, two months later, the pair were keeping their postponed luncheon date.

"I've wondered, Hank," Brett DeLosanto said. "How'd you get started with the auto parts bit?"

"Long story." Kreisel reached for the neat sourmash Bourbon which was his habitual drink and took an ample sip. He was relaxing and, while dressed in a well-cut business suit, had the buttons of his vest undone, revealing that he wore both suspenders and a belt. He added, "Tell you, if you like."

"Go ahead." Brett had worked through the past several nights at the Design-Styling Center, had caught up with sleep this morning, and now was relishing the daytime freedom before returning to his design board later this afternoon.

They were in a small private apartment a mile or so from the Henry Ford Museum and Greenfield Village. Because of its proximity, also, to Ford Motor Company headquarters, the apartment appeared on the books of Kreisel's company as his "Ford liaison office." In fact, the liaison was not with Ford but with a lissome, leggy brunette named Elsie, who lived in the apartment rent-free, was on the payroll of Kreisel's company though she never went there, and in return made herself available to Hank Kreisel once or twice a week, or more often if he felt like it. The arrangement was easygoing on both sides. Kreisel, a considerate, reasonable man, always telephoned before putting in an appearance, and Elsie saw to it that he had priority.

Unknown to Elsie, Hank Kreisel also had a General Motors and Chrysler liaison office, operating under the same arrangement.

Elsie, who had prepared lunch, was in the kitchen now.

"Hold it!" Kreisel told Brett. "Just remembered something. You know Adam Trenton?"

"Very well."

"Like to meet him. Word's out he's a big comer. Never hurts to make high-grade friends in this business." The statement was characteristic of Kreisel, a mixture of directness and amiable cynicism which men, as well as women, found appealing.

Elsie rejoined them, her every movement an overt sexuality which a simple, tight black dress accentuated. The ex-Marine patted her rump affectionately.

"Sure, I'll fix a meeting." Brett grinned. "Here?"

Hank Kreisel shook his head. "The Higgins Lake cottage. A weekend party. Let's aim at May. You choose a date. I'll do the rest."

"Okay, I'll talk with Adam. Let you know." When he was with Kreisel, Brett found himself using the same kind of staccato sentences as his host. As to a party, Brett had already attended several at Hank Kreisel's cottage hideaway. They were swinging affairs which he enjoyed.

Elsie seated herself at the table with them and resumed her lunch, her eyes moving between the two men as they talked. Brett knew, because he had been here before, that she liked to listen but seldom joined in.

Brett inquired, "What made you think of Adam?"

"The Orion. He okayed add-ons, I'm told. Last minute hot stuff. I'm making one of 'em."

"*You* are! Which one? The brace or floor reinforcement?"

"Brace."

"Hey, I was in on that! That's a big order."

Kreisel gave a twisted grin. "It'll make me or break me. They need five thousand braces fast, like yesterday. After that, ten thousand a month. Wasn't sure I wanted the job. Schedule's tough. Still plenty of headaches. But they figure I'll deliver."

Brett already knew of Hank Kreisel's reputation for reliability about deliveries, a quality which auto company purchasing departments cherished. One reason for it was a talent for tooling improvisations which slashed time and cost, and while not a qualified engineer himself, Kreisel could leapfrog mentally over many who were.

"I'll be damned!" Brett said. "You and the Orion."

"Shouldn't surprise you. Industry's full of people crossing each other's bridges. Sometimes pass each other, don't even know it. Everybody sells to everybody else. GM sells steering gears to Chrysler. Chrysler sells adhesives to GM and Ford. Ford helps out with Plymouth windshields. I know a guy, a sales engineer. Lives in Flint, works for General Motors. Flint's a GM company town. His main customer's Ford in Dearborn—for engineering design of engine accessories. He takes confidential Ford stuff to Flint. GM guards it from their own people who'd give their ears to see it. The guy drives a Ford car—to Ford, his customer. His GM bosses buy it for him."

Elsie replenished Hank Kreisel's Bourbon; Brett had declined a drink earlier.

Brett told the girl, "He's always telling me things I didn't know."

"He knows a lot." Her eyes, smiling, switched from the young designer's to Kreisel's. Brett sensed a private message pass.

"Hey! You two like me to leave?"

"No hurry." The ex-Marine produced a pipe and lit it. "You want to hear about parts?" He glanced at Elsie. "Not yours, baby." Plainly he meant: *Those are for me.*

"Auto parts," Brett said.

"Right." Kreisel gave his twisted grin. "Worked in an auto plant before I enlisted. After Korea, went back. Was a punch press operator. Then a foreman."

"You've made the big leagues fast."

"Too fast, maybe. Anyway, I'd watched how production worked—metal stampings. The Big Three are all the same. Must have the fanciest machines, high-priced buildings, big overhead, cafeterias, the rest. All that stuff makes a two-cent stamping cost a nickel."

Hank Kreisel drew on his pipe and wreathed himself in smoke. "So I went to Purchasing. Saw a guy I know. Told him I figured I could make the same stuff cheaper. On my own."

"Did they finance you?"

"Not then, not later. Gave me a contract, though. There and then for a million little washers. When I'd quit my job I had two hundred dollars cash. No building, no machinery." Hank Kreisel chuckled. "Didn't sleep that night. Dead scared. Next day I tore around. Rented an old billiard hall. Showed a bank the contract and the lease; they loaned me dough to buy scrap machinery. Then I hired two other guys. The three of us fixed the machinery up. They ran it. I rushed out, got more orders." He added reminiscently, "Been rushing ever since."

"You're a saga," Brett said. He had seen Hank Kreisel's impressive Grosse Pointe home, his half dozen bustling plants, the converted billiard hall still one of them. He supposed, conservatively, Hank Kreisel must be worth two or three million dollars.

"Your friend in Purchasing," Brett said. "The one who gave you the first order. Do you ever see him?"

"Sure. He's still there—on salary. Same job. Retires soon. I buy him a meal sometimes."

Elsie asked, "What's a saga?"

Kreisel told her, "It's a guy who makes it to the end of the trail."

"A legend," Brett said.

Kreisel shook his head. "Not me. Not yet." He stopped, more thoughtful suddenly than Brett had seen him at any time before. When he spoke again his voice was slower, the words less clipped.

"There's a thing I'd like to do, and maybe it could add up to something like that if I could pull it off." Aware of Brett's curiosity, the ex-Marine shook his head again. "Not now. Maybe one day I'll tell you."

His mood switched back. "So I made parts and made mistakes. Learned a lot fast. One thing: search out weak spots in the market. Spots where competition's least. So I ignored new parts; too much infighting. Started making for repair, replacement, the 'after market.' But only items no more than twenty inches from the ground. Mostly at front and rear. And costing less than ten dollars."

"Why the restrictions?"

Kreisel gave his usual knowing grin. "Most minor accidents happen to fronts and backs of cars. And down below twenty inches, all get damaged more. So more parts are needed, meaning bigger orders. That's where parts makers hit paydirt—on long runs."

"And the ten-dollar limit?"

"Say you're doing a repair job. Something's damaged. Costs more than ten dollars, you'll try to fix it. Costs less, you'll throw the old part out, use a replacement. There's where I come in. High volume again."

It was so ingeniously simple, Brett laughed aloud.

"I got into accessories later. And something else I learned. Take on some defense work."

"Why?"

"Most parts people don't want it. Can be difficult. Usually short runs, not much profit. But can lead to bigger things. And Internal Revenue are easier on you about tax deductions. They won't admit it." He surveyed his "Ford liaison office" amusedly. "But I know."

"Elsie's right. There's a whole lot you know."

Brett rose, glancing at his watch. "Back to the chariot factory! Thanks for lunch, Elsie."

The girl got up too, moved beside him, and took his arm. He was aware of her closeness, a warmth transmitted through the thinness of her dress. Her slim, firm body eased away, then once more pressed against his. Accidentally? He doubted it. His nostrils detected the soft scent of her hair, and Brett envied Hank Kreisel what he suspected would happen as soon as he had gone.

Elsie said softly, "Come in any time."

"Hey, Hank!" Brett said. "You hear that invitation?"

Momentarily the older man looked away, then answered gruffly, "If you accept, make sure I don't know about it."

Kreisel joined him at the apartment doorway. Elsie had gone back inside.

"I'll fix that date with Adam," Brett affirmed. "Call you tomorrow."

"Okay." The two shook hands.

"About that other," Hank Kreisel said. "Meant exactly what I told you. Don't let me know. Understand?"

"I understand." Brett had already memorized the number on the apartment telephone, which was unlisted. He had every intention of calling Elsie tomorrow.

As an elevator carried Brett downward, Hank Kreisel closed and locked the apartment door from inside.

Elsie was waiting for him in the bedroom. She had undressed and put on a sheer minikimono, held around her by a silk ribbon. Her dark hair, released, tumbled about her shoulders; her wide mouth smiled, eyes showing pleasurable knowledge of what was to come. They kissed lightly. He took his time about unfastening the ribbon, then, opening the kimono, held her.

After a while she began undressing him, slowly, carefully putting each garment aside and folding it. He had taught her, as he had taught other women in the past, that this was not a gesture of servility but a rite—practiced in the East, where he had learned it first—and a mutual whetting of anticipation.

When she had finished they lay down together. Elsie had passed Hank a *happi* coat which he slipped on; it was one of several he had brought home from Japan, was growing threadbare from long use, but still served to prove what Far Easterners knew best: that a garment worn during sexual mating, however light or loose, heightened a man's and woman's awareness of each other, and their pleasure.

He whispered, "Love me, baby!"

She moaned softly. "Love me, Hank!"

He did.

chapter fourteen

"You know what this scumbag world is made of, baby?" Rollie Knight had demanded of May Lou yesterday. When she hadn't answered, he told her. "Bullshit! There ain't nuthun' in this whole wide world but bullshit."

The remark was prompted by happenings at the car assembly plant where Rollie was now working. Though he hadn't kept score himself, today was the beginning of his seventh week of employment.

May Lou was new in his life, too. She was (as Rollie put it) a chick he had laid during a weekend, while blowing an early paycheck, and more recently they had shacked up in two rooms of an apartment house on Blaine near 12th. May Lou was currently spending her days there, messing with cook pots, furniture and bits of curtaining, making—as a barfly acquaintance of Rollie's described it—like a bush tit in the nest.

Rollie hadn't taken seriously, and still didn't, what he called May Lou's crapping around at playing house. Just the same he'd given her bread, which she spent on the two of them, and to get more of the same, Rollie continued to report most days of the week to the assembly plant.

What started this second go around, after he had copped out of the first training course, was—in Rollie's words—a big Tom nigger in a fancy Dan suit, who had turned up one day, saying his name was Leonard Wingate. That was at Rollie's room in the inner city, and they had a great big gabfest in which Rollie first told the guy to get lost, go screw himself, he'd had enough. But the Tom had been persuasive. He went on to explain, while Rollie listened, fascinated, about the fatso white bastard of an instructor who put one over with the checks, then got caught. When Rollie inquired, though, Wingate admitted that the white fatso wasn't going to jail the way a black man would have done, which proved that all the bullshit about justice was exactly that—bullshit! Even the black Tom, Wingate, admitted it. And it was just after he had—a bleak, bitter admission which surprised Rollie—that Rollie had somehow, almost before he knew it, agreed to go to work.

It was Leonard Wingate who had told Rollie he could forget about completing the rest of the training course. Wingate, it seemed, had looked up the records which said Rollie was bright and quick-witted, and so (Wingate said) they would put him straight on the assembly line next week, starting Monday, doing a regular job.

That (again, as Rollie told it) turned out to be bullshit, too.

Instead of being given a job in one place, which he might have managed, he was informed he had to be relief man at various stations on the line, which meant moving back and forth like a blue-assed fly, so that as soon as he got used to doing one thing, he was hustled over to another, then to something else, and something else, until his head was spinning. The same thing went on for the first two weeks so that he hardly knew— since the instructions he was given were minimal —what he was supposed to be doing from one minute to the next. Not that he'd have cared that much. Except for what the black guy, Wingate, had said, Rollie Knight—as usual—was not expecting anything. But it just showed that nothing they ever promised worked out the way they said it would. So . . . Bullshit!

Of course, nobody, *but nobody*, had told him about the speed of the assembly line. He'd figured that one for himself—the hard way.

On the first day at work, when Rollie had his initial view of a final car assembly line, the line seemed to be inching forward like a snail's funeral. He'd come to the plant early, reporting in with the day shift. The size of the joint, the mob flooding in from cars, buses, every other kind of wheels, you name it, scared him to begin with; also, everybody except himself seemed to know where they were going—all in one helluva hurry —and why. But he'd found where he had to report, and from there had been sent to a big, metal-roofed building, cleaner than he expected, but noisy. *Oh, man; that noise!* It was all around you, sounding like a hundred rock bands on bad trips.

Anyhow, the car line snaked through the building, with the end and beginning out of sight. And it looked as if there was time aplenty for any of the guys and broads (a few women were working alongside men) to finish whatever their job happened to be on one car, rest a drumbeat, then start work on the next. No sweat! For a cool cat with more than air between his ears, a cincheroo!

In less than an hour, like thousands who had preceded him, Rollie was grimly wiser.

The foreman he had been handed over to on arrival had said simply, "Number?" The foreman, young and white, but balding, with the harried look of a middle-aged man, had a pencil poised and said peevishly, when Rollie hesitated, "Social Security!"

Eventually Rollie located a card which a clerk in Personnel had given him. It had the number on it. Impatiently, with the knowledge of twenty other things he had to do immediately, the foreman wrote it down.

He pointed to the last four figures, which were 6469. "That's what you'll be known as," the foreman shouted; the line had already started up, and the din made it hard to hear. "So memorize that number."

Rollie grinned, and had been tempted to say it was the same way in prison. But he hadn't, and the foreman had motioned for him to follow, then took him to a work station. A partly finished car was moving slowly past, its brightly painted body gleaming. *Some snazzy wheels!* Despite his habit of indifference, Rollie felt his interest quicken.

The foreman bellowed in his ear: "You got three chassis and trunk bolts to put in. Here, here, and here. Bolts are in the box over there. Use this power wrench." He thrust it into Rollie's hands. "Got it?"

Rollie wasn't sure he had. The foreman touched another worker's shoulder. "Show this new man. He'll take over here. I need you on front suspension. Hurry it up." The foreman moved away, still looking older than his years.

"Watch me, bub!" The other worker grabbed a handful of bolts and dived into a car doorway with a power wrench, its cord trailing. While Rollie was still craning, trying to see what the man was doing, the other came out backward, forcefully. He cannoned into Rollie. "Watch it, bub!" Going around to the back of the car, he dived into the trunk, two more bolts in hand, the wrench still with him.

He shouted back, "Get the idea?" The other man worked on one more car, then, responding to renewed signals from the foreman, and with an "All yours, bub," he disappeared.

Despite the noise, the dozens of people he could see close by, Rollie had never felt more lonely in his life.

"*You! Hey! Get on with it!*" It was the foreman, shouting, waving his arms from the other side of the line.

The car which the first man had worked on was already gone. Incredibly, despite the line's apparent slowness, another had appeared. There was no one but Rollie to insert the bolts. He grabbed a couple of bolts and jumped into the car. He groped for holes they were supposed to go in, found one, then realized he had forgotten the wrench. He went back for it. As he jumped back in the car the heavy wrench dropped on his hand, his knuckles skinned against the metal floor. He managed to start turning the single bolt; before he could finish, or insert the other, the wrench cord tightened as the car moved forward. The wrench would no longer reach. Rollie left the second bolt on the floor and got out.

With the car after that, he managed to get two bolts in and made a pass at tightening them, though he wasn't sure how well. With the one after that, he did better; also the car following. He was getting the knack of using the wrench, though he found it heavy. He was sweating and had skinned his hands again.

It was not until the fifth car had gone by that he remembered the third bolt he was supposed to insert in the trunk.

Alarmed, Rollie looked around him. No one had noticed.

At adjoining work positions, on either side of the line, two men were installing wheels. Intent on their own tasks, neither paid the slightest heed to Rollie. He called to one, "Hey! I left some bolts out."

Without looking up, the worker shouted back, "Forget it! Get the next one. Repair guys'll catch the others down the line." Momentarily he lifted his head and laughed. "Maybe."

Rollie began inserting the third bolt through each car trunk to the chassis. He had to increase his pace to do it. It was also necessary to go bodily into the trunk and, emerging the second time, he hit his head on the deck lid. The blow half-stunned him, and he would have liked to rest, but the next car kept coming and he worked on it in a daze.

He was learning: first, the pace of the line was faster than it seemed; second, even more compelling than the speed was its relentlessness. The line came on, and on, and on, unceasing, unyielding, impervious to human weakness or appeal. It was like a tide which nothing stopped except a half-hour lunch break, the end of a shift, or sabotage.

Rollie became a saboteur on his second day.

He had been shifted through several positions by that time, from inserting chassis bolts to making electrical connections, then to installing steering columns, and afterward to fitting fenders. He had heard someone say the previous day there was a shortage of workers; hence the panic—a usual thing on Mondays. On Tuesday he sensed more people were at their regular jobs, but Rollie was still being used by foremen to fill temporary gaps while others were on relief or break. Consequently, there was seldom time to learn anything well, and at each fresh position several cars went by before he learned to do a new job properly. Usually, if a foreman was on hand and noticed, the defective work would be tagged; at other times it simply went on down the line. On a few occasions foremen saw something wrong, but didn't bother.

While it all happened, Rollie Knight grew wearier.

The day before, at the end of work, his frail body had ached all over. His hands were sore; in various other places his skin was bruised or raw. That night he slept more soundly than in years and awakened next morning only because the cheap alarm clock, which Leonard Wingate had left, was loudly insistent. Wondering why he was doing it, Rollie scrambled up, and a few minutes later addressed himself in the cracked mirror over a chipped enamel washbasin. *"You lovin' crazy cat, you dopehead, crawl back in bed and cop some Zs. Or maybe you fixin' to be a white man's nigger."* He eyed himself contemptuously but had not gone back to bed. Instead he reported to the plant once more.

By early afternoon his tiredness showed. Through the previous hour he had yawned repeatedly.

A young black worker with an Afro hairdo told him, "Man, you sleeping on your feet." The two were assigned to engine decking, their job to lower engines onto chassis, then secure them.

Rollie grimaced. "Them wheels keep comin'. Never did see so many."

"You need a rest, man. Like a rest when this mean line stops."

"Ain't never gonna stop, I reckon."

They maneuvered a hulking engine from overhead into the forward compartment of one more car, inserting the driveshaft in the transmission extension, like a train being coupled, then released the engine from suspension. Others down the line would bolt it into place.

The worker with the Afro hairdo had his head close to Rollie's. "You want this here line stopped? I mean it, man."

"Oh, sure, sure." Rollie felt more like closing his eyes than getting involved in some stupid gabfest.

"Ain't kiddin'. See this." Out of sight of others nearby, the worker opened a fist he had been holding clenched. In his palm was a black, four-inch steel bolt. "Hey, take it!"

"Why so?"

"Do like I say. Drop it there!" He pointed to a

groove in the concrete floor near their feet, housing the assembly line chain drive, an endless belt
like a monstrous bicycle chain. The chain drive
ran the length of the assembly line and back, im-
pelling the partially completed cars along the line
at even speed. At various points it sank underground, rose through extra floors above, passed
through paint booths, inspection chambers, or
simply changed direction. Whenever it did, the
moving chain clanked over cog points.

What the hell, Rollie thought. Anything to
pass the time, to help this day end sooner—even
a bunch of nothing. He dropped the bolt into the
chain drive.

Nothing happened except that the bolt moved
forward down the line; in less than a minute it
was out of sight. Only then was he aware of heads
lifting around him, of faces—mostly black—grinning at his own. Puzzled, he sensed others waiting
expectantly. For what?

The assembly line stopped. It stopped without warning, without sudden sound or jolting. The
change was so unremarkable that it took several
seconds before some, intent on work, were aware
that the line was now stationary in front of them
instead of passing by.

For perhaps ten seconds there was a lull.
During it, the workers around Rollie were grinning even more broadly than before.

Then, bedlam. Alarm bells clanged. Urgent
shouts resounded from forward on the line. Soon
after, somewhere in the depths of the plant a siren
wailed faintly, then increased in volume, growing
nearer.

The older hands who had watched, surreptitiously, the exchange between Rollie and the
worker with the Afro hairdo knew what had happened.

From Rollie Knight's work station the nearest

chain drive cog point was a hundred yards forward
on the line. Until that point, the bolt he had inserted in a link of the chain had moved unevent-
fully. But when it reached the cog, the bolt jammed
hard between cog and chain, so that something
had to give. The link broke. The chain drive
parted. The assembly line stopped. Instantly,
seven hundred workers were left idle, their wages
at union scale continuing while they waited for
the line to start again.

More seconds ticked away. The siren was
nearer, louder, traveling fast. In a wide aisle
alongside the line, those on foot—supervisors,
stock men, messengers and others—hastily moved
clear. Other plant traffic, fork-lifts, power carry-
alls, executive buggies—pulled aside and stopped.
Hurtling around a bend in the building, a yellow
truck with flashing red beacon swung into sight.
It was a crash repair unit carrying a three-man
crew with tools and welding gear. One drove, his
foot against the floor; two others hung on, bracing
themselves against welding cylinders in the rear.
Forward on the line a foreman had arms upraised,
signaling where the break had happened. The
truck tore past Rollie Knight's work station—a blur
of yellow, red, its siren at crescendo. It slowed,
then stopped. The crew tumbled out.

In any car assembly plant an unscheduled
line stoppage is an emergency, taking second
place only to a fire. Every minute of line production lost equates a fortune in wages, administration, factory cost, none of which can ever be
recovered. Expressed another way: when an assembly line is running it produces a new car
roughly every fifty seconds. With an unplanned
stoppage, the same amount of time means the full
cost of a new car lost.

Thus the objective is to restart the line first,
ask questions after.

The emergency crew, skilled in such contingencies, knew what to do. They located the chain drive break, brought the severed portions together. Cutting free the broken link, they welded in another. Their truck had scarcely stopped before acetylene torches flared. The job was hasty. When necessary, repairmen improvised to get the line moving again. Later, when production halted for a shift change or meal break, the repair would be inspected, a more lasting job done.

One of the repair crew signaled to a foreman —Frank Parkland—connected by telephone with the nearest control point. "Start up!" The word was passed. Power, which had been cut by circuit breaker, was reapplied. The chain drive clanked over cogs, this time smoothly. The line restarted. Seven hundred employees, most of them grateful for the respite, resumed work.

From the stoppage of the line to its restarting had occupied four minutes fifty-five seconds. Thus five and a half cars had been lost, or more than six thousand dollars.

Rollie Knight, though scared by now, was not sure what had happened.

He found out quickly.

The foreman, Frank Parkland—big-boned, broad-shouldered—came striding back along the line, his face set grimly. In his hand was a twisted four-inch bolt which one of the repair crew had given him.

He stopped, asking questions, holding up the mangled bolt. "It came from this section; had to. Some place here, between two sets of cogs. Who did it? Who saw it?"

Men shook their heads. Frank Parkland moved on, asking the questions over again.

When he came to the group decking engines, the young worker with the Afro hairdo was doubled up with laughter. Barely able to speak, he pointed to Rollie Knight. "There he is, boss! Saw him do it." Others at adjoining work stations were laughing with him.

Though Rollie was the target, he recognized, instinctively, no malice was involved. It was merely a joke, a diversion, a rambunctious prank. Who cared about consequences? Besides, the line had only stopped for minutes. Rollie found himself grinning too, then caught Parkland's eye and froze.

The foreman glared. "You did it? You put this bolt in?"

Rollie's face betrayed him. His eyes showed white from sudden fear combined with weariness. For once, his outward cockiness was absent.

Parkland ordered, "Out!"

Rollie Knight moved from his position on the line. The foreman motioned a relief man to replace him.

"Number?"

Rollie repeated the Social Security number he had learned the day before. Parkland asked his name and wrote it down also, his face remaining hard.

"You're new, aren't you?"

"Yeah." *For Cri-sake!*—it was always the same. Questions, gabbing, never an end. Even when Whitey kicked your ass, he dressed it up with bullshit.

"What you did was sabotage. You know the consequences?"

Rollie shrugged. He had no idea what "sabotage" meant, though he didn't like the sound of it. With the same resignation he had shown a few weeks earlier, he accepted that his job was gone. All that concerned him now was to wonder: What more could they throw at him? From the way this honky burned, he'd stir trouble if he could.

From behind Parkland, someone said, "Frank —Mr. Zaleski."

The foreman turned. He watched the approaching stocky figure of the assistant plant manager.

"What was it, Frank?"

"This, Matt." Parkland held up the twisted bolt.

"Deliberate?"

"I'm finding out." His tone said: *Let me do it my way!*

"Okay." Zaleski's eyes moved coolly over Rollie Knight. "But if it's sabotage, we throw the book. The union'll back us up; you know that. Let me have a report, Frank." He nodded and moved on.

Frank Parkland wasn't sure why he had held back in exposing the man in front of him as a saboteur. He could have done so, and fired him instantly; there would have been no repercussions. But momentarily it had all seemed too easy. The little, half-starved guy looked more a victim than a villain. Besides, someone who knew the score wouldn't leave himself that vulnerable.

He held out the offending bolt. "Did you know what this would do?"

Rollie looked up at Parkland, towering over him. Normally he would have glared back hate, but was too tired even for that. He shook his head.

"You know now."

Remembering the shouts, activity, siren, flashing lights, Rollie could not resist a grin. "Yeah, man!"

"Did somebody tell you to do it?"

He was aware of faces watching from the line, no longer smiling.

The foreman demanded, "Well, who was it?"

Rollie stayed mute.

"Was it the one who accused you?"

The worker with the Afro hairdo was bent over, decking another engine.

Rollie shook his head. Given the chance, there were debts he would pay back. But this was not the way.

"All right," Parkland said. "I don't know why I'm doing this, but I think you got suckered, though maybe I'm the sucker now." The foreman glared, begrudging his own concession. "What happened'll go on the record as an accident. But you're being watched; remember that." He added brusquely. "Get back to work!"

Rollie, to his great surprise, ended the shift fitting pads under instrument panels.

He knew, though, that the situation couldn't stay the way it was. Next day he was the subject of appraising glances from fellow workers, and the butt of humor. At first the humor was casual and tentative, but he was aware it could get rougher, much rougher, if the idea grew that Rollie Knight was a pushover for pranks or bullying. For someone unlucky or inept enough to get that reputation, life could be miserable, even dangerous, because the monotony of assembly line work made people welcome anything, even brutality, as a diversion.

In the cafeteria on his fourth day of employment there occurred the usual melee at lunch break in which several hundred men rushed from work stations, their objective to get in line to be served, and, after waiting, hastily swallow their food, go to the toilet, wash off their dirt and grease if so inclined (it was never practical to wash before eating), then make it back to work—all in thirty minutes. Amid the cafeteria crowd he saw the worker with the Afro hairdo surrounded by a group which was laughing, looking at Rollie speculatively. A few minutes later, after getting his own food, he was jostled roughly so that everything he had paid for cascaded to the floor where it was promptly trampled on—apparently an accident, too, though Rollie knew better. He did not eat that day; there was no more time.

During the jostling he heard a click and saw a switchblade flash. Next time, Rollie suspected, the jostling would be rougher, the switchblade used to nick him; or even worse. He wasted no time reasoning that the process was wildly illogical and unjust. A manufacturing plant employing thousands of workers was a jungle, with a jungle's lawlessness, and all that he could do was pick his moment to take a stand.

Though knowing time was against him, Rollie waited. He sensed an opportunity would come. It did.

On Friday, last day of his working week, he was assigned again to lowering engines onto chassis. Rollie was teamed with an older man who was the engine decker, and among others at adjoining work stations was the worker with the Afro hairdo.

"Man, oh man, I feel somethin' creepy-crawly," the latter declared when Rollie joined them near the end of a meal break, shortly before the line restarted. "You gonna give us all a special rest today?" He cuffed Rollie around the shoulders as others nearby howled with laughter. Someone else slapped Rollie from the other side. Both blows could have been good-natured, but instead slammed into Rollie's frailness and left him staggering.

The chance he had planned and waited for occurred an hour later. As well as doing his own work since rejoining the group, Rollie Knight had watched, minute by minute, the movements and positions of the others, which fell into a pattern, but now and then with variations.

Each engine installed was lowered from

overhead on chains and pulleys, its maneuvering and release controlled by three pushbuttons—UP, STOP, DOWN—on a heavy electric cord hanging conveniently above the work station. Normally the engine decker operated the pushbuttons, though Rollie had learned to use them too.

A third man—in this instance the Afro hairdo worker—moved between stations, aiding the other two as needed.

Though the installation team worked fast, each engine was eased into place cautiously and, when almost seated, before the final drop, each man made sure his hands were clear.

As one engine was almost lowered and in place, its fuel and vacuum lines became entangled in the chassis front suspension. The hangup was momentary and occurred occasionally; when it did, the Afro hairdo worker moved in, reaching under the engine to clear the tangled lines. He did so now. The hands of the other two—Rollie and the engine decker—were safely removed.

Watching, choosing his moment, Rollie moved slightly sideways, reached up casually, then depressed and held the DOWN button. Instantly, a heavy, reverberating "thunk" announced that half a ton of engine and transmission had dropped solidly onto mounts beneath. Rollie released the button and, in the same movement, eased away.

For an infinitesimal fraction of a second the Afro hairdo worker remained silent, staring unbelieving at his hand, its fingers out of sight beneath the engine block. Then he screamed—again and again—a shrieking, demented wail of agony and horror, piercing all other sounds around, so that all men working fifty yards away raised their heads and craned uneasily to see the cause. The screams continued, fiendishly, unceasing, while someone hit an alarm button to stop the line, another the UP control to raise the engine assembly. As it lifted the screams took on a new excruciating edge, while those who were nearest looked with horror at the squashed, mangled jigsaw of blood and bones which seconds earlier had been fingers. As the injured worker's knees buckled, two men held him while his body heaved, his face contorted as tears streamed over lips mouthing incoherent, animal moans. A third worker, his own face ashen, reached for the mashed and pulpy hand, easing loose what he could, though a good deal stayed behind. When what was left of the hand was clear, the assembly line restarted.

The injured worker was carried away on a stretcher, his screams diminishing as morphine took hold. The drug had been administered by a nurse summoned hurriedly from the plant dispensary. She had put a temporary dressing on the hand, and her white uniform was blood-spattered as she walked beside the stretcher, accompanying it to an ambulance waiting out of doors.

Among the workers, no one looked at Rollie.

The foreman, Frank Parkland, and a plant safety man questioned those closest to the scene during a work break a few minutes later. A union steward was present.

The plant men demanded: What exactly happened?

It seemed that no one knew. Those who might have had knowledge claimed to have been looking some other way when the incident occurred.

"It doesn't figure," Parkland said. He stared hard at Rollie Knight. "Somebody must have seen."

The safety man asked, "Who hit the switch?"

No one answered. All that happened was an uneasy shuffling of feet, with eyes averted.

"Somebody did," Frank Parkland said. "Who was it?"

Still silence.

Then the engine decker spoke. He looked older, grayer, than before, and had been sweating so that the short hairs clung damply to his black scalp. "I reckon it was me. Guess I hit that button, let her drop." He added, mumbling, "Thought she was clear, the guy's hands out."

"You sure? Or are you covering?" Parkland's eyes returned, appraisingly, to Rollie Knight.

"I'm sure." The engine decker's voice was firmer. He lifted his head; his eyes met the foreman's. "Was an accident. I'm sorry."

"You should be," the safety man said. "You cost a guy his hand. And look at that!" He pointed to a board which read:

THIS PLANT HAS WORKED
1,897,560 MAN HOURS
WITHOUT AN ACCIDENT

"Now our score goes back to zero," the safety man said bitterly. He left the strong impression that this was what mattered most.

With the engine decker's firm statement, some of the tenseness had eased.

Someone asked, "What'll happen?"

"It's an accident, so no penalties," the union man said. He addressed Parkland and the safety man. "But there's an unsafe condition at this work station. It has to be corrected or we pull everybody out."

"Take it easy," Parkland cautioned. "Nobody's proved that yet."

"It's unsafe to get out of bed in the morning," the safety man protested. "If you do it with your eyes closed." He glowered again at the engine decker as, still deliberating, the trio moved away.

Soon after, those who had been questioned returned to work, the absent worker replaced by a new man who watched his hands nervously.

From then on, though nothing was ever said, Rollie Knight had no more trouble with his fellow workers. He knew why. Despite denials, those who had been close by were aware of what had happened, and now he had the reputation of being a man not to cross.

At first, when he had seen the smashed, bloody hand of his former tormentor, Rollie, too, was shocked and sickened. But as the stretcher moved away, so did the incident's immediacy, and since it was not in Rollie's nature to dwell on things, by the next working day—with a weekend in between—he had accepted what occurred as belonging in the past, and that was it. He did not fear reprisals. He sensed that, jungle law or not, a certain raw justice was on his side, and others knew it, including the engine decker who protected him.

The incident had other overtones.

In the way that information spreads about someone who has achieved attention, word of Rollie's prison record leaked. But rather than being an embarrassment, it made him, he discovered, something of a folk hero—at least to younger workers.

"Hear you done big time," a nineteen-year-old from the inner city told him. "Guess you give them whitey pigs a run before they gotcha, huh?"

Another youngster asked, "You carry a piece?"

Although Rollie knew that plenty of workers in the plant carried guns at all times—allegedly for protection against the frequent muggings which occurred in toilets or in parking lots— Rollie did not, being aware of the stiff sentence he would get if, with his record, a firearm were ever discovered on him. But he answered, noncommittally, "Quit buggin' me, kid," and soon another rumor was added to the rest: The little guy, Knight, was always armed. It was an additional cause for respect among the youthful militants.

One of them asked him, "Hey, you want a joint?"

He accepted. Soon, though not as frequently as some, Rollie was using marijuana on the assembly line, learning that it made a day go faster, the monotony more bearable. About the same time he began playing the numbers.

Later, when there was reason to think about it more, he realized that both drugs and numbers were his introduction to the complex, dangerous understratum of crime in the plant.

The numbers, to begin with, seemed innocent enough.

As Rollie knew, playing the numbers game— especially in auto plants—is, to Detroiters, as natural as breathing. Though the game is Mafia-controlled, demonstrably crooked, and the odds against winning are a thousand to one, it attracts countless bettors daily who wager anything from a nickel to a hundred dollars, occasionally more. The most common daily stake in plants, and the amount which Rollie bet himself, is a dollar.

But whatever the stake, a bettor selects three figures—any three—in the hope they will be the winning combination for that day. In event of a win, the payoff is 500 to 1, except that some bettors gamble on individual digits instead of all three, for which the odds are lower.

What seems to bother no one who plays numbers in Detroit is that the winning number is selected by betting houses from those combinations which have least money wagered on them. Only in nearby Pontiac, where the winning number is geared to race results and published pari-

mutuel payoffs, is the game—at least in this regard
—honest.

Periodically, raids on the so-called "Detroit
numbers ring" are made much of by the FBI, Detroit police, and others. RECORD NUMBERS RAID
or BIGGEST RAID IN U.S. HISTORY are apt to be
headlines in the *Detroit News* and *Free Press*, but
next day, and without much searching, placing a
numbers bet is as easy as ever.

As Rollie worked longer, the ways in which
numbers operated in the plant became clearer.
Janitors were among the many taking bets; in
their pails, under dry cloths, were the traditional
yellow slips which numbers writers used, as well
as cash collected. Both slips and cash were
smuggled from the plant, to be downtown by a
deadline—usually race track post time.

A union steward, Rollie learned, was the
numbers supervisor for Assembly; his regular
duties made it possible for him to move anywhere
in the plant without attracting attention. Equally
obvious was that betting was a daily addiction
which a majority of workers shared, including
supervisors, office personnel, and—so an informant assured Rollie—some of the senior managers. Because of the immunity with which the
numbers game flourished, the last seemed likely.

A couple of times after the crushed fingers
incident, Rollie received oblique suggestions that
he himself might participate actively in running
numbers, or perhaps one of the other rackets in
the plant. The latter, he knew, included loan
sharking, drug pushing, and illegal check cashing;
also, overlapping the milder activities, were organized theft rings, as well as frequent robberies
and assaults.

Rollie's criminal record, by now common
knowledge, had clearly given him *ex-officio* stand-

ing among the underworld element directly involved with crime in the plant, as well as those
who flirted with it in addition to their jobs. Once,
standing beside Rollie at a urinal, a burly, normally
taciturn worker known as Big Rufe, announced
softly, "Guys say you dig okay, I should tell you
there's ways a smart dude can do better 'n the
stinkin' sucker money they pay square Joes here."
He emptied his bladder with a grunt of satisfaction. "Times, we need hep guys who know the
score, don't scare easy." Big Rufe stopped, zipping
his fly as someone else came to stand beside
them, then turned away, nodding, the nod convey-
ing that sometime soon the two of them would
talk again.

But they hadn't because Rollie contrived to
avoid another meeting, and did the same thing
after a second approach by another source. His
reasons were mixed. The possibility of a return
to prison with a long sentence still haunted him;
also he had a feeling that his life, the way it was
now, was as good or better than it had been before,
ever. A big thing was the bread. Square Joe sucker
money or not, it sure corralled more than Rollie
had known in a long time, including booze, food,
some grass when he felt like it, and little sexpot
May Lou, whom he might tire of sometime, but
hadn't yet. She was no grand door prize, no beauty
queen, and he knew she had knocked around
plenty with other guys who had been there ahead
of him. But she could turn Rollie on. It made him
horny just to look at her, and he laid pipe, sometimes three times a night, especially when May
Lou really went to work, taking his breath away
with tricks she knew, which Rollie had heard of
but had never had done to him before.

It was the reason, really, he had let May Lou
find the two rooms they shared, and hadn't pro-

tested when she furnished them. She had done the furnishing without much money, asking Rollie only to sign papers which she brought. He did so indifferently, without reading, and later the furniture appeared, including a color TV as good as any in a bar.

In another way, though, the price of it all came high—long, wearying work days at the assembly plant, nominally five days a week, though sometimes four, and one week only three. Rollie, like others, absented himself on Monday, if hung over after a weekend, or on Friday, if wanting to start one early; but even when that happened, the money next payday was enough to swing with.

As well as the hardness of the work, its monotony persisted, reminding him of advice he had been given early by a fellow worker: "When you come here, leave your brains at home."

And yet . . . there was another side.

Despite himself, despite ingrained thought patterns which cautioned against being suckered and becoming a honky lackey, Rollie Knight began taking interest, developing a conscientiousness about the work that he was doing. A basic reason was his quick intelligence plus an instinct for learning, neither of which had had an opportunity to function before, as they were doing now. Another reason—which Rollie would have denied if accused of it—was a rapport, based on developing mutual respect, with the foreman, Frank Parkland.

At first, after the two incidents which brought Rollie Knight to his attention, Parkland had been hostile. But as a result of keeping close tab on Rollie, the hostility disappeared, approval replacing it. As Parkland expressed it to Matt Zaleski during one of the assistant plant manager's periodic tours of the assembly line, "See that little guy? His first week here I figured him for a trouble-maker. Now he's as good as anybody I got."

Zaleski had grunted, barely listening. Recently, at plant management level, several new fronts of troubles had erupted, including a requirement to increase production yet hold down plant costs and somehow raise quality standards. Though the three objectives were basically incompatible, top management was insisting on them, an insistence not helping Matt's duodenal ulcer, an old enemy within. The ulcer, quiescent for a while, now pained him constantly. Thus, Matt Zaleski could not find time for interest in individuals—only in statistics which regiments of individuals, like unconsidered Army privates, added up to.

This—though Zaleski had neither the philosophy to see it, nor power to change the system if he had—was a reason why North American automobiles were generally of poorer quality than those from Germany, where less rigid factory systems gave workers a sense of individuality and craftsmen's pride.

As it was, Frank Parkland did the best he could.

It was Parkland who ended Rollie's status as a relief man and assigned him to a regular line station. Afterward, Parkland moved Rollie around to other jobs on the assembly line, but at least without the bewildering hour-by-hour changes he endured before. Also, a reason for the moves was that Rollie, increasingly, could handle the more difficult, tricky assignments, and Parkland told him so.

A fact of life which Rollie discovered at this stage was that while most assembly line jobs were hard and demanding, a few were soft touches. Installing windshields was one of the soft ones. Workers doing this, however, were cagey when being watched, and indulged in extra, unneeded motions to make their task look tougher. Rollie worked on windshields, but only for a few days because Parkland moved him back down the line to one of the difficult jobs—scrabbling and twisting around inside car bodies to insert complicated wiring harnesses. Later still, Rollie handled a "blind operation"—the toughest kind of all, where bolts had to be inserted out of sight, then tightened, also by feel alone.

That was the day Parkland confided to him, "It isn't a fair system. Guys who work best, who a foreman can rely on, get the stinkingest jobs and a lousy deal. The trouble is, I need somebody on those bolts who I know for sure'll fix 'em and not goof off."

For Frank Parkland, it was an offhand remark. But to Rollie Knight it represented the first time that someone in authority had leveled with him, had criticized the system, told him something honest, something which he knew to be true, and had done it without bullshit.

Two things resulted. First, Rollie fitted every out-of-sight bolt correctly, utilizing a developing manual skill and an improved physique which regular eating now made possible. Second, he began observing Parkland carefully.

After a while, while not going so far as admiration, he saw the foreman as a non-bullshitter who treated others squarely—black or white, kept his word, and stayed honestly clear of the crap and corruption around him. There had been few people in Rollie's life of whom he could say, or think, as much.

Then, as happens when people elevate others beyond the level of human frailty, the image was destroyed.

Rollie had been asked, once more, if he would

help run numbers in the plant. The approach was by a lean, intense young black with a scar-marred face, Daddy-o Lester, who worked for stockroom delivery and was known to combine his work with errands for plant numbers bankers and the loan men. Rumor tied the scar, which ran the length of Daddy-o's face, to a knifing after he defaulted on a loan. Now he worked at the rackets' opposite end. Daddy-o assured Rollie, leaning into the work station where he had just delivered stock, "These guys like you. But they get the idea you don't like them, they liable to get rough."

Unimpressed, Rollie told him, "Your fat mouth don't scare me none. Beat it!"

Rollie had decided, weeks before, that he would play the numbers, but no more.

Daddy-o persisted, "A man gotta do somethin' to show he's a man, an' you ain't." As an afterthought, he added, "Leastways, not lately."

More for something to say than with a specific thought, Rollie protested, "For Cri-sakes, how you fixin' I'd take numbers here, with a foreman around."

Frank Parkland, at that moment, hove into view.

Daddy-o said contemptuously, "Screw that motha! He don't make trouble. He gets paid off."

"You lyin'."

"If I show you I ain't, that mean you're in?"

Rollie moved from the car he had been working on, spat beside the line, then climbed into the next. For a reason he could not define, uneasy doubts were stirring. He insisted, "Your word ain't worth nothin'. You show me first."

Next day, Daddy-o did.

Under pretext of a delivery to Rollie Knight's work station he revealed a grubby, unsealed envelope which he opened sufficiently for Rollie to see the contents—a slip of yellow paper and two twenty-dollar bills.

"Okay, fella," Daddy-o said. "Now watch!"

He walked to the small, stand-up desk which Parkland used—at the moment unoccupied—and lodged the envelope under a paperweight. Then he approached the foreman, who was down the line, and said something briefly. Parkland nodded. Without obvious haste, though not wasting time, the foreman returned to the desk where he took up the envelope, glanced briefly under the flap, then thrust it in an inside pocket.

Rollie, watching between intervals of working, needed no explanation. Nothing could be plainer than that the money was a bribe, a payoff.

Through the rest of that day, Rollie worked less carefully, missing several bolts entirely and failing to tighten others. *Who the hell cared?* He wondered why he was surprised. Didn't everything stink? It always had. Wasn't everybody on the take in every way? These people; all people. He remembered the course instructor who persuaded him to endorse checks, then stole Rollie's and other trainees' money. The instructor was one; now Parkland was another, so why should Rollie Knight be different?

That night Rollie told May Lou, "You know what this scumbag world is made of, baby? Bullshit! There ain't nuthin' in this whole wide world but bullshit."

Later the same week he began working for the plant numbers gang.

chapter fifteen

The portion of northern Michigan which encloses Higgins Lake is described by the local Chamber of Commerce as "Playtime Country."

Adam Trenton, Brett DeLosanto, and others attending Hank Kreisel's cottage weekend in late May, found the description apt.

The Kreisel "cottage"—in fact, a spacious, luxuriously appointed, multibedroomed lodge—was on the west shoreline of Higgins Lake's upper section. The entire lake forms a shape resembling a peanut or a fetus, the choice of description depending, perhaps, on the kind of stay a visitor happens to be having.

Adam located the lake and cottage without difficulty after driving alone on Saturday morning by way of Pontiac, Saginaw, Bay City, Midland, and Harrison—most of the two-hundred-mile journey on Interstate 75. Beyond the cities he found the Michigan countryside lushly green, aspen beginning to shimmer and the shad-blow in full bloom. The air was sweetly fresh. Sunshine beamed from a near-cloudless sky. Adam had been depressed on leaving home but felt his spirits rise as his wheels devoured the journey northward.

The depression stemmed from an argument with Erica.

Several weeks ago, when he informed her of the invitation to a stag weekend party, which Brett DeLosanto had conveyed, she merely remarked, "Well, if they don't want wives, I'll have to find something to do myself, won't I?" At the time, her reasonableness gave Adam second thoughts about going at all; he hadn't been keen to begin with, but yielded to Brett's insistence about wanting Adam to meet Brett's supplier friend, Hank Kreisel. Finally, Adam decided to leave things the way they were.

But Erica had obviously not made plans of her own, and this morning when he got up and began packing a few things, she asked, "Do you really have to go?" When he assured her at this stage he did because he had promised, she inquired pointedly, "Does 'stag' mean no women or merely no wives?"

"No women," he answered, not knowing if it were true or not, though suspecting not, because he had attended suppliers' weekend parties before.

"I'll bet!" They were in the kitchen by then, Erica brewing coffee and managing to bang the pot about. "And I suppose there'll be nothing stronger to drink than milk or lemonade."

He snapped back, "Whether there is or isn't, it'll be a damn sight more congenial than around here."

"And who makes it uncongenial?"

Adam had lost his temper then. "I'll be goddamned if I know. But if it's me, I don't seem to have that effect on others apart from you."

"Then go to your blasted others!" At that, Erica had thrown a coffee cup at him—fortunately empty—and, also fortunately, he caught it neatly and set it down unbroken. Or perhaps it wasn't fortunate because he had started to laugh, which made Erica madder than ever, and she stormed out, slamming the kitchen door behind her. Thoroughly angry himself by this time, Adam had flung his few things in the car and driven away.

Twenty miles up the road the whole thing seemed ludicrous, as married squabbles so often are in retrospect, and Adam knew if he had stayed home the whole thing would have blown over by midmorning. Later, near Saginaw, and feeling cheerful because of the kind of day it was, he tried to telephone home, but there was no answer. Erica had obviously gone out. He decided he would call again later.

Hank Kreisel greeted Adam on arrival at the Higgins Lake cottage, Kreisel managing to look simultaneously trim and casual in immaculately pressed Bermuda shorts and an Hawaiian shirt, his lean, lanky figure as militarily erect as always. When they had introduced themselves, Adam parked his car among seven or eight others—all late models in the luxury ranges.

Kreisel nodded toward the cars. "Few people came last night. Some still sleeping. More arriving later." He took Adam's overnight bag, then escorted him onto a timbered, covered walkway which extended around the cottage from the roadway side. The cottage itself was solidly built, with exterior walls of log siding and a central gable, supported by massive hand-hewn beams. Down at lake level was a floating dock at which several boats were moored.

Adam said, "I like your place, Hank."

"Thanks. Not bad, I guess. Didn't build it, though. Bought it from the guy who did. He poured in too much dough, then needed cash." Kreisel gave a twisted grin. "Don't we all?"

They stopped at a door, one of several opening onto the walkway. The parts manufacturer strode in, preceding Adam. Directly inside was a bedroom in which polished woodwork gleamed. In a fireplace, facing a double bed, a log fire was laid.

"Be glad of that. Can get cold at night," Kreisel said. He crossed to a window. "Gave you a room with a view."

"You sure did." Standing beside his host Adam could see the bright clear waters of the lake, superbly blue, shading to green near the sandy shoreline. The Higgins Lake location was in rolling hills—the last few miles of journey had been a steady climb—and around cottage and lake were magnificent stands of jack pines, spruce, balsam, tamarack, yellow pine, and birch. Judging by the panoramic view, Adam guessed he was being given the best bedroom. He wondered why. He was also curious about the other guests.

"When you're ready," Hank Kreisel announced, "bar's open. So's the kitchen. Don't have meals here. Just drinks and food twenty-four hours. Anything else can be arranged." He gave the twisted grin once more as he opened a door on the opposite side of the room from where they had entered. "There's two doors in 'n out—this and the other. Both lock. Makes for private coming and going."

"Thanks. If I need to, I'll remember."

When the other had gone, Adam unpacked the few things he had brought and, soon after, followed his host through the second door. It opened, he discovered, onto a narrow gallery above a central living area designed and furnished in hunting lodge style. The gallery extended around the living room and connected with a series of stone slab steps which, in turn, formed part of an immense rock fireplace. Adam descended the steps. The living area was unoccupied and he headed for a buzz of voices outside.

He emerged onto a spacious sun deck high above the lake. People, in a group, had been talking; now, one voice raised above others argued heatedly, "So help me, you people in this industry are acting more and more like nervous Nellies. You've gotten too damn sensitive to criticism and too defensive. You're encouraging the exhibitionists, making like they're big time sages instead of publicity hounds who want their names in papers and on television. Look at your annual meetings! Nowadays they're circuses. Some nut buys one share of company stock, then tells off the chairman of the board who stands there and takes it. It's like letting a single voter, any voter, go to Washington and sound off on the Senate floor."

"No, it isn't," Adam said. Without raising his voice he let it penetrate the conversation. "A voter doesn't have any right on the Senate floor, but a shareholder has rights at an annual meeting, even with one share. That's what our system's all about. And the critics aren't all cranks. If we start thinking so, and stop listening, we'll be back where we were five years ago."

"Hey!" Brett DeLosanto shouted. "Listen to those entrance lines, and look who got here!" Brett was wearing an exotic outfit in magenta and yellow, clearly self-designed, and resembling a Roman toga. Curiously, it managed to be dashing and practical. Adam, in slacks and turtleneck, felt conservative by contrast.

Several others who knew Adam greeted him, including Pete O'Hagan, the man who had been speaking when he came in. O'Hagan represented one of the major national magazines in Detroit, his job to court auto industry brass socially—a subtle but effective way of soliciting advertising. Most big magazines had similar representation, their people sometimes becoming cronies of company presidents or others at high level. Such friendships became known to advertising agencies who rarely challenged them; thus, when advertising had to be cut, the publications with top bracket influence were last to be hurt. Typically, despite Adam's blunt contradiction of what had been said, O'Hagan showed no resentment, only smiles.

"Come, meet everybody," Hank Kreisel said. He steered Adam around the group. Among the guests were a congressman, a judge, a network TV personality, two other parts manufacturers and several senior people from Adam's own company, including a trio of purchasing agents. There was also a young man who offered his hand and smiled engagingly as Adam approached. "Smokey told me about you, sir. I'm Pierre Flodenhale."

"Of course." Adam remembered the youthful race driver whom he had seen, doubling as a car salesman, at Smokey Stephensen's dealership. "How are your sales?"

"When there's time to work at it, pretty good, sir."

Adam told him, "Cut the 'sir' stuff. Only first names here. You had bad luck in the Daytona 500."

"Sure did." Pierre Flodenhale pushed back his shock of blond hair and grimaced. Two months earlier he had completed a hundred and eighty grueling laps at Daytona, was leading with only twenty laps to go, when a blown engine head put him out of the race. "Felt like stomping on that old car after," he confided.

"If it had been me, I'd have pushed it off a cliff."

"Guess maybe I'll do better soon." The race driver gave a boyish smile; he had the same pleasant manner as when Adam had observed him previously. "Got a feeling this year I might pull off the Talladega 500."

"I'll be at Talladega," Adam said. "We're exhibiting a concept Orion there. So I'll cheer for you."

From somewhere behind, Hank Kreisel's voice cut in. "Adam, this is Stella. She'll do anything for you."

"Like getting a drink," a girl's pleasing voice said. Adam found a pretty, petite redhead beside him. She was wearing the scantiest of bikinis. "Hullo, Mr. Trenton."

"Hullo." Adam saw two other girls nearby

and remembered Erica's question: *Does "stag" mean no women or merely no wives?*

"I'm glad you like my swimsuit," Stella told Pierre, whose eyes had been exploring.

The race driver said, "Hadn't noticed you were wearing one."

The girl returned to Adam. "About that drink."

He ordered a Bloody Mary. "Don't go 'way," she told him. "Be back soon."

Pierre asked, "What's a 'concept' Orion, Adam?"

"It's a special kind of car made up for showing in advance of the real thing. In the trade we call it a 'one off.' "

"But the one at Talladega—it won't be a genuine Orion?"

"No," Adam said. "The real Orion isn't due until a month later. The 'concept' will resemble the Orion though we're not saying how closely. We'll show it around a lot. The idea is to get people talking, speculating on—how will the final Orion look?" He added, "You could say it's a sort of teaser."

"I can play that," Stella said. She had returned with Adam's drink and one for Pierre.

The congressman moved over to join them. He had flowing white hair, a genial manner and a strong, though pontifical voice. "I was interested in what you said about your industry listening, Mr. Trenton. I trust some of the listening is to what legislators are saying."

Adam hesitated. His inclination was to answer bluntly, as usual, but this was a party; he was a guest. He caught the eye of Hank Kreisel who seemed to have a knack of being everywhere and overhearing anything that mattered. "Feel free," Kreisel said. "A few fights won't hurt. We got a doctor coming."

Adam told the congressman, "What's coming out of legislatures right now is mostly foolishness from people who want their names in the news and know that blasting the auto industry, whether it makes sense or not, will do the trick."

The congressman flushed as Adam persisted, "A U.S. senator wants to ban automobiles in five years' time if they have internal combustion engines, though he hasn't any notion what will replace them. Well, if it happened, the only good thing is, he couldn't get around to make silly speeches. Some states have brought lawsuits in efforts to make us recall all cars built since 1953 and rebuild them to emission standards that didn't exist until 1966 in California, 1968 elsewhere."

"Those are extremes," the congressman protested. His speech slurred slightly, and the drink in his hand was clearly not his first of the day.

"I agree they're extremes. But they're representative of what we're hearing from legislators, and that—if I remember—was your question."

Hank Kreisel, reappearing, said cheerfully, "Was the question, all right." He slapped the congressman across the shoulders. "Watch out, Woody! These young fellas in Detroit got sharp minds. Brighter 'n you're used to in Washington."

"You'd never think," the congressman informed the group, "that when this character Kreisel and I were Marines together, he used to salute me."

"If that's what you're missing, General . . ." Hank Kreisel, still in his smart Bermuda shorts, snapped to rigid attention and executed a parade ground-style salute. Afterward he commanded, "Stella, get the senator another drink."

"I wasn't a general," the congressman complained. "I was a chicken colonel, and I'm not a senator."

"You were never a chicken, Woody," Kreisel

assured him. "And you'll make it to senator. Probably over this industry's corpse."

"Judging by you, and this place, it's a damn healthy corpse." The congressman returned his gaze to Adam. "Want to beat any more hell out of politicians?"

"Maybe a little." Adam smiled. "Some of us think it's time our lawmakers did a few positive things instead of just parroting the critics."

"Positive like what?"

"Like enacting some public enforcement laws. Take one example: air pollution. Okay, anti-pollution standards for new-built cars are here. Most of us in the industry agree they're good, are necessary, and were overdue." Adam was aware of the size of the group around them increasing, other conversations breaking off. He went on, "But what people like *you* ask of people like *us* is to produce an anti-pollutant device which won't go wrong, or need checking or adjustment, for the entire life of every car. Well, it can't be done. It's no more logical to expect it than to ask any piece of machinery to work perfectly forever. So what's needed? A law with teeth, a law requiring regular inspection of car pollutant devices, then repair or replacement when necessary. But it would be an unpopular law because the public doesn't really give two hoots about pollution and only cares about convenience. That's why politicians are afraid of it."

"The public does care," the congressman said heatedly. "I've mail to prove it."

"Some individuals care. The public doesn't. For more than two years," Adam insisted, "we've had pollution control kits available for older cars. The kits cost twenty dollars installed, and we *know* they work. They reduce pollution and make air purer—anywhere. The kits have been promoted, advertised on TV, radio, billboards, but almost nobody buys them. Extras on cars—even old cars—like whitewall tires or stereo tape decks are selling fine. But nobody wants antipollution kits; they're the least selling item we ever made. And the legislators you asked me about, who lecture us about clean air at the drop of a vote, haven't shown the slightest interest either."

Stella's voice and several others chorused, "Spare ribs! Spare ribs!"

The group around Adam and the congressman thinned. "About time," somebody said. "We haven't eaten for an hour."

The sight of piled food, now on a buffet at the rear of the sun deck presided over by a white-capped chef, reminded Adam that he had not had breakfast, due to his fight with Erica, and was hungry. He also remembered he must call home soon.

One of the purchasing agent guests, holding a plate heaped high with food, called out, "Great eating, Hank!"

"Glad you like it," his host acknowledged. "And with you guys here it's all deductible."

Adam smiled with the others, knowing that what Kreisel had said was true—that the purchasing agents' presence made this a business occasion, to be deducted eventually on Hank Kreisel's income tax return. The reasoning: auto company purchasing agents, who allocated millions of dollars' worth of orders annually, held a life or death authority over parts manufacturers like Kreisel. In older days, because of this, purchasing agents were accustomed to receive munificent gifts— even a lake cruiser or a houseful of furniture— from suppliers whom they favored. Now, auto companies forbade that kind of graft and an offender, if caught, was fired summarily. Just the same, perks for purchasing agents still existed, and being entertained socially, on occasions like

this or privately, was one. Another was having
personal hotel bills picked up by suppliers or their
salesmen; this was considered safe since neither
goods nor money changed hands directly, and
later, if necessary, a purchasing agent could deny
knowledge, saying he had expected the hotel to
bill him. And gifts at Christmastime remained one
more.

The Christmas handouts were forbidden annually by auto company managements in memos
circulated during November and December. But
just as inevitably, purchasing department secretaries prepared lists of purchasing staff home addresses which were handed out to suppliers' salesmen on request, a request considered as routine
as saying, "Merry Christmas!" The secretaries'
home addresses were always on the lists and,
though purchasing agents allegedly knew nothing
of what was going on, somehow their addresses
got there, too. The gifts which resulted—none
delivered to the office—were not as lavish as in
older days, but few suppliers risked failing to be-
stow them.

Adam was still watching the purchasing
agent with the piled plate when a soft, feminine
voice murmured, "Adam Trenton, do you always
say just what you're thinking?"

He turned. In front of him, regarding him
amusedly, was a girl of twenty-eight or thirty,
Adam guessed. Her high-cheekboned face was up-
tilted, her moist full lips lightly parted in a smile.
Intelligent bright eyes met his own directly. He
sensed a musky perfume, was aware of a lithe,
slender figure with small, firm breasts beneath a
tailored powder-blue linen dress. She was, Adam
thought, one of the most breathtakingly beautiful
women he had ever seen. And she was black. Not
brown, but black; a deep, rich black, her smooth

unblemished skin like silken ebony. He curbed an impulse to reach out, touching her.

"My name is Rowena," the girl said. "I was told yours. And I've been asked to see that you get something to eat."

"Rowena what?"

He sensed her hesitate. "Does it matter?" She smiled, so that he was aware of the full redness and moisture of her lips again.

"Besides," Rowena said, "I asked you a question first. You haven't answered it."

Adam remembered she had asked something about—did he always say what he was thinking?

"Not always. I don't believe any of us do really." He thought: *I'm sure as hell not doing it now*, then added aloud, "When I do say anything, though, I try to make it honest and what I mean."

"I know. I was listening to you talking. Not enough of us do that."

The girl's eyes met his own and held them steadily. He wondered if she sensed her impact on him, and suspected that she did.

The chef at the buffet, with Rowena's aid, filled two plates which they carried to one of the sun deck tables nearby. Already seated were the judge—a youngish Negro who was on the federal bench in Michigan—and another guest from Adam's company, a middle-aged development engineer named Frazon. Moments later they were joined by Brett DeLosanto, accompanied by an attractive, quiet brunette whom he introduced as Elsie.

"We figured this is where the action is," Brett said. "Don't disappoint us."

Rowena asked, "What kind do you have in mind?"

"You know us auto people. We've only two interests—business and sex."

The judge smiled. "It's early. Perhaps we

should take business first." He addressed Adam. "A while ago you were talking about company annual meetings. I liked what you said—that people, even with a single share, should be listened to."

Frazon, the engineer, as if rising to a bait, put down his knife and fork. "Well, I didn't. I don't agree with Adam, and there are plenty more who feel the way I do."

"I know," the judge said. "I saw you react. Won't you tell us why?"

Frazon considered, frowning. "All right. What the loudmouth one-share people want, including consumer groups and the so-called corporate responsibility committee, is to create disruption, and they do it by distortion, lies, and insult. Remember the General Motors annual meeting, when the Nader gang called everybody in the industry 'corporate criminals,' then talked about our 'disregard for law and justice,' and said we were part of 'a corporate crime wave dwarfing street crime by comparison'? How are we supposed to feel when we hear that? Grateful? How are we supposed to take clowns who mouth that kind of claptrap? Seriously?"

"Say!" Brett DeLosanto interjected. "You engineering guys were listening. We thought the only thing you ever heard was motor noises."

"They heard, all right," Adam said. "We all heard—those in General Motors, the other companies too. But what a lot of industry people missed was that the very words just quoted"—he motioned toward Frazon—"were intended to anger and inflame and prevent a reasonable response. The protesting crowd didn't want the auto industry to be reasonable; if it had, we'd have cut the ground from under them. And what they planned, worked. Our people fell for it."

The judge prompted, "Then you see invective as a tactic."

"Of course. It's the language of our times, and the kids who use it—bright young lawyers mostly—know exactly what it does to old men in board rooms. It curls their hair, raises their blood pressure, makes them rigid and unyielding. The chairmen and directors in our industry were reared on politeness; in their heyday, even when you knifed a competitor, you said 'excuse me.' But not any more. Now the dialogue is harsh and snarly, and points are scored by overstatement, so if you're listening—and smart—you underreact and keep cool. Most of our top people haven't learned that yet."

"I haven't learned it, and don't intend to," Frazon said. "I'll stick with decent manners."

Brett quipped, "There speaks an engineer, the ultimate conservative!"

"Adam's an engineer," Frazon pointed out. "Trouble is, he's spent too much time around designers."

The group at the table laughed.

Looking at Adam, Frazon said, "Surely you're not suggesting we should go along with what the militants at annual meetings want—consumer reps on boards of directors, all the rest?"

Adam answered quietly, "Why not? It could show we're willing to be flexible, and might be worth a try. Put somebody on a board—or on a jury—they're apt to take it seriously, not be just a maverick. We might even end up learning something. Besides, it will happen eventually and we'd be better off if we *made* it happen now instead of being forced into it later."

Brett asked, "Judge, what's your verdict now you've heard both sides?"

"Excuse me." The judge put a hand to his mouth, stifling a yawn. "For a moment I thought I was in court." He shook his head in mock solemnity. "Sorry. I never hand down opinions on week-ends."

"Nor should anyone," Rowena declared. She touched Adam's hand, letting her fingers travel lightly over his. When he turned toward her, she said softly, "Will you take me swimming?"

The two of them took a boat from the floating dock—one of Hank Kreisel's with an outboard which Adam used to propel them, unhurriedly, four miles or so toward the lake's eastern shore. Then, within sight of a beach with towering leafy trees behind, he cut the motor and they drifted on the blue translucent water. A few other boats, not many, came into sight and went away. It was mid-afternoon. The sun was high, the air drowsy. Before they left, Rowena had changed into a swim-suit; it was leopard patterned and what it revealed of her figure, as well as the soft, silken blackness of her skin, more than fulfilled the promise of the linen dress she had had on earlier. Adam was in trunks. When they stopped, he lighted cigarettes for them both. They sat beside each other on the cushions of the boat.

"Um," Rowena said. "This is nice." Her head was back, eyes closed against the brightness of the sun and lake. Her lips were parted.

He blew a smoke ring lazily. "It's called get-ting away from it all." His voice, for some reason, was unsteady.

She said softly, with sudden seriousness, "I know. It doesn't happen often. And it never lasts."

Adam turned. Instinct told him that if he reached for her she would respond. But for sec-onds of uncertainty he hesitated.

As if reading his mind, Rowena laughed lightly. She dropped her cigarette into the water. "We came to swim, remember?"

With a swift, single movement she rose and dived over the side. He had an impression of her lithe dark body, straight-limbed and like an arrow. Then, with a whipcrack sound and splash, she was out of sight. The boat rocked gently.

Adam hesitated again, then dived in too. After the sun's heat, the fresh lake water struck icily cold. He came up with a gasp, shivering, and looked around.

"Hey! Over here!" Rowena was still laughing. She bobbed under the surface, then re-emerged, water streaming down her face and hair. "Isn't it wonderful?"

"When I get my circulation back, I'll tell you."

"Your blood needs heating, Adam. I'm going ashore. Coming?"

"I guess so. But we can't leave Hank's boat to drift."

"Then bring it." Already swimming strongly toward the beach, Rowena called back, "That's if you're afraid of being marooned with me."

More slowly, towing the boat, Adam followed. Ashore, and welcoming the sun's warmth again, he beached the boat, then joined Rowena who was lying on the sand, her hands behind her head. Beyond the beach, sheltered in trees, was a cottage, but shuttered and deserted.

"Since you brought it up," Adam said, "at this moment I can't think of anyone I'd sooner be marooned with." He, too, stretched out on the sand, aware of being more relaxed than he had felt in months.

'You don't know me."

"You've aroused certain instincts." He propped himself on an elbow, confirming that the girl beside him was as breathtakingly lovely as she had seemed when he met her several hours ago, then added, "One of them is curiosity."

"I'm just someone you met at a party; one of Hank Kreisel's weekend parties where he employs hostesses. And in case you're wondering, that's *all* he employs us for. *Were* you wondering?"

"Yes."

She gave the soft laugh he had grown used to. "I knew you were. The difference between you and most men is that the others would have lied and said 'no.' "

"And the rest of the week, when there aren't parties?"

"I'm a high school teacher." Rowena stopped. "Damn! I didn't mean to tell you that."

"Then we'll even the score," Adam said. "There was something I didn't intend to tell *you*."

"Which is?"

He assured her softly, "For the first time in my life I know, really know, what it means when they say 'Black is Beautiful.' "

In the silence which followed, he wondered if he had offended her. He could hear the lapping of the lake, a hum of insects, an outboard motor in the distance. Rowena said nothing. Then, without warning, she leaned over and kissed him fully on the lips.

Before he could respond she sprang up, and ran down the beach toward the lake. From the water's edge she called back, "Hank said you had the reputation of being a sweet man when he told me to take special care of you. Now let's go back."

In the boat, heading for the west shore, he asked, "What else did Hank say?"

Rowena considered. "Well, he told me you'd be the most important person here, and that one day you'll be right at the top of your company."

This time, Adam laughed.

He was still curious, though, about Kreisel and his motives.

Sunset came, the party at the cottage continuing—and livening—as the hours passed. Before the sun disappeared, at last, behind a squad of white birches like silhoutted sentinels, the lake was alive with color. A breeze stirred its surface, bearing fresh, pine-scented air. Dusk eased in, then darkness. As stars came out, the night air cooled and the party drifted from the sun deck to indoors where, in the great rock fireplace, heaped brush and logs were blazing.

Hank Kreisel, an affable, attentive host, seemed everywhere, as he had throughout the day. Two bars and the kitchen were staffed and bustling; what Kreisel had said earlier about drinks and food available twenty-four hours each day seemed true. In the spacious, hunting lodge-style living room the party split into groups, some overlapping. A cluster around Pierre Flodenhale fired auto racing questions. ". . . *say a race is won or lost in the pits. Is that your experience?*" . . . "*Yes, but a driver's planning does it too. Before the race you plan how you'll run it, lap by lap. In the race you plan the next lap, changing the first plan . . .*" The network TV personality, who had been diffident earlier, had blossomed and was doing a skillful imitation of the U.S. President, supposedly on television with a car maker and an environmentalist, trying to appease both. "*Pollution, with all its faults, is part of our great American know-how . . . My scientific advisers assure me cars are polluting less than they used—at least, they would if there weren't more cars.*" (*Cough, cough, cough!*) . . . "*I pledge we'll have clean air again in this country. Administration policy is to pipe it to every home . . .*" Among those listening, one or two looked sour, but most laughed.

Some of the girls, including Stella and Elsie, moved from group to group. Rowena stayed close to Adam.

Gradually, as midnight came and went, the numbers thinned. Guests yawned, stretched tiredly, and soon after climbed the stone stairway at the fireplace, some calling down goodnights from the gallery to the holdouts who remained below. One or two exited by the sun deck, presumably reaching their rooms by the alternate route which Hank Kreisel had showed to Adam earlier. Eventually, Kreisel himself—carrying a sourmash Bourbon—went upstairs. Soon after, Adam noticed, Elsie disappeared. So did Brett DeLosanto and the redhead, Stella, who had spent the last hour close together.

In the great hearth the fire was burning down to embers. Apart from Adam and Rowena, both on a sofa near the fireplace, only one group remained at the room's opposite end, still drinking, noisy, and obviously with the intention of staying for a long time.

"A nightcap?" Adam asked.

Rowena shook her head. Her last drink—a mild Scotch and water—had lasted her an hour. Through the evening they had talked, mostly about Adam, though not by his choice but because Rowena adroitly parried questions about herself. But he had learned that her teaching specialty was English, which she admitted after laughingly quoting Cervantes: *"My memory is so bad, that many times I forget my own name."*

Now he stood up. "Let's go outside."

"All right."

As they left, no one in the other group glanced their way.

The moon had risen. The night was cold and clear. Moonbeams shimmered on the surface of the lake. He felt Rowena shiver, and put an arm around her.

"Almost everyone," Adam said, "seems to have gone to bed."

Again Rowena's gentle laugh. "I saw you noticing."

He turned her to him, tilted her head, and kissed her. "Let's us."

Their lips met again. He felt her arms around him tighten.

She whispered, "What I said was true. This isn't in the contract."

"I know."

"A girl can make her own arrangements here, but Hank sees to it she doesn't have to." She snuggled closer. "Hank would want you to know that. He cares what you think about him."

"At this moment," he whispered back, "I'm not thinking of Hank at all."

They entered Adam's bedroom from the outside walkway—the route he had used this morning on arrival. Inside, the room was warm. Someone, thoughtfully, had been in to light the fire; now, tongues of flame cast light and shadows on the ceiling. The coverlet was off the double bed, with sheets turned back.

In front of the fire, Adam and Rowena slipped out of what they were wearing. Soon after, he led her to the bed.

He had expected tenderness. He found, instead, a savagery in Rowena which at first amazed, soon after excited and, before long, inflamed him, too. Nothing in his experience had prepared him for the wild, tempestuous passion she unleashed. For both of them, it lasted—with gaps which human limits demanded—through the night.

Near dawn she inquired mischievously, "Do you still think black is beautiful?"

He told her, and meant it, "More than ever."

They had been lying, quietly, side by side. Now Rowena propped herself up and looked at him. She was smiling. "And for a honky, you're not bad."

As he had yesterday afternoon, he lit two

cigarettes and gave her one. After a while she said, "I guess black is beautiful, the way they say. But then I guess everything's beautiful if you look at it on the right kind of day."

"Is this that kind of day?"

"You know what I'd say today? Today, I'd say 'ugly is beautiful'!"

It was getting light. Adam said, "I want to see you again. How do we manage it?"

For the first time, Rowena's voice was sharp. "We don't, and both of us know it." When he protested, she put a finger across his lips. "We haven't lied to each other. Don't let's begin."

He knew she was right, that what had begun here would end here. Detroit was neither Paris nor London, nor even New York. At heart, Detroit was a small town still, beginning to tolerate more than it used to, but he could not have Detroit and Rowena—on any terms. The thought saddened him. It continued to, through the day, and as he left Higgins Lake for the return journey southward late that afternoon.

When he thanked his host before leaving, Hank Kreisel said, "Haven't talked much, Adam. Wish we'd had more chance. Mind if I call you next week?"

He assured Kreisel that he could.

Rowena, to whom Adam had said goodbye privately, behind two locked doors an hour earlier, was not in sight.

chapter sixteen

"Oh, Christ!" Adam said. "I forgot to phone my wife." He remembered, guiltily, intending since Saturday morning to call Erica and patch up the quarrel they had had before he left. Now it was Sunday evening and he still hadn't. In the meantime, of course, there had been Rowena, who eclipsed less immediate matters, and Adam had an unease, too, about facing Erica after *that*.

"Shall we turn off and find a pay phone?" Pierre Flodenhale asked. They were on Interstate 75, southbound, near the outskirts of Flint, and Pierre was driving Adam's car, as he had been since leaving the Higgins Lake cottage. The young race driver had come to the cottage with someone else who left early, and Adam had been glad to offer him a ride, as well as to have company on the way back to Detroit. Moreover, when Pierre offered to drive, Adam accepted gratefully and had dozed through the early part of the journey.

Now it was growing dark. Their headlights were among many slicing homeward from the country to the city.

"No," Adam said. "If we stop, it will waste time. Let's keep going."

He put out a hand tentatively to the Citizens Band radio beneath the instrument panel. They would be coming within range of Greater Detroit soon, and it was possible that Erica might have switched on the kitchen receiver, as she did on weekdays. Then he let his hand drop, deciding not to call. He was increasingly nervous, he realized, about talking with Erica, a nervousness which increased a half hour later as they passed Bloomfield Hills, then, soon after, left the freeway and turned west toward Quarton Lake.

He had intended to let Pierre, who lived in Dearborn, take the car on directly after dropping him off. Instead, Adam invited Pierre in and was relieved when he accepted. At least, Adam thought, he would have the foil of a stranger for a while before having to face Erica alone.

He need not have worried.

As the car crunched to a halt on the driveway gravel of the Trentons' house, lights went on, the front door opened, and Erica came out to greet Adam warmly.

"Welcome, darling! I missed you." She kissed him, and he knew it was her way of showing that Saturday's incident was over and need not be mentioned again.

What Adam did not know was that part of Erica's good spirits stemmed from a dress watch which she was wearing, the watch acquired during a further shoplifting adventure while he had been away.

Pierre Flodenhale climbed out from behind the wheel. Adam introduced him.

Erica gave her most dazzling smile. "I've seen you race." She added, "If I'd known you were driving Adam home, though, I might have been nervous."

"He's a lot slower than I am," Adam said. "Didn't break the speed limit once."

"How dull! I hope the party was livelier."

"Not all that much, Mrs. Trenton. Compared with some I've been at, it was quiet. Gets that way, I guess, when you only have men."

Don't push it, pal! Adam wanted to caution. He saw Erica glance at Pierre shrewdly, and suspected the young race driver was not used to the company of highly intelligent, perceptive women. Pierre was clearly impressed with Erica, though, who looked young and beautiful in silk Pucci pajamas, her long ash-blond hair falling around her shoulders.

They went into the house, mixed drinks, and took them to the kitchen where Erica made fried egg sandwiches for them all, and coffee. Adam left the other two briefly—to make a telephone call, and, tired as he was, to collect files he must work on tonight in preparation for the morning. When he returned, Erica was listening attentively to a discourse on auto racing—an extension, apparently, to Pierre's remarks to the group around him at the cottage.

Pierre had a sheet of paper spread out on which he had drawn the layout of a speedway track. ". . . so heading in to the mainstretch in front of the stands, you want the straightest line possible. At two hundred miles an hour, if you let the car wander you lose time bad. Wind's usually across the track, so you stay close to the wall, hug that old wall tight as you can . . ."

"I've seen drivers do it," Erica said. "It always frightens me. If you ever hit the wall at a speed like that . . ."

"If you do, you're safer hitting flat, Mrs. Trenton. I've been in a few walls . . ."

"Call me Erica," Erica said. "Have you really?"

Adam, listening, was amused. He had taken Erica to auto races, but had never known her to show this much concern. He thought: perhaps it was because she and Pierre liked each other instinctively. The fact that they did was obvious, and the young race driver was glowing, responding boyishly to Erica's interest. Adam felt grateful for the chance to regain his own composure without being the focus of his wife's attention. Despite his return home, thoughts of Rowena were still strong in Adam's mind.

"Every track you race on, Erica," Pierre was saying, "a driver has to learn to handle it like it was a . . ." He hesitated for a simile, then added, "like a violin."

"Or a woman," Erica said. They both laughed.

"You have to know where every bump is in that old track, the low spots, what the surface gets like with a real hot sun, or after a sprinkle of rain. So you practice and practice, driving and driving, 'til you find the best way, the fastest line around."

Seated across the room, his files now beside him, Adam threw in, "Sounds a lot like life."

The other two seemed not to have heard. Obviously, Adam decided, they would not mind if he got on with some work.

"When you're in a long race, say five hundred miles," Erica said, "does your mind ever wander? Do you ever think of something else?"

Pierre gave his boyish grin. "God, no! Not if you figure to win, or even walk away instead of being carried out." He explained, "You've a lot to keep checking and remember. How others in the race are doing, your plans for passing guys ahead, or how not to let guys past you. Or maybe there's trouble, like if you scuff a tire it'll take a tenth of a second off your speed. So you feel it happen, you remember, you do sums in your head, figure everything, then decide when to pit for a tire change, which can win a race or lose it. You watch oil pressure fifty yards before entering every corner, then, on the backstretch, check all gauges, and you keep both ears tuned to the way the engine sings. Then there's signals from the pit crew to look out for. Some days you could use a secretary . . ."

Adam, concentrating on memo reading, screened the voices of Pierre and Erica out.

"I never knew all that," Erica said. "It will

seem different watching now. I'll feel like an insider."

"I'd like to have you see me race, Erica." Pierre glanced across the room, then back. He lowered his voice slightly. "Adam said you'd be at the Talladega 500, but there's other races before that."

"Where?"

"North Carolina, for one. Maybe you could come." He looked at her directly and she was aware, for the first time, of a touch of arrogance, the star syndrome, the knowledge that he was a hero to the crowd. She supposed a lot of women had come Pierre's way.

"North Carolina's not so far." Erica smiled. "It's something to think about, isn't it?"

Some time later, the fact that Pierre Flodenhale was standing penetrated Adam's consciousness.

"I guess I'll be moving on, Adam," Pierre said. "Thanks a lot for the ride and having me in."

Adam returned a folder to his briefcase—a ten-year population shift estimate, prepared for study in conjunction with consumer car preference trends. He apologized, "I haven't been much of a host. I hope my wife made up for me."

"Sure did."

"You can take my car." He reached in his pocket for keys. "If you'll phone my secretary tomorrow, tell her where it is, she'll have it picked up."

Pierre hesitated. "Thanks, but Erica said . . ."

Erica bustled into the living room, pulling a light car coat over her pajamas. "I'll drive Pierre home."

Adam started to say, "There's no need . . ."

"It's a nice night," she insisted. "And I feel like some air."

Moments later, outside, car doors slammed, an engine revved and receded. The house was silent.

Adam worked a half hour more, then went upstairs. He was climbing into bed when he heard the car return and Erica come in, but was asleep by the time she reached the bedroom.

He dreamed of Rowena.

Erica dreamed of Pierre.

chapter seventeen

A belief among automobile product planners is that the most successful ideas for new cars are conceived suddenly, like unannounced star shell bursts, during informal, feet-on-desk bull sessions in the dead of night.

There are precedents proving this true. Ford's Mustang—most startling Detroit trend setter after World War II, and forerunner to an entire generation of Ford, GM, Chrysler, and American Motors products afterward—had its origins that way, and so, less spectacularly, have others. This is the reason why product teams sometimes linger in offices when others are abed, letting their smoke and conversation drift, and hoping—like prospicient Cinderellas—that magic in some form will touch their minds.

On a night in early June—two weeks after Hank Kreisel's cottage party—Adam Trenton and Brett DeLosanto nurtured the same kind of wish.

Because the Orion, also, was begun at night, they and others hoped that a muse for Farstar— next major project ahead—might be wooed the same way. Over several months past, innumerable think sessions had been held—some involving large groups, others small, and still more composed of duos like Adam and Brett—but from none of them yet had anything emerged to confirm a direction which must be decided on soon. The basement block work (as Brett DeLosanto called it) had been done. Projection papers were assembled which asked and answered, more or less: *Where are we today? Who's selling to whom? What are we doing right? Wrong? What do people think they want in a car? What do they really want? Where will they, and we, be five years from now? Politically? Socially? Intellectually? Sexually? What'll populations be? Tastes? Fashions? What new issues, controversies, will evolve? How will age groups shape up? And who'll be rich? Poor? In between? Where? Why?* All these, and a myriad other questions, facts, statistics, had sped in and out of computers. Now what was needed was something no computer could simulate: a gut feeling, a hunch, a shaft of insight, a touch of genius.

One problem was: to determine the shape of Farstar, they ought to know how Orion would fare. But the Orion's introduction was still four months away; even then, its impact could not be judged fully until half a year after that. So what the planners must do was what the auto industry had always done because of long lead times required for new models—guess.

Tonight's session, for Adam and Brett, began in the company teardown room.

The teardown room was more than a room; it was a department occupying a closely guarded building—a storehouse of secrets which few outsiders penetrated. Those who did, however, found it a source of unwaveringly honest information, for the teardown room's function was to dissect company products and competitors', then compare them objectively with each other. All big three auto companies had teardown rooms of their own, or comparable systems.

In the teardown environment, if a competitor's car or component was sturdier, lighter, more economical, assembled better, or superior in any other way, the analysts said so. No local loyalties ever swayed a judgment.

Company engineers and designers who had boobed were sometimes embarrassed by teardown room revelations, though they would be even more embarrassed if word leaked out to press or

public. It rarely did. Nor did other companies release adverse reports about defects in competitors'
cars; they knew it was a tactic which could boom-
erang tomorrow. In any case, objectives of the
teardown room were positive—to police the company's products and designs, and to learn from
others.

Adam and Brett had come to study three
small cars in their torndown state—the company's
own minicompact, a Volkswagen, and another import, Japanese.

A technician, working late at Adam's request,
admitted them through locked outer doors to a
lighted lobby, then through more doors to a large
high-ceilinged room, lined with recessed racks extending from floor to ceiling.

"Sorry to spoil your evening, Neil," Adam
said. "We couldn't make it sooner."

"No sweat, Mr. Trenton. I'm on overtime."
The elderly technician, a skilled mechanic who
had once worked on assembly lines and now
helped take cars apart, led the way to a section of
racks, some of which had been pulled out. "Everything's ready that you asked for."

Brett DeLosanto looked around him. Though
he had been here many times before, the teardown
operation never failed to fascinate him.

The department bought cars the way the
public did—through dealers. Purchases were in
names of individuals, so no dealer ever knew a
car that he was selling was for detailed study instead of normal use. The precaution ensured that
all cars received were routine production models.

As soon as a car arrived, it was driven to the
basement and taken apart. This did not mean
merely separating the car's components, but involved total disassembly. As it was done, each
item was numbered, listed, described, its weight
recorded. Oily, greasy parts were cleaned.

It took four men between ten days and two weeks to reduce a normal car to ordered fragments, mounted on display boards.

A story—no one really knew how true—was sometimes told about a teardown crew which, as a practical joke, worked in spare time to disassemble a car belonging to one of their number who was holidaying in Europe. When the vacationer returned, the car was in his garage, undamaged, but in several thousand separate parts. He was a competent mechanic who had learned a good deal as a teardown man, and he determinedly put it together again. It took a year.

Techniques of total disassembly were so specialized that unique tools had been devised—some like a plumber's nightmare.

The display boards containing the torn-down vehicles were housed in sliding racks. Thus, like dissected corpses, the industry's current cars were available for private viewing and comparison.

A company engineer might be brought here and told: "Look at the competition's headlamp cans! They're an integrated part of the radiator support instead of separate, complex pieces. Their method is cheaper and better. Let's get with it!"

It was called value engineering, and it saved money because each single cent of cost lopped from a car design represented thousands of dollars in eventual profit. Once, during the 1960s, Ford saved a mammoth twenty-five cents per car by changing its brake system master cylinder, after studying the master cylinder of General Motors.

Others, like Adam and Brett at this moment, did their viewing to keep abreast of design changes and to seek inspiration.

The Volkswagen on the display boards which the technician had pulled out had been a new one. He reported, with a touch of glumness, "Been taking VWs apart for years. Every damn time it's the same—quality good as ever."

Brett nodded agreement. "Wish we could say the same of ours."

"So do I, Mr. DeLosanto. But we can't. Leastways, not here."

At the display boards showing the company's own minicompact, the custodian said, "Mind you, ours has come out pretty well this time. If it wasn't for that German bug, we'd look good."

"That's because American small car assembly's getting more automated," Adam commented. "The Vega started a big change with the new Lordstown plant. And the more automation we have, with fewer people, the higher everybody's quality will go."

"Wherever it's going," the technician said, "it ain't gone to Japan—at least not to the plant that produced this clunker. For God's sake, Mr. Trenton! Look at that!"

They examined some of the parts of the Japanese import, the third car they had come to review.

"String and baling wire," Brett pronounced.

"I'll tell you one thing, sir. I wouldn't want anybody I cared about to be riding around in one of those. It's a motorbike on four wheels, and a poor one at that."

They remained at the teardown racks, studying the three cars in detail. Later, the elderly technician let them out.

At the doorway he asked, "What's coming up next, gentleman? For us, I mean."

"Glad you reminded me," Brett said "We came over here to ask *you*."

It would be some kind of small car; that much they all knew. The key question was: *What* kind?

Later, back at staff headquarters, Adam observed, "For a long time, right up to 1970, a lot of people in this business thought the small car was a fad."

"I was one," Elroy Braithwaite, the Product Development vice-president admitted. The Silver Fox had joined them shortly after Adam's and Brett's return from the teardown room. Now, a group of five—Adam, Brett, Braithwaite, two others from product planning staff—was sprawled around Adam's office suite, ostensibly doing little more than shoot the breeze, but in reality hoping, through channeled conversation, to awaken ideas in each other. Discarded coffee cups and overflowing ashtrays littered tables and window ledges. It was after midnight.

"I thought the small car fever wouldn't last," Braithwaite went on. He put a hand through his silver-gray mane, disordered tonight, which was unusual. "I was in some pretty high-powered company, too, but we've all been wrong. As far as I can see, this industry will be small-car oriented, with muscle cars on the outs, for a long time to come."

"Perhaps forever," one of the other product planners said. He was a bright young Negro with large spectacles, named Castaldy, who had been recruited from Yale a year earlier.

"Nothing's forever," Brett DeLosanto objected. "Hemlines or hair styles or hip language or cars. Right now, though, I agree with Elroy— a small car's the status symbol, and it looks like staying."

"There are some," Adam said, "who believe a small car is a nonsymbol. They say people simply don't care about status any more."

Brett retorted, "You don't believe that, any more than I do."

"I don't either," the Silver Fox said. "A good many things have changed these past few years, but not basic human nature. Sure, there's a 're- verse status' syndrome, which is popular, but it adds up to what it always did—an individual try- ing to be different or superior. Even a dropout who doesn't wash is a status seeker of a kind."

"So maybe," Adam prompted, "we need a car which will appeal strongly to the reverse-status seeker."

The Silver Fox shook his head. "Not entirely. We still have to consider the squares—that big, solid backlog of buyers."

Castaldy pointed out, "But most squares don't like to think of themselves that way. That's why bank presidents wear sideburns."

"Don't we all?" Braithwaite fingered his own.

Above the mild laughter, Adam injected, "Maybe that's not so funny. Maybe it points the way to the kind of car we *don't* want. That is— anything looking like a conventional car produced until now."

"A mighty big order," the Silver Fox said.

Brett ruminated. "But not impossible."

Castaldy, the young Yale man, reminded them, "Today's environment is part of reverse- status—if we're calling it that. I mean public opinion, dissent, minorities, economic pressures, all the rest."

"True," Adam said, then added, "I know we've been over this a lot of times, but let's list environ- mental factors again."

Castaldy looked at some notes. "Air pollu- tion: people want to do something."

"Correction," Brett said. "They want *other* people to do something. No one wants to give up personal transportation, riding in his own car. All our surveys say so."

"Whether that's true or not," Adam said, "the car makers are doing something about pollution and there isn't a lot individuals can do."

"Just the same," young Castaldy persisted, "a good many are convinced that a small car pollutes less than a big one, so they think they can contribute that way. Our surveys show that, too." He glanced back at his notes. "May I go on?"

"I'll try not to heckle," Brett said. "But I won't guarantee it."

"In economics," Castaldy continued, "gas mileage isn't as dominant as it used to be, but parking cost *is*."

Adam nodded. "No arguing that. Street parking space gets harder to find, public and private parking costs more and more."

"But parking lots in a good many cities *are* charging less for small cars, and the idea's spreading."

The Silver Fox said irritably, "We know all about that. And we've already agreed we're going the small car route."

Behind his glasses, Castaldy appeared hurt.

"Elroy," Brett DeLosanto said, "the kid's helping us think. So if that's what you want, quit pulling rank."

"My God!" the Silver Fox complained. "You birds are sensitive. I was just being myself."

"Pretend to be a nice guy," Brett urged. "Instead of a vice-president."

"You bastard!" But Braithwaite was grinning. He told Castaldy, "Sorry! Let's go on."

"What I really meant, Mr. Braithwaite . . ."

"Elroy . . ."

"Yes, sir. What I meant was—it's part of the whole picture."

They talked about environment and mankind's problems: over-population, a shortage of square footage everywhere, pollution in all forms, antagonisms, rebellion, new concepts and values among young people—the young who would soon rule the world. Yet, despite changes, cars would still be around for the foreseeable future; experience showed it. But what kind of cars? Some would be the same as now, or similar, but there must be other kinds, too, more closely reflecting society's needs.

"Speaking of needs," Adam queried, "can we sum them up?"

"If you wanted a word," Castaldy answered, "I'd say 'utility.'"

Brett DeLosanto tried it on his tongue. "The Age of Utility."

"I'll buy that in part," the Silver Fox said. "But not entirely." He motioned for silence while gathering thoughts. The others waited. At length he intoned slowly, "Okay, so utility's 'in.' It's the newest status symbol, or reverse-status—and we're agreed that whatever name you call it it means the same thing. I'll concede it's probably for the future, too. But that still doesn't allow for the rest of human nature: the impulse to mobility which is with us from the day we're born, and later a craving for power, speed, excitement which we never grow out of wholly. We're all Walter Mittys somewhere inside and, utility or not, pizzazz is 'in,' too. It's never been out. It never will be."

"I go with that," Brett said. "To prove your point look at the guys who build dune buggies. They're small car people who've found a Walter Mitty outlet."

Castaldy added thoughtfully, "And there are thousands and thousands of dune buggies. More all the time. Nowadays you even see them in cities."

The Silver Fox shrugged. "They take a utility Volkswagen without pizzazz, strip it to the chassis, then build pizzazz on."

A thought stirred in Adam's mind. It related to what had been said . . . to the torn-down Volkswagen he had seen earlier tonight . . . and to something else, hazy: a phrase which eluded him . . . He searched his mind while the others talked.

When the phrase failed to come he remembered a magazine illustration he had seen a day or two ago. The magazine was still in his office. He retrieved it from a pile across the room and opened it. The others watched curiously.

The illustration was in color. It showed a dune buggy on a rugged beach, in action, banked steeply on its side. All wheels were fighting for traction, sand spewing behind. Cleverly, the photographer had slowed his shutter speed so that the dune buggy was blurred with movement. The text with the picture said the ranks of dune buggy owners were "growing like mad"; nearly a hundred manufacturers were engaged in building bodies; California alone had eight thousand dune buggies.

Brett, glancing over Adam's shoulder, asked amusedly, "You're not thinking of building dune buggies?"

Adam shook his head. No matter how large the dune buggy population became, they were still a fad, a specialist's creation, not the Big Three's business. Adam knew that. But the phrase which eluded him was somehow linked . . . Still not remembering, he tossed the magazine on a table, open.

Chance, as happens so often in life, stepped in.

Above the table where Adam tossed the magazine was a framed photo of the Apollo 11 Lunar

Module during the first moon landing. It had been given to Adam, who liked it, and had had it framed and hung. In the photo, the module dominated; an astronaut stood beneath.

Brett picked up the magazine with the dune buggy picture and showed it to the others. He remarked, "Those things go like hell!—I've driven one." He studied the illustration again. "But it's an ugly son-of-a-bitch."

Adam thought: *So was the lunar module.*

Ugly indeed: all edges, corners, projections, oddities, imbalance; little symmetry, few clean curves. But because the lunar module did its job superbly, it defeated ugliness and, in the end, took on a beauty of its own.

The missing phrase came to him.

It was Rowena's. The morning after their night together she had said, "You know what I'd say today? I'd say, 'ugly is beautiful.'"

Ugly is Beautiful!

The lunar module was ugly. So was a dune buggy. But both were functional, utilitarian; they were built for a purpose and performed it. *So why not a car?* Why not a deliberate, daring attempt to produce a car, ugly by existing standards, yet so suited to needs, environment, and present time— the Age of Utility—that it would *become* beautiful?

"I may have an idea about Farstar," Adam said. "Don't rush me. Let me put it out slowly."

The others were silent. Marshaling thoughts, choosing words carefully, Adam began.

They were too experienced—all of them in the group—to go overboard, instantly, for a single idea. Yet he was aware of a sudden tension, missing before, and a quickening interest as he continued to speak. The Silver Fox was thoughtful, his eyes half-closed. Young Castaldy scratched an ear lobe—a habit when he concentrated—while

the other product planner, who had said little so
far, kept his eyes on Adam steadily. Brett DeLosanto's fingers seemed restless. As if instinctually,
Brett drew a sketch pad toward him.

It was Brett, too, who jumped up when
Adam finished, and began pacing the room.
He tossed off thoughts, incomplete sentences, like
fragments of a jigsaw . . . *Artists for centuries
have seen beauty in ugliness . . . Consider distorted, tortured sculpture from Michelangelo to
Henry Moore . . . And in modern times, scrap
metal welded in jumbles—shapeless to some, who
scoff, but many don't . . . Take painting: the*
avant-garde *forms; egg crates, soup cans in col-
lages . . . Or life itself!—a pretty young girl
or a pregnant hag: which is more beautiful?* . . .
It depended always on the way you saw it. Form,
symmetry, style, beauty were never arbitrary.

Brett thumped a fist into a palm. "With
Picasso in our nostrils, we've been designing cars
like they rolled off a Gainsborough canvas."

"There's a line in Genesis somewhere," the
Silver Fox said. "I think it goes, *'Your eyes shall
be opened.'* " He added cautiously, "But let's not
get carried away. We may have something. Even
if we do, though, there's a long road ahead."

Brett was already sketching, his pencil racing
through shapes, then discarding them. As he
ripped off sheets from his pad, they dropped to
the floor. It was a designer's way of thinking,
just as others exchanged ideas through words.
Adam reminded himself to retrieve the sheets
later and save them; if something came of this
night, they would be historic.

But he knew that what Elroy Braithwaite
had said was true. The Silver Fox, through more
years than any of the others here, had seen new
cars develop from first ideas to finished products,
but had suffered, too, through projects which

looked promising at birth, only to be snuffed out later for unforeseen reasons, or sometimes for no reason at all.

Within the company a new car concept had countless barriers to pass, innumerable critiques to survive, interminable meetings, with opposition to overcome. And even if an idea survived all these, the executive vice-president, president, and chairman of the board had veto powers . . .

But *some* ideas got through and became reality.

The Orion had. So . . . just barely possibly . . . might this early, inchoate concept, the seed sown here and now, for Farstar.

Someone brought more coffee, and they talked on, far into the night.

chapter eighteen

The OJL advertising agency, in the person of Keith Yates-Brown, was nervous and edgy because the documentary film *Auto City* was proceeding without a shooting script.

"There *has* to be a script," Yates-Brown had protested to Barbara Zaleski on the telephone from New York a day or two ago. "If there isn't, how can we protect the client's interests from here and make suggestions?"

Barbara, in Detroit, had felt like telling the management supervisor that the last thing the project needed was Madison Avenue meddling. It could transform the honest, perceptive film now taking shape into a glossy, innocuous mélange. But, instead, she repeated the views of the director, Wes Gropetti, a talented man with enough solid credits behind him to make his viewpoint count.

"You won't grab the mood of inner city Detroit by putting a lot of crud on paper because we don't *know* what the mood is yet," Gropetti had declared. "We're here with all this fancy camera and sound gear to find out."

The director, heavily bearded but diminutive in stature, seemed like a shaggy sparrow. He wore a black beret which he was never without, and was less sensitive about words than he was with visual images. He went on, "I want the inner city jokers, broads, and kids to tell us what they really think about themselves, and how they look on the rest of us lousy bums. That means their hates, hopes, frustrations, joys, as well as how they breathe, eat, sleep, fornicate, sweat, and what they see and smell. I'll get all that on film—their mugs, voices, everything unrehearsed. As to language, we'll let the crud fall where it may. Maybe I'll prick a few people in the ass to get them mad, but either way they'll talk, then while they do, I'll let the camera wander like a whore's attention, and we'll see Detroit the way they see it, through inner city eyes."

And it was working, Barbara assured Yates-Brown.

Using cinéma vérité technique, with a hand-held camera and a minimum of paraphernalia to distract, Gropetti was roaming the inner city with a crew, persuading people to talk frankly, freely, and sometimes movingly, on film. Barbara, who usually accompanied the expeditions, knew that part of Gropetti's genius lay in his instinct for selection, then making those he chose forget that a lens and lights were focused on them. No one knew what the little director whispered into ears before their owners began talking; sometimes he would bend his head down, confidentially, for minutes at a time. But it produced reactions: amusement, defiance, rapport, disagreement, sullenness, impudence, alertness, anger and once— from a young black militant who became impressively eloquent—a blazing hatred.

When he was sure of a reaction, Gropetti would spring instantly back so that the camera— already operating at the director's covert signal— would catch full facial expressions and spontaneous words. Afterward, with limitless patience, Gropetti would repeat the process until he had what he sought—a glimpse of personality, good or bad, amiable or savage, but vital and real, and without the clumsy intrusion of an interviewer.

Barbara had already seen rushes and rough cuts of the results, and was excited. Photographically, they had the quality and depth of Karsh portraits, plus Gropetti's magic mix of vibrant animation.

"Since we're calling the film *Auto City*," Keith Yates-Brown had commented when she told him all that, "maybe you should wise up Gropetti that there are motorcars around as well as people, and we'll expect to see some—preferably our client's—on the screen."

Barbara sensed that the agency supervisor was having second thoughts about the over-all authority she had been given. But he would also know that any film project needed to have someone firmly in charge and, until the OJL agency removed or fired her, Barbara was.

She assured Yates-Brown, "There *will* be cars in the picture—the client's. We're not emphasizing them, but we're not concealing them either, so most people will recognize the kind they are." She had gone on to describe the filming already done in the auto company's assembly plant, with emphasis on inner city hard core hiring—and Rollie Knight.

During the assembly plant filming, other workers nearby had been unaware that Rollie was the center of the camera's attention. Partly, this was out of consideration for Rollie, who wanted it that way, and partly to keep the atmosphere realistic.

Leonard Wingate of Personnel, who became interested in Barbara's project the night they met at Brett DeLosanto's apartment, had arranged the whole thing without fuss. All that anyone in the plant knew was that a portion of Assembly was being filmed, for purposes unexplained, while regular work went on. Only Wes Gropetti, Barbara, and the camera- and soundmen realized that a good deal of the time they appeared to be shooting, they were not, and that most of the footage taken featured Rollie Knight.

The only sound recording at this point was of assembly plant noises while they happened, and afterward Barbara had listened to the sound tape played back. It was a nightmare cacophony, incredibly effective as a background to the visual sequence.

Rollie Knight's voice, which would be dubbed in later, was to be recorded during a visit by Gropetti and the film crew to the inner city apartment house where Rollie and May Lou, his girl friend, lived. Leonard Wingate would be there. So—though Barbara did not report the fact to Keith Yates-Brown—would Brett DeLosanto.

On the telephone, Keith Yates-Brown had cautioned, "Just remember we're spending a lot of the client's money which we'll have to account for."

"We've stayed within budget," Barbara reported. "And the client seems to like what we've done so far. At least, the chairman of the board does."

She heard a sound on the telephone which could have been Keith Yates-Brown leaping from his chair.

"*You've* been in touch with the client's chairman of the board!" The reaction could not have been greater if she had said the Pope or the President of the United States.

"He came to visit our shooting on location. The day after, Wes Gropetti took some of the film and screened it in the chairman's office."

"You let that foul-mouthed hippie Gropetti loose on the fifteenth floor!"

"Wes seemed to think that he and the chairman got along well."

"*He* thought so! You didn't even go yourself?"

"I couldn't that day."

"Oh, my God!" Barbara could visualize the agency supervisor, his face paling, a hand clapped to his head.

She reminded him, "You told me yourself

that the chairman was interested, and I might report to him occasionally."

"But not *casually!* Not without letting us know here, in advance, so we could plan what you should say. And as for sending Gropetti on his own . . ."

"I was going to tell you," Barbara said, "the client's chairman phoned me next day. He said he thought our agency had shown commendable imagination—those were his words—in getting Wes Gropetti to begin with, and urged us to go on giving Wes his head because this was the kind of thing which ought to be a director's film. The chairman said he was putting all that in a letter to the agency."

She heard heavy breathing on the line. "We haven't got the letter yet. When it comes . . ." A pause. "Barbara, I guess you're doing fine." Yates-Brown's voice became pleading. "But *don't*, please don't, take chances, and let me know *anything instantly* about the client's chairman of the board."

She had promised that she would, after which Keith Yates-Brown—still nervously—repeated that he wished they had a script.

Now, several days later and scriptless as ever, Wes Gropetti was ready to film the final sequence involving hard core hiring and Rollie Knight.

Early evening.

Eight of them, altogether, were packed into the stiflingly hot, sketchily furnished room.

For Detroit generally, and especially the inner city, it had been a baking, windless summer day. Even now, with the sun gone, most of the heat—inside and out—remained.

Rollie Knight and May Lou were two of the eight because this was where—for the time being—they lived. Though the room was tiny by any

standard, it served the dual purpose of living and
sleeping, while a closet-sized "kitchen" adjoining
housed a sink with cold water only, a decrepit
gas cooker, and a few plain board shelves. There
was no toilet or bath. These facilities, such as they
were, were one floor down and shared with a
half dozen other apartments.

Rollie looked morose, as if wishing he had
not agreed to be involved with this. May Lou,
childlike and seeming to have sprouted like a
weed with skinny legs and bony arms, appeared
scared, though she was becoming less so as Wes
Gropetti, his black beret in place despite the heat,
talked quietly to her.

Behind the director were the camera operator
and soundman, their equipment deployed awkwardly in the confined space. Barbara Zaleski
stood with them, her notebook opened.

Brett DeLosanto, watching, was amused to
see that Barbara, as usual, had dark glasses
pushed up into her hair.

The camera lights were off. Everyone
knew that when they went on, the room would
become hotter still.

Leonard Wingate, from the auto maker's Personnel department and also the company's rank-
ing Negro executive, mopped his perspiring face
with a fresh linen handkerchief. Both he and
Brett were backed against a wall, trying to take as
little space as possible.

Suddenly, though only the two technicians
had seen Gropetti's signal, the lights were on, the
sound tape running.

May Lou blinked. But as the director continued to talk softly, she nodded and her face
adjusted. Then swiftly, smoothly, Gropetti eased
rearward, out of camera range.

May Lou said naturally, as if unaware of
anything but her own thoughts, "Ain't no good

worryin', not about no future like they say we should, 'cos it ain't ever looked as if there'd be one for some like us." She shrugged. "Don't look no different now."

Gropetti's voice. "Cut!"

Camera lights went out. The director moved in, whispering in May Lou's ear once more. After several minutes, while the others waited silently, the camera lights went on. Gropetti slid back.

May Lou's face was animated. "Sure they took our color TV." She glanced across the room toward an empty corner. "Two guys come for it, said we hadn't made no payments after the first. One of the guys wanted to know, why'd we buy it? I told him, 'Mister, if I got a down payment today, I can watch TV tonight. Some days that's all that matters.'" Her voice slipped lower. "I shoulda told him, 'Who knows about tomorrow?'"

"Cut!"

Brett whispered to Leonard Wingate beside him, "What's this all about?"

The Negro executive was still mopping his face. He said, low-voiced, "They're in trouble. The two of them had some real money for the first time in their lives, so they went wild, bought furniture, a color TV, took on payments they couldn't meet. Now, some of the stuff's been repossessed. That isn't all."

Ahead of them, Gropetti was having May Lou and Rollie Knight change positions. Now Rollie faced the camera.

Brett asked, still speaking softly, "What else has happened?"

"The word is 'garnishee,'" Wingate said. "It means a lousy, out-of-date law which politicians agree ought to be changed, but nobody does it."

Wes Gropetti had his head down and was talking to Rollie in his usual way.

Wingate told Brett, "Knight's had his wages

garnisheed once already. This week there was a second court order, and under the union agreement two garnishees mean automatic dismissal."

"Hell! Can't you do something?"

"Maybe. It depends on Knight. When this is over, I'll talk to him."

"Should he be spilling his guts on film?"

Leonard Wingate shrugged. "I told him he didn't have to, that it's his private business. But he didn't seem to mind, neither did the girl. Maybe they don't care; maybe they figure they can help somebody else. I don't know."

Barbara, who had overheard, turned her head. "Wes says it's part of the whole scene. Besides, he'll edit sympathetically."

"If I didn't think so," Wingate said, "we wouldn't be here."

The director was still briefing Rollie.

Wingate, speaking softly but his voice intense, told Barbara and Brett, "Half the problem with what's happening to Knight is our own attitudes—the establishment's; that means people like you two and me. Okay, we help somebody like these two kids, but as soon as we do, we expect them to have all our middle-class values which it took us years of living *our* way to acquire. The same goes for money. Even though Knight hasn't been used to it because none ever came his way, we expect him to handle money as if he'd had it all his life, and if he doesn't, what happens? He's shoved into court, his wages garnisheed, he's fired. We forget that plenty of us who've lived with money still run up debts we can't manage. But let this guy do the same thing"—the Negro executive nodded toward Rollie Knight—"and our system's all set to throw him back on the garbage heap."

"You're not going to let it happen," Barbara murmured.

Wingate shook his head impatiently. "There's only so much I can do. And Knight's just one of many."

Camera lights were on. The director glanced their way, a signal for silence. Rollie Knight's voice rose clearly in the quiet, hot room.

"Sure you find out things from livin' here. Like, most of it ain't gonna get better, no matter what they say. Besides that, nuthun' lasts." Unexpectedly, a smile flashed over Rollie's face; then, as if regretting the smile, a scowl replaced it. "So best not to expect nuthun'. Then it don't hurt none when you lose it."

Gropetti called, "Cut!"

Filming continued for another hour, Gropetti coaxing and patient, Rollie speaking of experiences in the inner city and the auto assembly plant where he was still employed. Though the young black worker's words were simple and sometimes stumbling, they conveyed reality and a true picture of himself—not always favorable, but not belittling either. Barbara, who had seen earlier sequences filmed, had a conviction that the answer print would be an eloquently moving document.

When camera lights went out after the concluding shot, Wes Gropetti removed his black beret and mopped his head with a large, grubby kerchief. He nodded to the two technicans. "Strike it! That's a wrap."

While the others filed out, with brief "goodnights" to Rollie and May Lou, Leonard Wingate stayed behind. Brett DeLosanto, Barbara Zaleski, and Wes Gropetti were going on to the Detroit Press Club for a late supper, where Wingate would join them shortly.

The Negro executive waited until the others had passed through the mean hallway outside, with its single, low-wattage light bulb and peeling paint, and were clattering down the worn wooden stairway to the street below. Through the hallway door, the odor of garbage drifted in. May Lou closed it.

She asked, "You want a drink, mister?"

Wingate started to shake his head, then changed his mind. "Yes, please."

From a shelf in the miniscule kitchen, the girl took a rum bottle with about an inch of liquor in it, which she divided equally between two glasses. Adding ice and Coke, she gave one to Wingate, the other to Rollie. The three of them sat down in the all-purpose room.

"There'll be some money coming to you from the film people for using your place tonight," Wingate said. "It won't be much; it never is. But I'll see you get it."

May Lou gave an unsure smile. Rollie Knight said nothing.

The executive sipped his drink. "You knew about the garnishee? The second one?"

Rollie still didn't answer.

"Somebody tol' him today at work," May Lou said. "They said he don't get his paycheck no more? That right?"

"He doesn't get part of it. But if he loses his job there'll be no more checks anyway—for anybody." Wingate went on to explain about garnishees—the attachment of a worker's pay at source by court order, which creditors obtained. He added that, while auto companies and other employers detested the garnishee system, they had no choice but to comply with the law.

As Wingate suspected, neither Rollie nor May Lou had understood the earlier garnishee, nor was Rollie aware that a second one—under company-union rules—could get him fired.

"There's a reason for that," Wingate said. "Garnishees make a lot of work for the payroll department, which costs the company money."

Rollie blurted, "Bullshit!" He got up and walked around.

Leonard Wingate sighed. "If you want my honest opinion, I think you're right. It's why I'll try to help you if I can. If you want me to."

May Lou glanced at Rollie. She moistened her lips. "He wants you to, mister. He ain't been himself lately. He's been . . . well, real upset."

Wingate wondered why. If Rollie had learned about the garnishee only today, as May Lou said, obviously he had not been worrying because of that. He decided not to press the point.

"What I can do," the executive told them, "and you must understand this is only if you want it, is have someone look over your finances for you, straighten them out if we can, and try to get you started fresh."

He went on, explaining how the system—devised by Jim Robson, a plant personnel manager for Chrysler, and copied nowadays by other companies—worked.

What they must do, he informed Rollie and May Lou, was give him, here and now, a list of all their debts. He would hand these to a senior Personnel man in Rollie's plant. The Personnel man, who did this extracurricular job on his own time, would go over everything to see how much was owing. Then he would phone the creditors, one by one, urging them to accept modest payments over a long period and, in return, withdraw their garnishees. Usually they agreed because the alternative was pointed out: that the man concerned would lose his job, in which event they would receive nothing, garnishee or not.

The employee—in this case Rollie Knight—would then be asked: What is the minimum amount of money you can live on weekly?

Once this was decided, Rollie's paycheck would be intercepted each week and routed to the

Personnel Department. There, every Friday, he would report and endorse the check over to the Personnel man making the arrangements. The Personnel man's office—Wingate told them—was usually crowded with fifty or so workers who had been in financial trouble and were being helped to straighten out. Most were grateful.

Afterward, the Personnel man would deposit Rollie's paycheck in a special account—in the Personnel man's name since the company took no official part in the arrangement. From this account he would issue checks to creditors for the sums arranged, giving Rollie another check—for the balance of his wages, on which he must live. Eventually, when all debts were cleared, the Personnel man would bow out and Rollie would receive his paycheck normally.

Records were open to inspection and the service operated solely to help workers in financial trouble, without charge of any kind.

"It won't be easy for you," Wingate warned. "To make it work, you'll have to live on very little money."

Rollie seemed about to protest, but May Lou interjected quickly, "We kin do it, mister." She looked at Rollie, and Wingate was aware of a mixture of authority and childlike affection in her eyes. "You'll do it," she insisted. "Yes, yo' will."

Half-smiling, Rollie shrugged.

But it was clear that Rollie Knight was still worried—really worried, Leonard Wingate suspected—about something else. Once more he wondered what it was.

"We've been sitting here," Barbara Zaleski said as Leonard Wingate joined them, "speculating on whether those two are going to make it."

Barbara, the only one in the group who was a Press Club member, was host to the other three.

She, Brett DeLosanto, and Wes Gropetti had waited at the bar. Now, the four of them moved to a table in the dining room.

As press clubs went, Detroit's was among the best in the country. It was small, well-run, with an excellent cuisine, and membership was sought after. Surprisingly, despite an exciting day-to-day affinity with the auto industry, the club's walls were almost bare—self-consciously, some thought —of mementos of the tie. The only one, which greeted visitors on entering, was a downbeat front page from 1947, its headline reading:

FORD DEAD
Dies in Oil-Lit, Unheated House

War and space travel, in contrast, were represented prominently, perhaps proof that newsmen sometimes suffer from hyperopia.

When they had ordered drinks, Wingate answered Barbara's question.

"I wish I could say yes. But I'm not sure, and the reason is the system. We talked about it earlier. People like us can cope with the system, more or less. Mostly, people like them can't."

"Leonard," Brett said, "tonight you've been sounding like a revolutionary."

"Sounding isn't being one." Wingate smiled dourly. "I don't think I have the guts; besides, I'm disqualified. I've a good job, money in the bank. As soon as anyone has those, they want to protect them, not blow it all up. But I'll tell you this: I know what makes people of my race revolutionaries."

He touched a bulge in the jacket of his suit. It was a collection of papers May Lou had given him before he left. They were invoices, time payment contracts, demands from finance companies. Out of curiosity, Wingate had gone over them briefly in his car, and what he had seen amazed and angered him.

He repeated to the other three the substance of his talk with Rollie and May Lou, omitting figures, which were private, but apart from that the others knew the story anyway, and he was aware they cared.

He said, "You saw the furniture they had in that room."

The others nodded. Barbara said, "It wasn't good, but . . ."

"Be honest," Wingate told her. "You know as well as I do, it was a bunch of shoddy junk."

Brett protested, "So what! If they can't afford much . . ."

"But you'd never *know* they couldn't, not from the price they paid." Once more, Wingate touched the papers in his pocket. "I just saw the invoice, and I'd say the invoice price is at least six times what the furniture was worth. For what they paid, or rather signed a finance contract for, those two could have had quality stuff from a reputable outfit like J. L. Hudson's or Sears."

Barbara asked, "Then why didn't they?"

Leonard Wingate put both hands on the table, leaning forward, "Because, my dear innocent, well-to-do friends, they didn't know any better. Because nobody ever taught them how to shop around or buy carefully. Because there isn't much point learning any of that if you've never had any real money. Because they went to a white-run store in a black neighborhood, which cheated them—but good! Because there are plenty of those stores, not just in Detroit, but other places too. I know. We've seen other people travel this route."

There was silence at the table. Their drinks had come, and Wingate sipped a neat Scotch on the rocks. After a moment he went on, "There's also a little matter of the finance charges on the furniture and some other things they bought. I did some figuring. It looks to me as if the interest rate was between nineteen and twenty percent."

Wes Gropetti whistled softly.

Barbara queried, "When your Personnel man talks to the creditors, the way you said he would, can he do anything to get the furniture bill or finance charges lowered?"

"The finance charges, maybe." Leonard Wingate nodded. "I'll probably work on that myself. When we call a finance outfit and use our company's name, they're apt to listen and be reasonable. They know there are ways a big auto manufacturer can put the squeeze on, if we take a mind to. But as to furniture . . ." He shook his head. "Not a chance. Those crooks'd laugh. They sell their stuff for as much as they can get, then turn their paper over to a finance company at a discount. It's little guys like Knight—who can't afford it—who pay the difference."

Barbara asked, "Will he keep his job? Rollie, I mean."

"Providing nothing else happens," Wingate said, "I think I can promise that."

Wes Gropetti urged, "For Christ sake, that's enough talk! Let's eat!"

Brett DeLosanto, who had been unusually quiet through most of the evening, remained so during the meal which followed. What Brett had seen tonight—the conditions under which Rollie Knight and May Lou lived; their cramped, mean room in the run-down, garbage-reeking apartment house; countless other buildings in the area, either the same or worse; the general malaise and poverty of the major portion of the inner city— had affected him deeply. He had been in the inner city before, and through its streets, but never with the same insight or sense of poignancy he had known within the past few hours.

He had asked Barbara to let him watch tonight's filming, partly from curiosity and partly because she had become so absorbed with the project that he had seen little of her lately. What he had not expected was to be drawn in, mentally, as much as he had.

Not that he had been unaware of ghetto problems of Detroit. When he observed the desperate grimness of housing, he knew better than to ask: *Why don't people move somewhere else?* Brett already knew that economically and socially, people here—specifically, black people—were trapped. High as living costs were in the inner city, in suburbs they were higher still, even if the suburbs would let blacks move there—and some wouldn't, still practicing discrimination in a thousand subtle and not-so-subtle ways. Dearborn, for example, in which Ford Motor Company had its headquarters, at last count didn't have a single black resident, due to hostility of white, middle-class families who supported wily maneuverings by its solidly established mayor.

Brett knew, too, that efforts to aid the inner city had been made by the well-meaning New Detroit Committee—more recently, New Detroit Inc.—established after the area's 1967 riots. Funds had been raised, some housing started. But as a committee member put it: "We're long on proclamations, short on bricks."

Another had recalled the dying words of Cecil Rhodes: *"So little done—so much to do."*

Both comments had been from individuals, impatient with the smallness of accomplishment by groups—groups which included the city, state, and federal governments. Though the 1967 riots were now years away, nothing beyond sporadic tinkering had been done to remedy conditions which were the riots' cause. Brett wondered: If so many, collectively, had failed, what could one person, an individual, hope to do?

Then he remembered: Someone had once asked that about Ralph Nader.

Brett sensed Barbara's eyes upon him and turned toward her. She smiled, but made no comment on his quietness; each knew the other well enough by now not to need explanations of moods, or reasons for them. Barbara looked her best tonight, Brett thought. During the discussion earlier her face had been animated, reflecting interest, intelligence, warmth. No other girl of Brett's acquaintance rated quite as high with him, which was why he went on seeing her, despite her continued, obstinate refusal to join him in bed.

Brett knew that Barbara had gained a lot of satisfaction from her involvement with the film, and working with Wes Gropetti.

Now Gropetti pushed back his plate, dabbing a napkin around his mouth and beard. The little film director, still wearing his black beret, had been eating Beef Stroganoff with noodles, washed down generously with Chianti. He gave a grunt of satisfaction.

"Wes," Brett said, "do you ever want to get involved—really involved—with subjects you do films about?"

The director looked surprised. "You mean do crusading crap? Chivvy people up?"

"Yes," Brett acknowledged, "that's the kind of crap I mean."

"A pox on that! Sure, I get interested; I have to be. But after that I take pictures, kiddo. That's all." Gropetti rubbed his beard, removing a fragment of noodle which the napkin had missed. He added, "A buttercup scene or a sewer—once I know it's there, all I want are the right lens, camera angle, lighting, sound synch. Nuts to involvement! Involvement's a full-time job."

Brett nodded. He said thoughtfully, "That's what I think, too."

In his car, driving Barbara home, Brett said, "It's going well, isn't it? The film."

"*So* well!" She was near the middle of the front seat, curled close beside him. If he moved his face sideways he could touch her hair, as he had already, several times.

"I'm glad for you. You know that."

"Yes," she said. "I know."

"I wouldn't want any woman I lived with *not* to do something special, something exclusively her own."

"If I ever live with you, I'll remember that."

It was the first time either of them had mentioned the possibility of living together since the night they had talked about it several months ago.

"Have you thought any more?"

"I've thought," she said. "That's all."

Brett waited while he threaded traffic at the Jefferson entrance to the Chrysler Freeway, then asked, "Want to talk about it?"

She shook her head negatively.

"How much longer will the film take?"

"Probably another month."

"You'll be busy?"

"I expect so. Why?"

"I'm taking a trip," Brett said. "To California."

But when she pressed him, he declined to tell her why.

chapter nineteen

The long, black limousine slowed, swung left, then glided smoothly, between weathered stone pillars, into the paved, winding driveway of Hank Kreisel's Grosse Pointe home.

Kreisel's uniformed chauffeur was at the wheel. Behind him, in the plush interior, were Kreisel and his guests, Erica and Adam Trenton. The car's interior contained—among other things —a bar, from which the parts manufacturer had served drinks as they drove.

It was late evening in the last week of July.

They had already dined—at the Detroit Athletic Club downtown. The Trentons had met Kreisel there, and a fourth at dinner had been a gorgeous girl, with flashing eyes and a French accent, whom Kreisel introduced merely as Zoë. He added that she was in charge of his recently opened export liaison office.

Zoë, who proved an engaging companion, excused herself after dinner and left. Then, at Hank Kreisel's suggestion, Adam and Erica accompanied him home, leaving their own car downtown.

This evening's arrangements had been an outcropping of Adam's weekend at Hank Kreisel's lakeside cottage. Following the cottage affair, the parts manufacturer telephoned Adam, as arranged, and they set a date. Inclusion of Erica in the invitation made Adam nervous at first, and he hoped Kreisel would make no references to the cottage weekend in detail, or Rowena in particular. Adam still remembered Rowena vividly, but she was in the past, and prudence and common sense dictated she remain there. He need not have worried. Hank Kreisel was discreet; they talked of other things—next season's prospects for the Detroit Lions, a recent scandel in city government, and later the Orion, some of whose parts Kreisel's company was now manufacturing in enormous quantities. After a while Adam relaxed, though he still wondered what, precisely, Hank Kreisel wanted of him.

That Kreisel wanted something he was sure, because Brett DeLosanto had told him so. Brett and Barbara had been invited tonight but couldn't make it—Barbara was busy at her job; Brett, who was leaving soon for the West Coast, had commitments to finish first. But Brett confided yesterday, "Hank told me what he's going to ask, and I hope you can do something because there's a lot more to it than just us." The air of mystery had irritated Adam, but Brett refused to say more.

Now, as the limousine stopped at Kreisel's sprawling, ivy-draped mansion, Adam supposed he would know soon.

The chauffeur came around to open the door and handed Erica out. With their host following, Erica and Adam moved onto the lawn nearby and stood together, the big house behind them, in the growing dusk.

The elegant garden, whose manicured lawn, well-trimmed trees and shrubs wore the patina of professional care, sloped downward to the uncluttered, boulevarded lanes of Lake Shore Road, the roadway offering no interruption—except for occasional traffic—to a panoramic view of Lake St. Clair.

The lake was still visible, though barely; a line of white wavelets marked its edge, and far out from shore, lights of lake freighters flickered. Closer at hand a tardy sailboat, using its outboard as a hurry-home, headed for a Grosse Pointe Yacht Club mooring.

"It's beautiful," Erica said, "though I always

think, when I come to Grosse Pointe, it isn't really part of Detroit."

"If you lived here," Hank Kreisel answered, "you'd know it was. Plenty of us still smell of gasoline. Or had grease under our fingernails once."

Adam said dryly, "Most Grosse Pointe fingernails have been clean for a long time." But he knew what Kreisel meant. The Grosse Pointes, of which there were five—all separate fiefdoms and traditional enclaves of great wealth—were as much a part of the auto world as any other segment of Greater Detroit. Henry Ford II lived down the street in Grosse Pointe Farms, with other Fords sprinkled nearby like rich spices. Other auto company wealth was here too—Chrysler and General Motors fortunes, as well as those of industry suppliers: big, older names like Fisher, Anderson, Olson, Mullen, and newer ones like Kreisel. The money's current custodians hobnobbed in socially exclusive clubs—at the apex the creaking, overheated Country Club, with a waiting list so long that a new, young applicant without family ties could expect to be admitted at senility. Yet for all its exclusiveness, Grosse Pointe was a friendly place—a reason why a soupçon of salaried auto executives made it their home, preferring its "family" scene to the more management-oriented Bloomfield Hills.

Once, older Grosse Pointers looked down patrician noses at automotive money. Now it dominated them, as it dominated all Detroit.

A sudden, night breeze from the lake stirred the air and set leaves rustling overhead. Erica shivered.

Hank Kreisel suggested, "Let's go in."

The chauffeur, who appeared to double in butlerage, swung heavy front doors open as they approached the house.

A few yards inside, Adam stopped. He said incredulously, "I'll be damned!"

Beside him, Erica, equally surprised, stood staring. Then she giggled.

The main floor living room into which they had stepped had all the accouterments of elegance —deep broadloom, comfortable chairs, sofas, sideboards, bookshelves, paintings, a hi-fi playing softly, and harmonious lighting. It also had a full-size swimming pool.

The pool, some thirty feet long, was attractively blue tiled, with a deep end, shallow end, and a three-tiered diving board.

Erica said, "Hank, I shouldn't have laughed. I'm sorry. But it's . . . surprising."

"No reason not to laugh," their host said amiably. "Most people do. Good many think I'm nuts. Fact is, I like to swim. Like to be comfortable, too."

Adam was looking around him with an amazed expression. "It's an old house. You must have ripped the inside out."

"Sure did."

Erica told Adam, "Quit making like an engineer and let's go swimming."

Obviously pleased, Kreisel said, "You want to?"

"You're looking at an Island girl. I could swim before I could talk."

He showed her to a corridor. "Second door down there. Lots of swimsuits, towels."

Adam followed Kreisel to another changing room.

Minutes later, Erica executed a dazzling swallow dive from the highest board. She surfaced, laughing. "This is the best living room I was ever in."

Hank Kreisel, grinning, dived from a lower board. Adam plunged in from the side.

When they had all swum, Kreisel led the way —the three of them dripping—across the broadloom to deep armchairs over which the butler-chauffeur had spread thick towels.

In a fourth chair was a gray-haired, frail-appearing woman, beside her a tray of coffee cups and liqueurs. Hank Kreisel leaned over, kissing her cheek. He asked, "How was the day?"

"Peaceful."

"This is my wife, Dorothy," Kreisel said. He introduced Erica and Adam.

Adam could understand why Zoë had been left downtown.

Yet, as Mrs. Kreisel poured coffee and they chatted, she seemed to find nothing strange in the fact that the others had had a dinner engagement in which—for whatever reason—she was not included. She even inquired how the food had been at the Detroit Athletic Club.

Perhaps, Adam thought, Dorothy Kreisel had come to terms with her husband's other life away from home—his various mistresses in "liaison offices," which Adam had heard of. In fact, Hank Kreisel seemed to make no secret of his arrangements, as witness Zoë tonight.

Erica chatted brightly. Obviously she liked Hank Kreisel, and the evening out, and now the swim, had been good for her. She appeared glowing, her youthfulness evident. She had found a bikini among the available swimwear; it was exactly right for her tall, slim figure, and several times Adam noticed Kreisel's eyes stray interestedly Erica's way.

After a while their host seemed restless. He stood up. "Adam, like to get changed? There's something I want to show you, maybe talk about."

So finally, Adam thought, they were coming to the point—whatever the point was.

"You sound mysterious, Hank," Erica said;

she smiled at Dorothy Kreisel. "Do I get to see this exposition too?"

Hank Kreisel gave his characteristic twisted grin. "If you did, I'd like it."

A few minutes later they excused themselves from Mrs. Kreisel who remained, placidly sipping coffee, in the living room.

When they had dressed, Hank Kreisel guided Adam and Erica through the main floor of the house, explaining it had been built by a long-dead auto mogul, a contemporary of Walter Chrysler and Henry Ford. "Solid. Outside walls as good as Hadrian's. Still are. So I tore the inside apart, put new guts in." The parts manufacturer opened a paneled doorway, revealing a spiral staircase, going down, then clattered ahead. Erica followed, more cautiously, Adam behind her.

They walked along a basement passageway, then, selecting a key from several on a ring, Hank Kreisel opened a gray metal door. As they entered the room beyond, bright fluorescent lighting flooded on.

They were, Adam saw, in an engineering experimental workshop. It was spacious, organized, among the best-equipped of its kind that he had seen.

"Spend a lot of time in this place. Do pilot stuff," Kreisel explained. "When new work comes up for my plants, bring it down here. Then figure out best way of production at cheapest unit cost. Pays off."

Adam remembered something which Brett DeLosanto had told him: that Hank Kreisel had no engineering degree, and his only training before beginning business for himself was as a machinist and plant foreman.

"Over here." Kreisel led the way to a low, wide work table. An object on it was covered by a cloth which he removed. Adam looked curiously at the metal structure underneath—an assemblage of steel rods, sheet metal, and connected internal parts, the size about equal to two bicycles. On the outside was a handle. As Adam turned it, experimentally, parts within the structure moved.

Adam shrugged. "Hank, I give up. What the hell is it?"

"Obviously," Erica said, "it's something he's submitting to the Museum of Modern Art."

"Maybe that's it. What I ought to do." Kreisel grinned, then asked, "Know much about farm machinery, Adam?"

"Not really." He turned the handle once again.

Hank Kreisel said quietly, "It's a threshing machine, Adam. Never been one like it, or this small. And it works." His voice took on an enthusiasm which neither Adam nor Erica had heard before. "This machine'll thresh any kind of grain —wheat, rice, barley. Three to five bushels an hour. Got pictures proving it . . ."

"I know enough about you," Adam said. "If you say it works, it works."

"Something else works, too. Cost. Mass-produced, it'd sell for a hundred dollars."

Adam looked doubtful. As a product planner, he knew costs the way a football coach knows standard plays. "Surely not including your power source." He stopped. "What *is* your power source? Batteries? A small gas motor?"

"Thought you'd get around to that," Hank Kreisel said. "So I'll tell you. Power source isn't any of those things. It's some guy turning a handle. Same way *you* did just now. Same handle. Except the guy I'm thinking of is an old Eastern geezer in a jungle village. Wearing a slope hat. When his arms get tired, a woman or a kid'll do it. They'll sit there, hours on end, just turn the handle. That's how we'll build this for a hundred bucks."

"No power source. Too bad we can't build cars that way." Adam laughed.

Kreisel told him, "Whatever else you do. Do me a favor now. Don't laugh."

"Okay, I won't. But I still can't see mass-producing, in Detroit of all places, a piece of farm machinery"—Adam nodded toward the thresher—"where you *turn a handle, for hours on end,* to make it work."

Hank Kreisel said earnestly, "If you'd been to places where I have, Adam, maybe you would. Parts of this world are a long way from Detroit. That's half our trouble in this town: we forget those other places. Forget that people don't think like we do. We figure everywhere else is like Detroit, or ought to be, so whatever happens should be our way: the way we see it. If others see different, they have to be wrong *because we're Detroit!* We've been like that about other things. Pollution. Safety. Those got so hot we had to change. But there's a lot more thinking left that's like religion."

"With high priests," Erica put in, "who don't like old beliefs challenged."

Adam shot her an annoyed glance which said: *Leave this to me.*

He pointed out, "A good many who are moving up in industry believe in rethinking old ideas and the effect is showing. But when you talk about a hand-operated machine—any kind of machine —*that* isn't a forward change; it's going backward to the way things were before the first Henry Ford." He added, "Anyway, I'm a car and truck man. This is farm machinery."

"Your company has a farm products division."

"I'm not involved with it, and don't expect to be."

"Your people at the top are. And you're involved with them. They listen to you."

"Tell me something," Adam said. "Did you put this up to our farm products people? Did they turn you down?"

The parts manufacturer nodded affirmatively. "Them and others. Need someone now to get me in a board room. So I can raise interest there. Hoped you'd see it."

At last it was clear precisely what Hank Kreisel wanted: Adam's help in gaining access to the corporate summit of his company, and presumably the ear of the president or chairman of the board.

Erica said, "Can't you do it for him?"

Adam shook his head, but it was Hank Kreisel who told her, "He'd have to believe in the idea first."

They stood looking at the contraption with its handle, so alien to everything in Adam's own experience.

And yet, Adam knew, auto companies often did become involved in projects having little or nothing to do with their principal activity of producing cars. General Motors had pioneered a mechanical heart for use in surgery, and other medical devices. Ford was working on space satellite communication, Chrysler dabbling in planned communities. There were other examples, and the reason for such programs—as Hank Kreisel shrewdly knew—was that someone high in each company had taken a personal interest to begin with.

"Been down to Washington about this thresher," Kreisel said. "Sounded out a lot of guys in State. They go for this. Talk of ordering two hundred thousand machines a year for foreign aid. It'd mean a start. But State Department can't do manufacturing."

"Hank," Adam said, "why work through another company at all? If you're convinced, why not build and market this yourself?"

"Two reasons. One's prestige. I don't have the name. Big company like yours does. Has the marketing setup, too. I don't."

Adam nodded. That much made sense.

"Other reason is finance. I couldn't raise the dough. Not for big production."

"Surely, with your track record, the banks . . ."

Hank Kreisel chuckled. "I'm into the banks already. So deep, some days they think I held 'em up. Never had much cash of my own. Surprising what you can do without it."

Adam understood that, too. Plenty of individuals and companies operated that way, and almost certainly Hank Kreisel's plants, their equipment, inventories, this house, his place at Higgins Lake, were mortgaged heavily. If Kreisel ever sold his business, or a part of it, he could reap millions in cash. Until he did, like others he would continue month by month with cash flow problems.

Again the parts manufacturer turned the thresher handle. Inside, the mechanism moved, though accomplishing nothing now; what it needed was grain to bite on, fed into a quart-size hopper at the top.

"Sure this is offbeat. Could say it's been a dream with me. Had it a long time." Hank Kreisel hesitated, seeming embarrassed by the admission, but went on, "Got the idea in Korea. Watched guys 'n dames in villages, pounding grain with rocks. Primitive: lots of muscle, small results. Saw a need, so started figuring this gizmo. Worked on it, on and off, ever since."

Erica was watching Hank Kreisel's face intently. She, too, knew something of his background, having learned it partly from Adam, partly elsewhere. Suddenly a picture took shape in her mind: of a tough, hard-fighting United States Marine in an alien, hostile land, yet observing native villagers with such understanding and compassion that, years afterward, an idea born at that time could stay with him like a flame.

"Tell you something, Adam," Kreisel said. "You too, Erica. This country's not selling farm machinery overseas. Leastways, not much. Ours is too fancy, too sophisticated. It's like a religion with us—the way I said: everything has to be powered. Must be electric, or use an engine, or whatever. What's forgotten is, Eastern countries have unending labor. You call for a guy to turn a handle, fifty come hurrying like flies—or ants. But we don't like that idea. Don't like to see dams built by coolies carrying stones. Idea offends us. We figure it's inefficient, not American; we say it's the way the pyramids were built. *So what*? Fact is: situation's there. Won't change for a long time, if ever. Another thing: out there, not many places to repair fancy machinery. So machines need to be simple." He took his hand away from the thresher whose handle he had continued turning. "This is."

Adam thought: Strangely, while Hank Kreisel had been speaking—eloquently for him—and demonstrating what he had built and believed in, he had a Lincolnesque quality which his tall, lean figure emphasized.

Would the idea work, Adam wondered? *Was* there a need, the way Hank Kreisel claimed? *Was* it a worthwhile project to which one of the Big Three auto companies might lend its world prestige?

Adam began firing questions based on his product planner's training in critical analysis. The questions embraced marketing, expected sales, distribution, local assembly, costs, parts, techniques for shipping, servicing, repair. Each point Adam raised, Kreisel seemed to have thought of and been prepared for, with the needed figures in his brain, and the responses showed why the parts manufacturer's own business had become the success it was.

Later, Hank Kreisel personally drove Adam and Erica to their car downtown.

Heading home, northward, on the John Lodge Freeway, Erica asked Adam, "Will you do what Hank wants? Will you get him in to see the chairman and the others?"

"I don't know." His voice betrayed doubts. "I'm just not sure."

"I think you should."

He glanced sideways, half-amused. "Just like that?"

Erica said firmly, "Yes, just like that."

"Aren't you the one who's always telling me I'm involved with too much already?" Adam was remembering the Orion, its introduction nearing week by week, with demands on his own time increasing, as they would for months ahead. Yet Farstar, now in early phases, was also requiring his concentration and working hours, at the office and at home.

Another thing on his mind was Smokey Stephensen. Adam knew he must resolve soon the question of his sister Teresa's investment in the auto dealership where he was overdue for another visit and a showdown with Smokey over several issues. Somehow, next week, he must try to fit *that* in.

He asked himself: Did he really want to take on something more?

Erica said, "It wouldn't take time. All Hank's asking is for an introduction so he can demonstrate his machine."

Adam laughed. "Sorry! It doesn't work that way." He explained: Any idea passed on for consideration at the summit of the company must have exhaustive analysis and views appended because nothing was ever dumped casually on the president's or chairman's desk. Even working through Elroy Braithwaite and Hub Hewitson, the executive vice-president—as Adam would have to—the ground rules still applied. Neither would authorize approach to the next higher echelon until an entire proposal had been sifted, costs worked out, market potential mapped, specific recommendations made.

And rightly so. Otherwise hundreds of crackpot schemes would clog the policymaking process.

In this instance—though other people might be involved later—Adam, initially, would have to do the work.

Something else: If farm products division had turned down Hank Kreisel's thresher scheme, as he admitted, Adam could make enemies by reviving it, whether success or failure followed. The farm products arm, though small by comparison with automotive operations, was still a part of the company, and making enemies anywhere was never a good idea.

In the end, tonight, Adam had been impressed by his host's demonstration and ideas. But would Adam gain by involvement? Would it be wise or foolish to become Hank Kreisel's sponsor?

Erica's voice cut through his thoughts. "Even if there were some work, I should think it might be a lot more useful than those other things you do."

He answered sarcastically, "I suppose you'd like me to drop the Orion, Farstar . . ."

"Why not? Those won't feed anybody. Hank's machine will."

"The Orion will feed you and me."

Even as he said it, Adam knew his last remark was smug and foolish, that they were drifting into a needless argument, but Erica flashed
back, "I suppose that's all you care about."

"No, it isn't. But there's a whole lot more to
think of."

"For instance, what?"

"For instance, Hank Kreisel's an opportunist."

"*I* liked him."

"So I noticed."

Erica's voice was ice. "Just what do you mean
by that?"

"Oh, hell!—nothing."

"I said: *What do you mean?*"

"All right," Adam answered, "while we were
by the pool, he was mentally undressing you.
You knew it, too. You didn't seem to mind."

Erica's cheeks were flushed. "Yes, I *did* know!
And no, I didn't mind! If you want the truth, I
liked it."

He said sourly, "Well, I didn't."

"I can't think why."

"What's that supposed to mean?"

"It means Hank Kreisel's a man, and acts like
one. That way, he makes a woman feel a woman."

"I suppose I don't."

"No, you bloody well don't!" Her anger filled
the car. It shook him. He had the sense to know
this had gone far enough.

Adam made his tone conciliatory. "Look,
maybe lately if I haven't been . . ."

"You objected because Hank made me feel
good. A woman. Wanted."

"Then I'm sorry. I suppose I said the wrong
thing, didn't think enough about it." He added,
"Besides, *I* want you."

"*Do you? Do you?*"

"Of course I do."

"*Then why don't you take me any more?*

*Don't you know it's two months since you did?
Before that, weeks and weeks. And you make me
feel so cheap telling you."*

They had left the freeway. Conscience-stricken, Adam stopped the car. Erica was sobbing, her face against the window on the other side. He reached gently for her hand.

She snatched it back. "Don't touch me!"

"Look," Adam said, "I guess I'm a first-class dope . . ."

"No! Don't say it! Don't say anything!" Erica choked back tears. "Do you think I want you to take me *now*? After asking? How do you think a woman feels who has to *ask*?"

He waited a while, feeling helpless, not knowing what to do or say. Then he started the car and they drove the rest of the way to Quarton Lake in silence.

As usual, Adam let Erica out before heading into the garage. Leaving, she told him quietly, "I've thought a lot, and it isn't just tonight. I want a divorce."

He said, "We'll talk about it."

Erica shook her head.

When he came in, she was already in the guest room with the door locked. That night for the first time since their marriage, they were in the same house and slept apart.

chapter twenty

"Gimme the bad news," Smokey Stephensen told Lottie Potts, his bookkeeper. "How much am I out of trust?"

Lottie, who looked and frequently behaved like a female Uriah Heep, but had a mind as sharp as razor blades, did quick arithmetic with a slim gold pencil.

"Counting those cars we just delivered, Mr. Stephensen, sir, forty-three thousand dollars."

"How much cash is in the bank, Lottie?"

"We can meet the payroll this week and next, Mr. Stephensen, sir. Not much more."

"Um." Smokey Stephensen rubbed a hand over his heavy beard, then leaned back, lacing his fingers over his belly which had grown larger lately; he reminded himself, absently, that he must do something about his weight soon, like going on a diet, though the thought depressed him.

Characteristically, Smokey was not alarmed about the financial crisis in which, this morning, he suddenly found himself. He had weathered others and would manage this one somehow. He pondered over Lottie's figures, doing further mental calculations of his own.

The day was Tuesday, in the first week of August, and the two of them were in Smokey's mezzanine office at the big suburban car dealership, Smokey behind his desk, wearing the blue silk jacket and brightly patterned tie which were like a uniform. Lottie, across from him, waited deferentially, several accounting ledgers spread open around her.

Smokey thought: There weren't many women around nowadays with Lottie's attitude. But then, if nature snarled at you at birth, making you as ugly as Lottie, you had to compensate in other ways. *By God!—she was a dog.* At thirty-five, or thereabouts, she looked fifty, with her lumpish lop-sided features, buck teeth, the suggestion of a squint, nondescript all-direction hair, appearing as if first grown on a coconut, a voice that grated like metal rims on cobblestones . . . Smokey switched his thoughts away, reminding himself that Lottie was utterly devoted, unquestionably loyal, unfailingly reliable, and that together they had clambered out of scrapes he might never have survived without her staff work.

Smokey had followed a dictum all his life: If you want a woman to stick beside you, pick an ugly one. Pretty girls were a luxury, but fickle. Ugly ones stayed to slice the meat and stir the gravy.

It was another ugly girl who had precipitated this morning's crisis. Smokey was grateful that she had.

Her name was Yolanda and she had telephoned him at home late last night.

Yolanda worked for the downtown bank which Smokey dealt with, and which financed his dealer's inventory of cars. She was a vice-president's secretary, with access to confidential information.

Another thing about Yolanda was that stripped to bra and panties she weighed two hundred pounds.

The moment Smokey had seen her, during a visit to the bank a year ago, he sensed a potential ally. Subsequently he telephoned, invited Yolanda to lunch and from that point let their friendship grow. Now, they met every two months or so; in between he sent her flowers, or candy which she devoured by the pound, and twice Smokey had taken her overnight to a motel. The latter occasions he preferred not to think about too much, but Yolanda—who had few such experiences come her way—remained pathetically grateful, a gratitude she repaid with periodic and useful intelligence from the bank.

"Our adjusters are planning some surprise dealer stock audits," she advised him on the phone last night. "I thought you'd want to know—your name is on the list."

He had asked, instantly alert, "When do the audits start?"

"First thing tomorrow, though no one's supposed to know." Yolanda added, "I couldn't call sooner because I've been working late and didn't think I should use an office phone."

"You're a bright kid. How long's the list?"

"Eight dealers are on it. I copied the names. Shall I read them?"

He blessed her thoroughness. "Please, baby."

Smokey was relieved to find his own name last but one. If the adjusters took the names in order, which was normal, it meant they wouldn't get to him until three days from now. So he had two days to work with, which wasn't much, but better than having a snap audit pulled tomorrow. He noted the other dealers' names. Three were acquaintances whom he would tip off; some other time they might repay the favor.

He told Yolanda, "You're a sweet kid to call me. We haven't seen enough of each other lately."

They ended with exchanges of affection, and Smokey sensed this was going to cost him another night at the motel, but it was worth it.

Next morning, early, he summoned Lottie, whom he also obliged in basic ways occasionally, but who never, at any time, failed to call him "Mr. Stephensen, sir." Her report—that the Stephensen dealership was seriously out of trust—resulted.

"Out of trust" meant that Smokey had sold cars, but had not turned the proceeds over to the bank which loaned him the money to buy them to begin with. The cars were the bank's security against its loan; therefore, since it had not been informed otherwise, the bank believed the cars were still safely in Smokey's inventory. In fact, forty-three thousand dollars worth of cars was gone.

Some sales had been reported to the bank over the past few weeks, but by no means all, and an audit of the dealership's stock—which banks and finance companies insisted on periodically—would reveal the deficiency.

The ex-race driver ruminated as he rubbed his beard again.

Smokey knew, as did all auto dealers, that it was normal for a dealership to be out of trust occasionally, and sometimes necessary. The trick was not to go too far, and not to get caught.

A reason for the problem was that car dealers had to find cash for each new car they took into stock, usually borrowing from banks or finance companies. But sometimes borrowing was not enough. A dealer's cash might be short, yet cash was needed—to pay for still more cars if the immediate sales outlook was good, or to meet expenses.

What dealers did, of course, was go slow in processing their paper work after any sale was consummated. Thus, a dealer might receive payment from a customer who bought a car, then subsequently the dealer would take a leisurely week or so to report the sale to his own creditors, the bank or finance company. During that time the dealer had the use of the money involved. Furthermore, at the end of it there would be more sales overlapping, which in turn could be processed slowly, so the dealer could use—again temporarily—the mony from those. In a way, it was like a juggling act.

Banks and finance companies knew the juggling went on and—within reason—condoned it by allowing dealers to be briefly, if unofficially "out of trust." They were unlikely, however, to tolerate an out-of-trust figure as large as Smokey's was at this moment.

Smokey Stephensen said softly, "Lottie, we gotta get some cars back in stock before those audit guys get here."

"I thought you'd say that, Mr. Stephensen, sir, so I made a list." The bookkeeper passed two clipped sheets across the desk. "These are all our customer deliveries for the past two weeks."

"Good girl!" Smokey scanned the list, noting approvingly that Lottie had included an address and telephone number against each name, as well as noting the model of car purchased and its price. He began ticking addresses which were reasonably near.

"We'll both get on the phone," Smokey said. "I've marked fourteen names to start. I'll take the top seven; you call the others. We need cars tomorrow morning, early. You know what to say."

"Yes, Mr. Stephensen, sir." Lottie, who had been through this before, was copying Smokey's notations on a duplicate list of her own. She would do her telephoning from the downstairs cubicle where she worked.

When Lottie had gone, Smokey Stephensen dialed the first number on his list. A pleasant female voice answered, and he identified himself.

"Just called," Smokey announced in his most mellifluous salesman's style, "to see how you good folks are enjoying that new car we had the privilege of selling you."

"We like it." The woman sounded surprised. "Why? Is anything wrong?"

"Nothing in the least wrong, ma'am. I'm simply making a personal check, the way I do with all my customers, to make sure everybody's happy. That's the way I run my business."

"Well," the woman said, "I guess it's a good way. Not many people seem to care that much nowadays."

"We care." Smokey had a cigar going by now; his feet were on the desk, chair tilted back. "All of us here care very much indeed. And about that, I have a suggestion for you."

"Yes?"

"Now that you've given your car some initial use, why not run it in to us tomorrow, let our service department give it a thorough check. That way we can see if anything wrong has shown up, as well as adjust anything else that's needed."

"But we've had the car less than a week . . ."

"All the more reason," Smokey said expansively, "for making sure everything's in tiptop shape. We'd like to do it for you; we really would. And there'll be no charge."

"You're certainly a *different* kind of car dealer," the woman on the phone said.

"I'd like to think that, ma'am. In any case, it's kind of you to say so."

They arranged that the car would be brought to the service department by eight o'clock the following morning. Smokey explained he wanted to allot one of his best mechanics to the job, and this would be easier if the car came early. The woman's husband, who usually drove to his office downtown, would either ride with someone else or take a bus.

Smokey made another call with similar results. With the two after that, he met resistance— tomorrow would not be convenient to release the cars; sensing firmness, he didn't press the point.

Making the fifth call he revised his tactics, though for no particular reason except as a change.

"We're not absolutely certain," Smokey informed the car's owner—a man who answered the telephone himself—"but we think your new car may have a defect. Frankly, I'm embarrassed to have to call you, but the way we feel about our customers, we don't like to take the slightest chance."

"No need to be embarrassed," the man said. "I'm glad you did call. What's the trouble?"

"We believe there may be a small exhaust leak, with carbon monoxide seeping into the passenger compartment. You or your passengers wouldn't smell it, but it might be dangerous. To be honest, it's something we've discovered on a couple of cars we received from the factory this week, and we're checking all others we've had recently to be on the safe side. I hate to admit it, but it looks as if there may have been a minor factory error."

"You don't have to tell me; I know how it is," the man said. "I'm in business myself, get labor problems all the time. The kind of help you get nowadays, they just don't care. But I sure appreciate your attitude."

"It's the way I run my shop," Smokey declared, "as I'm sure you do yours. So we can count on having your car here tomorrow morning?"

"Sure can. I'll run it in early."

"That's a big load off my mind. Naturally, there'll be no charge and, by the way, when you use the car between now and tomorrow, do me a favor and drive with a window open." The artist in Smokey could seldom resist the extra embellishment.

"Thanks for the tip! And I'll tell you something, mister—I'm impressed. Shouldn't be surprised if we do business again."

Smokey hung up, beaming.

At midmorning, Lottie Potts and her employer compared results. The bookkeeper had managed to get four cars promised for next day, Smokey five. The total of nine would have been enough if all the cars arrived, but between now and tomorrow morning some owners might change their minds or have problems arise to prevent them coming. Smokey decided to be safe. He selected another eight names from Lottie's list, and the two of them went back to telephoning. By noon, the owners of thirteen cars, in all, had agreed to return them to the Stephensen dealership early the following day for a variety of reasons.

Next was a conference between Smokey and his service manager, Vince Mixon.

Mixon was a cheerful whippet of a man, bald and in his late sixties, who ran the service department like a skillful maitre d'. He could diagnose instantly the ailments of any car, his organizational work was good, and customers liked him. But Vince Mixon had a weakness: he was an alcoholic. For ten months of each year he stayed on the wagon; twice a year, regularly, he fell off, sometimes with doleful consequences on the job.

No other employer would have tolerated the situation, and Mixon knew it; he also knew that if he lost his job, at his age he would never find another. Smokey, on the other hand, had shrewdly assessed the situation and figured advantages to himself. Vince Mixon was great when he functioned, and when he didn't Smokey managed. Smokey could also rely on his service manager not to be bothersome if ethics were bent occasionally; also, Mixon would do anything asked of him in tricky situations, such as now.

Together, they laid plans for tomorrow.

As each of the recalled cars arrived, it would

be whisked to the service department and washed, its interior vacuumed, the engine wiped over carefully to ensure a new appearance if the hood was raised. Glove compartments would be emptied of owners' possessions; these were to be stored in plastic bags, the bags tagged so that contents could be replaced later. License plates would be removed, their numbers carefully noted to ensure that eventually the right plates went back on the right cars. Tires must have a coat of black paint to simulate newness, especially where any tread wear showed.

The cars—a dozen, or thereabouts—would then be driven onto the fenced lot behind the dealership where new cars, not yet sold, were stored.

And that was all. No other work, of any kind, would be performed, and two days from now— apart from the cleaning job—the cars would be returned to their owners exactly as brought in.

In the meantime, however, they would be on the premises for counting and inspection by the bank's adjusters who would be satisfied, Smokey hoped, that his inventory of unsold cars was the size it should be.

Smokey said thoughtfully, "Those bank guys may not get here till the day after tomorrow. But the people'll be expecting their cars back tomorrow night. You'll have to phone everybody in the afternoon, invent a lot of excuses for holding 'em an extra day."

"Don't worry," Vince Mixon assured him, "I'll dream up good reasons."

His employer eyed him sternly. "I won't worry, long as you lay off the juice."

The whippet-like service manager held up a hand. "Not a teaspoonful till this is over. I promise."

Smokey knew from experience that the promise would be kept, but in exacting it he had ensured that a bender would soon follow. It was a strategy which the dealer seldom used, but he had to be sure of Vince Mixon for the next forty-eight hours.

"How about odometers?" the service man asked. "Some of those cars'll have a few hundred miles on by now."

Smokey pondered. There *was* a danger there; some bank adjusters were wise to dealer tricks and checked everything during a new car audit, odometers included. Yet messing with odometers nowadays was becoming tricky because of state laws; also, those in this year's models were the tamperproof kind.

"Nothing's tamperproof," Mixon asserted when Smokey reminded him of this. From a pocket the service manager produced a set of small, shaped metal keys. "See these? Made by a tool-and-die outfit called Expert Specialty in Greenville, South Carolina. Anybody can buy 'em and they'll reset odometers any which way; you name it."

"What about the new odometers—with white lines which drop if you change the numbers?"

"The lines are from plastic cases, set to break when you mess with them. But the same people who made those keys sell new plastic cases, which won't break, for a dollar each. I got two dozen outside, more on order." Mixon grinned. "Leave it to me, chief. Any odometer in that bunch showing over fifty miles, I'll turn back. Then before the owner gets the car again, I'll fix it the way it was."

Happily, Smokey clapped his employee on the shoulder. "Vince, we're in great shape!"

By the middle of next morning, it seemed they were.

As Smokey had anticipated, three of the

promised cars failed to show, but the other ten were brought in as arranged and were ample for his purpose. In the service department, washing, cleaning, and tire painting were going ahead briskly, taking priority over other work. Several of the cars had already been driven onto the storage lot, personally, by Vince Mixon.

Another item of good news was that the bank adjusters were conducting their audits in the order that the eight dealers' names appeared on Yolanda's list. Two of the three dealers whom Smokey tipped off yesterday had telephoned, with news from themselves and other dealerships which made this clear. It meant that Stephensen Motors could be sure of being checked tomorrow, though they would be ready by this afternoon.

Nor did Smokey have any real worries, provided he could get through today and tomorrow with his true stock posititon undetected. Business generally was excellent, the dealership sound, and he knew he could have his books back in order, and not be seriously out of trust, in a month or so. He admitted to himself: he *had* overextended a little, but then, he had gambled before and won, which was a reason he had lasted so long as a successful car dealer.

At 11:30 Smokey was relaxing in his mezzanine office, sipping coffee laced with brandy, when Adam Trenton walked in unannounced.

Smokey Stephensen had become slightly uneasy about Adam's visits, of which there had been several since their first meeting early in the year. He was even less pleased than usual to see Adam now.

"Hi!" he acknowledged. "Didn't know you were coming in."

"I've been here an hour," Adam told him. "Most of the time in the service department."

The tone of voice and a certain set to Adam's

face made Smokey uneasy. He grumbled, "Should think you might let me know when you get here. This is my shop."

"I would have, except you told me at the beginning . . ." Adam opened a black loose-leaf folder which he had carried during his last few visits and turned a page. "You told me the first time I came: 'Everything's wide open to you here, like a whorehouse with the roof off. You can see our books, files, inventories, just the way your sister would, as she's entitled to.' And later you said . . ."

Smokey growled. "Never mind! Didn't know I was talking to a recording machine." He stared suspiciously. "Maybe you been using one."

"If I had, you'd have known about it. I happen to have a clear memory, and when I'm involved in something I keep notes."

Smokey wondered what else was in the pages of the black folder. He invited Adam, "Sit down. Coffee?"

"No, thank you, and I'll stand. I came to tell you this is the last time I'll be in. I'm also informing you, because I think you're entitled to know, that I'm recommending my sister sell her stock in your business. Also"—Adam touched the black loose-leaf folder again—"I intend to turn this over to our company marketing department."

"*You what?*"

Adam said quietly, "I think you heard."

"*Then what the hell is in there?*"

"Among other things, the fact that your service department is, at this moment, systematically stripping several used cars of owner identification, faking them to look like new, and putting them with genuinely new cars on your storage lot. Your service manager, incidentally, has written bogus work orders on those cars for warranty which is not being performed but will be charged, no doubt, to our company. Right now I don't know the reason for what's happening, but think I can guess. However, since Teresa is involved, I'm going to call your bank, report what I've seen, and ask if they can enlighten me."

Smokey Stephensen said softly, *"Jesus Christ!"*

He knew the roof had fallen in, in a way he had least expected. He realized, too, his own mistake from the beginning: It was in being open with Adam Trenton, in giving him the run of the place the way he had. Smokey had sized up Adam as a bright, pleasant head office guy, undoubtedly good at his job or he wouldn't have it, but naïve in other areas, including the running of an auto dealership. It was why Smokey had reasoned that openness would be a kind of deception because Adam might sense if information was being held back, and it would make him curious, whereas frankness wouldn't. Also, Smokey believed that when Adam realized his sister's interest in the dealership was being dealt with honestly, he would not concern himself with other things. Too late, the dealer was learning he had been wrong on every count.

"Do me one favor," Smokey urged. "Gimme a minute to think. Then at least, let's talk."

Adam answered curtly, "All you'll be thinking of is a way to stop me, and it won't work. And we've done all the talking needed."

The dealer's voice rose. "How the hell you know what I'll be thinking?"

"All right; I don't know. But I know this: that you're a crook."

"That's a goddam lie! I could take you to court for it."

"I'm perfectly willing," Adam said, "to repeat

the statement in front of witnesses, and you can summon me into any court you want. But you won't."

"How a crook?" Smokey supposed he might as well find out what he could.

Adam dropped into a chair facing the desk and opened the black loose-leaf book.

"You want the whole list?"

"Damn right!"

"You cheat on warranty. You charge the manufacturer for work that isn't done. You replace parts that don't need replacing, then put the removed ones back in your own stock to use again."

Smokey insisted, "Give me *one* example."

Adam turned pages. "I've a lot more than one, but this is typical." An almost-new car had come into Stephensen Motors' service department, Adam recited, its carburetor needing minor adjustment. But instead of being adjusted, the carburetor was removed, a new one installed, the manufacturer billed for warranty. Afterward, the removed carburetor had been given the minor repair it needed to begin with, then was placed in the service department's stock from where it was later sold as a new unit. Adam had dates, work order and invoice numbers, the carburetor identification.

Smokey flushed. "Who said you could go snooping around my service records?"

"You did."

There were procedures to prevent that kind of fraud, as Adam knew. All Big Three manufacturers had them. But the vastness of organization, as well as the volume of work going through a big service depot, made it possible for dealers like Smokey to foil the system regularly.

He protested, "I can't keep tab of everything goes on in Service."

"You're responsible. Besides, Vince Mixon

runs that shop the way you tell him, the way he's running it today. Incidentally, another thing he does is pad customers' bills for labor. You want examples?"

Smokey shook his head. He had never suspected this son-of-a-bitch would be as thorough, or would even see and understand as much as he had. But even while Smokey listened, he was thinking hard, thinking the way he used to in a close race when he needed to pass or outmaneuver someone ahead of him on the track.

"Talking of customers," Adam said, "your salesmen still quote finance interest rates at so much a hundred dollars, even though the Truth in Lending Act makes that illegal."

"People prefer it that way."

"You mean *you* prefer it. Especially when an interest rate you quote as 'nine percent per hundred' means a *true* interest rate of over sixteen percent per year."

Smokey persisted, "That ain't so bad."

"I'll concede that. So would other dealers who do the same thing. What they might not like, though, is the way you cheat regularly on dealer sales contests. You postdate sales orders, change dates on others . . ."

Audibly, Smokey groaned. He waved a hand, surrendering. "Leave it, leave it! . . ."

Adam stopped.

Smokey Stephensen knew: *This guy Trenton had the goods.* Smokey might slide sideways out of some, or even all, the other finagling, but not this. Periodically, auto manufacturers awarded dealer bonuses—usually fifty to a hundred dollars a car—for every new car sale during specified periods. Since thousands of dollars were involved, such contests were carefully policed, but there were ways around the policing and Smokey, at times, had used them all. It was the kind of duplicity which a manufacturer's marketing department, if they learned of it, seldom forgave.

Smokey wondered if Adam knew, too, about the demonstrator cars—last year's models—which the dealership had sold as new after switching odometers. He probably did.

How in hell could one guy find out so much in just that little time?

Adam could have explained. Explained that to a top-flight automotive product planner, such matters as investigative research, detailed follow-through, analysis, the piecing together of fragmentary information, were all like breathing. Also, Adam was used to working fast.

Smokey had his eyes cast down on the desk in front of him; he appeared to be taking the time to think for which he had asked a few minutes ago. Now he lifted his head and inquired softly, "Whose side you on, anyway? Just whose interests you looking out for?"

Adam had anticipated the question. Last night and earlier today he had asked it of himself.

"I came here representing my sister, Teresa, and her forty-nine percent financial interest in this business. I still do. But that isn't to say I'll condone dishonesty, and neither would Teresa, or her husband, Clyde, if he were alive. It's why I'll go through with what I told you."

"About that. First thing you gonna do is call the bank. Right?"

"Right."

"Okay, Mr. Smart-ass-noble-high-'n-mighty, let me tell you what'll happen. The bank'll panic. Inspectors'll be around this afternoon, tomorrow they get a court order, padlock this place, seize the stock. Okay, next you say you'll hand them notes over to your company sales guys. Know what they'll do."

"At a guess, I'd say take away your franchise."

"No guessin'. It'll happen."

The two men eyed each other. The dealer leaned forward across the desk. "So where's that leave Teresa and them kids? How much you think forty-nine percent of a dead business'd be worth?"

"It wouldn't be a dead business," Adam said. "The company would put someone in temporarily until a new dealer could be named."

"A temporary guy! How well d'you think he'd run a business he doesn't know?—into bankruptcy maybe."

"Since you've brought up bankruptcy," Adam said, "that seems to be the way you're headed now."

Smokey slammed down a fist so hard and savagely that everything on his desk top shook. "There'll be no bankruptcy! Not if I play it my way. Only if we do it yours."

"So you say."

"*Never mind what I say!* I'll get my bookkeeper here right now! I'll prove it!"

"I've already been over the books with Miss Potts."

"Then, goddam, you'll go over them again with me!" Smokey was on his feet, raging, towering over Adam. The dealer's hands clenched and unclenched. His eyes were blazing.

Adam shrugged.

Smokey used an inside line to phone Lottie. When she promised to come at once, he slammed the phone down, breathing hard.

It took an hour.

An hour of argument, of assertions by Smokey Stephensen, of the dealer's penciled calculations with which the desk top was now strewn, of amplification of her bookkeeping by Lottie Potts, of examination of financial precedents reaching back to earlier years.

At the end Adam admitted to himself that it *could* be done. Smokey just might, just could, have the business back in shape financially a month from now, allowing for certain unorthodoxies and assuming a continuing upward trend in new car sales. The alternative was a temporary management which—as Smokey pointed out—might prove disastrous.

Yet to accomplish the survival of Stephensen Motors, Adam would be obliged to condone deception and defrauding of the bank's adjusters. He had the knowledge now; it was no longer a matter of guessing. During their rehash of the facts, Smokey admitted his out-of-trust position and his scheming to survive tomorrow's new car audit.

Adam wished he didn't know. He wished fervently that his sister, Teresa, had never involved him in this at all. And for the first time he understood the wisdom of his company's Conflict of Interest rules which forbade auto company employees to become involved—financially or otherwise—with auto dealerships.

As Lottie Potts gathered together her ledgers and left, Smokey Stephensen stood challengingly, hands on hips, his eyes on Adam. "Well?"

Adam shook his head. "Nothing's changed."

"It'll change for Teresa," Smokey said softly. "One month a nice fat check, next month, maybe, nothing. Another thing—all that stuff you accused me of. You never said I cheated Teresa."

"Because you haven't. That's the one area where everything's in order."

"If I'd wanted to, I could have cheated her. Couldn't I?"

"I suppose so."

"But I didn't, and ain't that what you came here to find out?"

Adam said wearily, "Not entirely. My sister wanted to take a long term view." He paused, then added, "I've also an obligation to the company I work for."

"*They* didn't send you here."

"I know that. But I didn't expect to discover all I have and now—as a company man—I can't ignore it."

"You sure you can't? Not for the sake of Teresa and them kids?"

"I'm sure."

Smokey Stephensen rubbed his beard and ruminated. His outward anger had gone, and when he spoke his voice was low, with a note of pleading. "I'll ask you to do one thing, Adam—and, sure, it'd help me—but you'd be doing it for Teresa."

"Doing what?"

Smokey urged, "Walk out of here right now! Forget what you know about today! Then gimme two months to get finances back in shape because there's nothing wrong with this business that that amount of time won't fix. You know it."

"I don't know it."

"But you know the Orion's coming, and you know what it'll do to sales."

Adam hesitated. The reference to the Orion was like a flag planted in his own back yard. If he believed in the Orion, obviously he believed that, with it, Stephensen Motors would do well.

Adam asked curtly, "Suppose I agreed. What happens at the end of two months?"

The dealer pointed to the black loose-leaf notebook. "You hand over them notes to your company marketing guys, the way you said you would. So, okay, I'd have to sell out or lose the franchise, but it'd be a growing business that was sold. Teresa'd get twice as much for her half, maybe more, than she would from a forced sale now."

Adam hesitated. Though it still involved dishonesty, the compromise held a compelling logic.

"Two months," the ex-race driver pleaded. "That ain't so much to ask."

"One month," Adam said decisively. "One month from today; that's all."

As Smokey visibly relaxed and grinned, Adam knew he had been conned. And now the decision was made, it left Adam depressed because he had acted against his own conscience and good judgment. But he was determined he *would* turn over to his company's marketing department, a month from now, the notes on Stephensen Motors.

Smokey, unlike Adam, was not depressed but buoyant. Though—with a dealer's instinct—he had asked for two months, he had wanted one.

In that time a lot might happen; something new could always turn up.

chapter twenty-one

A svelte United Air Lines ground hostess brought coffee to Brett DeLosanto who was telephoning from United's 100,000-Mile Club at Detroit Metropolitan Airport. It was close to 9 A.M., and the pleasantly appointed club lounge was quiet in contrast to the noisy, bustling terminal outside. No strident flight announcements were ever made here. The service—as became the VIP crowd—was more personal, and muted.

"There's no enormous hurry, Mr. DeLosanto," the girl said as she put the coffee on a table beside the tilt-back chair in which Brett was reclining while he phoned, "but Flight 81 to Los Angeles will begin boarding in a few minutes."

"Thanks!" Brett told Adam Trenton with whom he had been conversing for the past few minutes, "I have to go soon. The bird to Paradise awaits."

"Never thought of L.A. as being that," Adam said.

Brett sipped his coffee. "It's part of California, which viewed from Detroit is Paradise whichever way you slice the oranges."

Adam was speaking from his office at the company staff building, where Brett had called him. They had been discussing the Orion. A few days ago, with Job One—the first production Orion—only two weeks away, several color matching problems had arisen affecting soft trim inside the car. A design "surveillance group," which stayed with any new car through all its stages of production, had reported that some interior plastic delivered for manufacture looked "icy"—a serious fault—and upholstery, carpeting, and head lining were not the exact match they ought to be.

Colors were always a problem. Any car had as many as a hundred separate pieces which must match a color key, yet the materials had differing chemical compositions and pigment bases, making it difficult to achieve identical color shades. Working against a deadline, a design team and representatives from Purchasing and Manufacturing had finally rectified all differences, news just received by Adam with relief.

Brett had been tempted to mention the newer project, Farstar, on which work was proceeding excitingly on several fronts. But he caught himself in time, remembering he was on an outside telephone, also that this airline club room, where several other passengers relaxed while awaiting flights, was used by executives from competing companies.

"Something you'll be pleased to know," Adam told Brett. "I decided to try to help Hank Kreisel with his thresher. I sent young Castaldy over to Grosse Pointe to look at it; he came back full of enthusiasm, so then I talked with Elroy Braithwaite who seemed favorable. Now, we're preparing a report for Hub."

"Great!" The young designer's pleasure was genuine. He realized he had let emotion sway judgment in putting pressure on Adam to support Hank Kreisel's scheme, but so what? More and more, nowadays, Brett believed the auto industry had public obligations it was not fulfilling, and something like the thresher gave the industry a chance to utilize its resources in filling an admitted need.

"Of course," Adam pointed out, "the whole thing may never get past Hub."

"Let's hope you pick a 'cloud-of-dust' day to tell him."

Adam understood the reference. Hub Hewitson, the company's executive vice-president, when liking an idea, whirled himself and others into instant, feverish action, raising—as associates put it—clouds of dust. The Orion had been a Hub Hewitson dust cloud, and still was; so had other successes, failures too, though the latter were usually forgotten as fresh Hewitson dust erupted elsewhere.

"I'll look out for one of those days," Adam promised. "Have a good trip."

"So long, friend." Brett swallowed the remainder of his coffee, patted the airline hostess amiably on the rump as he passed her, then headed for the flight departure gate.

United's Flight 81—Detroit nonstop to Los Angeles—took off on schedule.

Like many who live frenetic lives on the ground, Brett enjoyed transcontinental air travel in the luxury of first class. Any such journey assured four or five hours of relaxation, interspersed pleasantly with drinks, good food and service, plus the complacent knowledge of not being reachable by telephone or otherwise, no matter how many urgencies boiled over down below.

Today, Brett used much of the journey merely to think, reviewing aspects of his life—past, present, future—as he saw them. Thus occupied, the time passed quickly and he was surprised to realize, during an announcement from the flight deck, that nearly four hours had elapsed since takeoff.

"We're crossing the Colorado River, folks," the captain's voice rattled on the p.a. "This is a point where three states meet—California, Nevada, Arizona—and it's a beautiful day in all of them, with visibility about a hundred miles. Those of you sitting on the right side can see Las Vegas and the Lake Mead area. If you're on the left, that water down there is Lake Havasu where London Bridge is being rebuilt."

Brett, on the port side with a seat section to himself, peered downward. The sky was cloudless and though they were high—at thirty-nine thousand feet—he could see, easily and sharply, the shape of the bridge below.

"Funny thing about that bridge," the captain went on chattily. "Story is—the people who bought it from the British got their bridges mixed. They thought they were buying the bridge on all those London travel posters, and no one told them until too late that *that* one is Tower Bridge, and London Bridge was a bitty old bridge upstream. Ha! ha!"

Brett continued to look down, knowing from the terrain below that they were now over California. He said aloud, "Forever bless my native state, its sunshine, oranges, screwball politics, religions, and its nuts."

A passing stewardess inquired, "Did you say something, sir?" She was young, willowy and tanned, as if her off-duty hours were spent exclusively at the beach.

"Sure did. I asked, 'What's a California girl like you doing for dinner tonight?'"

She flashed an impish smile. "Mostly depends on my husband. Sometimes he likes to eat at home; other times we go . . ."

"Okay," Brett said. "And the hell with women's lib! At least in the old days, when airlines fired girls who got married, you knew which were the unclipped wing ones."

"If it makes you feel any better," she told him, "if I weren't going home to my husband, I'd be interested."

He was wondering if that piece of blandishment was in the airline stewardess manual when the p.a. system came alive once more.

"This is your captain again, folks. Guess I should have told you to make the most of that hundred-mile visibility we've been enjoying. We've just received the latest Los Angeles weather. They're reporting heavy smog, with visibility in the L.A. area reduced to one mile or less."

They would be landing, the captain added, in another fifty minutes.

The first smog traces were evident over the San Bernardino Mountains. With Flight 81 still sixty miles from the Pacific Coast, Brett, looking out, reflected: *Sixty miles!* On his last trip, barely a year ago, no smog had appeared until Ontario, another twenty-five miles westward. Each time he came here, it seemed, the photochemical smog spread farther inland over the loveliness of the Golden State like an evil fungus. Their Boeing 720 was losing height now for the approach to Los Angeles International, but instead of land-marks below becoming clearer, they were blurring beneath an increasing gray-brown haze which nullified color, sunshine, seascape. The panoramic view of Santa Monica Bay which approaching air travelers used to behold was mostly, nowadays, a memory. As they continued descending and the smog grew worse, Brett DeLosanto's mood became increasingly melancholy.

Ten miles east of the airport, as the captain had predicted, visibility diminished to a mile, so that at 11:30 A.M. Pacific Daylight Time, the ground was barely visible.

After landing, in the United Terminal a brisk young man named Barclay from the company's regional office was awaiting Brett.

"I have a car for you, Mr. DeLosanto. We can drive directly to your hotel, or the college if you wish."

"Hotel first." Brett's official purpose in being here was to visit the Art Center College of Design, Los Angeles, but he would go there later.

Though the aerial view of his beloved California under its despoiling, filthy blanket had depressed him, Brett's spirits revived at the sight and sound of the airport's surging ground traffic at closer quarters. Cars, either singly or en masse, always excited him, especially in California where mobility was a way of life, with more than eleven percent of the nation's automobiles crammed within the state. Yet the same source had helped create an air pollution which was inescapable; already, Brett felt an irritation of the eyes, his nostrils prickled; without doubt the unclean brume was deeply in his lungs. He asked Barclay, "Has it been as bad as this for long?"

"About a week. Seems now, a partly clear day is an exception, a real clear one about as rare as Christmas." The young man wrinkled his nose. "We tell people it isn't all made by cars, that a lot is industrial haze."

"But do we believe it?"

"Hard to know what to believe, Mr. De-Losanto. Our own people tell us we have engine emission problems licked. Do you believe *that*?"

"In Detroit I believe it. When I get here I'm not so sure."

What it came down to, Brett knew, was the balance between economics and numbers. It was possible, now, to build a totally emission-free auto engine, but only at high cost which would make the cars employing it as remote from everyday use as a nobleman's carriage once was from the foot-slogging peasantry. To keep costs reasonable engineering compromises had to be made, though even with compromises, present emission control was excellent, and better by far than envisioned only a lustrum ago. Yet sheer numbers—the daily, weekly, monthly, yearly proliferation of cars— undid the end effect, as was smoggily evident in California.

They were at the car Brett would use during his stay.

"I'll drive," Brett said. He took the keys from Barclay.

Later, having checked in at the Beverly Hilton, and shed Barclay, Brett drove alone to the Art Center College of Design on West Third Street. CBS Television City towered nearby, with Farmers' Market huddled behind. Brett was expected, and was received with dual enthusiasm— as a representative of a company which hired many of each year's graduates, and as a distinguished alumnus himself.

The relatively small college buildings were, as usual, busily crowded, with all usable space occupied and nothing wasted on frills. The entrance lobby, though small, was an extension of classrooms and perpetually in use for informal conferences, interviews, and individual study.

The head of Industrial Design, who welcomed Brett amid a buzz of other conversations, told him, "Maybe someday we'll take time out to plan a quieter cloister."

"If I thought there was a chance," Brett rejoined, "I'd warn you not to. But you won't. This place should stay the pressure cooker it is."

It was an atmosphere he knew well—perpetually work-oriented, with emphasis on professional discipline. *This is not for amateurs,* the college catalogue declared, *this is for real.* Unlike many schools, assignments were arduously demanding, requiring students to produce, produce . . . over days, nights, weekends, holidays . . . leaving little time for extra interests, sometimes none. Occasionally, students protested at the unrelenting stress, and a few dropped out, but most adjusted and, as the catalogue put it too:

"Why pretend that the life they are preparing for is easy? It is not and never will be."

The emphasis on work and unyielding standards were reasons why auto makers respected the college and kept in touch with faculty and students. Frequently, companies competed for the services of top-line students in advance of graduation. Other design colleges existed elsewhere, but Los Angeles Art Center was the only one with a specific course in auto design, and nowadays at least half of Detroit's annual crop of new designers traveled the L.A. route.

Soon after arrival, surrounded by a group of students, Brett broke off to survey the tree-shaded inner courtyard where they had gathered, and were sipping coffee or soft drinks, and chewing doughnuts.

"Nothing's changed," he observed. "It's like coming home."

"Pretty packed living room," one of the students said.

Brett laughed. Like everything else here, the courtyard was too small, the students elbowing for space too many. Yet for all the congestion, only the truly talented were admitted to the school, and only the best survived the grueling three-year course.

The exchange of talk—a reason why Brett had come—went on.

Inevitably, air pollution was on the minds of students; even in this courtyard there was no escaping it. The sun, which should have been shining brightly from an azure sky, instead filtered dully through the thick gray haze extending from the ground to high above. Here, too, eye and nose irritation were constant and Brett remembered a recent U. S. Public Health warning that breathing New York's polluted air was equal to smoking a pack of cigarettes a day; thus nonsmokers innocently shared a smoker's probability of death from cancer. He presumed the same was true of Los Angeles, perhaps even more so.

On the subject of pollution, Brett urged, "Tell me what you characters think." A decade from now students like these would be helping shape industry policy.

"One thing you figure when you live here," a voice from the rear injected, "is something has to give. If we go on the way things are, one day everybody in this town will choke to death."

Brett pointed out, "Los Angeles is special. Smog is worse because of geography, temperature inversion, and a lot of sunlight."

"Not so special," someone else put in. "Have you been in San Francisco lately?"

"Or New York?"

"Or Chicago?"

"Or Toronto?"

"Or even little country towns on market days?"

Brett called across the chorus, "Hey! If you feel that way, maybe some of you are headed for the wrong business. Why design cars at all?"

"Because we're nutty about cars. Love 'em! Doesn't stop us thinking, though. Or knowing what's going on, and caring." The speaker was a gangling young man with untidy blond hair, at the forefront of the group. He put a hand through his hair, revealing the long slender fingers of an artist.

"To hear a lot of people out West, and other places"—Brett was playing devil's advocate—"you'd think the only future is in mass transportation."

"That old chestnut!"

"No one really wants to use mass transport," one of the few girls in the group declared. "Not if a car's practical and they can afford it. Besides, mass transit's a delusion. With subsidies, taxes, and fares, public transport delivers a lot less than automobiles for more money. So everybody gets taken. Ask New Yorkers! Soon—ask San Franciscans."

Brett smiled. "They'll love you in Detroit."

The girl shook her head impatiently. "I'm not saying it because of that."

"Okay," Brett told the others, "let's agree that cars will be the main form of transportation for another half century, probably a lot longer. What kind of cars?"

"Better," a quiet voice said. "A lot better than now. And fewer."

"Not much argument about being better, though the question's always: Which way? I'm interested, though, in how you figure fewer."

"Because we ought to think that way, Mr. DeLosanto. That's if we take the long view, which is for our own good in the end."

Brett looked curiously at the latest speaker who now stepped forward, others near the front easing aside to make room. He, too, was young, but short, swarthy, with the beginning of a pot belly and, on the surface, appearing anything but an intellectual. But his soft voice was compelling and others fell silent as if a spokesman had moved in.

"We have a good many rap sessions here," the swarthy student said. "Those of us taking Transportation Design want to be a part of the auto industry. We're excited by the idea. Cars turn us on. But it doesn't mean that any one of us is headed for Detroit wearing blinders."

"Let's hear the rest of it," Brett urged. "Keep talking!" Coming back, listening to forthright student views again—views unencumbered by defeats, disillusion, too much knowledge of practicalities or financial limitations—was an emotional experience like having personal batteries charged.

"A thing about the auto industry nowadays," the swarthy student said, "is it's tuned in to responsibility. Sometimes the critics won't admit it, but it has. There's a new feeling. Air pollution, safety, quality, all those things aren't just talking subjects any more. Something's being done, this time for real."

The others were still quiet. Several more students had joined the group; Brett guessed they were from other courses. Though a dozen art specialties beside automotive design were taught here, the subject of cars always evoked general interest within the school.

"Well," the same student continued, "the auto industry has some other responsibilities too. One of them is numbers."

It was curious, Brett thought, that at the airport earlier he had been thinking about numbers himself.

"It's the numbers that eat us up," the soft-voiced, swarthy student said. "They undo every effort the car people make. Take safety. Safer cars are engineered and built, so what happens? More get on the road; accidents go up, not down. With air pollution it's the same. Cars being made right now have the best engines ever, and they pollute less than any engine ever did before. There are even cleaner ones ahead. Right?"

Brett nodded. "Right."

"But the *numbers* keep going up. We're bragging now about producing ten million new cars a year, so no matter how good anybody gets at emission control, the total pollution gets worse. It's wild!"

"Supposing all that's true, what's the alternative? To ration cars?"

Someone said, "Why not?"

"Let me ask you something, Mr. DeLosanto,"

the swarthy student said. "You ever been in Bermuda?"

Brett shook his head.

"It's an island of twenty-one square miles. To make sure they keep room to move around, the Bermuda government does ration cars. First they limit engine capacity, body length and width. Then they allow only one car for every household."

A voice among the newcomers objected, "Nuts to that!"

"I'm not saying we should be that strict," the original speaker persisted. "I'm simply saying we ought to draw a line somewhere. And it isn't as if the auto industry couldn't stay healthy producing the same number of cars it does now, or that people couldn't manage. They manage in Bermuda fine."

"If you tried it here," Brett said, "you might have a new American Revolution. Besides, not being able to sell as many cars as people want to buy is an attack on free enterprise." He grinned, offsetting his own words. "It's heresy."

In Detroit, he knew, many *would* view the idea as heretical. But he wondered: Was it really? How much longer could the auto industry, at home and overseas, produce vehicles—with whatever kind of power plant—in continually increasing quantity? Wouldn't someone, somewhere, somehow, have to rule, as Bermuda had done: *Enough!* Wasn't the day approaching when a measure of control of numbers would become essential for the common good? Taxis were limited in number everywhere; so, to an extent, were trucks. Why not private cars? And if it didn't happen, North America could consist eventually of one big traffic jam; at times it was close to that already. Therefore, wouldn't auto industry leaders be wiser, more farsighted and responsible, if they took an initiative in self-restraint themselves?

But he doubted if they would.

A fresh voice cut in, "Not all of us feel the way Harvey does. Some think there's room for lots more cars yet."

"And we figure to design a few."

"Damn right!"

"Sorry, Harv! The world's not ready for you."

But there were several murmurs of dissent, and it was obvious that the swarthy student, Harvey, had a following.

The lanky blond youth who had declared earlier, *"We're nutty about cars,"* called, "Tell us about the Orion."

"Get me a pad," Brett said. "I'll show you."

Someone passed one, and heads craned over while he sketched. He drew the Orion swiftly in profile and head-on view, knowing the lines of the car the way a sculptor knows a carving he has toiled on. There were appreciative "wows," and "really great!"

Questions followed. Brett answered frankly. When possible, design students were fed these privileged tidbits, like heady bait, to keep their interest high. However, Brett was careful to fold and pocket his drawings afterward.

As students drifted back to classes, the courtyard session broke up. For the remainder of his time at the Art Center College of Design—through the same day and the next—Brett delivered a formal lecture, interviewed automotive design students individually, and critically appraised experimental car models which student teams had designed and built.

An instinct among this crop of students, Brett discovered, was toward severity of design, allied with function and utility. Curiously, it had been a similar combination of ideas agreed to by Brett, Adam Trenton, Elroy Braithwaite and the others, on the memorable night, two and a half months earlier, when the initial concept for Farstar had emerged. Through the time he had already spent on early Farstar designs, still being labored over in a closely guarded studio at Detroit, and now here, Brett was struck by the aptness of Adam's phrase: *Ugly is Beautiful!*

History showed that artistic trends—the latticework of all commercial designing—always began subtly and often when least expected. No one knew why artistic tastes changed, or how, or when the next development would come; it seemed simply that human virtuosity and perception were restless, ready to move on. Observing the students' work now—ignoring a degree of naïveté and imperfection—and remembering his own designs of recent months, Brett felt an exhilaration at being part of an obviously fresh, emerging trend.

Some of his enthusiasm, it seemed, transmitted itself to students whom he interviewed during his second day at the school. Following the interviews, Brett decided to recommend two potential graduates to the company Personnel and Organization staff for eventual hiring. One was the short, swarthy student, Harvey, who had argued forcefully in the courtyard; his design portfolio showed an ability and imagination well above average. Whichever auto company he worked for, Harvey was probably headed for trouble and collisions in Detroit. He was an original thinker, a maverick who would not be silenced, or dissuaded easily from strong opinions. Fortunately, while not always heeding mavericks, the auto industry encouraged them, knowing their value as a hedge against complacent thinking.

Whatever happened, Brett suspected, Detroit and Harvey would find each other interesting.

The other candidate he chose was the gangling youth with untidy blond hair whose talent, too, was obviously large. Brett's suggestion of future employment, so the student said, was the second approach made to him. Another auto firm among the Big Three had already promised him a design job, if he wanted it, on graduation.

"But if there's any chance of working near you, Mr. DeLosanto," the young man said, "I'll go with your company for sure."

Brett was touched, and flattered, but uncertain how to answer.

His uncertainty was based on a decision reached, alone in his Los Angeles hotel room, the previous night. It was now mid-August, and Brett had decided: at year end, unless something happened drastically to change his mind, he would quit the auto industry for good.

On the way back East, by air, he made another decision: Barbara Zaleski would be the first to know.

chapter twenty-two

Also in August—while Brett DeLosanto was in California—the Detroit assembly plant, where Matt Zaleski was assistant plant manager, was in a state of chaos.

Two weeks earlier, production of cars had ceased. Specialist contractors had promptly moved in, their assignment to dismantle the old assembly line and create a new one on which the Orion would be built.

Four weeks had been allotted for the task. At the end of it, the first production Orion—Job One—would roll off the line, then, in the three or four weeks following, a backlog of cars would be created, ready to meet expected demands after official Orion introduction day in September. After that, if sales prognostications held, the tempo would increase, with Orions flowing from the plant in tens of thousands.

Of the time allowed for plant conversion, two weeks remained and, as always at model changeover time, Matt Zaleski wondered if he would survive them.

Most of the assembly plant's normal labor force was either laid off or enjoying paid vacations, so that only a skeleton staff of hourly paid employees reported in each day. But far from the shutdown making the life of Matt Zaleski and others of the plant management group easier, work loads increased, anxieties multiplied, until an ordinary production day seemed, by comparison, an unruffled sea.

The contractor's staff, like an occupying army, was demanding. So were company headquarters engineers who were advising, assisting, and sometimes hindering the contractors.

The plant manager, Val Reiskind, and Matt were caught in a crossfire of requests for information, hurried conferences, and orders, the latter usually requiring instant execution. Matt handled most matters which involved practical running of the plant, Reiskind being young and new. He had replaced the previous plant manager, McKernon, only a few months earlier and while the new man's engineering and business diplomas were impressive, he lacked Matt's seasoned know-how acquired during twenty years on the job. Despite Matt's disappointment at failing to get McKernon's job, and having a younger man brought in over him, he liked Reiskind who was smart enough to be aware of his own deficiency and treated Matt decently.

Most headaches centered around new, sophisticated machine tools for assembly, which in theory worked well, but in practice often didn't. Technically, it was the contractor who was responsible for making the whole system function, but Matt Zaleski knew that when contractor's men were gone, he would inherit any inadequate situation they might leave. Therefore he stayed close to the action now.

The greatest enemy of all was time. There was never enough to make a changeover work so smoothly that by preassigned completion date it could be said: "All systems *go!*" It was like building a house which was never ready on the day set for moving in, except that a house move could be postponed, whereas a car or truck production schedule seldom was.

An unexpected development also added to Matt's burdens. An inventory audit, before production of the previous year's models ceased, had revealed stock shortages so huge as to touch off a major investigation. Losses from theft at any auto plant were always heavy. With thousands of workers changing shifts at the same time, it was a simple matter for thieves—either employees or walk-in intruders—to carry stolen items out.

But this time a major theft ring was obviously at work. Among items missing were more than three hundred four-speed transmissions, hundreds of tires, as well as substantial quantities of radios, tape players, air conditioners, and other components.

As an aftermath, the plant swarmed with security staff and outside detectives. Matt, though not remotely implicated, had been obliged to spend hours answering detectives' questions about plant procedure. So far there appeared to be no break in the case, though the Chief of Security told Matt, "We have some ideas, and there are a few of your line workers we want to interrogate when they come back." Meanwhile the detectives remained underfoot, their presence one more irritant at an arduous time.

Despite everything, Matt had come through so far, except for a small incident concerning himself which fortunately went unnoticed by anyone important at the plant.

He had been in his office the previous Saturday afternoon, seven-day work weeks being normal during model changeover, and one of the older secretaries, Iris Einfeld, who was also working, had brought him coffee. Matt began drinking it gratefully. Suddenly, for no reason he could determine, he was unable to control the cup and it fell from his hand, the coffee spilling over his clothing and the floor.

Angry at himself for what he thought of as carelessness, Matt got up—then fell full length, heavily. Afterward, when he thought about it, it semed as if his left leg failed him and he remembered, too, he had been holding the coffee in his left hand.

Mrs. Einfeld, who was still in Matt's office, had helped him back into his chair, then wanted to summon aid, but he dissuaded her. Instead, Matt sat for a while, and felt some of the feeling come back into his left leg and hand, though he knew he would not be able to drive home. Eventually, with some help from Iris Einfeld, he left the office by a back stairway and she drove him home in her car. On the way he persuaded her to keep quiet about the whole thing, being afraid that if word got around he would be treated as an invalid, the last thing he wanted.

Once home, Matt managed to get to bed and stayed there until late Sunday when he felt much better, only occasionally being aware of a slight fluttering sensation in his chest. On Monday morning he was tired, but otherwise normal, and went to work.

The weekend, though, had been lonely. His daughter, Barbara, was away somewhere and Matt Zaleski had had to fend for himself. In the old days, when his wife was alive, she had always helped him over humps like model changeover time with understanding, extra affection, and meals which—no matter how long she waited for him to come home—she prepared with special care. But it seemed so long since he had known any of those things that it was hard to remember Freda had been dead less than two years. Matt realized, sadly, that when she was alive he had not appreciated her half as much as he did now.

He found himself, too, resenting Barbara's preoccupation with her own life and work. Matt would have liked nothing more than to have Barbara remain at home, available whenever he came there, and thus filling—at least in part— her mother's role. For a while after Freda's death Barbara had seemed to do that. She prepared their meal each evening, which she and Matt ate together, but gradually Barbara's outside interests revived, her work at the advertising agency increased, and nowadays they were rarely in the Royal Oak house together except to sleep, and occasionally for a hurried weekday breakfast. Months ago Barbara had urged that they seek a housekeeper, which they could well afford, but Matt resisted the idea. Now, with so much to do for himself, on top of pressures at the plant, he wished he had agreed.

He had already told Barbara, early in August, that he had changed his mind and she could go ahead and hire a housekeeper after all, to which Barbara replied that she would do so when she could, but at the moment was too busy at the agency to take time out to advertise, interview, and get a housekeeper installed. Matt had bristled at that, believing it to be a woman's business— even a daughter's—to run a home, and that a man should not have to become involved, particularly when he was under stress, as Matt was now. Barbara made it clear, however, that she regarded her own work as equally important with her father's, an attitude he could neither accept nor understand.

There was a great deal else, nowadays, that Matt Zaleski failed to understand. He had only to open a newspaper to become alternately angry and bewildered at news of traditional standards set aside, old moralities discarded, established order undermined. No one, it seemed, respected anything any more—including constituted authority, the courts, law, parents, college presidents, the military, the free enterprise system, or the American flag, under which Matt and others of his generation fought and died in World War II.

As Matt Zaleski saw it, it was the young who caused the trouble, and increasingly he hated most of them: those with long hair you couldn't tell from girls (Matt still had a crewcut and wore it like a badge); student know-it-alls, choked up with book learning, spouting McLuhan, Marx, or Che Guevara; militant blacks, demanding the millennium on the spot and not content to progress slowly; and all other protestors, rioters, contemptuous of everything in sight and beating up those who dared to disagree. The whole bunch of them, in Matt's view, were callow, immature, knowing nothing of real life, contributing nothing . . . When he thought of the young his bile and blood pressure rose together.

And Barbara, while certainly no rebellious student or protestor, sympathized openly with most of what went on, which was almost as bad. For this, Matt blamed the people his daughter associated with, including Brett DeLosanto whom he continued to dislike.

In reality, Matt Zaleski—like many in his age group—was the prisoner of his long-held views. In conversations which sometimes became heated arguments, Barbara had tried to persuade him to her own conviction: that a new breadth of outlook had developed, that beliefs and ideas once held immutable had been examined and found false; that what younger people despised was not the morality of their parents' generation, but a façade of morality with duplicity behind; not old standards in themselves, but hypocrisy and self-deception which, all too often, the so-called standards shielded. In fact, it was a time of question, of exciting intellectual experiment from which mankind could only gain.

Barbara had failed in her attempts. Matt Zaleski, lacking insight, saw the changes around him merely as negative and destroying.

In such a mood, as well as being tired and having a nagging stomachache, Matt came home late to find Barbara and a guest already in the house. The guest was Rollie Knight.

Earlier that evening, through arrangements made for her by Leonard Wingate, Barbara had met Rollie downtown. Her purpose was to acquire more knowledge about the life and experiences of black people—Rollie in particular—both in the inner city and with the hard core hiring program. A spoken commentary to accompany the documentary film *Auto City*, now approaching its final edited form, would be based, in part, on what she learned.

To begin, she had taken Rollie to the Press Club, but the club had been unusually crowded and noisy; also, Rollie had not seemed at ease. So, on impulse, Barbara suggested driving to her home. They did.

She had mixed a whisky and water for each of them, then whipped up a simple meal of eggs and bacon which she served on trays in the living room; after that, with Rollie increasingly relaxed and helpful, they talked.

Later, Barbara brought the whisky bottle in and poured them each a second drink. Outside, the dusk—climaxing a clear, benevolent day— had turned to dark.

Rollie looked around him at the comfortable, tastefully furnished, though unpretentious room. He asked, "How far we here from Blaine and 12th?"

About eight miles, she told him.

He shook his head and grinned. "Eight hundred, more like."

Blaine and 12th was where Rollie lived, and where film scenes had been shot the night Brett DeLosanto and Leonard Wingate watched.

Barbara had scribbled Rollie's thought in a

few key words, thinking it might work well as
an opening line, when her father walked in.

Matt Zaleski froze.

He looked incredulously at Barbara and
Rollie Knight, seated on the same settee, drinks in
their hands, a whisky bottle on the floor between
them, the discarded dinner trays nearby. In her
surprise, Barbara had let the pad on which she
had been writing slip from her hand and out of
sight.

Rollie Knight and Matt Zaleski, though never
having spoken together at the assembly plant,
recognized each other instantly. Matt's eyes went,
unbelievingly, from Rollie's face to Barbara's.
Rollie grinned and downed his drink, making a
show of self-assurance, then seemed uncertain.
His tongue moistened his lips.

"Hi, Dad!" Barbara said. "This is . . ."

Matt's voice cut across her words. Glaring at
Rollie, he demanded, "What the hell are you doing
in my house, sitting there . . . ?"

Of necessity, through years of managing an
auto plant in which a major segment of the work
force was black, Matt Zaleski had acquired a
patina of racial tolerance. But it was never more
than a patina. Beneath the surface he still shared
the views of his Polish parents and their Wyandotte neighbors who regarded any Negro as in-
ferior. Now, seeing his own daughter entertaining
a black man in Matt's own home, an unreasoning
rage possessed him, to which tension and tiredness
were an added spur. He spoke and acted without
thought of consequences.

"Dad," Barbara said sharply, "this is my
friend, Mr. Knight. I invited him, and don't . . ."

"Shut up!" Matt shouted as he swung toward
his daughter. "I'll deal with you later."

The color drained from Barbara's face. "What
do you mean—you'll *deal* with me?"

Matt ignored her. His eyes still boring into Rollie Knight, he pointed to the kitchen door through which he had just come in. "Out!"

"Dad, don't you dare!"

Barbara was on her feet, moving swiftly toward her father. When she was within reach he slapped her hard across the face.

It was as if they were acting out a classic tragedy, and now it was Barbara who was unbelieving. She thought: *This cannot be happening.* The blow had stung and she guessed there were weal marks on her cheek, though that part was unimportant. What mattered was of the mind. It was as if a rock had been rolled aside, the rock a century of human progression and understanding, only to reveal a festering rottenness beneath —the unreason, hatred, bigotry living in Matt Zaleski's mind. And Barbara, because she was her father's daughter, at this moment shared his guilt.

Outside, a car stopped.

Rollie, as well, was standing. An instant earlier his confidence had deserted him because he was on unfamiliar ground. Now, as it came back, he told Matt, "Piss on you, honky!"

Matt's voice trembled. "I said get out. Now go!"

Barbara closed her eyes. *Piss on you, honky!* Well, why not? Wasn't that how life went, returning hate for hate?

For the second time within a few minutes the house side door opened. Brett DeLosanto came in, announcing cheerfully, "Couldn't make anybody hear." He beamed at Barbara and Matt, then observed Rollie Knight. "Hi, Rollie! Nice surprise to see you. How's the world, good friend?"

At Brett's easy greeting to the young black man, a flicker of doubt crossed Matt Zaleski's face.

"Piss on you too," Rollie said to Brett. He glanced contemptuously at Barbara. And left.

Brett asked the other two, "Now what in hell was that about?"

He had driven directly across town from Metropolitan Airport when his flight from California landed less than an hour ago. Brett had wanted to see Barbara, to tell her of his personal decision and plans he had begun formulating during the journey home. His spirits had been high and were the reason for his breezy entry. Now, he realized, something serious was wrong.

Barbara shook her head, unable to speak because of tears she was choking back. Brett moved across the room. Putting his arms around her, he urged gently, "Whatever it is, let go, relax! We can talk about it later."

Matt said uncertainly, "Look, maybe I was . . ."

Barbara's voice overrode him. "I don't want to hear."

She had control of herself, and eased away from Brett who volunteered, "If this is a family mishmash, and you'd prefer me to leave . . ."

"I want you here," Barbara said. "And when you go, I'm leaving with you." She stopped, then regarding him directly, "You've asked me twice, Brett, to come and live with you. If you still want me to, I will."

He answered fervently, "You know I do."

Matt Zaleski had dropped into a chair. His head came up. *"Live!"*

"That's right," Barbara affirmed icily. "We won't be married; neither of us wants to be. We'll merely share the same apartment, the same bed . . ."

"No!" Matt roared. "By God, no!"

She warned, "Just try to stop me!"

They faced each other briefly, then her father

dropped his eyes and put his head in his hands. His shoulders shook.

"I'll pack a few things for tonight," Barbara told Brett, "then come back for the rest tomorrow."

"Listen"—Brett's eyes were on the dejected figure in the chair—"I wanted us to get together. You know it. But does it have to be this way?"

She answered crisply, "When you know what happened, you'll understand. So take me or leave me—now, the way I am. If you don't, I'll go to a hotel."

He flashed a quick smile. "I'll take you."

Barbara went upstairs.

When the two men were alone, Brett said uncomfortably, "Mr. Z., whatever it was went wrong, I'm sorry."

There was no answer, and he went outside to wait for Barbara in his car.

For almost half an hour Brett and Barbara cruised the streets nearby, searching for Rollie Knight. In the first few minutes after putting her suitcase in the car and driving away, Barbara explained what had occurred before Brett's arrival. As she talked, his face went grim.

After a while he said, "Poor little bastard! No wonder he took off at me too."

"And me."

"I guess he figures we're all alike inside. Why wouldn't he?"

They drove down another empty street, then, near the end of it, their headlights picked up a shadowy figure, walking. It turned out to be a neighbor of the Zaleskis, going home.

"Rollie's gone." Brett glanced across the front seat of the car inquiringly. "We know where he lives."

Both knew the reason behind Brett's hesitation. It could be dangerous in downtown Detroit at night. Armed holdups and assaults were common-place.

She shook her head. "We can't do anything more tonight. Let's go home."

"First things first." He pulled to the curb and they kissed.

"Home for you," Brett said carefully, "is a new address—Country Club Manor, West Maple at Telegraph."

Despite their shared depression from to-night's events, he had an excited, breathless feeling as he swung the car northwest.

Much later, lying beside each other in the darkened bedroom of Brett's apartment, Barbara said softly, "Are your eyes open?"

"Yes." A few minutes previously Brett had rolled over onto his back. Now, hands behind his head, he was regarding the dimness of the ceiling.

"What were you thinking?"

"About something clumsy I once said to you. Do you remember?"

"Yes, I remember."

It had been the night Barbara had prepared dinner here and Brett had brought Leonard Win-gate home—the first meeting for the three of them. Afterward, Brett tried to persuade Barbara to stay the night with him, and when she wouldn't, had declared, *"You're twenty-nine; you can't possibly be a virgin, so what's our hangup?"*

"You didn't say anything when I said that," Brett pointed out, "but you were, weren't you?"

He heard her gentle, rippling laughter. "If anyone's in a position to know . . ."

"Okay, okay." She sensed him smiling, then he turned sideways so that their faces were together once again. "Why didn't you tell me?"

"Oh, I don't know. It isn't the sort of thing you talk about. Anyway, was it important, really?"

"It's important to me."

There was a silence, then Barbara said, "If you must know, it was important to me, too. You see, I always wanted the first time to be with someone I truly loved." She reached out, her fingers moving lightly down his face. "In the end, it was."

Brett's arms went around her, once more their bodies pressed together as he whispered, "I love you, too."

He had an awareness of savoring one of life's rare and precious moments. He had still not told Barbara of his own decision, made in Los Angeles, or spoken of his future plans. Brett knew that if he did, they would talk until morning, and talk was not what he wanted most tonight.

Then urgent desire, reciprocated, wiped out all other thoughts.

Afterward, again lying quietly, contentedly, beside each other, Barbara said, "If you like, I'll tell you something."

"Go ahead."

She sighed. "If I'd known it was as wonderful as this, I wouldn't have waited so long."

chapter twenty-three

Erica Trenton's affair with Pierre Flodenhale had begun early in June. It started shortly after their first encounter, when the young race driver accompanied Adam Trenton home, following the weekend cottage party at Higgins Lake.

A few days after that Sunday night, Pierre telephoned Erica and suggested lunch. She accepted. They met next day at an out-of-the-way restaurant in Sterling Heights.

A week later the met again and this time, after lunch, drove to a motel where Pierre had already checked in. With a minimum of fuss, they got into bed where Pierre proved an entirely satisfactory sex partner, so that when she went home, late that afternoon, Erica felt better, physically and mentally, than she had in months.

Through the remainder of June, and well into July, they continued to meet at every opportunity, both in daytime and during evenings, the latter when Adam had told Erica in advance that he would be working late.

For Erica the occasions were blissful sexual fulfillments of which she had been deprived far too long. She also relished Pierre's youth and freshness, as well as being excited herself by his lusty pleasure in her body.

Their meetings were sharply in contrast with the single assignation she had had, months earlier, with the salesman, Ollie. When Erica thought about that experience—though she preferred not to—it was with disgust at herself for letting it happen, even though she had been physically frustrated, to the point of desperation, at the time.

There was no desperation now. Erica had no idea how long the affair between herself and Pierre would last, though she knew it would never be more than an affair for either of them, and someday would inevitably end. But for the moment she was enjoying herself uninhibitedly and so, it seemed, was Pierre.

The enjoyment gave each of them a sense of confidence which led, in turn, to a carelessness about being seen together in public.

One of their favorite evening meeting places was in the pleasant colonial surroundings of the Dearborn Inn, where the service was friendly and good. Another attraction at the Dearborn Inn was a cottage—one of several on the grounds—a faithful replica of the one-time home of Edgar Allan Poe. Downstairs, the Poe cottage had two cozy rooms and a kitchen; upstairs, a tiny bedroom under the roof. The upstairs and downstairs portions were self-contained, and rented separately to Inn guests.

On two occasions when Adam was away from Detroit, Pierre Flodenhale occupied the lower portion of the Poe cottage, while Erica checked in upstairs. When the main outside door was locked, it was nobody's business who went up or down the inside staircase.

Erica so loved the historic little cottage, with its antique furnishings, that once she lay back in bed and exclaimed, "What a perfect place for lovers! It ought not to be used for anything else."

"Uh, huh," had been all that Pierre had said, which pointed up his lack of conversation and, in fact, a general absence of interest in anything not connected with motor racing or directly involving sex. About racing, Pierre could, and did converse animatedly and at length. But other subjects bored him. Confronted with current af-

fairs, politics, the arts—which Erica tried to talk
about sometimes—he either yawned or fidgeted
like a restless boy whose attention could not be
held for more than seconds at a time. Occasionally,
and despite all the satisfying sex, Erica wished
their relationship could be more rounded.

Around the time that the wish was developing
into a mild irritation with Pierre, an item linking
their names appeared in the *Detroit News*.

It was in the daily column of Society Editor
Eleanor Breitmeyer, whom many considered the
best society writer in North American newspaper-
dom. Almost nothing which went on in the Motor
City's social echelons escaped Miss Breitmeyer's
intelligence, and her comment read:

> Handsome, debonair race driver Pierre Flo-
> denhale and young and beautiful Erica
> Trenton—wife of auto product planner
> Adam—continue to relish each other's com-
> pany. Last Friday, lunching tête-à-tête at
> the Steering Wheel, neither, as usual, had
> as much as a glance for anyone else.

The words on the printed page were a startling jolt to Erica. Her first flustered thought as
she read them was of the thousands of people in
Greater Detroit—including friends of herself and
Adam—who would also see and talk about the
column item before the day was out. Suddenly,
Erica wanted to run into a closet and hide. She
realized how incredibly careless she and Pierre
had been, as if they were courting exposure, but
now it had happened she wished desperately they
hadn't.

The *News* items appeared in late July—a
week or so before the Trentons' dinner with Hank
Kreisel and their visit to his Grosse Pointe home.

The evening the item was published, Adam

had brought the *Detroit News* home, as he usually did, and the two of them shared it, in sections, while having martinis before dinner.

While Erica had the women's section, which included Society, Adam was leafing through the front news portion. But Adam invariably looked over the entire paper systematically, and Erica dreaded his attention turning to the section she was holding.

She decided it would be a mistake to remove any part of the newspaper from the living room because, however casually she did it, Adam would probably notice.

Instead, Erica went to the kitchen and served dinner immediately, taking a chance that the vegetables were done. They weren't, but when Adam came to the table he still hadn't opened any of the newspaper's back sections.

After dinner, returning to the living room, Adam opened his briefcase as usual and began work. When Erica had cleared the dining room, she came in, collected Adam's coffee cup, straightened some magazines and picked up the pieces of newpaper, putting them together to take out.

Adam had looked up. "Leave the paper. I haven't finished."

She spent the remainder of the evening on a knife edge of suspense. Pretending to read a book, Erica watched covertly each move which Adam made. When at last he snapped his briefcase closed, her tension mounted until, to Erica's unbelievable relief, he went upstairs to bed, apparently forgetting the newspaper entirely. She hid the paper then, and burned it next day.

But burning a single copy would not, she knew, prevent someone else showing the item to Adam or referring to it in conversation, which amounted to the same thing. Obviously, many on

Adam's staff, and others he associated with, had read or been told about the juicy piece of gossip, so for the next few days Erica lived in nervous expectation that when Adam came home he would bring the subject up.

One thing she was sure of: If Adam learned of the item in the *News*, Erica would know. Adam never dodged an issue, nor was he the kind of husband who would form a judgment without giving his wife the chance to state her case. But nothing was said, and when a week had gone by Erica started to relax. Afterward, she suspected what happened was that everyone assumed Adam knew, and hence avoided the subject out of consideration or embarrassment. For whatever reason, she was grateful.

She was also grateful for an opportunity to assess her relationships with both men: Adam and Pierre. The result—in everything except sex and the small amount of time they spent together, Adam came out far ahead. Unfortunately—or perhaps fortunately—for Erica, sex continued to be important in her life, which was the reason she agreed to meet Pierre again a few days later, though this time cautiously and across the river in Windsor, Canada. But of all their rendezvous, this latest proved the least successful.

The fact was: Adam had the kind of mind which Erica admired. Pierre didn't. Despite Adam's obsessive work habits, he was never out of touch with the sum of life around him; he had strong opinions and a social conscience. Erica enjoyed hearing Adam talk—on subjects other than the auto industry. In contrast, when she asked Pierre for his views on a Detroit civic housing controversy, which had been headline news for weeks, Pierre had never heard of it. "Figure all that stuff's none of my business," was a stock reply. Nor had he ever voted. "Wouldn't know how, and I'm not much interested."

Erica was learning: An affair, to be successful and satisfying, needed other ingredients than merely fornication.

When she asked herself the question: Who, of all the men she knew, would she soonest have an affair with, Erica came up with the revealing answer—Adam.

If *only* Adam would function as an *entire husband*.

But he rarely did.

The thought about Adam stayed foremost in her mind through several more days, carrying over to their evening at Grosse Pointe with Hank Kreisel. Somehow, it seemed to Erica, the ex-Marine parts manufacturer managed to bring out all that was best in Adam, and she followed the talk about Hank Kreisel's thresher, including Adam's cogent questioning, with fascination. It was only afterward, going home, when she remembered the other part of Adam she had once possessed—the eager lover, explorer of her body, now seemingly departed—that despair and anger overwhelmed her.

Her statement, later the same night, that she intended to divorce Adam had been real. It seemed hopeless to go on. Nor, next day or during others following, had Erica's resolve weakened.

It was true she did nothing specific to set the machinery of divorce in motion, and did not move out of the Quarton Lake house, though she continued sleeping in the guest bedroom. Erica simply felt that she needed a chance, in limbo, to adjust.

Adam did not object—to anything. Obviously he believed that time could heal their differences, though Erica did not. Meanwhile she continued to keep house, and also agreed to meet Pierre, who

had telephoned to say he would be briefly in
Detroit during an absence from the racing circuit.

"Something's wrong," Erica said. "I know it
is, so why don't you tell me?"

Pierre appeared uncertain and embarrassed.
Along with his boyishness, he had a transparent
manner which revealed his moods.

He said, in bed beside her, "It's nothing, I
guess."

Erica propped herself on an elbow. The
motel room was darkened because they had drawn
the drapes on coming in. Even so, enough light
filtered through for her to see the surroundings
clearly, which were much like those of other
motels they had been in—characterless, with
mass-produced furniture and cheap hardware.
She glanced at her watch. It was two in the afternoon, and they were in the suburb of Birmingham
because Pierre had said he would not have time to
drive across the river into Canada. Outside, the
day was dull and the midday forecast had predicted rain.

She turned back to study Pierre whose face
she could see clearly too. He flashed a smile,
though with a touch of wariness, Erica thought.
She noticed that his shock of blond hair was
mussed, undoubtedly because she had run her
hands through it during their recent love-making.

She had grown genuinely fond of Pierre. For
all his lack of intellectual depth, he had proved
agreeable, and sexually was every inch a man,
which was what Erica had wanted after all. Even
the occasional arrogance—the star syndrome she
had been aware of at their first meeting—seemed
to fit the masculinity.

"Don't mess about," Erica insisted. "Tell me
whatever's on your mind."

Pierre turned away, reaching for his trousers

beside the bed and searched in their pockets for cigarettes. "Well," he said, not looking at her directly, "I guess it's us."

"What about us?"

He had a cigarette alight and blew smoke toward the ceiling. "From now on I'll be more often at the tracks. Won't get to Detroit as much. Thought I ought to tell you."

There was a silence betwen them as a coldness gripped Erica which she struggled not to show. At length she said, "Is that all, or are you trying to tell me something else?"

Pierre looked uneasy. "Like what?"

"I should think you'd be the one to know that."

"It's just . . . well, we've been seeing a lot of each other. For a long time."

"It certainly is a long time." Erica tried to keep her voice light, knowing hostility would be a mistake. "It's every bit of two and a half months."

"Gee! Is that all?" His surprise seemed genuine.

"Obviously, to you it seems longer."

Pierre managed a smile. "It isn't like that."

"Then just how is it?"

"Hell, Erica, all it is—we won't be seeing each other for a while."

"For how long? A month? Six months? Even a year?"

He answered vaguely, "Depends how things go, I guess."

"What things?"

Pierre shrugged.

"And afterward," Erica persisted, "after this indefinite time, will you call me or shall I call you?" She knew she was pushing too hard but had become impatient with his indirectness. When he didn't answer, she added, "Is the band playing, 'It's Time to Say Goodbye'? Is this the brush-off? If it is, why not say so and have done with it?"

Clearly, Pierre decided to grasp the opportunity presented. "Yes," he said, "I guess you could say that's the way it is."

Erica took a deep breath. "Thank you for finally giving me an honest answer. Now, at least, I know where I stand."

She supposed she could scarcely complain. She had insisted on knowing and now had been told, even though, from the beginning of the conversation, Erica had sensed the intention in Pierre's mind. At this moment she had a mixture of emotions—the foremost, hurt pride because she had assumed that if either of them chose to end the affair it would be herself. But she wasn't ready to end it, and now, along with the hurt she had a sense of loss, sadness, an awareness of loneliness to come. She was realist enough to know that nothing would be gained by pleading or argument. One thing Erica had learned about Pierre was that he had all the women he needed or wanted; she knew, too, there were others whom Pierre had tired of ahead of herself. Suddenly she felt like crying at the thought of being one more, but willed herself not to. *She'd be damned* if she would feed his ego by letting him see how much she really minded.

Erica said coolly, "Under the circumstances there doesn't seem much point in staying here."

"Hey!" Pierre said. "Don't be mad." He reached under the bedclothes for her, but she evaded him and slipped from the bed, taking her clothes to the bathroom to dress. Earlier in their relationship, Pierre would have scrambled after her, seized her, and forced her playfully back to the bed, as had happened once before when they quarreled. Now he didn't, though she had been half-hoping that he would.

Instead, when Erica came out of the bathroom, Pierre was dressed too, and only minutes later they kissed briefly, almost perfunctorily, and parted. He seemed relieved, she thought, that their leave-taking had been accomplished with so little trouble.

Pierre drove away in his car, reaching speed with a squeal of tires as he left the motel parking lot. Erica followed more slowly in her convertible. Her last glimpse of him was as he waved and smiled.

By the time she reached the first intersection, Pierre's car was out of sight.

She drove another block and a half before realizing she had not the slightest notion where she was going. It was close to three in the afternoon and was now raining drearily, as the forecast said it would. Where to go, what to do? . . . with the rest of the day, with the rest of her life. Suddenly, like a pent-up flood released, the anguish, disappointment, bitterness, all of which she had postponed in the motel, swept over her. She had a sense of rejection and despair as her eyes filled with tears, which she let course down her cheeks unchecked. Still driving the car, mechanically, Erica continued through Birmingham, uncaring where she went.

One place she did not want to go was home to the house at Quarton Lake. It held too many memories, an excess of unfinished business, problems she had no capacity to cope with now. She drove a few more blocks, turned several corners, then realized she had come to Somerset Mall, in Troy, the shopping plaza where, almost a year ago, she had taken the perfume—her first act of shoplifting. It had been the occasion on which she had learned that a combination of intelligence, quickness, and nerve could be rewarding in diverse ways. She parked the car and walked through the rain to the indoor mall.

Inside, she wiped the rain and the tears together from her face.

Most stores within the shopping plaza were moderately busy. Erica wandered into several, glancing at Bally shoes, a display of F. A. O. Schwarz toys, the colorful miscellany of a boutique. But she was going through motions only, wanting nothing that she saw, her mood increasingly listless and depressed. In a luggage store she browsed, and was about to leave when a briefcase caught her attention. It was of English cowhide, gleaming brown. It lay on a glass-topped table at the rear of the store. Erica's eyes moved on, then inexplicably returned. She thought: there was no reason in the world why she should possess a briefcase; she had never needed one, nor was ever likely to. Besides, a briefcase was a symbol of so much that she detested—the tyranny of work brought home, the evenings Adam spent with his own briefcase opened, the countless hours which he and Erica had never shared. Yet she wanted the briefcase she had just seen, wanted it —irrationally—here and now. And intended to have it.

Perhaps Erica thought, she would give the briefcase to Adam as a parting, splendidly sardonic gift.

But was it necessary to pay for it? She *could* pay, of course, except that it would be more challenging to take what she wanted and walk away, as she had done so skillfully the other times. Doing so would add some zest to the day. There had been little enough so far.

Pretending to examine something else, Erica surveyed the store. As on other occasions when she had shoplifted, she felt a rising excitement, a heady, delicious combination of fear and daring.

There were three salespeople, she observed—

a girl and two men, one of the men older and presumably the manager. All were occupied with customers. Two or three other people in the store were, like Erica, browsing. One, a mousy grandmother-type, was examining luggage tags on a card.

By a roundabout route, pausing on the way, Erica sauntered to the display table where the briefcase lay. As if noticing it for the first time, she picked it up and turned it over for inspection. While doing so, a swift glance confirmed that the trio of salesclerks were still busy.

Continuing her inspection of the case, she opened it slightly and nudged two labels on the outside into the interior, out of view. Still casually, Erica lowered the case as if replacing it, but instead let it swing downward below the display table level, still in her hand. She looked boldly around the store. Two of the people who had been walking around were gone; one of the salesclerks had begun attending to another customer; otherwise, everything was the same.

Unhurriedly, swinging the briefcase slightly, she strolled toward the store doorway. Beyond it was the terraced indoor mall, connecting with other stores and protecting shoppers from the weather. She could see a fountain playing and hear its plash of water. Beyond the fountain, she noted, was a uniformed security guard, but he had his back toward the luggage store and was chatting with a child. Even if the guard saw Erica, once she had left the store there was no reason for him to be suspicious. She reached the doorway. No one had stopped her, or even spoken. Really!—it was all too easy.

"Just a moment!"

The voice—sharp, uncompromising—came from immediately behind. Startled, Erica turned.

It was the mousy grandmother-type who had

seemed to be engrossed with luggage tags. Except that now she was neither mousy nor grandmotherly, but with hard eyes and thin lips set in a firm line. She moved swiftly toward Erica, at the same time calling to the store manager, "Mr. Yancy! Over here!" Then Erica found her wrist gripped firmly and when she tried to free it, the grip tightened like a clamp.

Panic flooded through Erica. She protested, flustered, "Let me go!"

"Be quiet!" the other woman ordered. She was in her forties—not nearly as old as she had dressed herself to look. "I'm a detective and you've been caught stealing." As the manager hurried over, she informed him, "This woman stole that case she's holding. I stopped her as she was leaving."

"All right," the manager said, "we'll go in the back." His manner, like the woman detective's was unemotional, as if he knew what to do and would carry a distasteful duty through. He had barely glanced at Erica so that already she felt faceless, like a criminal.

"You heard," the woman detective said. She tugged at Erica's wrist, turning toward the rear of the store which presumably housed offices out of sight.

"No! No!" Erica set her feet firmly, refusing to move. "You're making a mistake."

"Your kind of people make the mistakes, sister," the woman detective said. She asked the store manager cynically, "Did you ever meet one who didn't say that?"

The manager looked uncomfortable. Erica had raised her voice; now heads had turned and several people in the store were watching. The manager, clearly wanting the scene removed from view, signaled urgently with his head.

It was at that moment Erica made her crucial

mistake. Had she accompanied the other two as they demanded, the procedure following would almost certainly have fitted a pattern. First, she would have been interrogated—probably harshly, by the woman detective—after which, more than likely, Erica would have broken down, admitted her guilt and pleaded for leniency. During the interrogation she would have revealed that her husband was a senior auto executive.

After admitting guilt, she would have been urged to make a signed confession. She would have written this out, however reluctantly, in her own handwriting.

After that she would have been allowed to go home with—so far as Erica was concerned—the incident closed.

Erica's confession would have been sent by the store manager to an investigative bureau of the Retail Merchants Association. If a record of previous offenses was on file, prosecution might have been considered. With a first offense—which, officially, Erica's was—no action would be taken.

Suburban Detroit stores, especially those near well-to-do areas like Birmingham and Bloomfield Hills, were unhappily familiar with women shoplifters who stole without need. It was not the store operators' business to be psychologists as well as retailers; nonetheless, most knew that reasons behind such stealing included sexual frustrations, loneliness, a need for attention—all of them conditions to which auto executives' wives were exceptionally vulnerable. Something else the stores knew was that prosecution, and publicity which the court appearance of an auto industry big name would bring, could harm their businesses more than aid them. Auto people were clannish, and a store which persecuted one of their number could easily suffer a general boycott.

Consequently, retail businesses used other

methods. Where an offender was observed and known, she was billed for the items taken, and usually such bills were paid without question. At other times, when identity was established, a bill followed in the same way; also, the scare of being detained, plus hostile questioning, were often enough to deter further shoplifting for a lifetime. But whichever method was used, the Detroit stores' objective, overall, was quietness and discretion.

Erica, panicky and desperate, left none of the quieter compromises open. Instead, she jerked her wrist free from the woman detective and—still clutching the stolen briefcase—turned and ran.

She ran from the luggage store into the mall, heading for the main outer door by which she had come in. The woman detective and the manager, taken by surprise, did nothing for a second or so. The woman recovered first. She sped after Erica, shouting, "Stop her! Stop that woman! She's a thief!"

The uniformed security guard in the mall, who had been chatting with a child, swung around at the shouts. The woman detective saw him. She commanded, "Catch that woman! The one running! Arrest her! She stole that case she's carrying."

Moving quickly, the guard ran after Erica as shoppers in the mall stood gaping, craning for a view. Others, hearing the shouting, hurried out of stores. But none attempted to stop Erica as she continued running, her heels tap-tap-tapping on the terrazzo floor. She went on, heading toward the outer door, the security guard still pounding behind.

To Erica, the ghastly shouts, people staring as she passed, the pursuing feet, now drawing closer, all were a nightmare. Was this really happening? It couldn't be! In a moment she must wake. But instead of waking, she reached the heavy outer door. Though she pushed hard, it opened with maddening slowness. Then she was outside, in the rain, her car on the parking lot only yards away.

Her heart was pounding, breath coming hard from the exertion of running and from fear. She remembered that fortunately she hadn't locked the car. Tucking the purloined briefcase under her arm, Erica fumbled open her handbag, scrabbling inside for car keys. A stream of objects fell from the handbag; she ignored them but located the keys. She had the ignition key ready as she reached the car, but could see that the security guard, a youngish, sturdily built man, was only yards away. The woman detective was following behind, but the guard was closest. Erica realized—she wouldn't make it! Not get inside the car, start the engine and pull away before he reached her. Terrified, realizing the consequences would be even greater now, despair engulfed her.

At that moment the security guard slipped on the rain-wet parking lot surface and fell. He went down fully, and lay a moment dazed and hurt before he scrambled up.

The guard's misfortune gave Erica the time she needed. Slipping into the car, she started the engine, which fired instantly, and drove away. But even as she left the shoppers' parking lot a new anxiety possessed her: Had her pursuers read the car license number?

They had. As well, they had the car's description—a current model convertible, candy apple red, distinctive as a blossom in winter.

And as if that were not enough, among the items spilled from Erica's handbag and left behind, was a billfold with credit cards and other identification. The woman detective was collecting the fallen items while the security guard, his uniform wet and soiled, and with a painfully sprained ankle, limped to a telephone to call the local police.

It was all so ridiculously easy that the two policemen were grinning as they escorted Erica from her car to theirs. Minutes earlier the police cruiser had pulled alongside the convertible and without fuss, not using flashing lights or siren, one of the policemen had waved her to stop, which she did immediately, knowing that anything else would be insane, just as attempting to run away to begin with had been madly foolish.

The policemen, both young, had been firm but also quiet and polite so that Erica felt less intimidated than by the antagonistic woman detective in the store. In any case, she was now totally resigned to whatever was going to happen. She knew she had brought disaster on herself, and whatever other disasters followed would happen anyway because it was too late to change anything, whatever she said or did.

"Our orders are to take you in, ma'am," one of the policemen said. "My partner will drive your car."

Erica gasped, "All right." She went to the rear of the cruiser where the policeman had the door open for her to enter, then shrank back when she realized the interior was barred and she would be locked inside as if in a cell.

The policeman saw her hesitate. "Regulations," he explained. "I'd let you ride up front if I could, but if I did they'd likely put *me* in the back."

Erica managed a smile. Obviously the two officers had decided she was not a major criminal.

The same policeman asked, "Ever been arrested before?"

She shook her head.

"Didn't think you had. Nothing to it after the

first few times. That is, for people who don't make trouble."

She entered the cruiser, the door slammed, and she was locked in.

At the suburban police station she had an impression of polished wood, and tile floors, but otherwise was only dully aware of the surroundings. She was cautioned, then questioned about what happened at the store. Erica answered truthfully, knowing the time for evasion was past. She was confronted by the woman detective and the security guard, both hostile, even when Erica confirmed their version of events. She identified the briefcase she had stolen, at the same time wondering why she had ever wanted it. Later, she signed a statement, then was asked if she wished to make a telephone call. To a lawyer? To her husband? She answered no.

After that, she was taken to a small room with a barred window at the rear of the police station, locked in, and left alone.

The chief of the suburban police force, Wilbur Arenson, was not a man who hurried needlessly. Many times during his career, Chief Arenson had found that slowness, when it could be managed, paid off later, and thus he had taken his time while reading several reports concerning an alleged shoplifting which occurred earlier in the afternoon, followed by a suspect's attempted flight, a police radio alert and, later, an interception and detention. The detained suspect, one Erica Marguerite Trenton, age twenty-five, a married woman living at Quarton Lake, had been cooperative, and further had signed a statement admitting the offense.

Under normal procedure the case would have gone ahead routinely, with the suspect charged, a subsequent court appearance and, most likely, a conviction. But not everything in a Detroit sub-urban police station proceeded according to routine.

It was not routine for the chief to review details of a minor criminal case, yet certain cases—at subordinates' discretion—found their way to his desk.

Trenton. The name stirred a chord of memory. The chief was not sure how or when he had heard the name before, but knew his mind would churn out the answer if he didn't rush it. Meanwhile, he continued reading.

Another departure from routine was that the station desk sergeant, familiar with the ways and preferences of his chief, had not so far booked the suspect. Thus no blotter listing yet existed, with a name and charges listed, for press reporters to peruse.

Several things about the case interested the chief. First, a need of money obviously was not a motive. A billfold, dropped on the shopping plaza parking lot by the fleeing suspect, contained more than a hundred dollars cash as well as American Express and Diners cards, plus credit cards from local stores. A checkbook in the suspect's hand-bag showed a substantial balance in the account.

Chief Arenson knew all about well-heeled women shoplifters and their supposed motivations, so the money aspect did not surprise him. More interesting was the suspect's unwillingness to give information about her husband or to telephone him when allowed the opportunity.

Not that it made any difference. The interrogating officer had routinely checked out ownership of the car she was driving, which proved to be registered to one of the Big Three auto manufacturers, and a further check with that company's security office revealed it was an official company car, one of two allocated to Mr. Adam Trenton.

The company security man had let that item of information about two cars slip out, though he hadn't been asked, and the police officer phoning the inquiry had noted it in his report. Now, Chief Arenson, a stockily built, balding man in his late fifties, sat at his desk and considered the notation.

As the police chief well knew, plenty of auto executives drove company cars. But only a senior executive would have *two* company cars—one for himself, another for his wife.

Thus it required no great deductive powers to conclude that the suspect, Erica Marguerite Trenton, now locked in a small interrogation room instead of in a cell—another intuitive move by the desk sergeant—was married to a reasonably important man.

What the chief needed to know was: How important? And how much influence did Mrs. Trenton's husband have?

The fact that the chief would take time to consider such questions at all was a reason why suburban Detroit communities insisted on maintaining their own local police forces. Periodically, proposals appeared for a merger of the score or more of separate police forces of Greater Detroit into a single metropolitan force. Such an arrangement, it was argued, would ensure better policing by eliminating duplication, and would also be less costly. The metropolitan system, its advocates pointed out, worked successfully elsewhere.

But the suburbs—Birmingham, Bloomfield Hills, Troy, Dearborn, the Grosse Pointes and others—were always solidly opposed. As a result, and because residents of those communities had influence where it counted, the proposal always failed.

The existing system of small, independent forces might not be the best means of providing equal justice for all, but it did give local citizens whose names were known a better break when they, their families or friends transgressed the law.

Presto!—the chief remembered where he had heard the name Trenton before. Six or seven months ago, Chief Arenson had bought a car for his wife from the auto dealer, Smokey Stephensen. During the chief's visit to the dealer's showroom— a Saturday, he recalled—Smokey had introduced him to an Adam Trenton from the auto company's head office. Afterward and privately, while Smokey and the chief made their deal about the car, Smokey mentioned Trenton again, predicting that he was going higher in the company, and one day would be its president.

Reflecting on the incident, and its implications at this moment, Chief Arenson was glad he had dawdled. Now, not only was he aware that the woman being detained was someone of consequence, but he had the further knowledge of where to get extra information which might be helpful in the case.

Using an outside line on his desk, the chief telephoned Smokey Stephensen.

chapter twenty-four

Sir Perceval McDowall Stuyvesant, Bart. and Adam Trenton had known each other and been friends for more than twenty years. It was a loose friendship. Sometimes two years or more slipped by without their meeting, or even communicating, but whenever they were in the same town, which happened occasionally, they got together and picked up the old relationship easily, as if it had never been set down.

A reason, perhaps, for the lasting friendship was their dissimilarity. Adam, while imaginative, was primarily a master of organization, a pragmatist who got things done. Sir Perceval, imaginative too and with a growing reputation as a brilliant scientist, was essentially a dreamer who had trouble mastering each day's practicalities—the kind of man who might invent a zipper but subsequently forget to zip up his own fly.

Their backgrounds were equally at variance. Sir Perceval was the last of a line of English squires, his father dead and the inherited title genuine. Adam's father had been a Buffalo, New York, steelworker.

The two met in college—at Purdue University. They were the same age and graduated together, Adam in Engineering; Perceval, whom his friends called Perce, in Physics. Afterward, Perce spent several more years gathering scientific degrees as casually as a child gathers daisies, then worked for a while for the same auto company as Adam. This had been in Scientific Research—the "think tank"—where Perce left his mark by discovering new applications for electron microscopes.

During that period they spent more time to-

gether than at any other—it had been before
Adam's marriage to Erica, and Perce was a bache-
lor—and they found each other's company increasingly agreeable.

For a while, Adam became mildly interested
in Perce's hobby of manufacturing pseudo-antique
violins—into each of which, with peculiar humor,
he pasted a Stradivari label—but rejected Perce's
suggestion that they learn Russian together. Perce
set out on that project alone, solely because someone had given him a subscription to a Soviet magazine, and in less than a year could read Russian
with ease.

Sir Perceval Stuyvesant had a lean, spindle-
shanked appearance and, to Adam, always looked
the same: mournful, which he wasn't, and perpetually abstracted, which he was. He also had an
easygoing nature which nothing disturbed, and
when concentrating on something scientific was
oblivious to everything around him, including
seven young and noisy children. This brood had
appeared at the rate of one a year since Perce's
marriage which took place soon after he left the
auto industry. He had wed a pleasant, sexy
scatterbrain, now Lady Stuyvesant, and for the
past few years the expanding family had lived
near San Francisco in a happy madhouse of a
home.

It was from San Francisco that Perce had
flown to Detroit specifically to see Adam. They
met in Adam's office in late afternoon of a day in
August.

When Perce had telephoned the previous day
to say that he was coming, Adam urged him not
to go to a hotel, but to come home to stay at
Quarton Lake. Erica liked Perce. Adam hoped that
an old friend's arrival would ease some of the tension and uncertainty still persisting between himself and Erica.

But Perce had declined. "Best if I don't, old boy. If I meet Erica this trip, she'll be curious to know why I'm there, and you'll likely want to tell her yourself in your own way."

Adam had asked, "Why *are* you coming?"

"Maybe I want a job."

But Sir Perceval hadn't wanted a job. As it turned out, he had come to offer one to Adam.

A West Coast company, involved with advanced electrical and radar technology, required an executive head. Perce, one of the company's founders, was currently its scientific vice-president, and his approach to Adam was on behalf of himself and associates.

He announced, "President is what we'd make you, old boy. You'd start at the top."

Adam said dryly, "That's what Henry Ford told Bunkie Knudsen."

"This could work out better. One reason—you'd be in a strong stock position." Perce gave the slightest of frowns as he regarded Adam. "I'll ask you a favor while I'm here. That's take me seriously."

"I always have." That was one of the things about their relationship, Adam thought—based on respect for each other's abilities, and with good reason. Adam had his own solid achievements in the auto industry and Perce, despite vagueness at times and his absent-mindedness about everyday matters, turned everything he touched in scientific fields into notable success. Even before today's encounter, Adam had heard reports about Perce's West Coast company which had gained a solid reputation for advanced research and development, electronically oriented, in a short time.

"We're a small company," Perce said, "but growing fast, and that's our problem."

He went on, explaining that a group of scientific people like himself had banded together in formation of the company, their objective to convert new, advanced knowledge with which the sciences abounded, into practical inventions and technology. A special concern was freshly emerging energy sources and power transmission. Not only would developments envisaged bring aid to beleaguered cities and industry, they would also augment the world's food supply by massive, powered irrigation. Already the group had scored successes in several fields so that the company was, as Perce expressed it, "earning bread and butter and some jam." Much more was expected.

"A good deal of our work is focusing on superconductors," Perce reported. He asked Adam, "Know much about that?"

"A little, not much."

"If there's a major breakthrough—and some of us believe it can happen—it'll be the most revolutionary power and metallurgical development in a generation. I'll tell you more of that later. It could be our biggest thing."

At the moment, Perce declared, what the company needed was a top-flight businessman to run it. "We're scientists, old boy. If I may say so, we've as many science geniuses as you'll find under one umbrella in this country. But we're having to do things we don't want to and are not equipped for—organization, management, budgets, financing, the rest. What *we* want is to stay in our labs, experiment, and *think*."

But the group didn't want just any businessman, Perce declared. "We can get accountants by the gross and management consultants in a dump truck. What we need is one outstanding individual —someone with imagination who understands and respects research, can utilize technology, channel invention, establish priorities, run the front office while we take care of the back, and still be a decent human being. In short, old boy, we need *you*."

It was impossible not to be pleased. Being offered a job by an outside company was no new experience for Adam, any more than it was to most auto executives. But the offer from Perce, because of who and what he was, was something different.

Adam asked, "How do your other people feel?"

"They've learned to trust my judgment. I may tell you that in considering candidates we made a short list. Very short. Yours was the only name on it."

Adam said, and meant it, "I'm touched."

Sir Perceval Stuyvesant permitted himself one of his rare, slow smiles. "You might even be touched in other ways. When you wish, we can talk salary, bonus, stock position, options."

Adam shook his head. "Not yet, if at all. The thing is, I've never seriously considered leaving the auto business. Cars have been my life. They still are."

Even now, to Adam, this entire exchange was mere dialectics. Greatly as he respected Perce and strong as their friendship was, for Adam to quit the auto industry voluntarily was inconceivable.

The two were in facing chairs. Perce shifted in his. He had a way of winding and unwinding while seated which made his long, lean figure seem sinuous. Each movement, too, signaled a switch in conversation.

"Ever wonder," Perce said, "what they'll put on your tombstone?"

"I'm not at all sure I'll have one."

Perce waved a hand. "I speak metaphorically, old boy. We'll all get a tombstone, whether in stone or air. It'll have on it what we did with the time we had, what we've left behind us. Ever thought of yours?"

"I suppose so," Adam said. "I guess we all do a little."

Perce put his fingertips together and regarded them. "Several things they could say about you, I suppose. For example: 'He was an auto company vice-president' or even maybe 'president' —that's if your luck holds and you beat out all the other strong contenders. You'd be in good company, of course, even though a *lot* of company. So *many* auto presidents and vice-presidents, old boy. Bit like the population of India."

"If you're making a point," Adam said, "why not get to it?"

"A splendid suggestion, old boy."

Sometimes, Adam thought, Perce overdid the studied Anglicisms. They had to be studied because, British baronet or not, Perce had lived in the U.S. for a quarter century and, with the exception of speech, all his tastes and habits were American. But perhaps it showed that everyone had human weaknesses.

Now Perce leaned forward, eying Adam earnestly. "You know what that tombstone of yours might say: 'He did something new, different, worthwhile. He was a leader when they carved new pathways, broke fresh ground. That which he left behind him was important and enduring.' "

Perce fell back in his chair as if the amount of talk—unusual in his case—and emotional effort had exhausted him.

Amid the silence which followed, Adam felt more moved than at any other point since the conversation began. In his mind he acknowledged the truth of what Perce had said, and wondered, too, how long the Orion would be remembered after its time and usefulness were ended. Farstar also. Both seemed important now, dominating the lives of many, including his own. But how important would they seem in time to come?

The office suite was quiet. It was late afternoon, and here as elsewhere within the staff building, pressures of the day were easing, secretaries and others beginning to go home. From where Adam sat, glancing outside he could see the freeway traffic, its volume growing as the exodus from plants and offices began.

He had chosen this time of day because Perce had asked particularly that they have at least an hour in which they would be undisturbed.

"Tell me some more," Adam said, "about superconductors—the breakthrough you were speaking of."

Perce said quietly, "They represent the means to enormous new energy, a chance to clean up our environment, and to create more abundance than this earth has ever known."

Across the office, on Adam's desk, a telephone buzzed peremptorily.

Adam glanced toward it with annoyance. Before Perce's arrival he had given Ursula, his secretary, instructions not to disturb them. Perce seemed unhappy about the interruption, too.

But Ursula, Adam knew, would not disregard instructions without good reason. Excusing himself, he crossed the room, sat at his desk and lifted the phone.

"I wouldn't have called you," his secretary's low-pitched voice announced, "except Mr. Stephensen said he has to speak to you, it's extremely urgent."

"Smokey Stephensen?"

"Yes, sir."

Adam said irritably, "Get a number where he'll be later this evening. If I can, I'll call him. But I can't talk now."

He sensed Ursula's uncertainty. "Mr. Trenton, that's exactly what I said. But he's most insistent. He says when you know what it's about, you won't mind him interrupting."

"Damn!" Adam glanced apologetically at Perce, then asked Ursula, "He's on the line now?"

"Yes."

"Very well, put him on."

Cupping a hand over the telephone, Adam promised, "This will take one minute, no more." The trouble with people like Smokey Stephensen, he thought, was that they always considered their own affairs to have overriding importance.

A click. The auto dealer's voice. "Adam, that you?"

"Yes, it is." Adam made no attempt to conceal his displeasure. "I understand my secretary has already told you I'm busy. Whatever it is will have to wait."

"Shall I tell that to your wife?"

He answered peevishly, "What's that supposed to mean?"

"It means, Mr. Big Executive too busy to take a phone call from a friend, your wife has been arrested. And not on a traffic charge, in case you're wondering. For stealing."

Adam stopped, in shocked silence, as Smokey went on. "If you want to help her, and help yourself, right now get free from whatever you're involved in and come to where I'm waiting. Listen carefully. I'll tell you where to go."

Dazedly, Adam wrote down the directions Smokey gave him.

"We need a lawyer," Adam said. "I know several. I'm going to phone one, get him over here."

He was with Smokey Stephensen, in Smokey's car, on the parking lot of the suburban police station. Adam had not yet been inside. Smokey had persuaded him to remain in the car while he recited the facts concerning Erica, which he had learned on the telephone from Chief Arenson, and during a visit to the chief's office before Adam's arrival. As Adam listened he had grown increasingly tense, his frown of worry deepening.

"Sure, sure," Smokey said. "Go phone a lawyer. While you're about it, why not call the *News*, *Free Press* and *Birmingham Eccentric*? They might even send photographers."

"What does it matter? Obviously, the police have made a stupid mistake."

"They ain't made a mistake."

"My wife would never . . ."

Smokey cut in exasperatedly, "Your wife *did*. Will you get that through your head? And not only did, she's signed a confession."

"I can't believe it."

"You'd better. Chief Arenson told me; he wouldn't lie. Besides, the police aren't fools."

"No," Adam said, "I know they're not." He took in a deep breath and expelled it slowly, forcing himself to think carefully—for the first time since hastily breaking off the meeting with Perceval Stuyvesant half an hour ago. Perce had been understanding, realizing that something serious had occurred, even though Adam hadn't gone into detail about the sudden phone call. They had arranged that Adam would call Perce at his hotel, either later tonight or tomorrow morning.

Now, beside Adam, Smokey Stephensen waited, puffing on a cigar, so the car reeked of smoke despite its air conditioning. Outside, the rain continued drearily, as it had since afternoon. Dusk was settling in. On vehicles and in buildings lights were coming on.

"All right," Adam said, "if Erica did what they say, there has to be something else behind it."

Out of habit, the auto dealer rubbed a hand over his beard. His greeting to Adam on arrival had been neither friendly nor hostile, and his voice was noncommittal now. "Whatever that is, I guess it's between you and your wife. The same goes for what's right or wrong; neither one's any business of mine. What we're talking about is the way things are."

A police cruiser pulled in close to where they were parked. Two uniformed officers got out, escorting a third man between them. The policemen took a hard look at Smokey Stephensen's car and its two occupants; the third man, whom Adam now saw was handcuffed, kept his eyes averted. While Smokey and Adam watched, the trio went inside.

It was an uncomfortable reminder of the kind of business transacted here.

"The way things are," Adam said, "Erica's inside there—or so you tell me—and needs help. I can either barge in myself, start throwing weight around and maybe make mistakes, or I can do the sensible thing and get a lawyer."

"Sensible or not," Smokey growled, "you'll likely start something you can't stop, and afterwards wish you'd done it some other way."

"What other way?"

"Like letting me go in there to begin. To represent you. Like my talking to the chief again. Like seeing what I can work out."

Wondering why he had not asked before, Adam queried, "Why did the police call *you?*"

"The chief knows me," Smokey said. "We're friends. He knows I know you." He forbore to tell Adam what he had already learned—that chances were good the store where the shoplifting had occurred would settle for payment of what had been taken and would not press charges; also, that Chief Arenson was aware the case might be sensitive locally, and therefore a favorable disposition might be arranged, depending on the co-operation and discretion of all concerned.

"I'm out of my depth," Adam said. "If you

think you can do something, go ahead. Do you want me to come with you?"

Smokey sat still. His hands were on the car's steering wheel, his face expressionless.

"Well," Adam said, "can you do something or not?"

"Yes," Smokey acknowledged, "I guess I could."

"Then what are we waiting for?"

"The price," Smokey said softly. "There's a price for everything, Adam. You, of all people, should know that."

"If we're discussing bribery . . ."

"Don't even *mention* bribery! Here or in there." Smokey gestured toward police headquarters. "And remember this: Wilbur Arenson's a reasonable guy. But if you offered him *anything,* he'd throw the book at your wife. You, too."

"I didn't intend to." Adam looked puzzled. "If it isn't that, then what . . ."

"*You son-of-a-bitch!*" Smokey shouted the words; his hands, gripping the steering wheel, were white. "You're putting me out of business, remember? Or is it so unimportant you've forgotten? One month, you said. One month before your sister puts her stock in my business on the block. A month before you turn that sneak's notebook of yours over to your company sales brass."

Adam said stiffly, "We have an agreement. It has nothing to do with this."

"You're damn right it has to do with this! If you want your wife out of this mess without her name, and yours, smeared all over Michigan, you'd best do some fast rethinking."

"It might be better if you explained what kind."

"I'm offering a deal," Smokey said. "It it needs explaining, you're not half as smart as I think."

Adam allowed the contempt he felt to express itself in his voice. "I suppose I get the picture. Let me see if I have it right. You are prepared to be an intermediary, using your friendship with the chief of police to try to free my wife and have any charges dropped. In return, I'm supposed to tell my sister not to dispose of her investment in your business and then ignore what I know about dishonesty in the way you run it."

Smokey growled. "You're pretty free with that word dishonesty. Maybe you should remember you got some in the family."

Adam ignored the remark. "Do I, or do I not, have the proposition right?"

"You're smart after all. You got it right."

"Then the answer's no. Under no circumstances would I change the advice I intend to give my sister. I'd be using her interests to help myself."

Smokey said quickly, "That means, then, you might consider the part about the company."

"I didn't say that."

"You didn't *not* say it either."

Adam was silent. Within the car the only sounds were a purr from the idling motor and the air-conditioning hum.

Smokey said, "I'll take the half of the deal. Never mind Teresa. I'll settle for you not snitching in the company." He paused, then expanded, "I'll not even ask for that black notebook of yours. Just that you don't use it."

Still Adam failed to answer.

"You might say," Smokey said, "you're choosing between the company and your wife. Be interesting to see who you put first."

Bitterly, Adam answered, "You know I've no choice."

He was aware that Smokey had tricked him, as had happened the day of their clash in the dealership when Smokey demanded twice as much as expected, then settled for what he had wanted to begin with. It was a hoary dealer's gambit, then as now.

But this time, Adam reminded himself, Erica had to be thought of. There was no other way.

Or was there? Even at this moment he was tempted to dispense with Smokey's help, to go to the police alone, learn what he could of what still seemed an unreal situation, then discover what, if anything, could be arranged. But it was a risk. The fact was: Smokey *did* know Chief Arenson, and equally obvious was that Smokey knew his way around this kind of situation, which Adam did not. When Adam had said a few minutes ago, "*I'm out of my depth,*" it was true.

But he knew he had acted against his own moral scruples and had compromised with conscience, whether for Erica's sake or not. He suspected gloomily it would not be the last time, and that personally, as well as in his work, he would make larger compromises as time went on.

Smokey, for his part, was concealing a bubbling cheerfulness within. On the day, only a short time ago, when Adam had threatened to expose him and Smokey won a month's reprieve, he had been convinced something would turn up. He had remained convinced. Now, it seemed, he had been right.

"Adam," Smokey said. He stubbed out his cigar, trying hard not to laugh. "Let's go get your missus out of the pokey."

Formalities were honored, the rituals observed.

In Adam's presence, Chief Arenson lectured Erica sternly. "Mrs. Trenton, if *ever* this happens again, the full force of the law will be applied. Do you clearly understand that?"

Erica's lips formed a barely audible, "Yes."

She and Adam were in separate chairs, facing the chief who was behind his desk. Despite the sternness, Chief Arenson appeared more like a banker than a policeman. Being seated emphasized his shortness; an overhead light beamed on his balding head.

No one else was in the room. Smokey Stephensen, who had arranged this meeting and its outcome, was waiting in the corridor outside.

Adam had been here with the chief when Erica was brought in, escorted by a policewoman.

Adam went toward Erica, his arms outstretched. She seemed surprised to see him. "I didn't tell them to call you, Adam. I didn't want you involved." Her voice was strained and nervous.

He said, as he held her, "That's what a husband's for, isn't it?"

At a nod from the chief, the policewoman left. After a moment, at the chief's suggestion, they all sat down.

"Mr. Trenton, in case you should have the idea there has been any misunderstanding in this matter, I believe you should read this." Chief Arenson passed a paper across his desk to Adam. It was a photocopy of Erica's signed statement in which she admitted guilt.

The chief waited while Adam read it, then asked Erica, "In your husband's presence, Mrs. Trenton, I now ask you: Were you offered any inducement to make that statement, or was any force or coercion of any kind employed?"

Erica shook her head.

"You are saying, then, that the statement was entirely voluntary?"

"Yes." Erica avoided Adam's eyes.

"Do you have any complaint, either about your treatment here or concerning the officers who arrested you?"

Again, Erica shook her head.

"Aloud, please. I want your husband to hear."

"No," Erica said. "No, I don't have any complaint."

"Mrs. Trenton," the chief said, "I'd like to ask you one other question. You don't have to answer, but it would be helpful to me if you did, and perhaps to your husband, too. I also promise that whatever the answer, nothing will happen as a result of it."

Erica waited.

"Have you ever stolen before, Mrs. Trenton? I mean recently, in the same kind of circumstances as today."

Erica hesitated. Then she said softly, "Yes."

"How many times?"

Adam pointed out, "You said one question and she answered it."

Chief Arenson sighed. "All right. Let it go."

Adam was aware of Erica glancing his way gratefully, then wondered if he had been wrong to intercede. Perhaps it might have been better if everything came out, since the chief had already promised immunity. Then Adam thought: The place for more revelations was in private, between himself and Erica.

If Erica chose to tell him. There seemed no certainty she would.

Even now, Adam had no idea how they were going to handle this when he and Erica got home. How *did* you handle the fact that your wife was a thief?

He had a sudden flash of anger: *How could Erica do this to him?*

It was then that Chief Arenson delivered his stern lecture to Erica, which she acknowledged.

The chief continued: "In this single special instance, because of your husband's standing in the community and the unfortunate effect which a prosecution would have on both of you, the store concerned has been persuaded not to press charges and I have decided to take no further action."

Adam said, "We know it was your initiative, Chief, and we're grateful."

Chief Arenson inclined his head in acknowledgment. "There are advantages sometimes, Mr. Trenton, in having a local suburban police force instead of a big metropolitan one. I can tell you that if this had occurred downtown, with the city police involved, the outcome would have been very different."

"If ever the question comes up, my wife and I will be among the strongest advocates of keeping a local force."

The chief made no acknowledgment. Politicking, he thought, should not become too obvious, even though it was good to have gained two more supporters of local autonomy. One day, if this man Trenton was going as high as predicted, he might prove a strong ally. The chief liked being a chief. He intended to do all he could to remain one until retirement, not become a precinct captain—as would happen under a metro force—taking orders from downtown.

He nodded, but did not stand—no sense in overdoing things—as the Trentons went out.

Smokey Stephensen was no longer in the corridor, but waiting in his car outside. He got out as Adam and Erica emerged from police headquarters. It was now dark. The rain had stopped.

While Adam waited as Smokey approached, Erica went on alone to where Adam's car was parked. They had arranged to leave Erica's convertible in the police garage overnight and pick it up tomorrow.

"We owe you some thanks," Adam told Smokey. "My wife doesn't feel up to it now, but she'll tell you herself later." It required an effort to be polite because Adam still resented bitterly the auto dealer's blackmailing tactics. Reason told him, however, that without Smokey on hand he might have fared worse.

Then Adam remembered his anger at Erica inside. Something else she had done, he realized, had been to put him at the mercy of Smokey Stephensen.

Smokey grinned and removed his cigar. "No need for thanks. So long as you keep your side of the bargain."

"It will be kept."

"Just one thing, and maybe you'll tell me it's none of my business, but don't be too hard on your wife."

"You're right," Adam said, "it is none of your business."

The auto dealer went on unperturbed, "People do funny things for funny reasons. Worth a second look sometimes to find out what the reasons really were."

"If I ever need some amateur psychology, I'll call you." Adam turned away. "Goodnight."

Thoughtfully, Smokey watched him go.

They had driven half the way to Quarton Lake.

"You haven't said anything," Erica said. "Aren't you going to?" She was looking straight ahead, and though her voice sounded tired, it had an edge of defiance.

"I can say what I have to in just one word: Why?" While driving, Adam had been struggling to control his indignation and temper. Now, both erupted. *"In God's name! Why?"*

"I've been asking myself that."

"Well, ask again and see if you can get some kind of sane answer. I'll be damned if I can."

"You don't have to shout."

"*You* don't have to steal."

"If we're only going to fight," Erica said, "we won't accomplish much."

"All I'm trying to accomplish is the answer to a simple question."

"The question being: Why?"

"Exactly."

"If you must know," Erica said, "I rather enjoyed doing it. I suppose that shocks you."

"Yes, it shocks me like hell."

She went on, musing aloud, as if explaining to herself. "Of course, I didn't want to get caught, but there was a thrill in knowing I might be. It made everything exciting and somehow sharper. In a way it was like the feeling you get when you've had one drink too many. Of course, when I *was* caught, it was awful. Much worse than anything I imagined."

"Well," Adam said, "at least we're making a start."

"If you don't mind, that's all I want to make tonight. I realize you have a lot of questions, and I guess you're entitled to ask them. But could we leave the rest until tomorrow?"

Adam glanced sideways. He saw that Erica had put her head back and her eyes were closed. She looked young and vulnerable and weary. He answered, "Okay."

She said, so softly that he had to strain to hear, "And thank you for coming. It's true what I said—I wasn't going to send for you, but I was glad when you were there."

He reached out and let his hand cover hers.

"You said something"—Erica still spoke dreamily, as if from a distance—"about making a start. If only we could make a whole new start!"

"In what way?"

"In every way." She sighed. "I know we can't."

On impulse, Adam said, "Perhaps we can."

It was strange, he thought, that today of all days Perceval Stuyvesant should have suggested one.

Sir Perceval and Adam were breakfasting together at the Hilton Hotel downtown, where Perce was staying.

Adam had not talked with Erica since their return home last night. She had gone exhausted to bed, fallen asleep immediately and was still sleeping soundly when he left the house early to drive into the city. He had considered waking her, decided against it, then half way to the breakfast appointment wished he had. He would have gone back, except that Perce had a midmorning flight to New York—the reason they made the arrangement by telephone last night; also, suddenly, Perce's proposition seemed more relevant and important than it had the day before.

One thing Adam had noticed last night was that while Erica went to sleep alone in the guest bedroom, as she had for the past month, she left the door open, and it was still open when he tiptoed in this morning.

He decided now: He would telephone home in another hour. Then, if Erica wanted to talk, he would rearrange his office schedule and go home for part of the morning.

Over their meal, Perce made no reference to the interruption in their talk the previous day; nor did Adam. Briefly Perce inquired about Adam's sons, Greg and Kirk, then they talked about superconductors—the area in which the small scientific company, now offering its presidency to Adam, was hopeful of a breakthrough.

"One extraordinary thing about superconductors, old boy, is that the public and the press know so little of them." Perce sipped his brew of mixed Ceylon and India teas which he carried with him in canisters and had prepared specially wherever he happened to be.

"As you probably know, Adam, a superconductor is a metal or wire which will carry a full load of electricity without any loss whatever."

Adam nodded. Like any eighth-grade physics student, he was aware that all present wires and cables caused at least a fifteen percent loss of power, called resistance.

"So a working superconductor with nil resistance," Perceval said, "would revolutionize the entire world's electric power systems. Among other things it would eliminate complex, expensive transmission equipment and provide fantastic amounts of power at unbelievably low cost. What has held back development until now has been the fact that superconductors would only function at very low temperatures—about 450 degrees below zero Fahrenheit."

Adam said, "That's pretty darned cold."

"Quite so. Which is why, in recent years, a scientific dream has been of a superconductor which will function at room temperature."

"Is it likely to be more than a dream?"

Perce thought before answering. "We've known each other a good many years, old boy. Have you ever known me to exaggerate?"

"No," Adam said. "Very much the reverse. You've always been conservative."

"I still am." Perce smiled and drank more tea, then went on. "Our group has not found a room temperature superconductor, but certain phenomena—the result of experiments we've made—have us excited. We wonder, some days, if we may not be very close."

"And if you are?"

"If we are, if there *is* a breakthrough, there's not an area of modern technology which won't be affected and improved. Let me give you two examples."

Adam listened with increasing fascination.

"I won't go into all the magnetic field hypotheses, but there's something called a superconducting ring. What it is is a wire which will store electric current in large amounts *and hold it intact*, and if we make the other breakthrough we'll be on top of this one, too. It'll make feasible the transfer of portable electric power in huge amounts, from place to place, by truck or boat or airplane. Think of its uses in the desert or the jungle—flown there in a package without a generator in sight, and more to follow when needed. And can you imagine another superconducting ring, this time in an electric operated car, making the battery as out of date as rushlight?"

"Since you ask," Adam said, "I have trouble imagining some of that."

Perce reminded him, "Not long ago people had trouble imagining atomic energy and space travel."

True, Adam thought, then pointed out, "You said two examples."

"Yes, I did. One of the interesting things about a superconductor is that it's diamagnetic—that's to say, when used in conjunction with more common magnets, immensely large repulsive forces can occur. Do you see the possibilities, old boy?—metals in any kind of machinery nestled close together yet never actually touching. Obviously we'd have frictionless bearings. And you could build a car without metal parts in contact with one another—hence, no wear. Those are just beginning possibilities. Others are endless."

It was impossible not to share some of Perce's conviction. From anyone else, Adam would have taken most of what was being described either as science fiction or a long-range possibility.

But not from Perce Stuyvesant who had a record of good judgment and accomplishment in deeply scientific fields.

"Somewhat fortunately," Perce said, "in the areas I've mentioned, and others, our group has been able to move along without attracting much attention. But there'll be attention soon—lots of it. That's another reason why we need you."

Adam was thinking hard. Perce's report and ideas excited him, though he wondered if the excitement would be as great or as sustained as he had experienced with cars—the Orion and Farstar, for example. Even now, the thought of not being a part of the auto industry was hard to accept. But there had been something in what Perce said yesterday about carving new pathways, breaking fresh ground.

Adam said, "If we do get down to this seriously, I'll want to come to San Francisco and talk with the rest of your people."

"We'd be more than delighted, old man, and I urge you to make it soon." Perce spread his hands in a deprecating gesture. "Of course, not everything I've described may work out the way we hope, nor is a breakthrough ever a breakthrough until it's happened. But there will be *some* important, exciting things; that much we know for sure and that I promise you. Remember that line? —'*There is a tide in the affairs of men, Which, taken at the flood* . . .' and so on."

"Yes," Adam said, "I remember."

He was wondering about timing, and a tide, for Erica and himself.

chapter twenty-five

The initial involvement of Rollie Knight in organized plant crime had begun in February. It started the same week that he saw the foreman Frank Parkland—whom Rollie had come close to admiring—take a bribe, prompting Rollie's later observation to May Lou, "There ain't nuthin' in this whole wide world but bullshit."

At first, to Rollie, his participation seemed slight enough. He began by taking and recording numbers bets each day in the area of Assembly where he worked. The money and yellow betting slips were passed by Rollie to the stockroom delivery man, Daddy-o Lester, who got them farther along their route toward a betting house downtown. From overheard remarks Rollie guessed the delivery system tied in with truck deliveries in and out of the plant.

Frank Parkland, still Rollie's foreman, gave him no trouble about occasional absences from his work station which the number running entailed. As long as the absences were brief and not too many, Parkland moved a relief man in without comment; otherwise, he cautioned Rollie mildly. Obviously the foreman was continuing to be paid off.

That was in February. By May, Rollie was working for the loan sharks and check cashers—two illegal plant enterprises which interlocked.

A reason for the new activity was that he had borrowed money himself and was having difficulty paying off. Also, the money Rollie was earning from his job, which at first had seemed a fortune, suddenly was no longer enough to keep pace with his own and May Lou's spending. So now Rollie persuaded others to accept loans and helped with their collection.

Such loans were made, and taken, casually—at extortionate rates of interest. A plant worker might borrow twenty dollars early in one week and owe twenty-five dollars by payday of the same week. Incredibly, the demand—including requests for larger sums—was brisk.

On payday, the loan sharks—company employees like everyone else—would become in-plant unofficial check cashers, cashing the paychecks of all who wished, but seeking out those who owed them money.

A check casher's fee was the odd cents on any check. If a check was made out for $100.99, the check casher took the 99¢, though his minimum fee was 25¢. Because of volume, and the fact that the check casher picked up his loans, plus interest, the operation involved big money and it was not unusual for a check casher-loan man to carry twenty thousand dollars in cash. When he did, he hired other workers as bodyguards.

Once a loan was made, it was wise for the borrower not to default. Anyone who did would find himself with a broken arm or leg, or worse—and would still owe the money, with more punishment to follow if it remained unpaid. A lucky few, like Rollie, were allowed to work off, in service, part of the interest owed. The principal sum—even for these—had to be repaid.

Thus, Rollie Knight, on all work days and especially paydays, became an intermediary for the flow of loan and check money back and forth. Despite this, he continued to be short of money himself.

In June, he began peddling drugs.

Rollie hadn't wanted to. Increasingly, as he became involved with plant rackets, he had a sense of being sucked in against his will, incurring the danger of exposure, arrest and—a dread which haunted him—a return to prison with a long sentence. Others who had no criminal records, though their activities were illegal, ran a lesser risk than himself. If caught and charged, they would be treated as first offenders. Rollie wouldn't.

It had been a growing anxiety on that score which made him morose and worried the night of the *Auto City* filming—also in June—in Rollie's and May Lou's apartment. Leonard Wingate, the company Personnel man, had sensed Rollie's deep-seated worry, but they had not discussed it.

Rollie also discovered, around that time, that it was easier to begin involvement with the rackets than to opt out. Big Rufe made that plain when Rollie demurred after being told he would be a part of the chain which brought marijuana and LSD into plants and distributed the drugs.

Months earlier, when the two had been side by side at a plant urinal, it was Big Rufe who approached Rollie with a hint about recruitment into plant crime. And now that the hint had become fact, it was clear that Big Rufe had a part in most of the illegal action going on.

"Don't cut no slice o' that pie for me," Rollie had insisted, when the subject of drug traffic came up. "You get some other dude, hear?"

They were on work break, talking behind a row of storage bins near the assembly line, and shielded from the view of others. Big Rufe had scowled. "You stink scared."

"Maybe."

"Boss don't like scared cats. Makes him nervous."

Rollie knew better than to ask who the boss was. He was certain that one existed—probably somewhere outside the plant—just as it was obvious that an organization existed, Rollie having seen evidence of it not long before.

One night, after his shift ended, instead of leaving, he and a half dozen others had remained inside the plant gates. Ahead of time they had been warned to make their way singly and inconspicuously to the Scrap and Salvage area. When they arrived, a truck was waiting and the group loaded it with crates and cartons already stacked nearby. It was obvious to Rollie that what was being loaded was new, unused material, and not scrap at all. It included tires, radios, and air conditioners in cases, and some heavy crates—which required loading with a hoist—and marked as containing transmissions.

The first truck left, a second came, and for three hours altogether the loading went on, openly, and although it was after dark and this portion of the plant saw little nighttime traffic, lights were blazing. Only toward the end did Big Rufe, who had appeared and disappeared several times, look around him nervously and urge everyone to hurry. They had, and eventually the second truck had gone too, and everyone went home.

Rollie had been paid two hundred dollars for the three hours he had helped load what was clearly a big haul of stolen goods. Equally evident was that the behind-scenes organization was efficient and large-scale, and there must have been payoffs to get the trucks safely in and out of the plant. Later, Rollie learned that the transmissions and other items could be bought cheaply at some of the many hot-rod shops around Detroit and Cleveland; also that the outflow through the Scrap and Salvage yard had been one of many.

"Guess you bought yourself a pack o' trouble by knowin' too much," Big Rufe had said when he and Rollie had their talk behind the storage bins. "That'd make the big boss nervous too, so if he figured you wasn't with us no more, he'd likely arrange a little party on the parking lot."

Rollie understood the message. So many beatings and muggings had occurred recently on the huge employee parking lots that even security patrols went around in pairs. Just the day before, a young black worker had been beaten and robbed —the beating so savage that he was hovering, in hospital, between life and death.

Rollie shuddered.

Big Rufe grunted and spat on the floor. "Yeah, man, I'd sure think about that if I was you."

In the end, Rollie went along with drug peddling, partly because of Big Rufe's threat, but also because he desperately needed money. The second garnishee of his wages in June had been followed by Leonard Wingate's financial austerity program, which left barely enough each week for Rollie and May Lou to live on, and nothing over to pay back loans.

Actually, the drug arrangement worked out easily, making him wonder if perhaps he had worried too much after all. He was glad that just marijuana and LSD were involved, and not heroin which was a riskier traffic. There *was* horse moving through the plant, and he knew workers who had habits. But a heroin addict was unreliable and likely to get caught, then under interrogation name his supplier.

Marijuana, on the other hand, was a pushover. The FBI and local police had told auto company managements confidentially that they would not investigate marijuana activity where less than one pound of the drug was involved. The reason was simple—a shortage of investigating officers. This information leaked, so that Rollie and others were careful to bring small amounts into the plant each time.

The extent of marijuana use amazed even Rollie. He discovered that more than half of the people working around him smoked two to three joints a day and many admitted it was the drug which kept them going. "For Cri-sakes," a regular purchaser from Rollie asserted, "if a guy wasn't spaced out, how else could he stand this rat run?" Just a half joint, he said, gave him a lift which lasted several hours.

Rollie heard another worker tell a foreman who had cautioned him for being obvious about marijuana use, "If you fired everybody smoking pot, you wouldn't build any cars around here."

Another effect of Rollie's drug peddling was that he was able to get squared away with the loan sharks, leaving some spare money which he used to indulge in pot himself. It was true, he found, that a day on the assembly line could be endured more easily if you were spaced, and you could get the work done too.

Rollie did manage to work to the continuing satisfaction of Frank Parkland, despite his extra activities which, in fact, took little time.

Because of his lack of seniority, he was laid off during two of the four weeks when the plant shut down for changeover to Orion production, then resumed work when the first Orions began to come down the line.

He took a keen interest in the Orion, describing it to May Lou when he returned from his first day of working on it, as "Hot pants wheels!" It even seemed to affect Rollie sexually because he added, "We gonna lay a lotta pipe tonight," at which May Lou giggled, and later they did, Rollie thinking about wheels most of the time and the chances of getting an Orion himself.

All was going well, it seemed, and for a while Rollie Knight almost forgot his own credo: *Nuthun' lasts.*

Until the last week of August, when he had cause to remember.

The message from Big Rufe came to Rollie's

work station via the stock man, Daddy-o Lester. The next night there would be some action. At the end of Rollie's shift tomorrow he was to stay in the plant. Between now and then he would be given more instructions.

Rollie yawned in Daddy-o's face. "I'll check my engagement book, man."

"You so smart," Daddy-o threw back, "but you don't hipe me. You'll be there."

Rollie knew he would be, too, and since the last after-shift episode at the Scrap and Salvage area produced an easy two hundred dollars, he assumed tomorrow's would be the same. Next day, however, the instructions he received half an hour before his work day ended were not what he expected. Rollie—so Daddy-o informed him—was to take his time about leaving the assembly line, hang around until the night shift began work, then go to the locker and washup area where others would meet him, including Daddy-o and Big Rufe.

Thus, when the quitting whistle shrilled, instead of joining the normal frenzied scramble for exits to the parking lots and bus stations, Rollie ambled away, stopping at a vending machine area to buy a Coke. This took longer than usual because the machines were temporarily out of use and being emptied of cash by two collectors from the vending company. Rollie watched while a stream of silver coins cascaded into canvas sacks. When a machine was available he bought his drink, waited a few minutes more, then took it to the employees' locker-washup room.

This was drab and cavernous, with a wet cement floor and a permanent stink of urine. A row of big stone washup basins—"bird baths"— was set centrally, at each of which a dozen men normally performed ablutions at once. Lockers, urinals, toilets without doors, crowded the remaining space.

Rollie rinsed his hands and face at a bird bath and mopped with paper towels. He had the washup area to himself since by now the day shift had gone and, outside, the new shift was settling down to work. Workers from it would begin drifting in here soon, but not yet.

An outside door opened. Big Rufe entered, moving quietly for a man of his bulk. He was scowling and looking at his wrist watch. Big Rufe's shirt sleeves were rolled back, the muscles rippling in his raised forearm. He motioned for silence as Rollie joined him.

Seconds later, Daddy-o Lester came through the same door that Big Rufe had used. The young black was breathing hard, as if he had been running; sweat glistened on his forehead and on the scar running the length of his face.

Big Rufe said accusingly, "I told you, hurry it . . ."

"I did! They runnin' late. Had trouble at one stand. Somethin' jammed, took longer." Daddy-o's voice was high-pitched and nervous, his usual swagger gone.

"Where they now?"

"South cafeteria. Leroy's watchin' out. He'll meet us where we said."

"South cafeteria's those guys' last stop." Big Rufe told the others, "Let's move it."

Rollie stood where he was. "Move where? An' what?"

"Now get on this fast." Big Rufe kept his voice low, his eyes on the outer door. "We gonna bust the vending machine guys. The whole deal's planned—a cincheroo. They carry a big load, 'n we got four guys to their two. You get a cut."

"I don't want it! Don't know enough."

"Want it or not, you got it. You got this, too." Big Rufe pressed a snub-nosed automatic into Rollie's hand.

He protested, "No!"

"What's the difference? You done time for armed. Now, if you carryin' a piece or you ain't, you get the same." Big Rufe shoved Rollie ahead of him roughly. As they left the locker-washup room, instinctively Rollie pushed the pistol out of sight into his trousers waistband.

They hastened through the plant, using out-of-the-way routes and keeping clear of observation —not difficult for anyone knowing the layout well. Though Rollie had not been inside the south cafeteria, which was a small one used by supervisors and foremen, he knew where it was. Presumably it had a battery of vending machines, as had the employees' area where he bought his Coke.

Over his shoulder, hurrying with the others, Rollie asked, "Why me?"

"Could be we like you," Big Rufe said. "Or maybe the boss figures the deeper a brother's in, the less chance he'll chicken out."

"The boss man in this too?"

"I tol' you this piece of action was planned. We bin studyin' them vending guys a month. Hard to figure why nobody knocked 'em off before."

The last statement was a lie.

It was not hard to figure—at least, for those with inside knowledge—why the vending machine collectors had gone unmolested until now. Big Rufe was among those who possessed such inside knowledge; also, he knew the special risks which he and the other three were running at this moment, and was prepared to accept and challenge them.

Rollie Knight had no such information. If he had, if he had known what Big Rufe failed to tell him, no matter what the consequences he would have turned and run.

The knowledge was: The vending concessions at the plant were Mafia-financed and -operated.

The Mafia in Wayne County, Michigan, of which Detroit is part, has a compass of activities ranging from the outright criminal, such as murder, to semilegal businesses. In the area, the name Mafia is more appropriate than Cosa Nostra since Sicilian families form its core. The "semi" of semilegal is also appropriate since no Mafia-controlled business ever operates without at least some ancillary knaveries—overpricing, intimidation, bribery, physical violence, or arson.

The Mafia is strong in Detroit's industrial plants, including auto plants. It controls the numbers rackets, finances and controls most loan sharks and takes a cut from others. The organization is behind the bulk of large-scale thefts from factories and helps with resale of stolen items. It has tentacles in plants through surface-legal operations such as service and supply companies, which are usually a cover-up for other activities or a means of hiding cash. Its dollar revenues each year are undoubtedly in the tens of millions.

But in recent years, with an aging Mafia chieftain declining physically and mentally in Grosse Pointe remoteness, a power struggle has erupted within Detroit Mafia ranks. And since a bloc within the power struggle consists solely of blacks, this substratum—in Detroit as elsewhere—has acquired the title Black Mafia.

Hence, black struggles within the Mafia for recognition and equality parallel the more deserving civil rights struggles of black people generally.

A cell of the Black Mafia, headed by a militant outside leader who remained under cover, and with Big Rufe as an in-plant deputy, had been testing and challenging the old established family rule. Months earlier, forays had begun into unauthorized areas—a separate numbers operation and increased Black Mafia loan sharking, extending through the inner city and industrial plants. Other operations included organized prostitution and "protection" shakedowns. All cut across areas where the old regime had once been absolute.

The Black Mafia cell had expected retaliation and it happened. Two black loan men were ambushed in their homes and beaten—one while his terrified wife and children watched—then robbed. Soon after, a Black Mafia numbers organizer was intercepted and pistol-whipped, his car overturned and burned, his records destroyed and money taken. All raids, by their ruthlessness and other hallmarks, were clearly Mafia work, a fact which victims and their associates were intended to recognize.

Now the Black Mafia was striking back. Robbery of the vending machine collectors would be one of a half dozen counterraids, all carefully timed for today and representing a test of strength in the power struggle. Later still, there would be more reprisals on both sides before the white-black Mafia war ended, if it ever did.

And, as in all wars everywhere, the soldiers and other victims would be expendable pawns.

Rollie Knight, Big Rufe, and Daddy-o had come through a basement corridor and were at the foot of a metal stairway. Immediately ahead was a halfway landing between floors, the top of the stairway out of sight.

Big Rufe commanded softly, "Hold it here!"

A face appeared, looking downward over the stairway rail. Rollie recognized Leroy Colfax, an intense, fast-talking militant who hung around with Big Rufe's crowd.

Big Rufe kept his voice low. "Them peckerwoods still there?"

"Yeah. Be two, three minutes more by the looks."

"Okay, we in place. You get clear now, but follow 'em down, 'n stay close. Understand?"

"I got it." With a nod, Leroy Colfax disappeared from sight.

Big Rufe beckoned Rollie and Daddy-o. "In here."

"Here" was a janitor's closet, unlocked and with space for the three of them. As they went inside, Big Rufe left the door slightly ajar. He queried Daddy-o. "You got the masks?"

"Yeah." Rollie could see that Daddy-o, the youngest, was nervous and trembling. But he produced three stocking masks from a pocket. Big Rufe took one and slipped it over his head, motioning for the others to do the same.

The basement corridor outside was quiet, the only noise a rumble, distantly above, where the assembly line was operating with the fresh eight-hour shift. This had been a shrewd time to pick. Traffic through the plant was never as great during the night shift as in daytime, and was even lighter than usual this early in the shift.

"You two watch me, move when I do." Through the mask, Big Rufe's eyes appraised Daddy-o and Rollie. "Ain't gonna be no trouble if we do this right. When we get them guys in here you both tie 'em up good. Leroy dumped the rope." He motioned to two coils of thin yellow cord on the closet floor.

They waited silently. As the seconds passed, Rollie found himself with a sense of resigned acceptance. He knew he was in this now, that his participation would not be changed or excused whatever happened, and if there were consequences he would share them equally with the other three. His choices had been limited; in fact, there were really no choices at all, merely decisions made by others and forced on him, which was the way it had always been, for as long as he remembered.

From the coveralls he was wearing, Big Rufe produced a heavy-handled Colt revolver. Daddy-o had a snub-nosed pistol—the same kind Rollie had been given. Reluctantly, reaching into his waistband, Rollie held his, too.

Daddy-o tensed as Big Rufe motioned with his hand. They could hear clearly—a clatter of feet coming down the metal stairway, and voices.

The door to the janitor's closet remained almost closed until the footsteps, now on the tile floor, were a few feet away. Then Big Rufe opened the door and the masked trio stepped out, guns raised.

The vending machine collectors looked as startled as any two men could.

Both wore gray uniforms with the vending company's insignia. One had a thatch of red hair and a pale pink face which, at the moment had turned even paler; the other, with heavy-lidded eyes, had the features of an Indian. Each carried two burlap bags slung over a shoulder and joined together with a chain and padlock. The pair were big-boned and burly, probably in their thirties, and looked as if they could handle themselves in a fight. Big Rufe gave them no chance.

He leveled his revolver at the red-haired man's chest and motioned with his head to the janitor's closet. "In there, baby!" He ordered the other, "You, too!" The words came out muffled through the stocking mask.

The Indian shot a glance behind him, as if to run. Two things happened. He saw a fourth masked figure—Leroy Colfax—armed with a long-bladed hunting knife, leaping down the stairs and cutting off escape. Simultaneously, the muzzle of

Big Rufe's revolver slammed into his face, opening his left cheek in a gash which spurted blood.

Rollie Knight jammed his own automatic against the ribs of the red-haired man who had swung around, clearly with the intention of aiding his companion. Rollie cautioned, "Hold it! It ain't gonna work!" All he wanted was to have done with this, without more violence. The red-haired man subsided.

Now the four ambushers shoved the others ahead of them into the little room.

The red-haired man protested, "Listen, if you guys knew . . ."

"Shaddup!" It was Daddy-o, who seemed to be over his fright. "Gimme that!" He grabbed the canvas sacks from redhead's shoulder, pushing the man so he tripped backward over mops and pails.

Leroy Colfax reached for the cash sacks of the other collector. But the Indian, despite his cheek wound, which was bleeding, had spirit. He lunged against Leroy, thrusting a knee into his groin and his left fist hard into the stomach. Then, with his right hand, he reached up and snatched the mask from Leroy's face.

For an instant the two glared at each other.

The vending machine collector hissed, "Now, I'll know who . . . aaaaaaah!"

He screamed—a loud, high-pitched sound which descended to a moan then subsided into nothingness. He fell forward heavily—on the long-bladed hunting knife which Leroy had thrust hard into his belly.

"*Jesus Christ!*" the red-haired man said. He stared down at the slumped, motionless form of his companion of a moment earlier. "You bastards killed him!"

They were his last words before unconsciousness as the butt of Big Rufe's gun crashed into his scalp.

Daddy-o, who was trembling more than he had originally, pleaded, "Did we hafta do that?"

"What's done's done," Big Rufe said. "And them two started it." But he sounded less sure of himself than at the beginning. Picking up two of the chained bags, he ordered, "Bring them others."

Leroy Colfax reached for them.

Rollie urged, "Wait!"

Outside, hurried footsteps were coming down the metal stairs.

Frank Parkland had stayed later than usual at the plant for a foremen's meeting in the office of Matt Zaleski. They discussed Orion production and some problems. Afterward he went to the south cafeteria where, at lunchtime, he had left a sweater and some personal papers. It was when he had recovered the items, and was leaving that he heard the scream from below and went down to investigate.

Parkland was past the closed door of the janitor's closet when something impinged on his consciousness. He turned back and saw what he had observed but not taken in at once—a series of blood spatters extending under the door.

The foreman hesitated. But since he was not a man given to fear, he opened the door and went in.

Seconds later, with an ugly head wound, he tumbled, unconscious, beside the vending machine collectors.

The three bodies were discovered an hour or so later—long after the quartet of Big Rufe, Daddy-o Lester, Leroy Colfax, and Rollie Knight had left the plant by climbing over a wall.

The Indian was dead, the other two barely alive.

chapter twenty-six

Matt Zaleski sometimes wondered if anyone outside the auto industry realized how little changed, in principle, a final car assembly line was, compared with the days of the first Henry Ford.

He was walking beside the line where the night shift, which had begun work an hour ago, was building Orions—the company's new cars, still not released to public view. Like others in senior plant management, Matt's own working day did not end when the day shift went home. He stayed on while the next shift settled down, dealing with production snafus as they occurred, which inevitably happened while the plant's people—management as well as workers—learned their new assignments.

Some assignments had been discussed during a foreman's meeting, held in Matt's office soon after the change of shifts. The meeting had ended fifteen minutes ago. Now Matt was patrolling—an alert surveillance, his experienced eyes searching for potential trouble spots.

While he walked, his thoughts returned to Henry Ford, the pioneer of mass production auto assembly.

Nowadays, the final assembly line in any auto plant was unfailingly the portion of car manufacturing which fascinated visitors most. Usually a mile long, it was visually impressive because an act of creation could be witnessed. Initially, a few steel bars were brought together, then, as if fertilized, they multiplied and grew, taking on familiar shapes like an exposed fetus in a moving womb. The process was slow enough for watchers to assimilate, fast enough to be exciting. The forward movement, like a river, was mostly in straight lines, though occasionally with bends or loops. Among the burgeoning cars, color, shape, size, features, frills, conveyed individuality and sex. Eventually, with the fetus ready for the world, the car dropped on its tires. A moment later an ignition key was turned, an engine sprang to life—as impressive, when first witnessed, as a child's first cry—and a newborn vehicle moved from the assembly line's end under its own power.

Matt Zaleski had seen spectators thronging through the plant—in Detroit they came like pilgrims, daily—marveling at the process and talking, uninformed and glibly, of the wonders of automated mass production. Plant guides, trained to regard each visitor as a potential customer, gave spiels to titillate the sense of wonder. But the irony was: a final assembly plant was scarcely automated at all; in principle it was still an old-fashioned conveyor belt on which pieces of an automobile were hung in sequence like decorations on a Christmas tree. In engineering terms it was the least impressive part of modern automobile production. In terms of quality it could swing this way or that like a wild barometer. And it was wholly susceptible to human error.

By contrast, plants making auto engines, though less impressive visually, were truly automated, with long series of intricate operations performed solely by machines. In most engine plants, row after row of sophisticated machine tools operated on their own, masterminded by computers, with the only humans in sight a few skilled tool men making occasional adjustments. If a machine did something wrong, it switched itself off instantly and summoned help through warning systems. Otherwise it did its job unvaryingly, to hairsbreadth standards, and stopped neither for meal breaks, toilet visits, nor to speak to another machine alongside. The system was a reason why engines, in comparison with more generally constructed parts of automobiles, seldom failed until neglected or abused.

If old Henry could come back from his grave, Matt thought, and view a car assembly line of the '70s, he might be amused at how few basic changes had been made.

At the moment, there were no production snags—at least, in view—and Matt Zaleski returned to his glass-paneled office on the mezzanine.

Though he could leave the plant now, if he chose, Matt was reluctant to return to the empty Royal Oak house. Several weeks had gone by since the bitter night of Barbara's departure, but there had been no *rapprochement* between them. Recently Matt had tried not to think about his daughter, concentrating on other thoughts, as he had on Henry Ford a few minutes earlier; despite this, she was seldom far from mind. He wished they could patch up their quarrel somehow, and had hoped Barbara would telephone, but she had not. Matt's own pride, plus a conviction that a parent should not have to make the first move, kept him from calling her. He supposed that Barbara was still living with that designer, DeLosanto, which was something else Matt tried not to think about, but often did.

At his desk, he leafed through the next day's production schedule. Tomorrow was a midweek day, so several "specials" would go on the line— cars for company executives, their friends, or others with influence enough to ensure that an automobile they ordered got better-than-ordinary treatment. Foremen had been alerted to the job numbers, so had Quality Control; as a result, all work on those particular cars would be watched with extra care. Body men would be cautioned to install header panels, seats, and interior trim more fussily than usual. Engine and power train sequences would receive close scrutiny. Later, Quality Control would give the cars a thorough going over and order additional work or adjustments before dispatch. "Specials" were also among the fifteen to thirty cars which plant executives drove home each night, turning in road test reports next morning.

Of course—as Matt Zaleski knew—there were dangers in scheduling "specials," particularly if a car happened to be for a plant executive. A few workers always had grievances, real or imagined, against management and were delighted at a chance to "get even with the boss." Then the legendary soft drink bottle, left loose inside a rocker panel so it would rattle through a car's lifetime, was apt to become reality. A loose tool or chunk of metal served the same purpose. Another trick was to weld the trunk lid closed from inside; a skilled welder, reaching through the back seat could do it in seconds. Or a strategic bolt or two might be left untightened. These were reasons why Matt and others like him used fictitious names when putting their own cars through production.

Matt put the next day's schedule down. There had been no need to review it, anyway, since he had gone over it earlier in the day.

It was time to go home. As he rose from the desk, he thought again of Barbara and wondered where she was. He was suddenly very tired.

On his way down from the mezzanine, Matt Zaleski was aware of some kind of disturbance—shouting, the sound of running feet. Automatically, because most things which happened in the plant were his business, he stopped, searching for the source. It appeared to be near the south cafeteria. He heard an urgent cry: "For God's sake get somebody from Security!"

Seconds later, as he hurried toward the disturbance, he heard sirens approaching from outside.

A janitor who discovered the huddled bodies of the two vending machine collectors and Frank Parkland, had the good sense to go promptly to a telephone. By the time Matt Zaleski heard the shouts, which were from others who had come on the scene subsequently, an ambulance, plant security men, and outside police were already on the way.

But Matt still reached the janitor's closet on the lower floor before any of the outside aid. Bulling his way through an excited group around it, he was in time to see that one of the three recumbent forms was that of Frank Parkland whom Matt had last seen at the foremen's meeting about an hour and a half before. Parkland's eyes were closed, his skin ashen, except where blood had trickled through his hair and clotted on his face.

One of the night shift office clerks who had run in with a first-aid kit, now lying unused beside him, had Parkland's head cradled in his lap and was feeling for a pulse. The clerk looked at Matt. "I guess he's alive, Mr. Zaleski; so's one of the others. Though I wouldn't want to say for how long."

Security and the ambulance people had come in then, and taken charge. The local police—uniformed men first, then plainclothes detectives—quickly joined them.

There was little for Matt to do, but he could no longer leave the plant, which had been sealed by a cordon of police cars. Obviously the police believed that whoever perpetrated the murder-robbery—it had been confirmed that one of the three victims was dead—might still be inside.

After a while, Matt returned to his office on the mezzanine where he sat, mentally numbed and listless.

The sight of Frank Parkland, who was clearly gravely hurt, had shocked Matt deeply. So had the knife protruding from the body of the man with the Indian face. But the dead man had been unknown to Matt, whereas Parkland was his friend. Though the assistant plant chief and foreman had had run-ins, and once—a year ago—exchanged strong words, such differences had been the result of work pressures. Normally, they liked and respected each other.

Matt thought: Why did it have to happen to a good man? There were others he knew over whom he would have grieved less.

At that moment, precisely, Matt Zaleski became aware of a sudden breathlessness and a fluttering in his chest, as if a bird were inside, beating its wings and trying to get out. The sensation frightened him. He sweated with the same kind of fear he had known years before in B-17F bombers over Europe when the German flak was barreling up, and now, as then, he knew it was the fear of death.

Matt knew, too, he was having some kind of attack and needed help. He began thinking in a detached way: He would telephone, and whoever came and whatever was done, he would ask them to send for Barbara because there was something he wanted to tell her. He was not sure exactly what, but if she came the words would find themselves.

The trouble was, when he made up his mind to reach for the telephone, he discovered he no longer had the power to move. Something strange was happening to his body. On the right side there was no feeling any more; he seemed to have no arm or leg, or any idea where either was. He tried to cry out but found, to his amazement and frustration, he could not. Nor, when he tried again, could he make any sound at all.

Now he knew what it was that he wanted to tell Barbara: That despite the differences they had had, she was still his daughter and he loved her, just as he had loved her mother, whom Barbara resembled in so many ways. He wanted to say, too, that if they could somehow resolve their present quarrel he would try to understand her, and her friends, better from now on . . .

Matt discovered he *did* have some feeling and power of movement in his left side. He tried to get up, using his left arm as a lever, but the rest of his body failed him and he slid to the floor between the desk and chair. It was in that position he was found soon after, conscious, his eyes mirroring an agony of frustration because the words he wanted to say could find no exit route.

Then, for the second time that night, an ambulance was summoned to the plant.

"You're aware," the doctor at Ford Hospital said to Barbara next day, "that your father had a stroke before."

She told him, "I know now. I didn't until today."

This morning, a plant secretary, Mrs. Einfeld, had reported, conscience-stricken, Matt Zaleski's mild attack a few weeks earlier when she had driven him home and he persuaded her to say nothing. The company's Personnel department had passed the information on.

"Taken together," the doctor said, "the two incidents fit a classic pattern." He was a specialist —a cardiologist—balding and sallow-faced, with a slight tic beneath one eye. Like so many in Detroit, Barbara thought, he looked as if he worked too hard.

"If my father hadn't concealed the first stroke, would it have changed anything?"

The specialist shrugged. "Perhaps; perhaps not. He'd have received medication, but the end result could have been the same. Either way, the question's academic now."

They were in an annex to an intensive care unit of the hospital. Through a glass window she could see her father in one of the four beds inside, a red rubber tube running from his mouth to a gray-green respirator on a stand close by. The respirator, wheezing evenly, was breathing for him. Matt Zaleski's eyes were open and the doctor had told Barbara that although her father was presently under sedation, at other times he could undoubtedly see and hear. She wondered if he was aware of the young black woman, also *in extremis*, in the bed nearest to him.

"It's probable," the doctor said, "that at some earlier period your father sustained valvular heart damage. Then, when he had the first mild stroke, a small clot broke off from the heart and went to the right side of his brain which, in a right-handed person, controls the body's left side."

It was all so impersonal, Barbara thought, as if a routine piece of machinery were being described, and not the sudden breakdown of a human being.

The cardiologist went on: "With the kind of stroke which your father had first, almost certainly the recovery was only apparent. It wasn't a real recovery. The body's fail-safe mechanism remained damaged and that was why the second stroke, to the left side of the brain, produced the devastating effect it did last night."

Barbara had been with Brett last night when a message was telephoned that her father had had a sudden stroke and been rushed to the hospital. Brett had driven her there, though he waited outside. "I'll come if you need me," he had said, taking her hand reassuringly before she went in, "but your old man doesn't like me, anyway, and being ill isn't going to change his mind. It might upset him more if he saw me with you."

On the way to the hospital, Barbara had had a guilty feeling, wondering how much her own act of leaving home precipitated whatever had happened to her father. Brett's gentleness, of which she saw more each day and loved him increasingly for, underlined the tragedy that the two men she cared most about had failed to know each other better. On balance, she believed her father mainly to blame; just the same, Barbara wished now that she had telephoned him, as she had considered doing several times since their estrangement.

At the hospital last night they had let her speak to her father briefly, and a young resident told her, "He can't communicate with you, but he knows you're there." She had murmured the things she expected Matt would want to hear: that she was sorry about his illness, would not be far away, and would come to the hospital frequently. While speaking, Barbara had looked directly into his eyes and while there was no flicker of recognition she had an impression the eyes were straining to tell her something. Was it imagination? She wondered again now.

Barbara asked the cardiologist, "What are my father's chances?"

"Of recovery?" He looked at her interrogatively.

"Yes. And please be completely candid. I want to know."

"Sometimes people don't . . ."

"I do."

The cardiologist said quietly, "Your father's chances of any substantial recovery are nil. My prognosis is that he will be a hemiplegic invalid as long as he lives, with complete loss of power on the right side, including speech."

There was a silence, then Barbara said, "If you don't mind, I'd like to sit down."

"Of course." He guided her to a chair. "It's a big shock. If you like, I'll give you something."

She shook her head. "No."

"You had to know sometime," the doctor said, "and you asked."

They looked, together, through the window of the intensive care unit, at Matt Zaleski, still recumbent, motionless, the machine breathing for him.

The cardiologist said, "Your father was with the auto industry, wasn't he? In a manufacturing plant, I believe." For the first time, the doctor seemed warmer, more human than before.

"Yes."

"I get a good many patients from that source. Too many." He motioned vaguely beyond the hospital walls toward Detroit. "It's always seemed to me like a battleground out there, with casualties. Your father, I'm afraid, was one."

chapter twenty-seven

No aid was to be given Hank Kreisel in the manufacture or promotion of his thresher.

The decision, by the board of directors' executive policy committee, reached Adam Trenton in a memo routed through the Product Development chief, Elroy Braithwaite.

Braithwaite brought in the memo personally and tossed it on Adam's desk. "Sorry," the Silver Fox said, "I know you were interested. You turned me on, too, and you might like to know we were in good company because the chairman felt the same way."

The last news was not surprising. The chairman of the board was noted for his wide-ranging interests and liberal views, but only on rare occasions did he make autocratic rulings and obviously this had not been one.

The real pressure for the negative decision, Adam learned later, came from the executive vice-president, Hub Hewitson, who swayed the triumvirate—the chairman, president, and Hewitson himself—which comprised the executive policy committee.

Reportedly, Hub Hewitson argued on the lines: The company's principal business was building cars and trucks. If the thresher didn't look like a money-making item to farm products division, it should not be foisted on any segment of the corporation merely on public-spirited grounds. As to extramural activities generally, there were already enormous problems in coping with public and legislative pressures for increased safety, less air pollution, employment of the disadvantaged, and kindred matters.

The argument concluded: We are not a philanthropic body but a private enterprise whose objective is to make profits for shareholders.

After brief discussion, the president supported Hub Hewitson's view, so that the chairman was outnumbered, and conceded.

"It's been left to us to inform your friend, Kreisel," the Silver Fox told Adam, "so you'd better do it."

On the telephone Hank Kreisel was philosophic when Adam gave him the news. "Figured the odds weren't the greatest. Thanks, anyway."

Adam asked, "Where do you go from here?"

"Can raise dough in more than one oven," the parts manufacturer said cheerfully. But Adam doubted if he would—at least, for the thresher, in Detroit.

He told Erica about the decision over dinner that evening. She said, "I'm disappointed because it was a dream with Hank—a good one—and I like him. But at least you tried."

Erica seemed in good spirits; she was making a conscious effort, Adam realized, even though, almost two weeks after her arrest for shoplifting, and release, their relationship was still unclear, their future undecided.

The day following the painful experience at the suburban police station, Erica had declared, "If you insist on asking a lot more questions, though I hope you won't, I'll try to answer them. Before you do, though, I'll tell you I'm sorry, most of all, for getting you involved. And if you're worrying about my doing the same thing again— don't. I swear there'll never be anything like it as long as I live."

He had known she meant it, and that the subject could be closed. But it had seemed a right time to tell Erica about the job offer from Perce Stuyvesant and the fact that Adam was considering it seriously. He added, "If I do accept, it will mean a move, of course—to San Francisco."

Erica had been incredulous. "You're considering leaving the auto industry?"

Adam had laughed, feeling curiously lightheaded. "If I didn't, there'd be problems about dividing my time."

"You'd do *that* for me?"

He answered quietly, "Perhaps it would be for both of us."

Erica had seemed dazed, shaking her head in disbelief, and that subject had been dropped too. However, Adam had telephoned Perce Stuyvesant next day to say he was still interested, but would not be able to fly West until after the Orion's debut in September, now barely a month away. Sir Perceval had agreed to wait.

Another thing that had happened was that Erica moved back into their bedroom from the guest room, at Adam's suggestion. They had even essayed some sex, but there was no escaping that it was not as successful as in the old days, and both knew it. An ingredient was missing. Neither was sure exactly what it was; the only thing they knew with certainty was that in terms of their marriage they were marking time.

Adam hoped there would be a chance for them both to talk things over—away from Detroit —during two days of stock car racing they would be attending soon in Talladega, Alabama.

chapter twenty-eight

A page one banner headline of the *Anniston Star* ("Alabama's Largest Home-Owned Newspaper") proclaimed:

300 GOES AT 12:30

The news story immediately following began:

Today's Canebreak 300, as well as tomorrow's Talladega 500, promise some of the hottest competition in stock car racing history.

For the grueling 300-mile race today, and even tougher 500-miler Sunday, super fast cars and drivers have pushed qualifying speeds close to 190 mph.

What drivers, car owners, mechanics, and auto company observers now wonder is how the power-packed racers will act over the 2.66 mile trioval of Alabama International Speedway, at those speeds, when 50 cars are fighting for position on the track . . .

Lower on the same page was a sidebar story:

Severe Blood Shortage
Will Not Diminish
Big Race Precautions

Local alarm had been manifest (so the secondary news story said) because of an area Blood Bank shortage. The shortage was critical "because of the possibility of serious injuries to race drivers and a need for transfusions over Saturday's and Sunday's racing."

Now, to conserve supplies, all elective surgery at Citizens Hospital for which use of blood was predicted had been postponed until after the weekend. Additionally, appeals were being made to race visitors and residents to donate blood at a special clinic, opening Saturday at 8 A.M. Thus, a supply of blood for racing casualties would be assured.

Erica Trenton, who read both news reports while breakfasting in bed at the Downtowner Motor Inn, Anniston, shuddered at the implications of the second, and turned to the paper's inside pages. Among other race news on page three was an item:

New 'Orion' on Display
This One's a 'Concept'

The Orion's manufacturers, it was reported, were being closemouthed about how nearly the "styling concept" model, currently on view at Talladega, resembled the soon-to-appear, real Orion. However, public interest had been high, with pre-race crowds thronging the infield area where the model could be seen.

Adam would have had that news by now, Erica was sure.

They had come here together yesterday, having flown in on a company plane from Detroit, and this morning Adam left their suite at the motor inn early—almost two hours ago—to visit the Speedway pit area with Hub Hewitson. The executive vice-president, who was the senior company officer attending the two-day race meet, had a rented helicopter at his disposal, which had picked up Hewitson and Adam, and later several more. The same helicopter would make a second series of trips shortly before race time to collect Erica and a few other company wives.

Anniston, a pleasant green-and-white country town, was six miles or so from the Talladega track.

Officially, Adam's company, like other car manufacturers, was not directly involved in auto racing, and the once strongly financed factory teams had been disbanded. Yet no official edict could wipe out an ingrained enthusiasm for racing which most auto executives shared, including Hub Hewitson, Adam, and others in their own and competitive companies. This was one reason why most major auto races attracted strong contingents from Detroit. Another was that auto corporation money continued to flow into racing, through back doors, at division level or lower. In this way—in which General Motors had set a pattern across the years—if a car bearing a manufacturer's name won, its makers could cheer publicly, reaping plaudits and prestige. But if a car carrying their name lost, they merely shrugged and disclaimed association.

Erica got out of bed, took a leisurely bath, and began dressing.

While doing so, she thought about Pierre Flodenhale whose picture had been featured prominently in the morning paper. Pierre, in racing garb and crash helmet, was shown being kissed by two girls at once and was beaming—undoubtedly because of the girls but also, probably, because most prognosticators had picked him as among the two or three drivers most likely to win both today's and tomorrow's races.

Adam and others in the company contingent here were also happy about Pierre's prospects, since in both races he would be driving cars with their company's name.

Erica's feelings about Pierre were mixed, as she was reminded when they met briefly last night.

It had been at a crowded cocktail-supper party—one of many such affairs taking place around town, as always happened on the eve of any major auto race. Adam and Erica had been invited to six parties and dropped in on three. At the one where they met Pierre, the young race driver was a center of attention and surrounded by several glamorous but brassy girls—"pit pussies," as they were sometimes known—of the type which auto racing and its drivers seemed always to attract.

Pierre had detached himself on seeing Erica, and made his way across the room to where she was standing alone, Adam having moved away to talk with someone else.

"Hi, Erica," Pierre said easily. He gave his boyish grin. "Wondered if you'd be around."

"Well, I am." She tried to be nonchalant, but unaccountably felt nervous. To cover up, she smiled and said, "I hope you win. I'll be cheering for you both days." Even to herself, however, her words sounded strained, and in part, Erica realized, it was because the physical presence of Pierre aroused her sensually, still.

They had gone on chatting, not saying very much, though while they were together Erica was aware of others in the room, including two from Adam's company, glancing their way covertly. No doubt some were remembering gossip they had heard, including the *Detroit News* item about Pierre and Erica, which distressed her at the time.

Adam had strolled over to join them briefly, and wished Pierre well. Soon after, Adam moved away again, then Pierre excused himself, saying that because of the race tomorrow he must get to bed. "You know how it is, Erica," he said, grinning again, then winked to make sure she did not miss the unsubtle humor.

Even that reference to bed, clumsy as it was,

had left an effect, and Erica knew she was far from being completely over her affair with Pierre.

Now, it was noon next day and the first of the two big races—the Canebreak 300—would begin in half an hour.

Erica left the suite and went downstairs.

In the helicopter, Kathryn Hewitson observed, "This *is* rather ostentatious. But it beats sitting in traffic, I suppose."

The helicopter was a small one which could carry only two passengers at a time, and the first to be whirled from Anniston to the Talladega Speedway were the executive vice-president's wife and Erica. Kathryn Hewitson was a handsome, normally self-effacing woman in her early fifties, with a reputation as a devoted wife and mother, but also one who, on occasions, could handle her dynamic husband firmly, as no one else knowing him could or dared to. Today, as she often did, she had brought along her needlepoint which she worked on, even during their few minutes in the air.

Erica smiled an acknowledgment because the helicopter's noise as they were airborne precluded conversation.

Beneath the machine, the ochre-red earth of Alabama, framing lush meadowland, slid by. The sun was high, the sky unclouded, the air warm with a dry, fresh breeze. Though it would be September in a few days more, no sign of fall was yet apparent. Erica had chosen a light summer dress; so had most other women whom she saw.

They landed in the Speedway infield, already massed with parked vehicles and race fans, some of whom had camped here overnight. Even more cars were streaming in through two double-lane traffic tunnels beneath the track. At the helicopter landing pad, a car and driver were waiting for

Kathryn Hewitson and Erica; briefly, traffic in one of the incoming tunnel lanes was halted, the lane control reversed, while they sped through to the grandstand side of the track.

The grandstands too—North, South, and Over Hill—were packed with humanity, waiting expectantly in the now hot sun along their mile-long length. As the two women reached one of the several private boxes, a band near the starting line struck up "The Star-Spangled Banner." A singer's soprano voice floated over the p.a. Wherever they were, most spectators, contestants, and officials stood. The cacophony of speedway noises hushed.

A clergyman with a Deep South drawl intoned, "Oh God, watch over those in peril who will compete . . . We praise Thee for today's fine weather, and give our thanks for business Thou hast brought this area . . ."

"Damn right," Hub Hewitson asserted in the front row of his company's private box. "Lots of cash registers jingling, including ours, I hope. Must be a hundred thousand people." The phalanx of company men and wives surrounding the executive vice-president smiled dutifully.

Hewitson, a small man with close-cropped, jet black hair, whose energy seemed to radiate through his skin, leaned forward so he could better view the throngs which jammed the Speedway. He declared again, "Motor racing's come up to be the second most popular sport; soon it'll be the first. All of 'em out there are interested in power under the hood, thank God!—and never mind the sanctimonious sons-of-bitches who tell us people aren't."

Erica was two rows from the front, with Adam beside her. Kathryn Hewitson had gone to the rear of the box, which had tiered seats rising from front to rear, and was sheltered from the sun. Kathryn told Erica as they came in, "Hub likes me along, but I don't really care for racing. It makes me frightened at times, and sad at others, wondering what's the point of it all." Erica could see the older woman in the back row now, busy with her needlepoint.

The private box, like several others, was in the South grandstand and commanded a view of the entire Speedway. The start-finish line was immediately in front, banked turns to left and right, the backstretch visible beyond the infield. On the nearer side of the infield were the pits, now thronged with overalled mechanics. Pit row, as it was known, had ready access to and from the track.

In the company box, among other guests, was Smokey Stephensen, and Adam and Erica had spoken with him briefly. Ordinarily, a dealer would not make it in here with the high command, but Smokey enjoyed privileges at race meets, having once been a big star driver, with many older fans still revering his name.

Next to the company box was the press enclosure, with long tables and scores of typewriters, also ranged in tiers. The press reporters, alone among most others present today, self-importantly hadn't stood for the national anthem. Now, most were clattering on typewriters, and Erica, who could view them through a glass window at the side, wondered what they could be writing so much bout when the race hadn't even started.

But starting time was close. The praying was done clergy, parade marshals, drum majorettes, bar `s, and other nonessentials had removed themsel `s. Now the track was clear, and fifty competing cars were in starting positions—a long double line. Throughout the Speedway, as always in final moments before a race, tension grew.

Erica saw from her program that Pierre was

in row four of the starting lineup. His car was
number 29.

The control tower, high above the track, was
the Speedway's nerve center. From it, by radio,
closed circuit TV, and telephone, were controlled
the starters, track signal lights, pace cars, service
and emergency vehicles. A race director presided
at a console; he was a relaxed and quietly spoken
young man in a business suit. In a booth beside
him sat a shirt-sleeved commentator whose voice
would fill the p.a. system through the race. At a
desk behind, two uniformed Alabama State Troop-
ers directed traffic in the nontrack areas.

The race director was communicating with
his forces: "Lights work all the way 'round? . . .
okay . . . Track clear? . . . all set . . . Tower
to pace car: Are you ready to go? . . . All right,
fire 'em up!"

Over the Speedway p.a., voiced by a visiting
fleet admiral on an infield dais, went the traditional command to drivers: "Gentlemen, start
your engines!"

What followed was racing's most exciting
sound: The roar of unmuffled engines, like fifty
Wagnerian crescendos, which swamped the
Speedway with sound and extended for miles
beyond.

A pace car, pennants billowing, swung onto
the track, its speed increasing swiftly. Behind the
pace car, competing cars moved out, still two
abreast, maintaining their starting lineup as they
would for several preliminary, nonscoring laps.

Fifty cars were scheduled to begin the race.
Forty-nine did.

The engine of a gleaming, vivid red sedan, its
identifying number 06 painted in high visibility
gold, wouldn't start. The car's pit crew rushed forward and worked frantically, to no avail. Eventu-

ally the car was pushed by hand behind the wall of pit row and, as it went, the disgusted driver flung his helmet after it.

"Poor guy," somebody in the tower said. "Was the best-looking car on the field."

The race director cracked, "He spent too much time polishing it."

During the second preliminary lap, with the field still bunched together, the director radioed the pace car, "Pick up the tempo."

The pace car driver responded. Speeds rose. The engines' thunder grew in intensity.

After a third lap the pace car, its job done, was signaled off the track. It swung into pit row.

At the start-finish line in front of the grandstand, the starter's green flag slashed the air.

The 300 mile race—113 grueling laps—began.

From the outset the pace was sizzling, competition strong. Within the first five laps a driver named Doolittle, in number 12, charged through massed cars ahead to take the lead. Shooting up behind came car number 38, driven by a jut-jawed Mississippian known to fans as Cutthroat. Both were favorites, with racing pundits and the crowd.

A dark horse rookie driver, Johnny Gerenz in number 44, ran an unexpected third.

Pierre Flodenhale, clearing the pack soon after Gerenz, moved up to fourth in number 29.

For twenty-six laps the lead switched back and forth between the two front cars. Then Doolittle, in 12, pitted twice in quick succession with ignition trouble. It cost him a lap, and later, with smoke pouring from his car, he quit the race.

Doolittle's departure put the rookie, Johnny Gerenz, in 44, in second place. Pierre, in 29, was now third.

In the thirtieth lap a minor mishap, with debris and spilled oil, brought out caution flags, slowing the race while the track was cleared and sanded. Johnny Gerenz and Pierre were among those who pitted, taking advantage of the non-competing laps. Both had tire changes, a fill of gas, and were away again in seconds.

Soon after, the caution flag was lifted. Speed resumed.

Pierre was drafting—staying close behind other cars, using the partial suction they created, saving his own fuel and engine wear. It was a dangerous game but, used skillfully, could help win long races. Experienced onlookers sensed Pierre was holding back, saving a reserve of speed and power for later in the race.

"At least," Adam told Erica, "we hope that's what he's doing."

Pierre was the only one among present leaders in the race who was driving one of the company's cars. Thus, Adam, Hub Hewitson, and others were rooting for Pierre, hopeful that later he would move into the lead.

As always, when she went to auto races, Erica was fascinated by the speed of pit stops—the fact that a crew of five mechanics could change four tires, replenish gasoline, confer with the driver, and have a car moving out again in one minute, sometimes less.

"They practice," Adam told her. "For hours and hours, all year-round. And they never waste a movement, never get in one another's way."

Their seat neighbor, a manufacturing vice-president, glanced across. "We could use a few of their kind in Assembly."

Pit stops, too, as Erica knew, could win or lose a race.

With the race leaders in their forty-seventh lap, a blue-gray car spun out of control on the

steeply banked north turn. It came to rest in the
infield, right side up, the driver unhurt. In course
of its gyrations, however, the blue-gray car clipped
another which slid sideways into the track wall
amid a shower of sparks, then deep red flames
from burning oil. The driver of the second car
scrambled out and was supported by ambulance
men as he left the track. The oil fire was quickly
extinguished. Minutes later the p.a. announced
that the second driver had sustained nose lacera-
tions only; except for the two wrecked cars, no
other damage had been done.

The race proceeded under a yellow caution
flag, competitors holding their positions until the
caution signal should be lifted. Meanwhile, wreck-
ing and service crews labored swiftly to clear the
track.

Erica, a little bored by now, took advantage
of the lull to move rearward in the box. Kathryn
Hewitson, her head down, was still working on
needlepoint, but when she looked up, Erica saw
to her surprise that the older woman's eyes were
moist with tears.

"I really can't take this," Kathryn said. "That
man who was just hurt used to race for us when
we had the factory team. I know him well, and
his wife."

Erica assured her, "He's all right. He was
only hurt slightly."

"Yes, I know." The executive vice-president's
wife put her needlepoint away. "I think I could
use a drink. Why don't we have one together?"

They moved to the rear of the private box
where a barman was at work.

Soon after, when Erica returned to rejoin
Adam, the caution flag had been lifted, the race
was running full-out again, under green.

Moments later, Pierre Flodenhale, in 29,
crammed on a burst of speed and passed the

rookie driver, Johnny Gerenz, in 44, moving into second place.

Pierre was now directly behind Cutthroat, clinging to the lead in number 38, his speed close to 190 mph.

For three laps, with the race in its final quarter, the two fought a blistering duel, Pierre trying to move up, almost succeeding, but Cutthroat holding his position with skill and daring. But in the homestretch of the eighty-ninth lap, with twenty-four more laps to go, Pierre thundered by. Cheers resounded across the Speedway and in the company box.

The p.a. boomed: *"It's 29, Pierre Flodenhale, out front!"*

It was at that moment, with the lead cars approaching the south turn, directly in front of the south grandstand and private boxes, that it happened.

Afterward there was disagreement concerning precisely what had occurred. Some said a wind gust caught Pierre, others that he experienced steering trouble entering the turn and overcorrected; a third theory maintained that a piece of metal on another car broke loose and struck 29, diverting it.

Whatever the cause, car 29 snaked suddenly as Pierre fought the wheel, then at the turn slammed head on into the concrete retaining wall. Like a bomb exploding, the car disintegrated, breaking at the fire wall, the two main portions separating. Before either portion had come to rest, car 44, with Johnny Gerenz, plowed between both. The rookie driver's car spun, rolled, and seconds later was upside down in the infield, its wheels spinning crazily. A second car smashed into the now spread-out wreckage of 29, a third into that. Six cars altogether were in the pileup at the turn; five were eliminated from the race, one limped on for a few laps more before shedding a wheel and being towed to the pits. Apart from Pierre, all other drivers involved were unhurt.

The group in the company box, like others elsewhere, watched in shocked horror as ambulance attendants rushed to the two separate, shattered portions of car 29. A group of ambulance men had surrounded each. They appeared to be bringing objects to a stretcher placed midway between the two. As a company director, with binoculars to his eyes, saw what was happening he paled, dropped the binoculars, and said in a strangled voice, "Oh, Jesus Christ!" He implored his wife beside him, "Don't look! Turn away!"

Unlike the director's wife, Erica did not turn away. She watched, not wholly understanding what was happening, but knowing Pierre was dead. Later, doctors declared, he died instantly when car 29 hit the wall.

To Erica, the scene from the moment of the crash onward was unreal, like a reel of film unspooling, so her personal involvement was removed. With a dulled detachment—the result of shock—she witnessed the race continuing for twenty-or-so laps more, then Cutthroat the winner being acclaimed in Victory Lane. She sensed relief in the crowd. After the fatality the gloom around the course had been almost palpable; now it was cast off as a triumph—any triumph—erased the scar of defeat and death.

In the company box the despondency did not lift, unquestionably because of the emotional impact of the violent death a short time earlier, but also because a car of another manufacturer had gained the Canebreak 300 victory. A degree of talk—quieter than usual—centered around the possibility of success next day in the Talladega 500. Most in the company group, however, dispersed quickly to their hotels.

Only when Erica was back in the privacy of the Motor Inn suite, alone with Adam, did grief sweep over her. They had driven together from the Speedway in a company car, Adam saying little, and had come directly here. Now, in the bedroom, Erica flung herself down, hands to her face, and moaned. What she felt was too deep for tears, or even for coherence in her mind. She only knew it had to do with the youthfulness of Pierre, his zest for life, the good-natured charm which on balance outweighed other faults, his love of women, and the tragedy that no woman, anywhere, would ever know or cherish him again.

Erica felt Adam sit beside her on the bed.

He said gently, "We'll do whatever you want —go back to Detroit right now, or stay tonight and leave tomorrow morning."

In the end they decided to stay, and had dinner quietly in the suite. Soon after, Erica went to bed and dropped into exhausted sleep.

Next morning, Sunday, Adam assured Erica they could still leave at once if she preferred it. But she had shaken her head, and told him no. An early northward journey would mean having to pack hurriedly, and would entail an effort which seemed pointless since there was nothing to be gained by rushing to Detroit.

Pierre's funeral, so the *Anniston Star* reported, would be on Wednesday in Dearborn. His remains were to be flown to Detroit today.

Soon after her early morning decision, Erica told Adam, "You go to the 500. You want to, don't you? I can stay here."

"If we don't leave, I'd like to see the race," he admitted. "Will you be all right alone?"

She told him that she would, and was grateful for the absence of questioning by Adam, both yesterday and today. Obviously he sensed that the experience of watching someone whom she knew die a violent death had been traumatic and, if he was wondering about any extra implications of her grief, he had the wisdom not to voice his thoughts.

But when the time came for Adam to leave for the Speedway, Erica decided she did not want to be alone, and would go with him after all.

They went by car, which took a good deal longer than the helicopter trip the previous day and allowed something of the insulation which had helped her through yesterday to creep over Erica. In any case, she was glad to be out of doors. The weather was glorious, as it had been the entire weekend, the Alabama countryside as lovely as any she had seen.

In the company's private box at the Speedway everything seemed back to normal, as compared with yesterday afternoon, with cheerful talk centering on the fact that two strong favorites in today's Talladega 500 would be driving cars of the company's make. Erica had met one of the drivers briefly; his name was Wayne Onpatti.

If either Onpatti or the other favored driver, Buddy Undler, won today, it would eclipse yesterday's defeat since the Talladega 500 was the longer and more important race.

Most major races were on Sunday, and manufacturers of cars, tires, and other equipment acknowledged the dictum: *Win on Sunday, sell on Monday*.

The company box was just as full as yesterday, with Hub Hewitson again in the front row and clearly in good spirits. Kathryn Hewitson, Erica saw, sat alone near the rear, still working on her needlepoint and seldom looking up. Erica settled into a corner of the third row, hoping that despite the crowd she could be, to a degree, alone.

Adam stayed in his seat beside Erica, except

for a short period when he left the box to talk outside with Smokey Stephensen.

The auto dealer had motioned with his head to Adam just before starting time, while the race preliminaries were in progress. The two of them left the company box by the rear exit, Smokey preceding, then stood outside in the bright, warm sunshine. Though the track was out of sight, they could hear the roar of engines as the pace car and fifty competing cars began to move.

Adam remembered it was on his first visit to Smokey's dealership, near the beginning of the year, that he had met Pierre Flodenhale, then working as a part-time car salesman. He said, "I'm sorry about Pierre."

Smokey rubbed a hand across his beard in the gesture Adam had grown used to. "Kid was like a son to me, some ways. You tell yourself it can always happen, it's part of the game; I knew it in my time, so did he. When it comes, though, don't make it no easier to bear." Smokey blinked, and Adam was aware of a side to the auto dealer's nature, seldom revealed.

As if to offset it, Smokey said roughly, "That was yesterday. This is today. What I want to know is—you talked to Teresa yet?"

"No, I haven't." Adam had been aware that the month's grace he had given Smokey before his sister disposed of her interest in Stephensen Motors would be over soon. But Adam had had not acted to inform Teresa. Now he said, "I'm not sure I intend to—advise my sister to sell out, I mean."

Smokey Stephensen's eyes searched Adam's face. They were shrewd eyes, and there was little that the dealer missed, as Adam knew. The shrewdness was a reason why Adam had re-examined his convictions about Stephensen Motors over the past two weeks. Many reforms were coming in the auto dealership system, most of them overdue. But Adam believed Smokey would survive such changes because survival was as natural to him as being in his skin. That being so, in terms of an investment, Teresa and her children might find it hard to do better.

"I guess this is a time for the soft sell," Smokey said. "So I won't push; I'll just wait, and hope. One thing I know, though. If you change your mind from what you figured to begin with, it'll be for Teresa and not as any favor to me."

Adam smiled, "You're right about that."

Smokey nodded. "Is your wife all right?"

"I think so," Adam said.

They could hear the tempo of the race increasing, and went back into the company box.

Auto races, like wines, have vintage years. For the Talladega 500 this proved to be the best year ever—a fast and thrilling contest from its swift-paced outset to a spectacular down-to-the-wire finish. Through a total of 188 laps—a fraction over 500 miles—the lead switched many times. Wayne Onpatti and Buddy Undler, the favorites of Adam's company, stayed near the front, but were challenged strongly by a half dozen others, among them the previous day's victor, Cutthroat, who was out ahead for a large part of the race. The sizzling pace took its toll of a dozen cars, which quit through mechanical failure, and several others were wrecked, though no major pileup occurred as on the previous day, nor was any driver injured. Yellow caution flags and slowdowns were at a minimum; most of the race was full-out, under green.

Near the end, Cutthroat and Wayne Onpatti vied for the lead, with Onpatti slightly ahead, though moans resounded through the company box when Onpatti swung into the pits, stopping for a late tire change, which cost him half a lap and put Cutthroat solidly out front.

But the tire change proved wise and gave Onpatti what he needed—an extra bite on turns, so that by the backstretch of the final lap he had caught up with Cutthroat, and the two were side by side. Even thundering down the homestretch together with the finish line in sight, the result was still in doubt. Then, foot by foot, Onpatti eased past Cutthroat, finishing a half car length ahead—the victor.

During the final laps, most people in the company box had been on their feet, cheering hysterically for Wayne Onpatti, while Hub Hewitson and others jumped up and down like children, in unrestrained excitement.

When the result was known, for a second there was silence, then pandemonium broke.

Cheers, even louder than before, mingled with victorious shouts and laughter. Beaming executives and guests pummeled one another on backs and shoulders; hands were clasped and wrung; in the aisle, between benches, two staid vice-presidents danced a jig. "Our car won! We won!" echoed around the private box, with other cries. Someone chanted the inevitable, "Win on Sunday, sell on Monday." With still more shouts and laughter the chant was taken up. Instead of diminishing, the volume grew.

Erica surveyed it all, at first in detachment, then in disbelief. She could understand the pleasure of a share in winning; despite her own aloofness earlier, in the tense, final moments of the race she had felt involved, had craned forward with the rest to watch the photo finish. But *this* . . . this crazed abandonment of every other thought . . . was something else.

She thought of yesterday: its grief and awful cost; the body of Pierre, at this moment en route for burial. And now, so soon, the quick dismissal . . . *"Win on Sunday; sell on Monday."*

Coldly, clearly, and distinctly, Erica said, *"That's all you care about!"*

The hush was not immediate. But her voice carried over other voices close at hand, so that some paused, and in the partial silence Erica spoke again. "I said, 'That's all you care about!' "

Now, everyone had heard. Inside the box, the noise and other voices stilled. Across the sudden silence someone asked, "What's wrong with that?"

Erica had not expected this. She had spoken suddenly, from impulse, not wanting to be a focus of attention, and now that it was done, her instinct was to back away, to save Adam more embarrassment, and leave. Then anger surged. Anger at Detroit, its ways—so many of them mirrored in this box; what they had done to Adam and herself. She would *not* let the system shape her to a mold: a complaisant company wife.

Someone had asked: *"What's wrong with that?"*

"It's wrong," Erica said, "because you don't live—*we* don't live—for anything but cars and sales and winning. And if not all the time, then most of it. You forget other things. Such as, yesterday a man died here. Someone we knew. You're so full of winning: *'Win on Sunday!'* . . . *He was Saturday* . . . You've forgotten him already . . ." Her voice tailed off.

She was conscious of Adam regarding her. To Erica's surprise, the expression on his face was not critical. His mouth was even crinkled at the corners.

Adam, from the beginning, caught every word. Now, as if his hearing were heightened, he was aware of external sounds: the race running down, tail end cars completing final laps, fresh cheers for the new champion, Onpatti, heading for the pits and Victory Lane. Adam was conscious, too, that Hub Hewitson was frowning; others were embarrassed, not knowing where to look.

Adam supposed he ought to care. He thought objectively: Whatever truth there was in what Erica had said, he doubted if she had picked the best time to say it, and Hub Hewitson's displeasure was not to be taken lightly. But he had discovered moments earlier: *He didn't give a damn! To hell with them all!* He only knew he loved Erica more dearly than at any time since he had known her.

"Adam," a vice-president said, not unkindly, "you'd better get your wife out of here."

Adam nodded. He supposed for Erica's sake —to spare her more—he should.

"Why should he?"

Heads turned—to the rear of the company box, from where the interruption came. Kathryn Hewitson, still holding her needlepoint, had moved into the center aisle and stood facing them all, tight-lipped. She repeated, "Why should he? Because Erica said what *I* wanted to say, but lacked the moral courage? Because she put into words what every woman here was thinking until the youngest of us all spoke up?" She surveyed the silent faces before her. "*You men!*"

Suddenly Erica was aware of other women looking her way, neither embarrassed nor hostile, but—now the barrier was lifted—with eyes which registered approval.

Kathryn Hewitson said firmly, "Hubbard!"

Within the company Hub Hewitson was treated, and at times behaved, like a crown prince. But where his wife was concerned he was a husband—no more, no less—who, at certain moments, knew his obligations and his cues. Nodding, no longer frowning, he stepped to Erica and took both her hands. He said, in a voice which carried through the box, "My dear, sometimes in haste, excitement, or for other reasons we forget some simple things which are important. When we do, we need a person of conviction to remind us of our error. Thank you for being here and doing that."

Then suddenly, all tension gone, they were pouring from the box into the sunshine.

Someone said, "Hey, let's go over, shake hands with Onpatti."

Adam and Erica walked away arm in arm, knowing something important had happened to them both. Later, they might talk about it. For the moment there was no need for talk; their closeness was all that mattered.

"Mr. and Mrs. Trenton! Wait, please!"

A company public relations man, out of breath from running, caught them at a ramp to the Speedway parking lot. He announced, between puffs, "We just called the helicopter in. It'll be landing on the track. Mr. Hewitson would like you both to use it for the first trip. If you give me your keys, I'll take care of the car."

On their way to the track, with his breath more normal, the p.r. man said, "There's something else. There are two company planes at Talladega Airport."

"I know," Adam said. "We're going back to Detroit on one."

"Yes, but Mr. Hewitson has the jet, though he won't be using it until tonight. What he wondered is if you would like to have it first. He suggests you fly to Nassau, which he knows is Mrs. Trenton's home, then spend a couple of days there. The plane could go down and back, and still pick up

Mr. Hewitson tonight. We'd send it to Nassau again for you, on Wednesday."

"It's a great idea," Adam said. "Unfortunately I've a whole string of appointments in Detroit, starting early tomorrow."

"Mr. Hewitson told me you'd probably say that. His message was: For once, forget the company and put your wife first."

Erica was glowing. Adam laughed. One thing could be said for the executive vice-president: When he did something, he did it handsomely.

Adam said, "Please tell him we accept with thanks and pleasure."

What Adam did not say was that he intended to be sure, on Wednesday, he and Erica were in Detroit in time for Pierre's funeral.

They were in the Bahamas, and had swum from Emerald Beach, near Nassau, before the sun went down.

On the patio of their hotel, at sunset, Adam and Erica lingered over drinks. The night was warm, with a soft breeze riffling palm fronds. Few other people were in sight since the mainstream of winter visitors would not arrive here for another month or more.

During her second drink, Erica took an extra breath and said, "There's something I should tell you."

"If it's about Pierre," Adam answered gently, "I think I already know."

He told her: Someone had mailed him, anonymously in an unmarked envelope, a clipping from the *Detroit News*—the item which caused Erica concern. Adam added, "Don't ask me why people do those things. I guess some just do."

"But you didn't say anything." Erica remembered—she had been convinced that if he found out, he would.

"We seemed to have enough problems, without adding to them."

"It was all over," she said. "Before Pierre died." Erica recalled, with a stab of conscience, the salesman, Ollie. That was something she would *never* tell Adam. She hoped, one day, she could forget that episode herself.

From across the table dividing them, Adam said, "Whether it was over or not, I'd still want you back."

She looked at him, emotion brimming. "You're a beautiful man. Maybe I haven't been appreciating you as much as I should."

He said, "I guess that goes for both of us."

Later, they made love, to find the old magic had returned.

It was Adam, drowsily, who spoke their epilogue: "We came close to losing each other, and our way. Let's never take that chance again."

While Adam slept, Erica lay awake beside him, hearing night sounds through windows opened to the sea. Later still, she too fell asleep; but at daybreak they awoke together and made love again.

chapter twenty-nine

In early September the Orion made its debut before the press, company dealers, and the public.

The national press preview was in Chicago—a lavish, liquor-laced freeload which, it was rumored, would be the last of its kind. The reason behind the rumor: Auto firms were belatedly recognizing that most newsmen wrote the same kind of honest copy whether fed champagne and beluga caviar, or beer and hamburgers. So why bother with big expense?

Nothing in the near future, however, was likely to change the nature of a dealer preview which, for the Orion, was in New Orleans and lasted six days.

It was a spectacular, show biz extravaganza to which seven thousand company dealers, car salesmen, their wives and mistresses were invited, arriving in waves of chartered aircraft, including several Boeing 747s.

All major hotels in the Crescent City were taken over. So was the Rivergate Auditorium—for a nightly musical extravaganza which, as one bemused spectator put it, "could have run on Broadway for a year." A stupendous climax to the show was the descent, amid a shimmering Milky Way and to music from a hundred violins, of a huge shining star which, as it touched center stage, dissolved to an Orion—the signal for a wild ovation.

Other fun, games, and feasting continued through each day, and at nights, fireworks over the harbor, with a magnificent set piece spelling ORION, closed the scene.

Adam and Erica Trenton attended, as did

Brett DeLosanto; and Barbara Zaleski flew in to join Brett briefly.

During one of the two nights Barbara was in New Orleans, the four of them had dinner together at Brennan's in the French Quarter. Adam, who had known Matt Zaleski slightly, asked Barbara how her father was.

"He's able to breathe on his own now, and he can move his left arm a little," she answered. "Apart from that, he's totally paralyzed."

Adam and Erica murmured sympathy.

Barbara left unexpressed her daily prayer that her father would die soon, releasing him from the burden and agony she sensed each time she looked into his eyes. But she knew that he might not. She was aware, too, that the elder Joseph Kennedy, one of history's more famous victims of a stroke, had lived for eight years after being totally disabled.

Meanwhile, Barbara told the Trentons, she was making plans to move her father home to the Royal Oak house with full-time nursing care. Then, for a while, she and Brett would divide their time between Royal Oak and Brett's Country Club Manor apartment.

Speaking of the Royal Oak house, Barbara reported, "Brett's become an orchid grower."

Smiling, she told Adam and Erica that Brett had taken over the care of her father's orchid atrium, and had even bought books on the subject.

"I dig those orchids' lines, the way they flow," Brett said. He speared an Oyster Roffignac which had just been served him. "Maybe there's a whole new generation of cars hung in there. Names, too. How about a two door hardtop called *Aerides masculosum?*"

"We're here for the Orion," Barbara reminded him. "Besides, it's easier to spell."

She did not tell Adam and Erica about one

incident which had happened recently, knowing that if she did it would embarrass Brett.

On several occasions after her father's stroke, Barbara and Brett stayed overnight at the Royal Oak house. One evening Brett arrived there first. She found him with an easel set up, a fresh canvas, and his paints. He had sketched on the canvas, and now was painting, an orchid. Afterward Brett told her that his model was a *Catasetum saccatum* —the bloom which he and Matt Zaleski had both admired the night, almost a year ago, when the older man flared up at Brett and, later, Barbara forced her father to apologize. "Your old man and I agreed it was like a bird in flight," Brett said. "I guess it was the only thing we did agree on."

A little awkwardly Brett had gone on to suggest that when the painting was finished, Barbara might like to take it to her father's room at the hospital and position it where he could see it. "The old buzzard hasn't got a lot to look at. He enjoyed his orchids, and he might like this."

Then, for the first time since Matt's affliction, Barbara broke down and wept.

It had been a relief, and afterward she felt better, aware that her emotions had remained pent up until Brett's simple act of kindness released them. Barbara valued even more what Brett was doing because of his deep involvement with a new car planning project, Farstar, soon to be presented at a top-level strategy meeting of company officers. Farstar was occupying Brett's days and nights, leaving time for little else.

Obliquely, at the New Orleans dinner table, Adam referred to Farstar, though cautiously not naming it. "I'll be glad when this week is over," he told Barbara. "The Orion is Sales and Marketing's baby now. Back at the farm we've new things borning."

"Only two weeks to the big-you-know-wot parley," Brett put in, and Adam nodded.

Barbara sensed that Adam and Brett were tremendously caught up in Farstar, and wondered if, after all, Brett would go through with his private plan to leave the auto industry at year end. She knew that Brett had not discussed the possibility yet with Adam who, Barbara was convinced, would try to persuade him to stay.

Barbara revealed some professional news of her own. The documentary film *Auto City*, now complete, had been enthusiastically received at several critical advance showings. The OJL advertising agency, Barbara personally, and the director, Wes Gropetti, had received warm letters of praise from the client's chairman of the board and—even more significant—a major TV network had committed itself to showing *Auto City* as a public service during prime viewing time. As a result, Barbara's own standing at OJL had never been higher, and she and Gropetti had been asked to work together on a new film for another agency client.

The others congratulated her, Brett with obvious pride.

Soon after, the talk returned to the Orion and the dealer preview extravaganza. "I can't help wondering," Erica said, "if all this week is really necessary."

"It is," Adam said, "and I'll tell you why. Dealers and salesmen at a preview see any car at its best—like a jewel in a Tiffany setting. So from that, plus all the carnival, they go back charged up about the product that in a few days will be dropped off in front of their dealerships."

"Dropped off dusty," Brett said. "Or maybe grimy from the journey, with hub caps off, bumpers greasy, stickers and sealing tape all over. A mess."

Adam nodded. "Right. But the dealer and salesmen have already seen the car as it should be. They know how great it is when prepared for a showroom. Their enthusiasm doesn't leave them, and they do a better selling job."

"Not forgetting, advertising helps," Barbara said. She sighed. "I know that critics think a lot of the hoopla's corny. But we know it works."

Erica said softly, "Then mostly because all three of you care so much, I hope it works for the Orion."

Under the table, Adam squeezed her hand. He told the others, "Now we can't miss."

A week later, when the Orion was on view in dealer showrooms throughout North America, it seemed that he was right.

"Rarely," reported *Automotive News,* the industry's weekly holy writ, "has a new car evoked such a remarkable response so soon. Already, a huge backlog of orders has its manufacturers elated, their production men harried, competitors alarmed."

A press consensus reflected the same view. The *San Francisco Chronicle* declared, "The Orion has most of the safety and clean air hardware we've been promised for years, and looks beautiful too." The *Chicago Sun-Times* conceded, "Yessir! This one's zazzy!" *The New York Times* pontificated, "Conceivably, the Orion may mark the end of an era which, while admittedly encouraging engineering advances, often subordinated them to styling needs. Now, both out-of-view engineering and external form appear to be proceeding hand-in-hand."

Newsweek and *Time* both featured Hub Hewitson and the Orion on their covers. "The last time that happened," a gleeful p.r. man told anybody who would listen, "was with Lee Iacocca and the Mustang."

Not surprisingly, the company's top echelon was in a happy mood when, soon after the Orion's public introduction, it met to consider Farstar.

It was a final product policy meeting—last of a series of three. The Farstar project had survived the preceding two. Here, it would either go forward as a firm commitment—a new car to be introduced in two years' time—or would be discarded forever, as many projects were.

The previous meetings had involved intensive study, presentations, argument, and tough interrogation, but were relatively informal. The final meeting would still feature the same kind of study and dissection but, as to formality, would be like a black-tie dinner party compared with casual lunch.

The product policy board, which today would total fifteen people, began assembling shortly after 9 A.M. The meeting would commence at 10 A.M. promptly, but it was traditional for informal discussions, between groups of two and three, to occupy most of the hour beforehand.

The meeting place was on the fifteenth floor of the company staff building—a smallish, luxuriously appointed auditorium, with a horseshoe-shaped table of polished walnut. Around the closed end of the horseshoe were five black leather, high-backed chairs for the chairman of the board, president, and three executive vice-presidents of whom Hub Hewitson was senior. In the remaining lower-backed chairs the remaining participants would sit, in no particular order.

At the horseshoe's open end was a raised lectern for use by whoever was making a presentation. Today it would be occupied mainly by Adam Trenton. Behind the lectern was a screen for slide and film projection.

A smaller table beside the horseshoe was for

the meeting's two secretaries. In the wings and a projection booth were staff backup men, with thick black notebooks containing—as a wag once put it—every answer known to man.

And as always, despite the prevailing Orion happiness and a surface ease which might deceive an outsider, the underlying tone of the product policy meeting would be deadly serious. For here was where an auto corporation put millions of dollars on the line, along with its reputation and its life. Some of the world's greatest gambles were launched here, and they *were* gambles because, despite research and backup, an "aye" or "nay" decision in the end must be based on instinct or a hunch.

Coffee service in the auditorium began with first arrivals. That was traditional, as was a waiting pitcher of chilled orange juice—for the chairman of the board who disliked hot drinks in daytime.

The room was filling when Hub Hewitson breezed in near 9:30. He first got coffee for himself, then beckoned Adam and Elroy Braithwaite, who were chatting.

Looking pleased with himself, Hewitson opened a folder he had carried in and spread out several drawings on the horseshoe table. "Just got these. Timely, eh?"

The Design-Styling vice-president strolled to join them and the four pored over the drawings. No one needed to ask what they were. Each sheet bore the insignia of another of the Big Three manufacturers and included illustrations and specifications of a new car. Equally obvious was that this was the competitive car which Farstar would face two years from now, if today's proposals were approved.

The Silver Fox whistled softly.

"It's extraordinary," the Design-Styling vice-president mused, "how, in some ways, their thinking has paralleled ours."

Hub Hewitson shrugged. "They keep an ear to the ground just as we do, read the same newspapers, study trends; they know the way the world's moving. Got some bright boys on their payroll, too." The executive vice-president shot a glance at Adam. "What do you say?"

"I say we have a far better car. We'll come out ahead."

"You're pretty cocky."

"If that's the way it seems," Adam said, "I guess I am."

Hub Hewitson's face relaxed into a grin. "I'm cocky, too. We've another good one; let's sell it to the others."

He began folding the drawings. Later, Adam knew, they would analyze the competitive car in detail, and perhaps make changes in their own as a result.

"I've often wondered," Adam said, "what we have to pay to get this stuff."

Hub Hewitson grinned again. "Not as much as you'd think. Ever hear of a well-paid spy?"

"I suppose not." Adam reflected: Spying was something which all big auto companies practiced, though denying that they did. His own company's espionage center—under an innocuous name—occupied cramped, cluttered quarters in the Design-Styling Center and was a clearinghouse for intelligence from many sources.

For example, research engineers of competitive companies were a mother lode of information. Like all scientific researchers, engineers loved to publish, and papers at technical society meetings often contained a phrase or sentence, by itself insignificant, but, taken in conjunction with other fragments from elsewhere, gave clues to a competitor's thinking and direction. Among those engaged in auto espionage it was accepted that "engineers are innocents."

Less innocent was a flow of intelligence from the Detroit Athletic Club, where senior and middle-rank executives from all companies drank together. A result of their drinking was that some, relaxed and off-guard, tried to impress others with their inside knowledge. Across the years, finely tuned ears in the D.A.C. had garnered many tidbits and occasionally news of great importance.

Then there were leakages through tool-and-die companies. Sometimes the same tooling companies served two, or even three, major auto makers; thus, a seemingly casual dropper-in to a die-making shop might see work in progress for an auto firm other than his own. An experienced designer looking at the female portion of a die could sometimes tell what the entire rear or front end of a competitor's car looked like—then go away and sketch it.

Other tactics were sometimes used by outside agencies whose *modi operandi* were not scrutinized too closely. They included enlistment of competitors' disaffected employees to purloin papers, and sifting of garbage was not unknown. Once in a while an employee, unconcerned about conflicting loyalties, might be "planted" in another company. But these were grubby methods which top executives preferred not to hear about in detail.

Adam's thoughts switched back to Farstar and the product policy board.

The auditorium clock showed 9:50 and the company chairman had just arrived, accompanied by the president. The latter, a dynamic leader in the past but now considered "old school" by Adam and others, would be retiring soon, with Hub Hewitson predicted to succeed him.

A voice beside Adam asked, "What variances will Farstar have for Canada?" The questioner was head of the company's Canadian subsidiary, invited here today by courtesy.

"We'll be going into that," Adam said, but he described the variances anyway. One of the Farstar lines would be given a differing name—Independent—exclusive to Canada, and the exterior hood emblem would be changed to include a maple leaf. Otherwise the can would be identical with Farstar models in the U.S.

The other nodded. "As long as we have some difference we can point to, that's the main thing."

Adam understood. Although Canadians drove U.S. cars, produced by U.S. controlled subsidiaries employing U.S. union labor, national vanity in Canada fostered the delusion of an independent auto industry. The Big Three had humored these pretensions for years by naming the heads of their Canadian branches presidents, although in fact such presidents were answerable to vice-presidents in Detroit. The companies, too, had introduced a few "distinctively Canadian" models. Nowadays, however, Canada was being regarded more and more by all auto makers as just another sales district, and the special models—never more than a façade—were being quietly dropped. The "Canadianized" Farstar Independent would probably be the last.

At a minute to ten, with the fifteeen decision makers seated, the chairman of the board sipped orange juice, then said whimsically, "Unless anyone has a better suggestion, we might as well begin." He glanced at Hub Hewitson. "Who's starting?"

"Elroy."

Eyes turned to the Product Development vice-president.

"Mr. Chairman and gentlemen," the Silver Fox said crisply, "today we are presenting Farstar with a recommendation to proceed. You've all read your agendas, you know the plan, and you've seen the models in clay. In a moment we'll get down to details, but first this thought: Whatever we call this car, it will not be Farstar. That code name was merely chosen because, compared with Orion, this project seemed a long way distant. But suddenly it isn't distant any more. It's no longer a Farstar; the need is here, or will be in two years' time which in production terms, as we know, is the same thing."

Elroy Braithwaite paused, passing a hand across his silver mane, then went on, "We think this kind of car, which some will call revolutionary, is inevitable anyway. And incidentally"—the Silver Fox motioned to the folder of competitor's drawings on the table in front of Hub Hewitson—"so do our friends on the other side of town. But we also believe that instead of letting Farstar, or something like it, be forced on us the way some of our activities have been in recent years, we can make it happen, now. I, for one, believe that as a company and an industry it's time we took the offensive more strongly once again, and did some way-out pioneering. That, in essence, is what Farstar is about. Now we'll consider details." Braithwaite nodded to Adam, waiting at the lectern. "Okay, let's go."

"The slides you are now seeing," Adam announced as the screen behind him filled, "show what market research has demonstrated to be a gap in availability, which Farstar will fill, and the market potential of that gap two years from now."

Adam had rehearsed this presentation many times and knew the words by rote. Generally, through the next two hours, he would "follow the book," now open in front of him, though as usual at these meetings there would be interruptions and pointed, penetrating questions.

As the half dozen slides went through, with Adam making brief commentaries, he still had time to think of what Elroy Braithwaite had said moments earlier. The remarks about the company taking a strong offensive had surprised Adam, first because it had not been necessary to make a comment of that kind at all, and also because the Silver Fox had a reputation for caginess and gauging wind directions carefully before committing himself to anything. But perhaps Braithwaite, too, was infected with some of the new thinking and impatience pervading the auto industry as old war horses retired or died and younger men moved up.

Braithwaite's phrase "way-out pioneering" had reminded Adam, too, of similar words used by Sir Perceval Stuyvesant during their own conversation five weeks ago. Since then, Adam and Perce had spoken by telephone several times. Adam's interest had grown in the possibility of accepting the presidency of Sir Perceval's West Coast company, but Perce continued to agree that any kind of decision be delayed until the Orion's launching and today's presentation of Farstar. After today, however, Adam must decide—either to go to San Francisco for more discussions or to decline Perce's offer entirely.

Adam had talked with Erica, for the second time, about the proffered West Coast job during their two days in the Bahamas. Erica had been definite. "It has to be your decision absolutely, darling. Oh, of course I'd love to live in San Francisco. Who wouldn't? But I'd rather have you happy in Detroit than unhappy somewhere else, and either way we'll be together."

Her declaration cheered him, but even after

that he remained in doubt, and was still uncertain now.

Hub Hewitson's voice cut brusquely across the Farstar presentation. "Let's stop a minute and talk about something we might as well face up to. This Farstar is the ugliest son-of-a-bitching car I ever saw."

It was typical of Hewitson that, while he might support a program, he liked to bring out possible objections himself for frank discussion.

Around the horseshoe table there were several murmurs of assent.

Adam said smoothly—the point had been anticipated—"We have, of course, been aware of that all along."

He began explaining the philosophy behind the car: a philosophy expressed by Brett DeLosanto during the after-midnight session months earlier when Brett had said, "With Picasso in our nostrils, we've been designing cars like they rolled off a Gainsborough canvas." That had been the night when Adam and Brett had gone together to the teardown room, moving on later to the bull session with Elroy Braithwaite and two young product planners, of whom Castaldy was one. They had emerged with the question and concept: Why not a deliberate, daring attempt to produce a car, ugly by existing standards, yet so suited to needs, environment, and present time—the Age of Utility—that it would become beautiful?

Though there had been adaptations and changes in outlook since, Farstar had retained its basic concept.

Here and now Adam was circumspect about the words he used because a product policy board meeting was no place to wax overly poetic, and notions about Picasso took second place to pragmatism. Nor could he speak of Rowena, though it had been the thought of her which inspired his own thinking that night. Rowena was still a beautiful memory, and while Adam would never tell Erica about her, he had a conviction that even if he did Erica would understand.

The discussion about the visual look of Farstar ended, though they would return to the subject, Adam knew.

"Where were we?" Hub Hewitson was turning pages of his own agenda.

"Page forty-seven," Braithwaite prompted.

The chairman nodded. "Let's get on."

An hour and a half later, after prolonged and inconclusive discussion, the group vice-president of manufacturing pushed away his papers and leaned forward in his chair. "If someone had come to me with the idea for this car, I'd not only have thrown it out, but I'd have suggested he look for employment elsewhere."

Momentarily, the auditorium was silent. Adam, at the lectern, waited.

The manufacturing head, Nolan Freidheim, was a grizzled auto industry veteran and the dean of vice-presidents at the table. He had a forbidding, craggy face which seldom smiled, and was noted for his bluntness. Like the company president, he was due for retirement soon, except that Freidheim had less than a month of service remaining and his successor, already named, was here today.

While the others waited, the elderly executive filled his pipe and lit it. Everyone present knew that this was the last product policy meeting he would attend. At length he said, "That's what I'd have done, and if I had, we'd have lost a good man and probably a good car too."

He puffed his pipe and put it down. "Maybe that's why my time's come, maybe that's why I'm glad it has. There's a whole lot that's happening nowadays I don't understand; plenty of it I dislike and always will. Lately, though, I've found I don't care as much as I used to. Another thing: Whatever we decide today, while you guys are sweating out Farstar—or whatever name it gets eventually —I'll be fishing off the Florida Keys. If you've time, think of me. You probably won't have."

A ripple of laughter ran around the table.

"I'll leave you with a thought, though," Nolan Freidheim said. "I was against this car to begin with. In a way I still am; parts of it, including the way it looks, offend my notion of what a car should be. But down in my gut, where plenty of us have made good decisions before now, I've a feeling that it's right, it's good, it's timely, it'll hit the market when it should." The manufacturing chief stood up, his coffee cup in hand to replenish it. "My gut votes 'yes.' I say we should go with Farstar."

The chairman of the board observed, "Thank you, Nolan. I've been feeling that way myself, but you expressed it better than the rest of us."

The president joined in the assent. So did others who had wavered until now. Minutes later a formal decision was recorded: For Farstar, all lights green!

Adam felt a curious emptiness. An objective had been gained. The next decision was his own.

chapter thirty

Since the last week of August, Rollie Knight had lived in terror.

The terror began in the janitor's closet at the assembly plant where Leroy Colfax knifed and killed one of the two vending machine collectors, and where the other collector and the foreman, Parkland, were left wounded and unconscious. It continued during a hasty retreat from the plant by the four conspirators—Big Rufe, Colfax, Daddy-o Lester, and Rollie. They had scaled a high, chain-link fence, helping each other in the darkness, knowing that to leave through any of the plant gates would invite questioning and identification later.

Rollie gashed his hand badly on the fence wire, and Big Rufe fell heavily, limping afterward, but they all made it outside. Then, moving separately and avoiding lighted areas, they met in one of the employee parking lots where Big Rufe had a car. Daddy-o had driven because Big Rufe's ankle was swelling fast, and paining him. They left the parking lot without using lights, only turning them on when reaching the roadway outside.

Looking back at the plant, everything seemed normal and there were no outward signs of an alarm being raised.

"Man, oh man," Daddy-o fretted nervously as he drove. "If I ain't glad to be clear o' that!"

From the back seat, Big Rufe grunted. "We ain't clear o' nuthin' yet."

Rollie, in front with Daddy-o and trying to stem the bleeding of his hand with an oily rag, knew that it was true.

Despite his fall, Big Rufe had managed to get

one set of chained cash bags over the fence with him. Leroy Colfax had the other. In the back seat they hacked at the bags with knives, then poured the contents—all silver coins—into several paper sacks. On the freeway, before reaching the city, Colfax and Big Rufe threw the original cash bags out.

In the inner city they parked the car on a dead-end street, then separated. Before they did, Big Rufe warned, "Remember, all we gotta do is act like there ain't nuthun' different. We play this cool, ain't nobody gonna prove we was there tonight. So tomorrow, everybody shows their faces just like always, same as any other day." He glared at the other three. "Somebody don't, that's when the pigs start lookin' our way."

Leroy Colfax said softly, "Might be smarter to run."

"You run," Big Rufe snarled, "I swear I'll find 'n kill you, the way you did that honky, the way you got us all in this . . ."

Colfax said hastily, "Ain't gonna run. Just thinkin' is all."

"Don't think! You showed already you ain't got brains."

Colfax was silent.

Though he had not spoken, Rollie wished he could run. But to where? There was nowhere; no escape, whichever way you turned. He had a sense of his own life seeping out, the way blood was still seeping from his injured hand. Then he remembered: The chain of happenings leading to tonight had begun a year ago, when the white cop baited him, and the black cop gave a card with a hiring hall address. Rollie's mistake, he recognized, had been to go there. Or had it? If what had overtaken him had not happened in this way, there would have been some other.

"Now listen good," Big Rufe had said, "we

all in this together, we stick together. If nobody
of us four blabs, we gonna be okay."

Perhaps the others believed. Rollie hadn't.

They parted then, each taking one of the
paper sacks of coins which Big Rufe and Colfax
had divided in the back seat of the car. Big Rufe's
was bulkier than the others.

Choosing his route cagily, conscious of the
implications of the paper sack of coins if he should
be stopped by a police patrol, Rollie reached the
apartment house on Blaine near 12th.

May Lou wasn't in; she had probably gone to
a movie. Rollie bathed the gash in his hand, then
bound it roughly with a towel.

After that he counted the money in the paper
sack, dividing the coins into piles. It totaled
$30.75—less than a day's pay at the assembly
plant.

If Rollie Knight had had the erudition or
philosophy, he might have debated, within himself,
the nature of risks which human beings take for
trifling amounts such as $30.75, and their degrees
of losing. There had been earlier risks which
frightened him—the risk of refusing to be swept
along into deeper involvement with plant crime,
and the risk of backing out tonight, which he
could have taken, but didn't, when Big Rufe thrust
the gun into his hand.

These risks had been real, not just imagined.
A savage beating, accompanied by broken limbs,
could have been ordered for Rollie by Big Rufe as
easily as groceries are ordered from a store. Both
men knew it; and that way Rollie would have
been a loser too.

But in the end the losing could have been less
than the total disaster—life imprisonment for
murder—which threatened now.

In essence the risks which Rollie chose to

take, and not to take, were those which—in degree
—face all men in a free society. But some, within
the same society, are born with cruelly limited
choices, belying the hoary bromide that "all men
are created equal." Rollie, and tens of thousands
like him, hedged in from birth by poverty, in-
equality, scant opportunity, and with the sketchiest
of education providing poor preparation for such
choices as occur, are losers from the beginning.
Their degree of losing remains the only thing to
be determined.

Thus, the tragedy of Rollie Knight was two-
fold: The darker side of the earth that he was
born to, and society's failure to equip him mentally to break away.

But thinking none of this, knowing only
bleak despair and fear of what would come tomorrow, Rollie thrust the $30.75 in silver beneath
his bed, and slept. He did not awaken later when
May Lou came in.

In the morning, May Lou dressed Rollie's
hand with a makeshift bandage, her eyes asking
questions which he did not answer. Then Rollie
went to work.

At the plant, plenty of talk was circulating
about the murder-robbery of the night before,
and there had been reports on radio, TV, and in
the morning newspaper. Local interest in Rollie's
area of Assembly centered on the bludgeoning of
Frank Parkland, who was in the hospital, though
reportedly with mild concussion only. "Just proves
all foremen are thickheaded," a humorist pronounced at break time. There was immediate
laughter. No one seemed distressed by the robbery,
or greatly concerned about the murdered man,
who was otherwise unknown.

Another report said one of the plant managers
had had a stroke, brought on by the whole affair

plus overwork. However, the last was clearly an exaggeration since everyone knew a manager's job was a soft touch.

Apart from the talk, no other activity concerning the robbery-murder was visible from the assembly line. Nor, as far as Rollie could see, or hear through scuttlebutt, was anyone on the day shift questioned.

No rumors, either, tied any names to the crime.

Despite Big Rufe's warning to the other three, he alone failed to show up at the plant that day. Daddy-o conveyed the news to Rollie at midmorning that Big Rufe's leg was so swollen he could not walk, and had reported sick, putting out a story of having been drunk the night before and falling down stairs at home.

Daddy-o was shaky and nervous, but had recovered some of his confidence by early afternoon, when he paid a second call to Rollie's work station, obviously wanting to gab.

Rollie had snarled at him, low-voiced, "For Cri-sakes quit hangin' round me. And keep that stinkin' mouth shut!" If anyone blabbed, causing word to spread, Rollie feared most of all it would be Daddy-o.

Nothing more that was notable occurred that day. Or on the one after. Or through an entire week following that.

As each day passed, while Rollie's anxiety remained, his relief increased a little. He knew, however, there was still plenty of time for the worst to happen. Also he realized: while the sheer numbers of lesser unsolved crimes caused police investigations to ease or end, murder was in a different league. The police, Rollie reasoned, would not give up quickly.

As it happened, he was partly right and partly wrong.

The timing of the original robbery had been shrewd. It was the timing also which caused police investigation to center on the plant night shift, even though detectives were unsure that the men they sought were company employees at all. Plenty of auto plant crimes were committed by outsiders, using fake or stolen employee identification badges to get in.

All the police had to work with was a statement by the surviving vending machine collector that four men were involved. All had been masked and armed; he believed all four were black; he had only the vaguest impressions of their physical size. The surviving collector had not seen the face of the briefly unmasked robber, as had his companion who was knifed.

Frank Parkland, who was struck down instantly on entering the janitor's closet, had observed nothing.

No weapons had been discovered, no fingerprints found. The slashed cash bags were eventually recovered near a freeway, but provided no clue, apart from suggesting that whoever discarded them was headed for the inner city.

A team of four detectives assigned to the case began methodical sifting through names and employment dockets of some three thousand night shift employees. Among these was a sizable segment with criminal records. All such individuals were questioned, without result. This took time. Also, part way through the investigation the number of detectives was reduced from four to two, and even the remaining pair had other duties to contend with.

The possibility that the wanted men might be part of the day shift, and had remained in the plant to stage the robbery, was not overlooked. It was simply one of several possibilities which the police had neither time nor manpower to cope with all at once.

What investigators really hoped for was a break in the case through an informer, which was the way many serious crimes, in greater Detroit as elsewhere, were solved. But no information came. Either the perpetrators were the only ones who knew the names involved, or others were remaining strangely silent.

The police were aware that the vending concessions at the plant were Mafia-financed and run; they knew, too, that the dead man had Mafia connections. They suspected, but had no means of proving, that both factors were related to the silence.

After three and a half weeks, because of a need to assign detectives to newer cases, while the plant murder-robbery case was not closed, police activity slackened off.

The same was not true elsewhere.

The Mafia, generally, does not look kindly on any interference with its people. And when interference is from other criminals, repercussions are stern, and of a nature to be a warning against repetition.

From the instant that the man with the Indian features died from the knife wound inflicted by Leroy Colfax, Colfax and his three accomplices were marked for execution.

Doubly assuring this was that they were pawns in the Mafia-Black Mafia war.

When details of the murder-robbery were known, the Detroit Mafia family worked quietly and effectively. It had channels of communication which the police did not.

First, feelers were put out for information. When none resulted, a reward was quietly offered: a thousand dollars.

For that much, in the inner city, a man might sell his mother.

Rollie Knight heard of the Mafia involvement and reward one week and two days after the debacle at the plant. It was at night and he was in a dingy Third Avenue bar, drinking beer. The beer, and the fact that whatever official investigation was going on had not come close to him so far, had relaxed a little of the terror he had lived with for the past nine days. But the news, conveyed by his companion at the bar—a downtown numbers runner known simply as Mule—increased Rollie's terror tenfold and turned the beer he had drunk into bile, so that he was hard pressed not to vomit there and then. He managed not to.

"Hey!" Mule said, after he conveyed the news of the Mafia-proffered reward. "Ain't you in that plant, man?"

With an effort, Rollie nodded.

Mule urged, "You find out who them guys was, I pass the word, we split the dough, okay?"

"I'll listen around," Rollie promised.

Soon after, he left the bar, his latest beer untouched.

Rollie knew where to find Big Rufe. Entering the rooms where the big man lived, he found himself looking into the muzzle of a gun—the same one, presumably, used nine days before. When he saw who it was, Big Rufe lowered the gun and thrust it in his trousers waistband.

He told Rollie, "Them crummy wops come, they ain't gonna find no pushover."

Beyond his readiness, Big Rufe seemed strangely indifferent—probably, Rollie realized later, because he had known of the Mafia danger in the first place, and accepted it.

There was nothing to be gained by staying, or discussion. Rollie left.

From that moment, Rollie's days and nights were filled with a new, more omnipresent dread. He knew that nothing he could do would counter it; he could only wait. For the time being he continued working, since regular work—too late, it seemed—had become a habit.

Though Rollie never knew the details, it was Big Rufe who betrayed them all.

He foolishly paid several small gambling debts entirely with silver coins. The fact was noticed, and later reported to a Mafia underling who passed the information on. Other pieces of intelligence, already known about Big Rufe, were found to fit a pattern.

He was seized at night, taken by surprise while sleeping, and given no chance to use his gun. His captors brought him, bound and gagged, to a house in Highland Park where, before being put to death, he was tortured and he talked.

Next morning Big Rufe's body was found on a Hamtramck roadway, a road much traveled at night by heavy trucks. It appeared to have been run over several times, and the death was listed as a traffic casualty.

Others, including Rollie Knight—who heard the news from a terrified, shaking Daddy-o— knew better.

Leroy Colfax went into hiding, protected by politically militant friends. He remained hidden for almost two weeks, at the end of which time it was demonstrated that a militant, like many another politician, has his price. One of Colfax's trusted companions, whom each addressed as brother, quietly sold him out.

Leroy Colfax, too, was seized, then driven to a lonely suburb and shot. When his body was found, an autopsy disclosed six bullets but no other clues. No arrest was ever made.

Daddy-o ran. He bought a bus ticket to New

York and tried to lose himself in Harlem. For a while he succeeded, but several months later was tracked down and, soon after, killed by knifing.

Long before that—on hearing of Leroy Colfax's slaying—Rollie Knight began his own time of waiting, and meanwhile went to pieces.

Leonard Wingate had trouble identifying the thin female voice on the telephone. He was also irritated at being called in the evening, at home.

"May Lou *who*?"

"Rollie's woman. Rollie Knight."

Knight. Wingate remembered now, then asked, "How did you get my phone number? It isn't listed."

"You wrote it on a card, mister. Said if we was in trouble, to call."

He supposed he had—probably the night of the filming in that inner city apartment house.

"Well, what is it?" Wingate had been about to leave for a Bloomfield Hills dinner party. Now he wished he had gone before the phone rang, or hadn't answered.

May Lou's voice said, "I guess you know Rollie ain't been workin'."

"Now, how in the world would I know that?"

She said uncertainly, "If he don't show up . . ."

"Ten thousand people work in that plant. As a Personnel executive I'm responsible for most of them, but I don't get reports about individuals . . ."

Leonard Wingate caught sight of himself in a wall mirror and stopped. He addressed himself silently: *Okay, you pompous, successful, important bastard with an unlisted phone, so you've let her know what a wheel you are, that she's not to assume you've anything in common just because you happen to be the same color. Now what?*

In his own defense, he thought: It didn't happen often, and he had caught it now; but it showed how an attitude could grow, just as he had heard black people in authority treat other black people like dirt beneath their feet.

"May Lou," Leonard Wingate said, "you caught me in a bad moment and I'm sorry. Do you mind if we start again?"

The trouble, she told him, was with Rollie. "He ain't eatin', sleepin', don't do nuthun'. He won't go out. Just sits and waits."

"Waits for what?"

"He won't tell me, won't even talk. He looks awful, mister. It's like . . ." May Lou stopped, groping for words, then said, "Like he's waitin' to die."

"How long since he went to work?"

"Two weeks."

"Did he ask you to call me?"

"He don't ask nuthun'. But he needs help bad. I know he does."

Wingate hesitated. It really wasn't his concern. It was true he had taken a close interest in hard core hiring, and still did; had involved himself, too, in a handful of individual cases. Knight's was one. But there was just so much help that people could be given, and Knight had quit working—voluntarily it seemed—two weeks ago. Yet Leonard Wingate still felt self-critical about his attitude of a few minutes earlier.

"All right," he said, "I'm not sure I can do anything, but I'll try to drop by in the next few days."

Her voice said pleadingly, "Could you, tonight?"

"I'm afraid that's impossible. I've a dinner engagement which I'm late for already."

He sensed hesitation, then she asked, "Mister, you remember me?"

"I already said I do."

"I ever ask you for anythin' befo'?"

"No, you haven't." He had the feeling May Lou had never asked much of anyone, or of life, nor received much either.

"I'm askin' now. Please! Tonight. For my Rollie."

Conflicting motivations pulled him: ties to the past, his ancestry; the present, what he had become and might be still. Ancestry won. Leonard Wingate thought ruefully: It was a good dinner party he would miss. He suspected that his hostess liked to demonstrate her *liberalitas* by having a black face or two at table, but she served good food and wine, and flirted pleasantly.

"All right," he said into the telephone, "I'll come, and I think I remember where it is, but you'd better give me the address."

If May Lou had not warned him beforehand, Leonard Wingate thought, he would scarcely have recognized Rollie Knight, who was emaciated, his eyes sunken in a haggard face. Rollie had been sitting at a wooden table facing the outer door and started nervously as Wingate came in, then subsided.

The company Personnel man had had the forethought to bring a bottle of Scotch. Without asking, he went to the closet-like kitchen, found glasses and carried them back. May Lou had slipped out as he arrived, glancing at him gratefully and whispering, "I'll just be outside."

Wingate poured two stiff, neat Scotches and pushed one in front of Rollie. "You'll drink this," he said, "and you can take your time about it. But after that, you'll talk."

Rollie's hand went out to take the drink. He did not look up.

Wingate took a swallow of his own Scotch and felt the liquor burn, then warm him. He put the glass down. "We might save time if I tell you I know exactly what you think of me. Also, I know all the words, most of them stupid—white nigger, Uncle Tom—as well as you. But whether you like or hate me, my guess is, I'm the only friend you'll see tonight." Wingate finished his drink, poured another and pushed the bottle toward Rollie. "So start talking before I finish this, or I'll figure I'm wasting time and go."

Rollie looked up. "You act pretty mad. When I ain't said a word."

"Try some words then. Let's see how it goes." Wingate leaned forward. "To start: Why'd you quit work?"

Draining the first Scotch poured for him, Rollie replenished his glass, then began talking—and went on. It was as if, through some combination of Leonard Wingate's timing, acts, and speech, a sluice gate had been opened, so that words tumbled out, channeled by questions which Wingate interposed, until the whole story was laid bare. It began with Rollie's first hiring by the company a year ago, continued through his experiences at the plant, involvement with crime—small at first, then larger—to the robbery-murder and its aftermath, then the knowledge of the Mafia and word of his ordained execution which, with fear and resignation, Rollie now awaited.

Leonard Wingate sat listening with a mixture of impatience, pity, frustration, helplessness, and anger—until he could sit no more. Then, while Rollie went on talking, Wingate paced the tiny room.

When the recital was done, the Personnel man's anger exploded first. He stormed, "You goddam fool! You were given a chance! You had it made! And then you blew it!" Wingate's hands clenched and unclenched with a complex of emotions. *"I could kill you!"*

Rollie's head came up. Briefly, the old impudence and humor flashed. "Man, you gonna do that, you take a card 'n stand in line."

The remark brought Wingate back to reality. He knew he was faced with an impossible choice. If he helped Rollie Knight to escape his situation, he would compound a crime. Even failing to act on his own knowledge at this moment probably made him an accessory to murder, under the law. But if he failed to help, and merely walked away, Wingate knew enough of the inner city and its jungle law to be aware that he would be leaving Rollie to his death.

Leonard Wingate wished he had ignored the telephone bell tonight, or had not yielded to May Lou's plea to come here. If he had done one or the other, he would now be seated comfortably at a table with congenial people, white napery, and gleaming silver. But he *was* here. He forced himself to think.

He believed what Rollie Knight had told him. Everything. He remembered, too, reading in the press of the discovery of Leroy Colfax's bullet-punctured body, and it had been drawn to his notice in another way because, until recently, Colfax had been an assembly plant employee. That was barely a week ago. Now, with two of the four conspirators dead and a third having dropped from sight, Mafia attention was likely to move to Rollie soon. But how soon? Next week? Tomorrow? Tonight? Wingate found his own eyes going nervously toward the door.

He reasoned: What he must have, without delay, was another opinion, a second judgment to reinforce his own. Any decision was too crucial to make unaided. But whose opinion? Wingate was sure that if he went to his own senior in the company, the vice-president of Personnel, the advice given would be coldly legalistic: Murder had been committed, the name of one of the murderers was known; therefore inform the police, who would handle it from there.

Wingate knew—whatever the consequences to himself—he wouldn't do it. Or at least, not without seeking other counsel first. An idea occurred to him: Brett DeLosanto.

Since their first encounter last November, Leonard Wingate, Brett, and Barbara Zaleski had become good friends. In course of an increasing amount of time in one another's company, Wingate had come to admire the young designer's mind, realizing that beneath a surface flippancy he possessed instinctive wisdom, common sense, and a broad compassion. His opinion now might be important. Also, Brett knew Rollie Knight, having met him through Barbara and the *Auto City* filming.

Wingate decided: He would telephone and, if possible, meet Brett tonight.

May Lou had slipped into the apartment unnoticed. Wingate didn't know how much she had heard or knew. He supposed it didn't matter.

He motioned to the door. "Can you lock that?"

May Lou nodded. "Yes."

"I'm going now," Leonard Wingate told Rollie and May Lou, "but I'll be back. Lock the door after me and keep it locked. Don't let anyone else in. When I come, I'll identify myself by name and voice. You understand?"

"Yes, mister." May Lou's eyes met his. Small as she was, scrawny and unimpressive, he was aware of strength.

Not far from the Blaine apartment house, Leonard Wingate found a pay phone in an all-night Laundromat.

He had the phone number of Brett's apartment in a notebook and dialed it. The Laundromat's washers and dryers were noisy and he covered one ear so he could hear the ringing tone at the other end. The ringing continued unanswered, and he hung up.

Wingate remembered a conversation with Brett a day or two ago in which Brett mentioned that he and Barbara would be meeting Adam and Erica Trenton—whom Leonard Wingate knew slightly—later in the week. Wingate decided to try there.

He called Directory Assistance for the Trentons' suburban number. But when he dialed it, there was no answer either.

More than ever now, he wanted to reach Brett DeLosanto.

Leonard Wingate recalled something else Brett had told him: Barbara's father was still on the critical list at Ford Hospital. Wingate reasoned: The chances were, Barbara and Brett were together, and Barbara would leave word at the hospital about where she could be reached.

He dialed the hospital's number. After waiting several minutes, he spoke with a floor nurse who admitted, yes they did have means of getting in touch with Miss Zaleski.

Wingate knew he would have to lie to get the information. "I'm her cousin from Denver and I'm calling from the airport." He hoped the Laundromat's noises sounded sufficiently like airplanes. "I've flown here to see my uncle, but my cousin wanted me to meet her first. She said if I called the hospital you'd always know where I could find her."

The nurse observed tartly, "We're not running a message agency here." But she gave him the information: Miss Zaleski was at the Detroit Symphony tonight with Mr. and Mrs. Trenton and

Mr. DeLosanto. Barbara had even left the seat numbers. Wingate blessed her thoroughness.

He had left his car outside the Laundromat. Now he headed for Jefferson Avenue and the Civic Center, driving fast. A fine rain had begun while he was telephoning; road surfaces were slick.

At Woodward and Jefferson, crowding his chances, he beat an amber light and swung into the forecourt of the Ford Auditorium—blue-pearl-granite-and-marble-faced showplace of the Detroit Symphony Orchestra. Around the Auditorium, other Civic Center buildings towered—Cobo Hall, Veterans' Memorial, the City-County Building—modern, spacious, brightly floodlit. The Civic Center area was often spoken of as a fountainhead—the beginning of a vast urban renewal program for downtown Detroit. Unfortunately, while the head was finished, almost nothing of the body was in sight.

A uniformed attendant by the Auditorium's main doors stepped forward. Before the man could speak, Leonard Wingate told him, "I have to locate some people who are here. It's an emergency." In his hand he held the seat numbers he had copied down while speaking with the hospital nurse.

The doorman conceded: Since the performance was in progress and there was no other traffic, the car could remain "just for a few minutes," with the key in the ignition.

Wingate passed inside through two sets of doors. As the second doors closed, music surrounded him.

An usherette turned from watching the stage and the orchestra. She said, low-voiced, "I won't be able to seat you until intermission, sir. May I see your ticket?"

"I don't have one." He explained his purpose and showed the girl the seat numbers. A male usher joined them.

The seats, it seemed, were near the front and center.

"If you'd take me to the row," Wingate urged, "I could signal Mr. DeLosanto to come out."

The usher said firmly, "We couldn't allow that, sir. It would disturb everybody."

"How long to intermission?"

The ushers were unsure.

For the first time, Wingate was aware of what was being played. He had been a music lover since childhood and recognized Prokofiev's *Romeo and Juliet* Orchestral Suite. Knowing that conductors used varying arrangements of the suite, he asked, "May I see a program?" The usherette gave him one.

The passage he had identified was the opening of the "Death of Tybalt." With relief, he saw it was the final portion of the work before an intermission.

Even waiting impatiently, the music's magnificence swept over him. The swift-surging opening theme moved on to a quickening timpani solo with strokes of death-like hammer blows . . . *Tybalt had killed Romeo's friend Mercutio. Now, on the dying Tybalt, Romeo wreaked vengeance he had sworn* . . . Horn passages wailed the tragic paradox of human destructiveness and folly; the full orchestra swelled to a crescendo of doom . . .

Wingate's skin prickled, his mind drawing parallels between the music and the reason for his presence here.

The music ended. As a thunder of applause swept through the Auditorium, Leonard Wingate hurried down an aisle, escorted by the usher. Word was passed quickly to Brett DeLosanto whom Wingate saw at one. Brett appeared surprised, but began moving out, followed by Barbara and the Trentons.

In the foyer, they held a hurried conference.

Without wasting time on details, Wingate revealed that his search for Brett had been because of Rollie Knight. And since they were still downtown, Wingate's intention was that the two of them go directly to Rollie and May Lou's apartment.

Brett agreed at once, but Barbara raised difficulties, wanting to go with them. They argued briefly, Leonard Wingate opposing the idea, and Brett supported him. In the end it was agreed that Adam would take Erica and Barbara to Brett's Country Club Manor apartment and await the others there. Neither Adam, Erica, nor Barbara felt like returning to the concert.

Outside, Wingate led Brett to his waiting car. The rain had stopped. Brett, who was carrying a topcoat, threw it on the back seat, on top of one of Wingate's already there. As they pulled away, Leonard Wingate began a swift-paced explanation, knowing the journey would be short. Brett listened, asking an occasional question. At the description of the murder-robbery, he whistled softly. Like countless others he had read published reports of the killing at the plant; also, there was a personal link since it seemed likely that events that night had hastened Matt Zaleski's stroke.

Yet Brett felt no enmity toward Rollie Knight. It was true that the young black worker was no innocent, but there were degrees of guilt, whether recognized in law or not. Wingate obviously believed—and Brett accepted—that Rollie had become enmeshed a little at a time, in part unwillingly, his freedom of choice diminishing like a weakening swimmer drawn toward a vortex. Nonetheless, for what Rollie Knight had done, there were debts he would have to pay. No one could, or should, help him escape them.

"The one thing we can't do," Brett said, "is help him get away from Detroit."

"I figured that, too." If the crime had been lesser, Wingate thought, they might have chanced it. But not with murder.

"What he needs is something he didn't have those other times—the best lawyer you can get with money."

"He doesn't have money."

"Then I'll raise it. I'll put some up myself, and there'll be others." Brett was already thinking of people to approach—some, outside the usual ranks of charity bestowers, who felt strongly about social injustice and racial prejudice.

Wingate said, "He'll have to surrender to the police; I can't see any other way. But if we've a strong lawyer he can insist on protection in jail." He wondered—though not aloud—how effective the protection would be, lawyer or not.

"And with a good trial lawyer," Brett said, "he might, just might, get a break."

"Maybe."

"Will Knight do as we say?"

Wingate nodded. "He'll do it."

"Then we'll find a lawyer in the morning. He'll handle the surrender. Tonight, the two of them—the girl as well—had better stay with Barbara and me."

The Personnel man shot a glance across the car's front seat. "You sure?"

"I'm sure. Unless you've a better idea."

Leonard Wingate shook his head. He was glad he had found Brett DeLosanto. Though nothing the young designer had said or done so far was beyond Wingate's own powers of reasoning and decision, Brett's presence and clearheadedness was reassuring. He possessed an instinctive leadership, too, which Wingate, with his training, recognized. He wondered if Brett would be content to remain designing all his years.

They were at the 12th and Blaine intersection. Outside the rundown, paint-peeling apartment house, they got out of the car and Wingate locked it.

As usual, the odor of garbage was strong.

Ascending the worn wooden stairway to the apartment house third floor, Wingate remembered he had told Rollie and May Lou he would identify himself from outside by name and voice. He need not have bothered.

The door he warned them to keep locked was open. Part of the lock was hanging loose where some force—undoubtedly a violent blow—had splintered it.

Leonard Wingate and Brett went in. Only May Lou was inside. She was putting clothes into a cardboard suitcase.

Wingate asked, "Where's Rollie?"

Without looking up, she answered, "Gone."

"Gone where?"

"Some guys come. They took him."

"How long ago?"

"Right after you went, mister." She turned her head. They saw she had been crying.

"Listen," Brett said, "if we get descriptions we can warn the police."

Leonard Wingate shook his head. He knew it was too late. He had a feeling it had been too late from the beginning. He knew, too, what he and Brett DeLosanto were going to do now. They would walk away. As so many in Detroit walked away or, like the priest and Levite, crossed over on the other side.

Brett was silent.

Wingate asked May Lou, "What will you do?"

She closed the cardboard suitcase. "I'll make out."

Brett reached into a pocket. With a gesture, Wingate stopped him. "Let me."

Without counting them, he took what bills he had and pressed them into May Lou's hand. "I'm sorry," he said. "I guess it doesn't mean much, but I'm sorry."

They went downstairs.

Outside, when they came to the car, its near-side door hung open. The window glass was broken. The two topcoats which had been on the car's back seat were gone.

Leonard Wingate cradled his head in his arms on the car roof. When he looked up, Brett saw his eyes were wet.

"Oh, God!" Wingate said. He raised his arms beseechingly to the black night sky. *"Oh, God! This heartless city!"*

Rollie Knight's body was never found. He simply disappeared.

chapter thirty-one

"It's your life, not mine," Adam told Brett DeLosanto. "But I wouldn't be a friend if I didn't say that I think you're being hasty, and making an enormous mistake."

It was close to midnight, and the five of them —Adam and Erica, Barbara and Brett, and Leonard Wingate—were in the Country Club Manor apartment. Brett and Wingate had joined the others half an hour ago, having driven from the inner city. The conversation had been gloomy. When they had exhausted all that could be said about Rollie Knight, Brett announced his intention to leave the automobile industry and to submit a letter of resignation tomorrow.

Adam persisted, "In another five years you could be heading up Design-Styling."

"There was a time," Brett said, "when that was the only dream I had—to be a Harley Earl, or a Bill Mitchell, or Gene Bordinat, or an Elwood Engel. Don't misunderstand me—I think they've all been great; some are still. But it isn't for me, that's all."

Leonard Wingate said, "There are other reasons, though, aren't there?"

"Yes, there are. I don't think car manufacturers, who do so much long-range planning for themselves, have done more than a thimbleful of planning and service for the community they live in."

Adam objected, "That may have been true once; it isn't any more. Everything's changed or changing fast. We see it every day—in management attitudes, community responsibility, the kind of cars we're building, relations with government, acknowledgment of consumers. This isn't the same business it was even two or three years ago."

"I'd like to believe it," Brett said, "if only because obviously you do. But I can't, and I'm not alone. Anyway, from now on I'll be working on the outside."

Erica asked, "What will you do?"

"If you want the truth," Brett told her, "I'll be damned if I know."

"It wouldn't surprise me," Adam said, "if you got into politics. I'd like you to know that if you do, I'll not only vote for you, I'll contribute to your campaign."

Wingate said, "Me, too." It was strange, he thought, that only this evening he had sensed Brett's leadership and wondered how long he would stay in design.

Brett grinned. "One of these days that may cost you both. I'll remember."

"One thing he's going to do," Barbara told the others, "is paint. If I have to chain him to an easel and bring his meals. If I have to support the two of us."

"Speaking of support," Brett said, "I've thought of starting a small design business of my own."

"If you do," Adam predicted, "it won't stay small because you can't help being a success. Also, you'll work harder than you ever did."

Brett sighed. "That's what I'm afraid of."

But even if it happened, he thought, he would be his own man, would speak with an independent voice. That was what he wanted most, and so did Barbara. Brett glanced at her with a love which seemed to increase day by day. Whatever unknown quantities were coming, he knew that they would share them.

"There were rumors," Barbara said to Adam, "that you might leave the company too."

"Where did you hear that?"

"Oh, around."

Adam thought: It was hard to keep any secret in Detroit. He supposed Perce Stuyvesant, or someone close to him, had talked.

Barbara pressed him. "Well, *are* you leaving?"

"An offer was made to me," Adam said. "I thought about it seriously for a while. I decided against it."

He had telephoned Perce Stuyvesant a day or two ago and explained: There would be no point in going to San Francisco to speak of terms and details; Adam was an automobile man and would remain one.

As Adam saw it, a good deal was wrong with the auto industry, but there was a great deal more that, overwhelmingly, was right. The miracle of the modern automobile was not that it sometimes failed, but that it mostly didn't; not that it was costly, but that—for the marvels of design and engineering it embodied—it cost so little; not that it cluttered highways and polluted air, but that it gave free men and women what, through history, they had mostly craved—a personal mobility.

Nor, for an executive to spend his working life, was there any more exciting milieu.

"All of us see things in different ways," Adam told Barbara. "I guess you could say I voted for Detroit."

Soon afterward they said goodnight.

On the short drive from Maple and Telegraph to Quarton Lake, Adam said, "You didn't say much tonight."

"I was listening," Erica answered. "And thinking. Besides, I wanted you to myself, to tell you something."

"Tell me now."

"Well, it rather looks as if I'm pregnant. Look out!—don't swerve like that!"

"Just be glad," he said, as he pulled into a driveway, "you didn't tell me on the Lodge at rush hour."

"Whose driveway is this?"

"Who the hell cares?" He put out his arms, held her, and kissed her tenderly.

Erica was half laughing, half crying. "You were such a tiger in Nassau. It must have happened there."

He whispered, "I'm glad I was," then thought: It could be the very best thing for them both.

Later, when they were driving again, Erica said, "I've been wondering how Greg and Kirk will feel. You've two grown sons, then suddenly a baby in the family."

"They'll love it. Because they love you. Just as I do." He reached for her hand. "I'll phone and tell them tomorrow."

"Well," she said, "between us we seem to be creating things."

It was true, he thought happily. And his life was full.

Tonight he had Erica, and this.

Tomorrow, and in days beyond, there would be Farstar.

about the author

Born in Luton, England, in 1920, Arthur Hailey was educated in English schools until age 14. He joined the British Royal Air Force in 1939 and served as a pilot and flight lieutenant during World War II and in the Middle and Far East. In 1947 Mr. Hailey emigrated to Canada, where he was a real estate salesman, a business paper editor, and then a sales and advertising executive. In 1956 he scored his first writing success with a TV drama, "Flight Into Danger," which was subsequently a movie and a novel, RUNWAY ZERO-EIGHT.

Mr. Hailey, one of the great storytellers of our time, has millions of devoted readers, and his novels are published in every major language. His sensational bestsellers include HOTEL, AIRPORT, THE FINAL DIAGNOSIS, IN HIGH PLACES—and his newest one, WHEELS.

Mr. Hailey lives in the Bahamas with his wife Sheila and their teen-age children: Jane, Steven, and Diane. Arthur Hailey cherishes his family privacy, avoiding publicity except—as he puts it—"when a new book comes out, and my publishers insist I do my duty."